REVIEWERS PRAISE *THE*

"Entertaining. . . . Kellogg lightful quartet . . . neatly of-time experiences with N' encounters real magic for the first time with a sense of awe." —*Starlog*

"A fun romp with some creatively surreal moments, and a frightening view of a too-possible future." —*Locus*

"From first page to last, this is an excellent book. . . . This book has magic, love, humor, action, and dragons: something for everyone!" —*KLIATT*

"Enchanting fantasy, filled with adventure, villains, romance, and hope . . . a heroine with some spunk . . . a magical tapestry of intrigue and daring . . . weaves a spell over the reader. A must for all those dragon lovers of other writers like Wrede and McCaffrey. I can't wait for the next book in the series." —*VOYA*

"Dragon fans are really going to love THE BOOK OF EARTH . . . the dragon is absolutely irresistible. When he's on stage, sparks of excitement leap through the pages. By the end of the book and the dramatic introduction of Water, you will indeed find it hard to wait for the next tale." —*Romantic Times*

Be sure to read all four novels
in MARJORIE B. KELLOGG'S
powerful DAW fantasy series—

The Dragon Quartet:
THE BOOK OF EARTH (Volume One)
THE BOOK OF WATER (Volume Two)
THE BOOK OF FIRE (Volume Three)
THE BOOK OF AIR (Volume Four)

MARJORIE B. KELLOGG

THE BOOK OF

AIR

Volume Four of
The Dragon Quartet

DAW BOOKS, INC.

DONALD A. WOLLHEIM, FOUNDER

375 Hudson Street, New York, NY 10014

ELIZABETH R. WOLLHEIM
SHEILA E. GILBERT
PUBLISHERS

www.dawbooks.com

YA
kee

First Printing, November 2003
1 2 3 4 5 6 7 8 9

For **Dorothy Koehler**, and all other friends of dragons.

And for **Jim Hansen**, who told it like it is.

As always, thanks are due to Lynne Kemen and Bill Rossow, literary critics *par excellence*, to Vicki Davis, to my agent, Joshua Bilmes, and to my oh-so-patient editor and publisher, Sheila Gilbert.

Apologies are due to all the readers of THE DRAGON QUARTET who had to wait so long for this final volume! Real life just got the better of me.

PROLOGUE

The Creation

IN THE BEGINNING,
and a little after . . .

In the Beginning, four mighty dragons raised of elemental energies were put to work creating the World. They were called Earth, Water, Fire, and Air. No one of them had power greater than another, and no one of them was mighty alone.

When the work was completed and the World set in motion, the four went to ground, expecting to sleep out this World's particular history and not rise again until World's End.

The first to awaken was Earth.

He woke in darkness, as innocent as a babe, with only the fleeting shadows of dreams to hint at his former magnificence. But one bright flame of knowledge drove him forth: he was Called to Work again, if only he could remember what the Work was.

He found the World grown damp and chill, over-run by the puniest of creatures, Creation's after-thought, the ones called Men. Earth soon learned that Men, too, had forgotten their Origin. They had abandoned their own intended Work in the World and thrived instead on superstition, violence, and self-righteous oppression of their fellows. They had forgotten as well their primordial relationship with dragons—all, that is, but a few.

One in particular awaited Earth's coming, a young girl who knew nothing of the secret duty carried down through the countless generations of her blood. Her name was Erde, and she knew her Destiny when she faced a living dragon and was not afraid.

Thereafter, Earth's Quest became her own, and together they searched her World for answers to his questions. Some they found and slowly, along with his memory, Earth's powers reawakened. But the girl's World was dark and dangerous and ignorant, and the mysterious Caller who summoned Earth could not be found within it. One day, blindly following the Call, Earth took them Somewhere Else.

In that Somewhere Else, they found Earth's sister Water, and her Companion N'Doch. N'Doch's World was hot and crowded and full of noise, and mysterious to Erde until she understood that she had traveled to Sometime, as well as to Somewhere. It became her task to teach N'Doch about the dragons and their Quest, for he did not know his Destiny, and did not join them willingly at first.

Water, too, had heard the Caller. She could answer some of Earth's questions about the Work, but added many of her own. Soon, the dragons were convinced that an unknown Power not only blocked their Search, but threatened their safety. Evidence pointed to the dragon Fire, but why would their own brother conspire against them?

When the dangers of N'Doch's World, both human and inhuman, closed in around them, the four in desperation returned to Erde's time, with nothing but N'Doch's recurring dream of a Burning Land to tell them where to go to continue the Search.

But in Erde's time, conditions were deteriorating. . . .

N'Doch's nightmare vision took the four to a farther Future, where the results of Mankind's carelessness and greed were only too evident. War, disease and ecological collapse had razed the landscape and brought human society to ruin. Here, the four found undeniable evidence of Fire's villainy. In the planet's final days, he ruled as a tyrannical god over a dwindling population, preaching Apocalypse and plotting against his siblings. He even boasted of how cleverly he'd hidden away their sister Air.

But the four found surprising allies in that hot and desiccated land, resourceful men and women who knew that their survival depended on a more sympathetic relationship with Nature. The most astonishing addition to the Quest was Fire's own dragon guide, Paia. Her fated bond with her fellow guides allowed her to repudiate her dragon's misdeeds, and join the efforts to free Air from her mysterious prison and Paia's people from Fire's cruel yoke.

From out of this rebellion, an old friend appeared in a new guise, and was revealed as the fourth dragon guide. But he didn't know where his dragon was, either.

Yet, was Fire merely evil, or was there truth to his claim of knowledge that only he possessed?

At last, Earth, Water, and Fire came face-to-face. A fiery confrontation on a barren mountaintop forced Fire into temporary retreat. But not before he had threatened murder and mayhem against all that the humans knew and loved. . . .

PART ONE

The Summoning
of the Hero

Chapter One

Gone. The Fire-breather is gone.

Seconds afterward, the Librarian senses a change. A difference inside. Like the twitching of muscles he'd not even known were paralyzed.

Smoke still hangs in the heated air, the Fire-breather's sulfurous trace. It's the same dry dawn on the same dry mountaintop. The Librarian is alive when he didn't expect to be, but he is not the same as he was a moment ago.

His dragon has touched him, he's sure of it. A feather-light glancing contact, almost too brief to be noticed, yet inside him now, this entire . . . what? A reordering, an enlarging—of thought, of perception, of understanding. A more *outward* focus.

And the connection felt deliberate this time. Not like it's always been for him before, at the mercy of his peculiar inner circuitry, picked out by random roving beams that stun and blind, then swing away through the fog. This was . . . almost directed. Behind the walls of the dragon's enigmatic prison, something has changed for her, too.

She knows where to find me.

The others must hear of this, immediately. But as the Librarian tries for words, none will come, aloud or otherwise. This has *not* changed. Besides, the others are not ready for another dose of revelation. Not yet. Though the terrifying confrontation passed within mere moments of real time, they're as stunned and spent as if it had been hours. Distracted. Sluggish with terror and awe. Struggling with watery knees and weakened bowels. And wondering, as he is, how they managed to come through the conflagration alive. Though urgency thrills through the Librarian's nervous system like a drug, he knows he must allow them space for recovery.

The smoke is persistent and sullen. Unnatural, like the creature that made it. Acid, like his tongue. The Librarian coughs, waving his arms uselessly. The Fire-breather's stench is not so easily dispelled. And it's a long time since he's been outside in the unconditioned air. His pampered lungs have forgotten the acrid stink of combustion and the punishment of daylight. The constant dry weight of the heat, even at dawn. The arid mountain ledges still radiate yesterday's baking. Already they're being baked all over again. Heat upon heat. Even stone has a life that can be burned away. The Librarian sways, overcome by a moment of synchronicity with the rock.

. . . *deep-anchored to slow-time, swelling sun seared, shattered, wind-battered, groaning with the revolutions of the dying planet* . . .

Motion recalls him to the mountaintop, to the dawn, to the rocky plateau that was once a landing pad. Once. When men still ruled. The Librarian sees the soldier is stirring. Has it been hours or seconds since? He mustn't let himself drift like that, not now.

He must remember how to act. He must recall decisiveness, now that his eternal waiting has ended, and time suddenly matters. Events matter. The Firebreather has come and gone. The dragon Air has touched him. Six hundred men, women, and children wait in the caverns below, anxious about the outcome of the confrontation above. His people, who have faith in him, who believe he has the knowledge to hold off the Last Days. Does he? Of course not. It's her knowledge, the dragon's, that he believes in, that he preaches about. Which is why he must . . . must . . . her touch . . . there is little time left . . . she is searching, too.

Drifting . . .

The Librarian struggles to get hold of himself. He wishes for the animal body of his former days, when the ability to shake one's self vigorously was all that was needed to feel put back in order. *Every hair in place.* He longs for the cool darkness of his den beneath the mountain, for the remote comforts of his screens and sensors and console. When his dragon finds him there, he can almost concentrate. Reflect rather than absorb. Deflect to the machines the bright roar of her energies. Keep the explosion in his senses within the limits of sanity . . . most of the time. With the expansion of her power over the years, the danger to him has grown also. This last century or so, without the buffer of the machines, his brain would have been burned to the proverbial cinder. The Librarian shudders. Though there is power to spare in her sendings, there is little coherency. Sometimes he fears that his dragon is not entirely sane.

But this time, *this* time . . . there *was* something different. Along with the usual kaleidoscope of images, there was a hint of meaning. More than a hint.

As if a new circuit had opened, to run a message on an infinite loop: *Hurry! Hurry! Hurry!* No, it's not so articulate as that. The Librarian supplies the words, which barely describe the imperative within. It sighs like wind. It tumbles like water. It groans like the earth. He is eager to get back down below, to see if the machines can detect it, deflect it, interpret it.

Across the circular pad, the soldier dusts soot from his bare forearms and scowls at the brightening skies, as if to assure himself that the Fire-breather is truly gone. He lays a hand on the bowed head of the Fire-breather's guide. She who was lately so bold has slid weeping to the ground beside him. The soldier murmurs soundlessly without bending toward her, seeming to know that no mere word or gesture will console her. He is familiar with the aftershock of battles. The Librarian watches him as he quietly steps away across the tarmac to inspect the arc of scorched rock and heat-fused sand laid down around them by the Fire-breather's wrath. He is not a big man, but sturdy, with a blunt, determined jaw and a restless glance. He moves quickly, economically, unmindful of the gathering heat. The rising sun glints off the carved and gilded hilt of the sword slung sheathed across his back. The sword. The Librarian remembers that sword and this man, in a more youthful version. But the memory is from a former life, and hazy. Most clearly, he recalls the man this man once served, an elder knight. Battle-scarred, a weary idealist. One has grown much like the other, over time—not physically, for the soldier is shorter, blonder, more intent. But maturity and ill-fortune have blunted his youthful arrogance, so the Librarian's memories of both men blend in a tightening fabric. He follows the

weave for a while, interested in the complex patterning of human lives. Then he catches himself.

Drifting again, Gerrasch. Not now, not now!

He flexes his pink-palmed hands, his clever fingers,
his only sure anchor to the world. He sighs. His life
is about to get very complicated.

The Earth-mover's guide stirs next. As if waking
suddenly, she starts and staggers to her feet, then
pivots in an aimless circle, running down like a spinning top until she ends up gazing numbly at the
Librarian. Her dark curls are frizzed with singe.
Tears streak the ash dusting her pale smooth cheeks.
But though she is the youngest of them all, almost a
child, she does not give in to sobs. She gathers herself
again quickly. She looks away to the others, counting
heads, assessing their welfare. Beside her, the Water-
bearer's tall guide swears softly and at length, grinding his fists into his eyes.

In the Librarian's gut, the wordless signal steps up
its urgent thrum: *Hurry! Hurry! Hurry!*

The Earth-mover and Water-bearer themselves are
still hunkered down in a silent conference of dragon
outrage. They, most of all, must hear of the change
in him, but though he's only just met them, the Librarian knows enough of dragons to understand that
they'll not be disturbed until they're good and ready,
no matter what. He forgives them. They are dragons,
after all. No matter the urgency, impatience is a lesson the Librarian has yet to learn. Not so the soldier,
who has finished his inspection tour and has already
begun to pace, though he attempts to disguise it as
patrolling and limbering up, that is, useful movement. While the rest pull themselves together, the
Librarian welcomes the chance for a moment of

dragon study, his first since the pair's sudden arrival to save their humans from the Fire-breather's vicious tantrum. The Librarian has lived with a dragon inside him for all his life, yet he's never seen one in the flesh. Suddenly, he's seen three in less than half an hour.

Earth is vast, bronze, and plated. He crouches like a mountain of veined brown marble, rough-carved in the form of a beast. His neck is thickly muscled, his haunches massive. His tail is short and wide, and grounds him to the rock like an ancient tree root. His curved ivory horns and scimitar claws reflect the glow of the rising sun. In contrast to this unrelenting solidity, Water could be a swirl of a billion blue-green butterflies, ephemeral and phosphorescent, infinitely changeable. The Librarian understands this is only the shape she's chosen for the moment. He wonders if there is a shape she calls her own, in which her own identity rests and is at home. Earth and Water are as different from each other as they are from their fire-breathing, golden-scaled, deadly-minded brother.

How will his own dragon look, the Air-bringer, once she's set free to appear before him? The Librarian has no data to work with, only gut feeling and instinct. He's built a picture in his imagination. When he thinks of his dragon, he sees the tall cloud towers of ancient summers, the white-topped, fair-weather spires that once brought soft air and warm breezes. Clouds. Only a memory from a time when the planet's cycle of respiration was still normal. But the Librarian remembers them in passionate detail, as an icon in the landscape of Paradise. Of Arcadia. Of all that is lost.

Drifting, Gerrasch. Again, again. Focus on the dragon!

What else was new in this precious instant of contact? The Librarian replays it in his mind: reverse, fast forward, reverse, fast forward. The cloud image seems a bit more architectural than before, a sort of cloud city. An anomaly? The Librarian stores it for further analysis.

The pale girl and the tall young man have gathered themselves enough to turn to the older man behind them. Together, they ease him up from his knees and pat away his shudders of terror and outrage. For this man's sake, the Librarian at last wills his big clumsy body toward an idea of motion. Stillness would be vastly easier, but this dark-skinned man is neither soldier nor dragon guide. Only his faith in the Librarian's visions has brought him so near to death on a bleak and bitter mountaintop. He deserves some soothing and support.

No wind among the rocks, wreathed in heat and stubborn smoke, pressed down by the yellow dome of sky. No sound. Only the brittle rattle of pebbles beneath the soldier's boots as he paces out the blackened circle for a third or fourth time. No one has said a word, the Librarian notes, since the Firebreather vanished.

Ah, good, he muses, when his feet more or less respond to his orders, and shuffle him forward. *Perhaps now the words will follow.*

The pale girl finally finds her tongue. "We have to go after him!"

In her widened eyes, the Librarian sees the stark

reflection of the Fire-breather's long list of parting threats, each one pointed and personal. "Now! Before he . . . we have to warn everyone!"

Her name is Erde von Alte, and she is fourteen. The Librarian has met her before, in earlier times. The same time as the elder knight. Even then, she was given to overemphasis and passionate exaggeration, in the way of fourteen year olds, which is unsurprising since in the eleven hundred years since he first encountered her, she has aged but two months. The Librarian feels he has permission to note her overzealousness, having been a fourteen year old himself several times in his life, though never a girl. Besides, young Erde came to the present the easy way, dragon-back, while he has had to live each day and every year in between.

"Everyone! Please! If we don't hurry, he'll get to them first! He'll . . . !"

"Whoa, girl, easy." The tall youth stops rubbing his eyes and stands blinking. His lanky ebony body cuts a hard profile against the sun-splashed rock. "Can't just race on off. Gotta figure where he's headed."

The Citadel, thinks the Librarian, so sure he's spoken aloud that he's confused when none of them react to the visions of seared flesh and broken bodies writhing so vividly inside his own eyes.

The girl shoves away the dark youth's raised palms. "We'll go everywhere, then! We'll have to split up!"

"Maybe. I don't know." He shrugs, an uneasy dance of flatly muscled shoulders beneath his charred T-shirt. "Let's see what *they* say." He glances toward the two dragons and spots the soldier, still in restless, impatient motion. "Hey, Dolph! C'mon over! Battle conference!"

The tall youth is called N'Doch. He is West African, and from a time in the world's history when his homeland was not yet under water. The older man is Luther Williams, a local in the present time, from one of the itinerant Tinker clans. The soldier is from the girl's place and time. The Librarian is not yet sure about this one's preference in a name. A different version is used by each of the dragon guides. The knight's squire he met so long ago was Adolphus Michael von Hoffmann, heir to the sizable estates of Köthen. Germany, it was. Tenth century. A baron, he thinks. The Librarian cares little about such things.

The soldier glances up at N'Doch's summons. He frowns, already pondering solutions as he paces across the tarmac to join them. Gently but firmly, as he passes, the baron scoops up the Fire-breather's guide and urges her forward under the shelter of his arm. She leans into him, drying her eyes, flicking dubious and apologetic glances though damp lashes at her fellow guides. The Librarian feels shy as she approaches, uncomfortably conscious of his wild hair and his shambling, graceless bulk.

For this is Paia, after all. The High Priestess of the Temple of the Apocalypse, the Fire-breather's cult. The Librarian knows everything about her. His machines beneath the mountain are hooked to her machines in the Fire-breather's lair, though she was unaware of the connection—and of him—until their meeting mere hours ago. He's always known Fire's priestess was a beautiful woman, but he finds the reality of her . . . *go ahead, Gerrasch, say it* . . . her flesh quite overwhelming. Small wonder that Dolph or Hoffmann or Baron Köthen or whatever the soldier wishes to be called soothes her along like something precious. She is that rare occurrence, especially nowadays: unblemished, unmutated, undeformed. A perfect physical specimen. Of course the soldier is in love with her. Who could blame him?

A loose circle coalesces in the center of the old landing pad. First, all of them talk at once, a burst of babble that manages to express only their relief at being still alive. Then they fall silent to gaze expectantly at the Librarian, as if an urgent meeting has been called to order, of which he has unaccountably been elected Chair.

Not so unaccountably, the Librarian reminds himself. Not a moment to waste, and there's a major language barrier here.

He visualizes the problem as an interlinked flow chart. For him, an image is always more articulate than words, and so, words are a wonder to him. Words are his long life's study, which is why he comes armed with a solution.

Erde, N'Doch, and Baron Köthen have been speaking tenth century German. Though N'Doch's native languages are twenty-first century Wolof and sub-Saharan French, he's learned the antique German recently and precipitously from the dragons, who can download entire databases into a linked human mind, the only issue being how fast the mind can accept the input. Köthen speaks German and passable Old French, but is not dragon-linked like the guides. Still, he has a quick ear and a quicker mind, so he's fast picking up the contemporary English that is Luther's only tongue, as it is Paia's—except Luther speaks his own "Tinker" dialect of English, which sounds different from Paia's. But Paia, as Fire's guide, is mind-linked to the other guides. Translation is automatic. Maybe the worst of this chaos is N'Doch's slang-ridden English, learned watching old twentieth century American videos. It makes the Librarian's teeth itch.

The conundrum is, of course, what language to use in spoken conversation? Once Köthen is more fluent, English will be the obvious *lingua franca*. For now, only the Librarian can resolve the confusion. Hence their breathless attention.

He fishes in the deep pockets of his jumpsuit for his remote keypad and activates the translator program. He holds up his little device like a beacon, nodding around the circle. Again, they all start in at once.

"He'll go right to . . ."

"We gotta see what . . ."

"What about the . . ."

The soldier shakes his head and backs off a step.

"He'll go to Deep Moor first!" Erde exclaims breathlessly.

"Why would he?"

"Wait!" rumbles Luther. "Fust t'ing, we gudda tell da uddahs."

The Librarian is still struggling to vocalize. His voice is stuck, like an unoiled hinge. "Yes," he manages finally, grateful for any coherent sound at all.

YES.

The echo booms in his chest as well as in his head. It makes him want to cough. The dragons have ended their private conference. The Librarian feels his brain crowd up as the other guides drop into mental contact.

Earth lifts his horned head. WE MUST POSTPONE THE QUEST UNTIL OUR FRIENDS ARE SAFE.

Yes! Erde's slim fists ball up for emphasis. *We'll go now and warn Deep Moor!*

N'Doch shakes his head. *Faster if we stopped by Papa Dja's on the way!*

The Citadel is closest! We should go there first!

The Librarian recalls that he must tell them about his new difference, about his true moment with his dragon, the missing sister, and the object of their Quest. But time and minds run breakneck in the Meld. So long-schooled in waiting, the Librarian is like a timid driver on a freeway ramp at rush hour. He can't get a word in edgewise. *Need info,* he offers instead.

YES. WE MUST GATHER TO DISCUSS THE BEST COURSE OF ACTION.

A chorus of distress rises from the minds in the Meld, who know how long a dragon discussion can take.

Dear dragon, we haven't time!

So many lives are in danger!

JUST HOLD ON, ALL OF YOU. Water's music for once rings harsh. THERE ARE A LOT OF INTER-ESTS AT STAKE HERE, INCLUDING A FEW YOU SEEM TO HAVE FORGOTTEN ABOUT! OUR SIS-TER AIR STILL LANGUISHES IN CAPTIVITY, FAR AHEAD ALONG THE TIME LINE.

Where?

Farther in the future?

The Librarian recalls now what terror had pushed from his mind. In the midst of the firefight, the drag-ons' hasty revelation: *We know where she is!*

Erde subsides with an anxious frown. She would never contradict a dragon, not even someone else's.

But no one's been there. We can't go there dragon-back without an image to travel to.

Fire's been there. Let's send Paia to pick his brain.

WE HAVE BEEN PONDERING THIS, AND AS YET, SEE NO SOLUTION, Earth told them.

Water reluctantly agrees. YES, FOR NOW, WE'LL

DO WHAT WE CAN DO. WE'LL HELP OUR FRIENDS.

ASK THOSE BELOW TO CLEAR SPACE IN THE LARGEST CAVERN. WE ARE COMING TO JOIN THEM.

The Future. An image. A future image. What if . . . ?

Can't hold on to that train of thought against the pull of a dragon imperative. The Librarian gives up and thumbs his remote, calling up the gawky boy he's left listening at the console in the complex far below. He summons words enough to be understood. Mattias is used to supplying the ones in between. The Librarian often dreams of vocalizing his thought-images. If, when he opened his mouth, the pictures just flowed out, as detailed and coherent as they are in his head, or as words are in the mouths of others, he'd have no problem communicating with the world. But what would the response be, he wonders, to his cloud-tower image of the dragon Air?

"Wow!" squeaks the remote. "Dragons?" The receding slap of bare feet is audible over the open line as Mattias abandons the console and hotfoots it down the corridor.

"Join hands!" Erde urges. "Lord Earth will take us down!"

Baron Köthen mutters a warning to Luther about the nauseating effects of dragon transport.

Luther says, "Mebbe we 'umins shud take da elevader."

"Too late," N'Doch replies.

Seconds later, the hot glare of the summit has been eclipsed by the opaque weight of the mountain. They are in darkness. Wavering points of light surround them like a sea of stars. The nervous waiting silence is broken only by the resonant, far-off thump of the circulating fans. The Librarian sucks in cool air, filtered and humidified, and expels a gasping sigh of relief. He'll be able to think more clearly now, he's sure of it. He sees the soldier shudder just once and swallow hard. Luther groans faintly. The Librarian has felt nothing, as if traveling disembodied through tons of solid rock is perfectly natural. As if he's been doing it for years. Sometimes he suspects he is not yet entirely "umin."

For instance, his nose is far too sensitive. The chill air of the cavern is redolent with the smell of humans and animals, yet he can pick out familiar individuals by their scent alone. He can still read their emotions, their lingering fear, the surge of adrenaline caused by Mattias' announcement. In the vast, high-vaulted space, the rows of wagons and carts and campsites have been hastily hauled back. The open center is ringed by lanterns and receding, dim-lit ranks of weary, worried, awe-filled faces. Hot meals and a good night's sleep have been rare down here for several days now. Their astonishment tickles the Librarian's nose—a tang of citrus. After all, six people have just materialized out of nowhere, right in front of them.

The most familiar scent of all steps out of the darkness. Leif Cauldwell—a mixed scent of smoke, leather, and a hint of cinnamon. Every eye follows him: tall and golden, head priest of the Fire Temple turned rebel leader. No living human has had more experience with the Fire-breather, except Paia herself.

Right now, Cauldwell smells like a man trying hard to look optimistic. Behind his firmly sculpted mouth, his teeth worry the inside of his lip. The Tinker elder Reuben Stokes limps along at his side—brisk odors of salt and pine sap. Luther immediately goes to greet them. Cauldwell's body is in its prime and powerful, and though Luther's chin-forward stoop betrays his age, they both tower over little Stoksie. But no matter. All three clasp hands as if they'd last parted unsure of ever seeing each other again.

"Yu wudnta b'leeved it, Leif!" Luther's murmur is heartfelt and grateful. "Dey sentim packin', dey did!"

For the soldier's sake, the Librarian thumbs his translator up to max.

"No, Luther. He *left*, in a rage!" The remote unit mimics Erde's girlish stridency to perfection. "You know that's nowhere near the end of it. People everywhere are in terrible danger!"

Luther nods, but her rebuke does little to dampen his enthusiasm.

Leif Cauldwell's worried gaze flicks toward the Librarian. "So what happened up there?"

"Left, yes." The Librarian offers his pudgy shortcut of a shrug. "Now what?" He knows what. *Hurry, hurry.* The message throbs in his chest like a second heartbeat. But he will not tell people what to do. He will not give orders. He's seen far too much of that in his many lives.

N'Doch rests both hands on Erde's shoulders, solicitous but restraining. "Yeah, that's it, chief. We got some hard decisions to make, and we gotta do it fast."

"But . . . he came? The Beast?" Cauldwell squints into the darkness behind them. "Is Paia with you? Did he take her? Is she all right?"

"She's here. She's fine," says N'Doch.

"Yes. No." The Librarian feels dragon pressure building behind his brow like a foul-weather headache. Not his dragon. It's the other two. They've been patient so far, but silent anonymity is not their strong suit. "Not. But . . ."

"It was rough on her," N'Doch supplies. "But she told him where to go."

Cauldwell spies his former superior, mute and lovely, within the curve of the soldier's arm. "Congratulations, cuz!" His smile offers both approval and awe: she has faced down the Fire-breather and lived. Then his edginess returns. "Mattias said you were bringing the other . . ."

"Draguns, Leif! Yu kin sayit." Luther's wide grin reflects the flicker of lantern light. "Da gud uns!" He points to a peculiar zone of darkness in the middle of the cleared area. A blue light dances at its center. "Dey's sistah an' brudder ta da One!"

A murmur rustles across the cavern, the very breath of hope and reverence. "The One!"

The One who will save us all. The Librarian ponders his mantra, and the tall cloud towers bloom behind his eyelids. *Air, Air, Air.* But now is no time for preaching on his visions, even if he could get the words out right.

Because Cauldwell needs help. This brave and seasoned warrior has backed away before he can stop himself, retreating from the mysterious looming darkness and its companion glow, though he sees Stoksie and Luther smiling and unalarmed. The Librarian smells his reflex terror, and the effort it takes for the big man to plant his feet and gaze about, as if he'd merely been making room. Leif Cauldwell has good reason to fear dragons, from his long and bitter years in the Fire-breather's employ. The Librarian brushes away the phantoms rushing into his head— fire, smoke, human sacrifice—and shuffles over to stand close by the rebel leader's side. Cauldwell glances down at him.

"Ah. Gerrasch." He grips the Librarian's soft shoulder. "Ah."

Earth speeds up his metabolism toward visibility, and the huge cavern seems to shrink, relative to the dragon's great, glimmering shadow. His eyes precede his solid form, appearing as disembodied oval lamps, as tall as a man and glowing like the sky before dawn. The crowd stirs and murmurs. His head alone is as big as their tallest wagons. His curved ivory claws and horns shine with his own interior gleam. Cauldwell stares, his jaw set, as the phosphorescent blue eddy drops to hover at the brown dragon's side.

The Librarian gazes up at the rebel leader, willing him toward acceptance and calm. If it would help, he would embrace the man, and each and every one of the throng withdrawing cautiously into the deeper shadows. These are his people, who have gifted him with their faith for so long. Not all of them, to be sure, especially among the Tinkers. Stoksie, for one, has remained an unbeliever, even while accepting the more secular aspects of Cauldwell's rebellion. But Tinkers are by nature broad-minded, and Stoksie was always open to proof, so it thrills the Librarian to at last be able to offer him some. Proof of what he's been promising and preaching, that great Powers will appear to oppose the Fire-breather's tyranny, to help free the One and restore the dying planet. He couldn't warn them that those Powers would also be dragons. His visions hadn't been that specific.

He watches an entire spectrum of loathing shiver across Leif Cauldwell's handsome face as the man tries to come to grips.

An odd sound, half moan, half sigh, escapes the High Priestess. She slips out from under the soldier's protective arm. He takes a step after her, then falls back as she glides forward to grasp Cauldwell's hand.

"These are not like him," she whispers.

Her voice is hoarse. No wonder. She's just been shouting down the Fire-breather, inhaling the smoke and sulfur of his wrath. *Her dragon. Fire.* The Librarian hears grief and guilt and confusion in every word. The soldier waits, watching his woman like the hawk he very much resembles.

"Come. Meet them." Paia leads Cauldwell across the open floor toward the dragons. He tries not to seem unwilling. The blue glow coalesces into something nearer form: wings webbed with gossamer, a long neck, a shimmering fish tail, appearing, disappearing, changeable. An impression of music hovers in the air. Earth lowers his huge head. His eyes are like lighted doorways. His nostrils flare gently. Warm, sweet breezes ruffle the rebel leader's hair. Scents of moist loam and bruised grass. The Librarian cannot help but smile, though his heart pounds with that other urgency. *Leaves. Grass.* It's been far too long since he's inhaled such treasures. Paia lays her own hand and Cauldwell's on the dragon's shining claw. Cauldwell's hand trembles, then steadies.

Behind them, Luther says, "Wuz dem dat saved uz, Leif."

"Not a moment too soon, either," N'Doch agrees.

Stoksie whistles softly. "Heeza big un, all ri'."

N'Doch grins. "And getting bigger every day.

When I first met him, he wasn't much bigger than an elephant."

"Yeah? Wuzza nelefant?"

"Yu know, Stokes," Luther mutters. "Yu seen 'em in pitchers."

Stoksie looks dubious.

"Later, dude, okay?" N'Doch watches Cauldwell ease a half step closer to the big dragon. "Later, I'll sing you about elephants."

The girl strays to the Librarian's side. He feels like he's being force-fed the entire world's impatience and anxiety. He sends Erde easeful messages. If he could reach his dragon, he'd send her some, too. Cauldwell's absolute trust must be won, or the forces for good will be a force divided.

Cauldwell lets his hand slide across the waist-high ivory curl of claw, broader than his own muscular thigh. "Is this what it was like?" he asks Paia, "With . . . him?"

Paia's choked laugh is the most rueful sound the Librarian has ever heard. "Oh, no, cousin. Oh, no. No. Not at all."

Cauldwell takes a breath, then lifts his head and looks the dragon in the eye: a tall, golden man caught in a benign and golden stare. Benign, but awe-inspiring. Even the Librarian finds it so. Cauldwell licks his lips. "Let's see . . . you must be . . ."

"He is Lord Earth." Erde has moved up on his other side. Paia steps back, into the soldier's waiting embrace. They move in concert, these dragon guides, the Librarian muses, forgetting for a moment that he is one of them.

"Earth." Cauldwell cannot tear his gaze away. "Ah. Yours?"

The girl wags her singed curls faintly. "Say rather,

I am his. His servant, and guide in the world of men. As your cousin is Lord Fire's, only . . ."

"Only. Only?"

"It's my fault," murmurs Paia from behind. "It must be. Yet Earth tells me otherwise. He says I am meant to help the Go . . . um, that is, Fire . . . see the error of his ways."

Cauldwell's mouth twists. "He'll only see what's in his own interest."

The Librarian agrees. He worries that Earth's assessment is too generous. The dysfunction seems profound, and the dragon in question entirely intractable.

"Earth," repeats Cauldwell. His hand rests more easily on the dragon's claw. "Earth and . . . ?"

"Water," N'Doch supplies.

As Cauldwell turns, Water settles her form still further. The Librarian watches closely. When she's done settling, he silently applauds her cleverness. She's become a lovely, swan-necked blue dragon, cloaked in velvet like a seal, and no bigger than one of the Tinker mules that's whickering greetings from the far corners of the cavern. A phrase comes to his mind, from another former life: *good cop, bad cop.* The Librarian grins. Next to her looming, mountainous, and terrifying brother, Water is just the cutest little dragon you ever did see.

Luther's murmur is equal parts awe and delight. "Sheez a shape-shiftah, Leif. Ain'dat sumting?"

"It's something, all right."

"We should . . ." Erde urges. "Isn't it time to . . . ?"

Her anxiety brims over and swirls around the Librarian like surf. This time, he agrees. With Fire on the rampage who knows where, laying waste to who knows which of their near and dear, it's high time they got moving. He's lingered only to savor the luxury of someone else doing the talking for him. Three someones, his fellow guides, who can tap directly into his image-driven brain and translate for him. Except about the machines. That's beyond all understanding. The machines and his connection to them are his contribution to the four-way destiny. That much, at least, he is sure of, among so little else.

N'Doch and Erde snatch a brief reunion with Stoksie, asking after the rest of Blind Rachel, his Tinker crew. Seven out of ten of the local crews made it into the Refuge before Fire began torching the countryside. The Librarian worries about the fate of the other three.

He waves his arms. "We should. Now. The Library."

N'Doch grabs Leif Cauldwell's elbow familiarly. "Time to go to work, chief. See if the computers can tell us what Fire's up to."

Cauldwell eases free of the younger man's grip. "Leif. Call me Leif. There are no chiefs around here."

"Sure, sure. Whatever." N'Doch's round ebony face is open and guileless. He scuffs one foot along the polished stone floor. "But it's gonna make such a cool rhyming lyric when I get to writing a song about you."

Cauldwell stares at him.

"N'Doch . . ." Erde warns.

Cauldwell takes in the girl's prim and disapproving frown, makes a quick assessment and lets his testiness fade. "Yeah? Can't wait to hear it." He turns away to the Librarian. "Who do we need downstairs?"

"All. All."

N'Doch adds, "Everyone who can fit. All of us and all of you . . . y'know, your non-chiefs."

Erde's glower deepens. "He will not behave. Do not expect it."

But Cauldwell is already in motion, heading off into darkness, along a path among the crowded wagons. He has no problem with giving orders. "Luther, Stoksie, you're with us. Where's Ysa? And Stanze? We'll need Constanze." He halts, scanning the crowd.

Luther joins him, smiling. "Sheez ovah deah, Leif. Lookit dat, willya?"

Cauldwell's wife Constanze, with their little daughter clasped in her arms, trails a pack of children out of the throng, heading straight for the brown dragon's tall snout, which he's cushioned comfortably on crossed forepaws in order to greet them. Cauldwell starts. "Stanze . . . !"

"S'okay, Leif." Luther restrains him with a raised palm. "S'awri'. We shudn't teach 'em all owah feahs, ri'?"

"But . . ."

"But nuttin, Leif. Look fer yerself."

One of the smallest children is already snuggled against the dragon's rough jaw. Earth is impressive, but he is not lovely like his sister. The Librarian admits that he's seen prettier horned toads. But the child's eyes are only adoring. Constanze shoots a helpless glance in her husband's direction. The child in her grasp struggles for freedom. She shrugs and sets the girl down beside the dragon's claws. The girl crows delightedly and wraps her arms around the nearest pillar of ivory. Constanze backs away, bemused, then with another shrug, she turns and comes toward Cauldwell. The Librarian notes that the water dragon has stealthily sidestepped out of child-range.

Beside him, N'Doch chuckles dryly. "They'll leave

her alone. She's not talking to 'em like he is. He's still a kid despite his size, but she came into the world a grown-up. I sang her into kid-form once. My little brother. Died when he was five. Don't think she liked it much."

Cauldwell's arm slides automatically around Constanze's waist. They watch their little girl slipping and sliding as she tries to climb the dragon's claw. "Are we just going to leave them alone together?" Cauldwell asks.

Constanze leans into his side. "She told me, distinctly and even grammatically, that the dragon had assured her he wasn't eating children today."

"She said that? What an imagination!"

"No. I got the impression she was relaying what he actually said. All the children say he's talking to them."

"Really?" Cauldwell looks to the Librarian in alarm. "Is that possible?"

"Possible. Yes."

"Something you taught them? By the One, what are we raising?"

"The future," says the Librarian before he's even thought it over. And it's true that what the children have become is as much his fault as anyone's. He's been their tutor and their mascot. It's his dark den that's their favorite place of play. If he himself is not entirely human, how can he teach the children to be?

"Lord Earth urges us to action," Erde announces.

"We should get a move on," N'Doch nods. "The dragons'll listen in through us."

"Ah, if only Sir Hal were here!" Erde mourns.

"Sure, just what we need," N'Doch mutters. "Another chief."

Cauldwell gives the dragons one last glance of misgiving, then expels a long breath and leads his war council toward the elevator. The Librarian trots after him, his fingers itching for his keypad. N'Doch falls in behind, beside Paia and the soldier.

"Taking up the rear as usual, yer lordship?"

"One day you'll sass the wrong man, Dochmann." Köthen jerks his thumb toward Cauldwell's retreating back.

"Jeez, if you ain't blown me away yet, no one will. The world loves a clown, Dolph, doncha know?"

"I wouldn't bet money on it. Or your life."

"Like I'd better not sass the Fire dude, is that what you're getting at?"

The soldier adjusts the sword across his back to a more comfortable angle. "It wouldn't be my first advice."

"The God . . . I mean, Fire . . . doesn't take well to mockery," agrees Paia quietly. "He only knows how to give it out."

"Then I'm gonna be in deep shit," N'Doch predicts. " 'Cause there's one thing I just can't leave alone, and that's a guy who takes himself too seriously."

Köthen groans. "I'll rue the day I swore my sword to your safety."

"Cheer up, Dolph. You used to be one of those too-serious guys, remember, and we worked it out okay, didn't we?"

"It's hardly analogous."

"Yeah, well." At the open door of the elevator, silhouetted against the bright light from the cab, N'Doch glances back at the big, dirt-colored dragon, besieged by a pack of noisy little children.

He laughs softly. "That's one hell of a baby-sitter!"

Chapter Two

N'doch is pondering that song he'll make up about Leif Cauldwell as he trails the others into the shadowed Communications Room. He lets the base rhythm of the HVAC underline the melody, and longs for an instrument to play it on.

The group piles up in front of the bright wall screen, still running feed from the helipad security camera. N'doch stands at the back. He's taller than any of them, except Luther and Cauldwell. Besides, the image is so large and so clear, it's like he's inside of it, like he's back up there on the mountaintop, in the heat and the smoke, a sitting duck for dragon-fire. Makes him sweat just to think about it. And about what Fire might be up to. Even packed in here like sardines, it's tough to keep still, tough to fight the worry down. His grandpa's got power, N'doch is sure of it, but is his magic strong enough to stand against the malign wizardry of Fire?

Papa Dja, Papa Dja, keep your head low, old man, he intones silently.

The boy Mattias jumps up from the console as Gerrasch approaches. N'Doch thinks the kid looks a whole lot tighter around the eyes than when they'd left him here before. No surprise, given what he's just seen, courtesy of the video feed. But he's trying to play it cool. N'Doch would've done the same at his age. Hell, he's doing it now.

"Weah's da dragins?" Mattias demands immediately.

Gerrasch elbows him gently aside and rolls into his padded chair, his soft pink hands working the keys before he's even settled his bulk.

N'Doch jerks his thumb. "Upstairs."

Mattias looks to Gerrasch, who's already hunched down and oblivious, then to Leif Cauldwell. His entire gawky-teen body pleads. "Kin I go, Leif, huh, huh?"

Cauldwell nods. A bit grudgingly, N'Doch thinks, but he's willing to cut the rebel leader some slack. A day ago, before all these mouthy strangers showed up out of nowhere, the dude was running his own show, the whole show, no matter what he says about chiefs or no chiefs. But his rebellion was doomed— ill-equipped and undermanned—and the man has the grace to see it, even if he won't say it out loud. Two dragons suddenly on his side gives him and his people a serious fighting chance.

The kid practically lays rubber scooting on out of there. N'Doch shoulders his way out of the press to wander restlessly among the rows of darkened workstations while late arrivals trot in from upstairs and the Librarian fiddles with his keypad. The walls to either side of the screen are gridded with smooth-faced, rectangular units adorned with svelte pull handles and tiny green idiot lights. Probably some sort of data storage. N'Doch wonders about the people who used to live and work here, sunk so deep into the mountain bedrock. What happened to them? What did they do while the world outside fell apart around them? He slides a palm along the slick surface. What is it? Metal? Plastic? He can't tell. For him, it's . . . well, the *future*. He can't repress a little private speculation about what all this super high-tech equipment could do if retrofitted and put to work mixing one of his songs. He doubts he'll get the chance to find out. Too much serious shit going down.

The yellow glow bathing the racks of alien equipment flicks over to blue. N'Doch pivots and moves toward the screen. The big world map is back, with its too-great expanse of hot, empty ocean and its overlay of satellite orbits. He scans for the blinking indicators.

"Uh-oh," he murmurs, and scans again.

There's the one for Air, parked off the map in the lower corner, signifying her imprisonment who-knows-where, and there's the two active signals poised over a position that looks to be right about where he's standing, only several levels up in the big cavern. "Where is he? Where's the fourth signal?"

He hears a weird chittering noise. It's Gerrasch, something he's doing with his teeth. "Gone," he says. "Already."

"Gone?" moans Erde. "Oh, I knew it! We shouldn't have waited!"

"Hold on, hold on." But N'Doch is offering comfort he doesn't feel.

Stoksie peers at the screen. "Gone weah?"

"To another time," says Cauldwell grimly, "If I understand this right."

N'Doch nods. "Question is, which one? Who do we warn first?"

Again, they're all talking at once, filling the room with more noise than there are people. Luther explains to Ysa what the blinking lights mean. Constanze asks if the indicator would change if the Beast assumed man-form. N'Doch thinks about his mama, alone in front of her vid set. Grandpapa Djawara can't be much help to her. He's an old man, living by himself out in the bush with only distant neighbors who fear and mistrust him anyway. He'll need all his witchy powers to keep his own self safe.

Cauldwell lets everyone yammer out their anxiety. Meanwhile, he leans over the Librarian's round shoulder and gets to work. "Gerrasch, call up House. What's happening at the Citadel?"

The Librarian keys in the connection. He and Caldwell have worked together a long time. N'Doch moves in, interested. He's learned in the Meld how, when Fire awoke, he commandeered the Cauldwell family fortress as his temple and stronghold. But Paia's presence in the Meld is emotional more than visual, despite her being a painter and all. N'Doch is eager for a clearer look at this place he's heard so much about. And then there's the Citadel's sentient computer, this "House" that Leif's asking about. The machine that's been Paia's mentor in the dragon lore, like Papa Dja for N'Doch and Hal Engle for Erde. N'Doch still can't quite get his brain around it. There was no full-tilt AI back in his time. He always talked a lot of sci-fi, but he didn't believe in much of it. So he's startled by the voice that floats up from the console speakers. Doesn't sound synthesized at all. Not like the AIs in the old sf vids, which always talked like they'd swallowed a big dose of Prozac. This sounds like just a human, and a kinda panicky one at that. N'Doch has never heard a computer whine before.

"Finally! Where have you been? I've been calling for hours and Mattias kept saying, 'they went upstairs, they went upstairs,' but he didn't know how to patch me through, or maybe he thought, well, I don't know what he thought! Really, Gerrasch, you have to train your people better! Is he there? He's not here. He . . ."

"Was here," intones the Librarian. "Gone already."

"Gone? Gone? Where?"

"Away."

'What do you mean, away? You mean, *downtime*? Is everyone all right? Is Paia all right?"

Funny how everyone keeps asking that, muses N'Doch.

"She's fine, House." Cauldwell leans in to be heard over the background din of questions and debate.

"Leif! You made it! I was so concerned!"

"Everyone here's fine. A bit shell-shocked, but fine. What's going on there? Can you put the monitors on-line?"

"Working on it. Such excitement you've missed, Leif! There's been a palace coup, just as you predicted. Second Son Branfer has declared himself First Son in your absence!"

"Branfer! That clod can't manage his breakfast, never mind the whole Temple!"

"And one of the Faceless Twelve, I forget which, has elevated herself to High Priestess."

N'Doch detects conflict on Cauldwell's sculpture-perfect face. There goes his other seat of authority, poof! Swept from beneath him. But he'd engineered that usurping himself. So dedicated to his cause, he gave up what had to be a real cushy job. Except for having Fire as your boss.

"Hope she and Branfer hate each other," Caldwell mutters darkly.

"If not now, they will soon, particularly if I have anything to say about it. The Temple is doomed. They'll all be eating each other alive by noon!"

N'Doch marvels at the computer's unconcealed relish for violence and intrigue. Like lots of teenagers he's known. Proof enough for him that this machine is sentient.

Cauldwell is less gleeful. "Any injuries? Much damage? What about Christoff and Ark?"

"Safe. Holed up here in the Rare Books Room with the others. I was able to warn them in time."

"Can you keep them safe?"

"Until *he* comes looking for them . . ."

"Then we'll have to get them out of there before that happens."

"I'll tell them. Then we have to figure out a way to rescue me." There's a pause, entirely without static. The Librarian's typing fingers go slack. Cauldwell gnaws his lip. Finally, its voice gone flat, the computer says, "Patching through the monitors."

The big blue map on the wall is quickly papered over by a grid of smaller images: rooms, interior vistas, some populated, others not, some obscured by signal static, a few entirely blank. N'Doch sees long windowless corridors, paneled in gleaming wood, furnished with carpets and paintings and the occasional ornate, stiff-backed chair. People racing to and fro. He sees a vast, bustling kitchen, though he can't really tell if a meal is being prepared or if the food stores are being raided. He sees a huge dining hall with the tables laid out in a blatantly hierarchical pattern. He sees sun-blasted walled courtyards and a long view down the nave of an elaborate, gilded basilica he supposes to be the Temple. A small gathering huddles in noisy prayer near what must be the altar.

"Not many signs of fighting," notes Cauldwell. "House did the job right."

Paia drifts over to the console with Köthen in tow. "Look! My home. Or it was . . ."

Köthen looks, with his usual intensity. N'Doch doubts the good baron knows how to do anything casual.

"And will be again," Cauldwell insists. "We're not surrendering the Citadel. We're encouraging the Temple to self-destruct while the Beast is distracted."

Paia peers at her tall cousin as if just now registering who he is and what he's done. "You've planned this a long time, haven't you, Luco."

"Leif. Luco is past."

"Yes. I see that now."

N'Doch decides she's finally pulling herself together. This is the first unambiguous statement he's heard out of her since she confronted her rogue dragon up on the mountaintop and bravely denied him. He understands how devastated that's left her. No matter how fiercely he resisted the pull of dragon destiny at first, he'd be a hollow shell if Water was taken from him now.

Paia leans toward the console's one visible mike. N'Doch is sure it's an anachronism. The sensors in this room could likely pick up a mouse sneeze. Old Gerrasch must prefer the illusion of focus. Or maybe this future's too future even for him.

"Hello, House."

"Hello, Paia." The computer's voice goes deeper,

calmer, like a new persona has kicked in. "How are you getting along out there in the world?"

Paia sinks into the chair that Köthen has found for her. "Oh, House! I wouldn't know where to begin! There's so much you never told me!"

N'Doch swallows a rueful guffaw, though it nearly chokes him. He eases over beside Köthen to study the Citadel up close. Searching for clues, both of them. N'Doch's still struggling to encompass this world he's landed in, how it got the way it is from the way it was in his time. Not just the rising oceans and the global drought, but the people, and how they coped, how they live now. As for Köthen, he's even farther out of the loop, but he's a sponge for useful information, plus he's dead eager to learn all about this woman he's fallen for, so hard and so suddenly.

"Big joint, huh?" N'Doch is taken by the sheer size and scope of the Citadel, at least as far as he can see from these images. "Whacha think, Dolph? Look anything like your palace at home?"

The baron snorts quietly. "Castle Köthen is hardly a palace, Dochmann. Attractively situated, comfortable enough, but modest by comparison. What it is, however, is secure and easily defended."

"Yeah? You ever have to do that?"

Köthen cuts him a look of amused disbelief. "If not me, then who?"

"Well, I mean, I guess . . . Yeah. Stupid question." When he first met Köthen, the man wore bloodied armor and wrist shackles. Putting a sword back in his hand was like grafting on a lost arm.

"Not stupid. Not really." Cauldwell has been eavesdropping. "I'd like to know, too."

"Hey, chief. Forgot you speak Kraut." N'Doch gives way, bringing the rebel leader and Köthen face-to-face. These two alpha dudes, he figures, have some deep shit to work out if they're gonna work together, so better sooner than later. And let them do it here, in a crowd, where nothing much can happen.

But Cauldwell's negotiating skills haven't gone near as rusty as his diplomat's German. He offers Köthen a serious, collegial smile. "Here. I'll show you around my place first." He guides the baron along the tapestry of images to point out a long view of barren red hills. "The cameras trained on the entrance went belly-up a while ago, but these ones up on the cliff face are still working. You see, the Citadel's a natural fortress. Dug deep into the side of a mountain." He nods to the next image, where the camera stares straight down into the empty inner courtyard. "It's proved impossible to take when its defense is well organized—I know. I've held it myself a few times."

Köthen folds his arms, as if listening out of mere good manners.

"But now, in the midst of a power grab," Cauldwell continues smoothly, "it'll be chaos in there. Which is exactly the point. House, can we look at a cross section, a plan? Give me a few screens' worth."

"Working," mutters the computer.

The image collage breaks down and reassembles quickly, but not before N'Doch has taken in a flash of blue overlaid with one bright word: *HURRY.*

"Wait! What was that? Did anyone see that? I thought I saw . . ."

But no one's listening. Several big diagrams replace the image and whatever had followed it. As Köthen moves in to look them over, his eyes narrow with interest.

"Like what you see?" Cauldwell taps a lower-level plan, tracing out access routes.

Köthen allows him the faintest motion, more shrug than nod. "What soldier wouldn't? Though I'd prefer to be defending it rather than taking it."

"Of course, and when you do get inside, it's close quarters for a fight. Hand-to-hand all the way. Which is why . . ." Cauldwell eyes the long sword sheathed across the shorter man's back. "You any good with that thing?"

N'Doch steps between them, planting a palm against the baron's chest. A short time ago, he wouldn't have dared to do this. Now it's Cauldwell he's worried about. "He is, chief. You can take it from me."

But Cauldwell knew that. He smiles his challenge. "Ready to use it?"

Köthen's glance flicks back to the feed from the Citadel. "Never a better time . . . "

"That's what I was thinking."

"Hey, wait a minute . . ." N'Doch recognizes complicity when he hears it, and it's caught him completely by surprise. He'd never have figured the rough medieval fighting man and the sleek high-tech warrior for such instant allies. Suddenly something about it worries him. "I mean, hold on . . . !"

Caldwell ignores him. "I've got people inside, good ones, in computer contact. But I have to pull them before the Beast returns, or they're char and cinder, every one of them. The sooner we move . . ."

Köthen nods, though N'Doch knows for a fact that he'd never heard of a computer until yesterday. "The dragons could take us. Paia could show them the way, isn't that right, Dochmann?"

"Er . . . yeah."

Cauldwell blinks. "All of us?"

"I don't know. If they were horses, I could tell you

their carrying capacity to the ounce." He offers up one of his rare grins, rueful and charming. "We'll just have to ask them."

"Like you said, there'll never be a better moment."

"What, now? *Now?*" N'Doch's sharp exhalation gets everyone's attention. Even Gerrasch, intent at the console, glances up. "You can't do this now! We've got relatives and friends to take care of first!" He glares from one to the other. "Dolph! Whadda you thinking?"

Köthen gazes back with that look of his that's so much like a shrug.

"I also have friends and relatives to rescue," Cauldwell jabs a stern finger at the screen. "In there. Men and women who've risked their lives to overthrow the Beast."

"But . . ." N'Doch rubs his eyes. "Aww, shit!"

"It does not require an army to deliver a warning or conduct a spot rescue," Köthen observes. "And the sooner you're about it, the better."

"Me? What about you?"

Köthen looks away, as if to check on the latest events on the wall screen. When he looks back, he says nothing, knowing he doesn't have to.

"C'mon, Dolph! Don't desert me, man! I need your help!"

"We all do!" exclaims a voice from behind. "My lord baron, you can't possibly mean to . . ."

"My lady."

Erde pushes through the crowd to face him. "Surely you will come with us to save Deep Moor! Rose and the others—they're in terrible danger!"

N'Doch doesn't blame Köthen for avoiding Erde's eyes. Her pleading desperation would melt stones. Most stones, maybe. Not this one.

"My place is here. My *duty* is here."

He says it to N'Doch, but really, he's telling her, with an arch touch of vengefulness that N'Doch can't really admire. And the girl is so appalled, she forgets to temper her preemptory tone. N'Doch hears a fight brewing.

"Our duty is where the dragons lead us!"

"Who are you to tell me where my duty lies?"

N'Doch watches Cauldwell kick back and let it happen, like he already knows which way it's gonna go. But N'Doch can't keep his own stupid mouth from dragging him into the middle. "You brought him, girl. You lectured him all about dragons and destiny. I guess you gotta live with the consequences."

"But Deep Moor is in danger! Your sword is needed, my lord!"

"So you said when you hauled me away from Deep Moor. Now you wish to haul me back again?" Köthen rounds on her, and the flare in his dark eyes isn't warm or pleasant. "What should I care for Deep Moor? Have you forgotten, my lady? Deep Moor was to be my silk-lined cell."

"Only to keep you alive, my lord!"

"Alive for what? To win a crown for another?"

"For the rightful prince, my lord baron!" She looks entirely bewildered, like she can't believe she has to explain such obviousness to a man of honor such as himself. Their raised voices have carried over the noise in the rest of the room. Luther and Stoksie wander over, ever so casually.

"If he's rightful, then let him have it!" Köthen flings up an angry fist, then collects himself. "You said yourself, my lady, that I might discover my destiny here, and so I have. It isn't the one you had planned for me, apparently, but isn't that just the way with destinies? They control us rather than the other way around?"

"But my lord . . . *Deep Moor*! All our friends . . . !"

"Go warn Hal Engle. He'll see to Deep Moor and his witch-lady. He doesn't need me. He's made that abundantly clear."

N'Doch at last takes pity on the girl's stunned disbelief. "My guess is he'll think different about that, Dolph, when Fire shows up on his doorstep."

Köthen shrugs. "What's done is done."

"Not really. It may feel like we're a thousand years from Deep Moor, but remember, Time's gone all elastic on us, Dolph."

Cauldwell clears his throat. "Listen, if the man wants to fight for us, I could sure use him. What does it matter if he's here or there? We're all working toward the same end, right? The defeat of the Beast."

Luther and Stoksie murmur their agreement.

Then other murmurs rise around them, and die into sudden silence.

"Yes, but . . . !" Erde's last syllable rings loudly, alone.

The room has turned hot with reflected yellow glare. Astonished faces stare past N'Doch to the screen behind him, lit to molten gold by the surreal glow. N'Doch knows that glow, like he knows his hands, or the sound of his own voice. He turns slowly, afraid of what he's going to see.

It's what he's expected. Sun. Sand. Bright-painted fishing boats. Palm trees.

Home.

It's like the wall's been blown away without a scrap left, and what's outside is not a mountain's worth of rock, but . . . the beach. Outside the seaside

African town that N'Doch always thought he'd grow old and die in . . . until he met a certain dragon.

Without thinking, he steps toward the screen.

Köthen grabs his arm. "Dochmann, no."

"Lemme go, Dolph."

He can feel the heat shimmering off the glistening white sand. Just past the bright curve of that hull, he knows, is a path through the palm grove to the town gates and the market. Köthen's hard fingers bruise his flesh as he struggles to free himself. "What's it to you? You don't wanna go, fine, but I gotta! I can go now, and warn them!"

"No. It is not real, Dochmann, remember? It's a wall, and moving pictures. You told me that, remember?"

"I can smell the damn salt! Can't you? And the fish? Can't you smell it, Dolph?" What N'Doch remembers is what Paia said, in the Meld when only the dragon guides could hear. When the wall turned up a full-screen image of Deep Moor, so real-looking you were sure you could walk right into it, she said, Well, *you could.*

It's a portal, she said. *A doorway.* Her own dragon had told her so. Why believe anything out of the slimy renegade's lying mouth? Because of the heat and the smell: the drying seaweed and the pungent smoke blowing off the kebob vendors' carts. And because of the sounds: the roll and break of the surf, and the tinny distant music from the market stalls.

"Off me, Dolph! Lemme go!" N'Doch tries a quick, breaking twist, unsuccessfully. Köthen is shorter than he is, but stronger and just as fast. "Look, this'll fix our transport problem! No dragons needed. I'm there!" He swings himself a few steps closer to the screen. "Dolph, they're sitting ducks! Please! Lemme go!" Another jerk and twist, another step closer.

Now Paia's hanging on his other side like her life depended on it. "It could be a trap! It's just the sort of thing he'd do!"

Köthen is talking and Paia is talking, and Erde's throwing her two cents in. N'Doch doesn't listen. He's so . . . *drawn*. It's . . . home, right in front of him. Only has to step through. He'll just be there, he knows it. Check up on his mama and Papa Dja, get them into hiding, then the dragons could pick him up on their way back from Deep Moor. He's got it all worked out. Save everyone a lot of trouble and debate if he just did it. . . .

Now.

N'Doch feints with his body. With his mind, he calls the dragon upstairs.

I'm taking a little shortcut, kiddo. Come get me when you're ready.

DO NOT . . . !

Too late. N'Doch leans hard into his feint, then shifts his weight and—a miracle—throws Köthen off-balance, not enough to break his grip but enough to be able to pivot toward him fast and slam in with a full body block. The baron staggers, his soldier's fists still welded to N'Doch's wrist and elbow. N'Doch pivots again and flings Köthen away from the screen. The force shoves Paia through it . . . and drags him after.

The passage is instantaneous. From dim cool to searing glare in the span of a heartbeat. The bright shock of the heat and the sudden grainy softness beneath them startles Paia into letting go. Both tumble headlong into hot, white sand and lie gasping for the briefest of seconds.

N'Doch looks up, and groans.

Why is it things never work out like he's intended? There's the High Priestess sprawled on the beach beside him, two hundred years away from the man who would do anything to keep her safe. No sign anywhere of a return portal. Just sand, palm trees, and hot, hot ocean. N'Doch's eyes squeeze shut. All he can think of is how many pieces Köthen is going to cut him into when the dragons arrive to rescue them.

Chapter Three

Wide-eyed, Erde watches N'Doch flail, stumble into searing white light, then collapse in a heap in the powdery sand with the High Priestess on top of him. Her gasp is half giggle, for they do look comical, that is, until the hot beach vanishes, she's back in the darkened room, staring at a bright blue wall, and N'Doch and Paia are gone.

Erde shudders, her foolish half grin frozen. For between the brightness and the blue, for an instant so brief she almost doubts her senses, she'd glimpsed something else. She'd seen Deep Moor in flames.

"What . . . what happened?" Leif Cauldwell looks to Gerrasch. "Where'd they go?"

The Librarian rises in horror. Has he seen it, too? "There. Are. No!"

Erde blinks away the fiery afterimage and tries not to panic. "To Africa. It's N'Doch's home." She alerts the dragons. But they know already.

What do we do?

GO AFTER THEM, OF COURSE.

To Africa? Now? But I saw Deep Moor burning!

OVERANXIOUS IMAGININGS, GIRL.
IT'S FIRE'S AFTERMATH.
How can you be sure?

Cauldwell stares at the wall of blue. "You can get them back again, right?"

"Noo, noo . . ." Gerrasch is tapping, tapping at his rows of little square buttons, making soft sounds of animal distress.

HELP THE LIBRARIAN. LEND HIM YOUR VOICE.

The dragons are right, as usual, even Lady Water, always less patient with youthful folly. Erde hurries to Gerrasch's side. She must not give in to her terrors. "I think . . . it's not like a door. He can't open this portal when he wants to. It has its own . . . magic." She hesitates at the word. Notions of magic are scoffed at in this future world, despite the obvious presence of dragons. But how else to describe her intuition about the portal, without N'Doch here to help with his knowledge of what he calls "technology?"

"Can't open it?" Cauldwell repeats. "Well, that's a problem."

Baron Köthen stares tight-lipped at the empty blue expanse. "He did it on purpose."

"No, my lord, he . . ." Erde turns to him, wary of his hot temper, now that his lady has been stolen from him.

"He did! The young whelp!"

"He didn't mean to take Paia," asserts Cauldwell's wife reasonably. "Why would he?"

Erde is surprised by Constanze's innocence. Surely it's an obvious possibility that N'Doch abducted the High Priestess in order to entice Köthen away from Leif Cauldwell's military preoccupations. Now the baron will have to require the dragon to take him to his lady right away, as any devoted knight would do.

But Köthen makes no such demand. He stands with his arms folded and his brows drawn down in an inward stare. A conflict of interest, no doubt. He feels honor bound, Erde decides, having already promised his sword to Cauldwell's rebellion. If so, then Cauldwell must release him, and surely will quickly volunteer to do so.

Again, she is confounded. Both Cauldwells wait silently, observing Köthen's inner debate.

"Is Paia in any danger there?" asks Constanze at last.

"Of course!" Erde cries. "Of course she is!"

Köthen sends the Cauldwells an even glance. "No more so than here."

"Not true, my lord! It's beastly hot there, and the air is full of poison!"

"And so it is here."

"But there are guns everywhere! N'Doch was killed with guns, until the dragon healed him!"

"Healed?" Cauldwell asks Köthen.

"It's true," admits Köthen, "or so the lad tells me. I wasn't there."

"Huh. Never heard of Fire doing anything like that."

Constanze murmurs, "He'd rather destroy people than save them."

"Healing is Lord Earth's special gift!" Erde declares, though she knows that pride is a sin and that Cauldwell's interest is only in the military value of such an asset.

"My lady Erde." Köthen looses his arms as if breaking an invisible bond and bows so formally, she suspects him of mockery. "I would be eternally grateful if you and your esteemed dragon would effect a rescue at your earliest possible convenience. The whelp will keep my lady safe until you get there. He knows I'll have his liver for breakfast if he doesn't."

Cauldwell nods, and his wife relaxes against him in relief. Constanze is brown-skinned and eagle-eyed. She reminds Erde of the women of Deep Moor, and of her dead grandmother, the Baroness. Women of power. She'll not relent.

Erde gazes imploringly at the trio of Tinkers. "Help me convince him!"

"Dockman'll do it jus' gud, nah," Stoksie soothes. "Yu'll see."

Ysabel nods, and Luther merely shrugs. There is sympathy in his dark face, but no voice on her side. The crisis here and now is more real to these people than a crisis somewhere so far away, and Erde can hardly blame them. But the image of burning Deep Moor still flares in her mind's eye. Was it only, as Lady Water said, her fearful imaginings? Or was it a true Seeing? She looks to Gerrasch. His eyes are dark and round, and fixed on her as if he has shared her awful vision.

"Yes. Go. Quickly! Come back!"

"What? Must I go alone?"

The flames burn so fiercely in her head, and among them move the shadows of men and horses. Swords flash. She sees . . .

The hell-priest! Oh, dragon!

"You'll have the dragons, after all." Köthen puts out a hand to steady her. "Could you be better armed?"

Terror and outrage push Erde toward the edge of a tantrum, which only frightens her further. She's never been given to tantrums. Of course they are right to send off the least valuable fighter. Doubtless her real, her innermost reason for demanding Köthen's company is that she can't bear to part with him. Every day, for the two weeks since she dragged him unwilling into the dragons' Quest, she has been able to think of him as part of her life. His stern grace and beauty have been the chief pleasure of her days—except, of course, for the dragon. She even thrust her own feelings aside when the arrival of the High Priestess woke Köthen from his gloom, for Passion is one of the High Ideals, and Erde can recognize—and must honor—a True Passion when she sees it, even though she is not its object.

But here is Baron Köthen refusing to bow to the Ideal and let it rule him, as a True Knight should. She should not love him. And yet, she does. Nor should she waste another moment arguing. And yet, she does. Because to allow his willfulness to go unchallenged means forsaking her own Ideals.

"Adolphus Michael Hoffman," she hears herself declaiming. "Thou art not a man of honor, to leave thy lady thus endangered!"

Ah! She's touched him. He looks quite taken aback. But only long enough to study her with that dark gaze, so surprising beneath his shock of blond hair. She seems to have done something he approves of, though she can't understand what or how. Despite the faint, satirical gleam in his eyes, Erde blunders onward. "Nor is it worthy of a True Knight to send a lady unchaperoned into the wilderness!"

"Two dragons are not chaperone enough? Then we'll find a knight more honorable than I to guard your journey." Köthen lifts his head, unable any longer to subdue his ironical grin, and scans the faces crowded around. "Who's for a quest on dragon-back?"

Erde is stunned speechless. This is mockery for certain! Is the dragons' sacred Purpose mere child's play in his mind, and only war the work of adults?

A portentous silence gathers around her, but for the shuffling of feet on the hard, smooth floor. In the back, murmuring. Someone clears her throat. Then Luther Williams steps forward.

"I, fer one." He turns to Cauldwell. "S'all ri', Leif?"

Cauldwell nods, surprised. "Good choice. What d'you think, Gerrasch?"

"Yes. Yes. Go."

"Are you armed?" Köthen asks him.

Luther pats the large knife shoved into his waist-band.

It's like being put up for auction. Erde cannot believe how badly her efforts have turned out. But she must get to Deep Moor somehow, and it will be good to have Luther along. The Tinkers are extremely resourceful, and Luther is a man of piety and principle. "Thank you, Luther! Will you really come?"

"Betcha!"

With that, the matter is settled. Baron Köthen turns away to talk strategy with the Cauldwells. Gerrasch bends over his keypad, the chatty disembodied voice of the machine called House nattering in his ear. The wall again fills with ranks of moving pictures from the Citadel. For a moment, Erde could almost weep from loneliness, so she calls to the only being whose love she is sure of.

Oh, dragon! I am so weary!

YOU NEED FOOD AND REST, CHILD.

And when shall I find them?

SOON.

But not yet.

FOOD, PERHAPS. BUT NOT REST. NOT YET. NO
REST FOR ANY OF US UNTIL OUR SISTER AIR IS
FOUND AND LIBERATED. ASK LUTHER IF FOOD
CAN BE SPARED FOR OUR JOURNEY.

And you, dear dragon? How long since you've eaten?

TOO LONG. THE LAND HERE IS BARREN.
NOTHING LIVING BUT HUMANS AND THE
TAME CREATURES LEFT TO THEM.

Lady Water chimes in impatiently. I'LL TAKE
YOU FISHING WHEN WE GET THERE!

Erde hopes the dragon can wait just a little while
longer. For time is of the essence and since everyone
is so sure that N'Doch can handle his situation, she
plans to head to Deep Moor first. She can warn the
women about Lord Fire's threats, and tell them of
her vision of flames. They will understand. Then she
can rush back to N'Doch's time with a clear con-
science. It's a good plan. But to forestall further argument, she'll not inform the other humans of this
minor alteration.

While the warriors gather to plan the assault on
the Citadel, Erde draws Luther aside, fingering his
thin shirt and woven string vest. "You'll need some
warmer clothing when we get to Deep Moor. Would
N'Doch's fit you? I think his pack is put away somewhere in your wagon."

Stoksie has tagged along to help them prepare. "I
know weah dat is."

Luther says, "Cold deah, izzit? Mebbe snow,
eben?"

"Snow, for sure."

"Snow. Dat I wanna see." Luther elbows the
smaller man. "Yu wanna make da trip, Stokes?"

"Nah. My daddy saw't, wontime. Leas' das what he sed. But den, he sed a lotta t'ings." Stoksie grins and trots off to find N'Doch's pack.

Erde worries that these cheerful men have no real idea of the frigid dangers of true winter. Heat and drought are their only reference points. "I'm sure you have never been as cold as you will be in Deep Moor," she tells Luther earnestly.

But Luther is sweating by the time he's tried on as many layers of N'Doch's heavy clothing as will fit him. Erde shakes out her own woolens and slides her feet into her sheepskin boots. They make her feel safer, like putting on armor, or some sort of shell, though she's no longer ashamed to be seen in the scant, loose clothing that's the only sensible thing in this desiccated future. She's gotten used to being so aware of her body—and of everyone else's—all the time. For the sake of her little deception, she lets Stoksie fold all the clothing away again in N'Doch's pack. She will carry it, and Luther will shoulder the sturdy sack of food Stoksie has thrown together while up in the caverns. Blind Rachel provisions, she's sure, and gladly given, from wagons recently restocked from the sale of Erde's dragon brooch, which also purchased the fine and venerable sword that Baron Köthen wears across his back.

Does she now regret that sacrifice? She doesn't think so. Despite her failure to make events turn out the way she wanted, Erde von Alte retains her belief that what is meant to happen, will happen. Destiny is too essential a force to be turned aside by one man's stubborn perversity, or for that matter, by the stubborn scheming of a perverse dragon.

As if aware of her thoughts, Köthen glances up

from his huddle with the Cauldwells. "Don't be long."

She looks for a trace of gloating or victory or whatever she imagines a man might feel. But all that is gone now. She sees only dispassionate concern, that of a commander sending his man off on a mission.

"What?" he demands, for she is staring back at him intently.

Erde blinks, looks away. How can she explain what she's just understood? How can she admit to it? She's interpreted all of Köthen's actions as meant specifically to thwart her personally, to make her miserable—revenge for having been brought away against his will. Now, as a larger vision opens up to her, she sees the entire folly of this assumption. Certainly he is not above rubbing a bit of salt into her wounds, but she is not his target. She's hardly within range of his aim at all. And if she catches an arrow, it's because he sees no need to be careful. Like a leaf to the sun, he turns toward what he knows best, what he's trained to do, what makes him feel worthy. And that is to get things moving, men and things, to maximize the use of slim resources, both personal and physical, in order to accomplish the task at hand. Whatever the task might be. Even though the dragons' Quest is not his own, and despite a foolish girl often putting herself in his way.

No. Not child's play. Not child's play at all. Rather, he's assigned her the danger she is best equipped to cope with and live through. A blush warms Erde's cheeks. Had she really thought that leadership only meant waving a sword about more skillfully than anyone else?

"What is it, girl?" Köthen asks, more forcefully.

Erde stares down at her sandaled feet. "I'm sorry. So very sorry."

"Pardon?" He takes a step toward her. "I don't think I heard you correctly."

"I said, I'm sorry, my lord."

"For what?"

"For all the trouble I've caused you."

"An apology?" He's actually at a loss for words. He glances back at the intent faces around Gerrasch's swiftly moving fingers. The glow from the many rows of little buttons lights his profile, and Erde's heart turns over yet again. She can't say which part of his face is most beautiful to her, or why, but she knows she could stare at him forever, and be happy. She cannot deny the truth of the sigh that wells up, as if from the very bottom of her soul.

When Köthen's gaze returns, it is milder than she's ever seen it. He grips her shoulder to shake it lightly. "On your way, then. Grab up my lady Paia and that kidnapping young whelp, then do what you can for the witchy women on your way back. Be quick about it!"

"Aye, my lord."

"Luther!"

"Yeah!" The Tinker hefts the heavy sack.

"Bring them back safe!"

"Betcha!"

Erde readies the image of Deep Moor in her mind. WE ARE GOING TO . . . ?

Yes, Dragon. To Deep Moor first. Fearful imaginings or not, it seems only right. Will Lady Water agree?

IF WE DO IT QUICKLY, I'LL AGREE TO ANYTHING.

Erde grasps Luther's arm. "Hang on tight!"

Chapter Four

When it's clear she's off-balance and falling, Paia gives in and lets the momentum take her. The instant the sun-bright image came up on the screen, she'd known what it was. The portal had opened again. So she is not surprised to find herself thrown flat on burning sand with the breath knocked out of her. Nor is she surprised to find the tall young African's limbs entangled with her own. Serves her good and right. She shouldn't have hung onto him. She looks for the soldier, but sees he's been left behind. When panic wells up, she fights it down easily enough. He'll be worried about her, but maybe it's all right to be without him for a while. A good thing, to be on her own. For the first time ever. In her life.

Catching her breath, Paia contemplates this sudden urge toward solitude. The air is heavy, as if it would take less of it than usual to fill up her lungs. It leaves the oddest taste of salt on her tongue. She's aware of a certain inner numbness. Her brain is a slow-turning maelstrom. Better just to concentrate on what to do for the next few seconds. Like, get out of the sun and the punishing heat. Then she sees the ocean, and the parts of her scattered self draw together. She scrambles to her knees like a worshiper at the altar.

"Steady, now," wheezes the young man, though he hardly sounds steady himself. He frees his leg and arms and edges away, then gets up to scan the beach warily.

"The water! Ah! It's so . . . beautiful!" Blue from side to side. Water as wide as the sky. The hot light dancing off a billion shifting surfaces. She's seen the ocean on computer screens, more of it than she's seen dry land. But the reality is overwhelming. It's awe-inspiring. It's so animated, so very . . . wet. The rolling of the surf is hypnotic. Paia has only known still water, like the Sacred Pool in the Citadel. Immediately, she wants to paint it, to try to capture that dance of reflected light, to work with all those colors she's never had use for before. "Are we in . . . ?"

N'Doch nods as if he had something to be ashamed of. "My place."

The western coast of Africa, then, in the year 2013. Half a day ago, she and N'Doch were total strangers. But they have been in the Meld together, and know everything there is to know about each other. By contrast, she knows almost nothing about the soldier, Adolphus of Köthen, except that they are fated together. But this sharing of minds, what a gift and privilege! Paia recalls that N'Doch at first felt invaded by his fellow dragon guides, but at least he's come around enough not to resist entirely. A sense of the merging still lingers, like an intimate scent. Intimate enough to be compromising, but N'Doch won't take advantage, even if he'd welcome the chance. It's too much like incest. Even better, he doesn't believe in running other people's lives—unlike most of the men she's met. Paia smiles up at him. He's as beautiful in his own way as the soldier is. It would be comforting just to flirt a little, as she used to with Luco, in the security of knowing nothing would come of it. But she senses it would upset this young man, at least until they know each other better. Delicately, she offers him a hand, asking to be helped to her feet.

He looks away, frowning. "He's gonna kill me, y'know. Just absolutely murder me."

Paia laughs, picturing the soldier's handsome, rough-hewn glower. Like a rock at sunset. A bright block of unpolished marble. The memory of his beauty distracts her momentarily. "I won't let him. I promise."

"Easy for you to say."

He's watching her like she's a bomb primed to go off. Waiting for the weeping and panic. But Paia's had enough of all that. For now, she prefers her numbness. It allows her to get on with things. She rises on her own, brushing sand from her long white shirt and soft pants. The open beach is as hot as a griddle. She's sweating already, and knows she must look a sight. In the Temple, looking ugly and concealing her body was her idea of rebellion. Now she's glad for the protection of long sleeves and pant legs. The sunlight may be as lethal here in 2013 as it is in her own time. Paia doesn't recall her history lessons all that well. What's the point of history when you know the world is ending? Besides, whenever she wanted actual information, she could always ask House. But House is two hundred years away. Ignorance, she realizes, can be a dangerous liability.

Farther along the beach, she sees an unimaginable thing: children running about naked, their dark little bodies as shiny as wet stones.

"Look!" she cries.

"Shhh! What? Keep it down!" N'Doch's eyes dart about. "Oh. That's just kids. Nothing to be worried about."

"But they're out in the sun! What are their mothers thinking?"

"That they might get a moment's rest if their kids have something to keep them busy." He shades his brow to study a group of colorful boats beached a short distance away. "Don't see anything that looks like a return portal, do you? How does this thing work?"

"I don't know. The God . . . I'm sorry, I mean, Fire. He never said. But the other dragons will know where we are, won't they?"

"More or less. And they're not going to be too happy with me either." He probes the sand with his toe, unearthing a mean-looking scrap of metal. "You're taking this very calmly."

"Shouldn't I be?" Paia wants to smile, but that seems to make him suspicious, like he's afraid he'll start smiling back. Will he understand if she tells him she's not feeling much of anything right now?

He's scanning the beach again. "Not the safest spot in the world."

At least there's no golden dragon spitting his fire and venom in your eyes. At least, not yet. "After this morning, nothing could scare me."

"Gotcha." His grin flicks past her like a shard of light reflected off seawater. "And just let me say, girl, you were awesome!"

I did what I had to do, Paia thinks. So why don't I feel better about it?

She realizes she's waiting for him, for the God, as she always has when he's not around. Waiting for him to appear in a wreath of flame to mock and upbraid and flatter and pamper her. How will she learn to live without him? She must root out every lingering shred of devotion and desire, and let only her fear and hatred of him flourish.

She calls up the soldier's face to banish the God's forbidden image. She studies the slender, swaying trees that raise a tall gray wall across the top of the beach. Palm trees, a memory suggests. Paia would have expected them to be greener. She imagines touching their stiff fronds into the landscape with the edge of her palette knife.

Beside her, N'Doch straightens, listening. "Quick! This way!"

She looks up, instinctively searching for dragon shadow. But the sky is still empty and blue. Then she hears a low growling from behind the palms. "What's that?"

He grabs her arm. "Cover first, questions later!" He pulls her across the superheated sand toward the beached flotilla. The boats looked like painted toys from a distance, but as N'Doch hauls her into the shadow of the nearest one, its bright prow towers over them in a rising curve, its mast at a crazy tilt.

"Hunh. That's strange." N'Doch runs a palm along the planking. Paint falls away like peeling bark. "Doesn't look like she's been out in a while." His hand snags in a rough spot, then another and another. The tip of his finger disappears into the scarred wood. "Aw, no wonder! Bullet holes."

Paia's nose wrinkles. "What's that awful smell?"

"Fish. That's fish, girl. You never smelled dead fish in your life?"

"Where would I find a fish in the Citadel?"

"Damn, woman, you need to get out more!"

The growling sound is louder. Nearing, Paia realizes, and rapidly. N'Doch draws her around the pointed end of the boat, putting a stinking pile of crates between them and the noise. Paia needs no urging to hunker down behind the smelly barricade. She knows what that sound is. Engines. She hasn't heard engines since she was a child. They were a rare event, and usually they brought bad news.

"Jeeps," N'Doch mutters.

"Who is it?"

"No one we'll want to know, you can bet on that."

He ducks behind the curve of the boat as four dusty green vehicles roar through a gap between the palm trunks and out onto the beach. They fling up long arcs of sand as they turn and speed down the beach, swerving left and right, horns blaring. Paia hears a popping sound, like gunfire. The children scatter, screaming. Raucous male laughter echoes up the beach, over the boom and whine of the motors.

"Muthafuckahs." N'Doch slides a hand down the long knife sheath on his belt. "Let's get out of here. Now's when we'll wish we had the dragons with us. Step where I step, and don't you linger! Watch out for the shit in the sand."

Paia wonders if the danger in the sand is living or dead. She scoots after him along the line of boats, from hull shadow to hull shadow, away from the mayhem down the beach. Using the crates and the few ragged shacks as cover, N'Doch heads for the tree line. Shards of rusting metal and sun-bleached plastic are scattered everywhere. The beach might as well be mined with knife blades.

"Where did all this come from?" Paia asks.

"Folks just leave things where they fall. The Tinker crews could live for a year off this beach!" Hardly slowing, he stoops to snatch a rusted metal rod out of the sand.

"What's that?"

"A perfectly good tire iron."

"Is it a weapon?" She sees how neatly it fits into his fist.

"It is now." He glances up as they near the line of palms. "Man, these trees have seen better days. Guess I wasn't looking, last time I was out here."

Most of the palm leaves are stiff and brown, the source of the dry rattling that Paia has heard under the roar of the engines and the roll of the surf. Dead fronds lie in spiky heaps at the base of the trees.

Another burst of gunfire erupts down the beach.

"C'mon, keep moving! We're almost there." N'Doch hurries her forward, shoving her into the speckled shade between the slim, curved trunks just as the jeeps wheel around and head back toward the boats. Three of them race side by side, jostling each other with a great revving of engines and the squeal of bruised metal. "Don't let 'em see you!"

Pressed behind a palm trunk, Paia asks, "Why are they doing that?"

"Because they can." He's gripping the tire iron like a club.

His bitter tone makes Paia stare curiously after the careening vehicles as they smash heedlessly through a stack of crates. "They must be very rich. I mean, to be able to waste fuel and vehicles so recklessly."

"And it's your kids and mine who'll pay for it,

girl!" N'Doch's dark face relaxes into momentary confusion. "Well, I mean, mine already have. If I even had any. If I ever had the time." He waves the tire iron irritably. "Never mind. Let's go find Fâtime."

"Who?"

"My mother."

He strides off through the palm trunks, heading inland. Within five minutes of struggling to keep up, Paia is winded. She feels awkward, running full tilt. Arms and legs all over the place. The hot grit in her sandals rasps painfully against her soft indoor soles.

"N'Doch! Please! I can't . . . !"

Startled, he glances back, then stops to wait. In his haste, he's almost forgotten her. "Sorry. If there was any place safe, I'd leave you there."

"No!"

"I mean, to rest, while I find Fâtime."

"I'll be okay," she gasps. "Just please don't leave me."

He grins sourly. "You're in luck. I can't."

Paia slumps against a palm trunk. She doesn't want to be a burden to him. But being High Priestess of the Temple of the Apocalypse did not involve a lot of physical labor. She's had a life of being merely decorative, at least since the God . . . no, she must, must call him Fire . . . since Fire arrived at the Citadel. Before that, she was her father's protected little girl.

She tries a rueful sort of smile. "I'm out of shape, I'm afraid. But if Fire is here, I'm your best chance of dealing with him."

"Your shape looks just fine to me." N'Doch grins down at her, then looks away sheepishly. "Sorry again. It's habit. Don't mean anything by it, y'know. He'd have my head if he heard me.''

He. The soldier. For a moment, she was sure he meant Fire. ''Does it matter so much to you what he thinks?''

''Well, yeah. I guess it does. He's the dude, y'know?'' He chews his lip, considering, then suddenly he's off again through the trees.

Paia pushes herself harder, breathing more deeply, imitating N'Doch's steady stride. It's easier now that they're not slogging through deep sand. She studies his lean, muscular frame moving ahead of her. What would it take to acquire his strength and endurance? Paia envisions her soft curves bulked up with muscle. She rather likes the idea. Certainly, being so very decorative gives her a kind of power. But it's mostly the power to manipulate others—men, of course, but not only—into doing things for you. Paia would like to be able to do things for herself. Like the girl Erde—still a young teenager, yet so confident in her role as dragon guide, so totally in tune with her dragon. Paia wishes she had so clear a view of life. She wishes for a truer dragon.

Musing distractedly with her body on autopilot, Paia slams smack into N'Doch's back. He's halted, with the tire iron at the ready. They've jogged into the middle of a village without even noticing. Or perhaps it's more of an encampment. People are milling about, aimless and slow, as if exhausted. Smoke rises among them in pale columns like ephemeral palm trunks. Ragged blankets are spread on the ground and tied between trees. Small piles of possessions are strewn here and there, but Paia sees little in the way of shelter. The people are ebony-skinned, like N'Doch. Her own café-au-lait looks pale by comparison. She hears babies crying, and a murmur of argument and desperation and other kinds of prayer. Somewhere among the palms and hanging blankets, a woman is wailing. Long thin exhalations of grief.

Paia shivers. "What's happened here?"

N'Doch shakes his head. "Things are . . ."

"Are what?"

"Don't know . . . I mean, this is the *bidonville*. It's always been here, but it's . . . different than it was. Stick close. I mean it, okay?"

He waits until she nods her agreement. When he starts forward, she hooks a finger through one of his belt loops, so that she can peer around without losing him.

She sees mostly women and children. And old people. As they move into the settlement, makeshift tents appear, and lean-tos cobbled together out of scrap wood, rusted sheet metal, and corrugated plastic. There's sickness everywhere, and lassitude and injury. Moaning bodies sprawl in the shade with no one to tend to them. The children are dull-eyed and malnourished. An old man with no legs is propped up against a nearby palm trunk. He spies Paia, and stretches out a stick-thin hand. His scabbed lips mouth unintelligible beseechings.

When N'Doch elbows her along, Paia realizes she's been caught by the old man's desperate gaze. Her memory, stirred by horror and disgust, again offers up a reference. During the collapse that isolated her family fortress, the Citadel's communications links provided news, more news than anyone could want, except her father, who watched the global video feed compulsively, obsessively, in those final days. In addition to storm devastation and killing grounds, there were all those awful refugee camps, crowded with starved, exhausted populations forced to flee the rising oceans, the waves of plague, the tides of war.

Is this the beginning, or is the collapse already at full throttle?

Paia notes the change in N'Doch's body language. Wary but confident before, he has lost his bravado. His eyes flick about restlessly as he walks. She wonders if he's taken a wrong turn.

"I don't get it," he mutters.

"What? Tell me." His unease is contagious.

"It wasn't like this . . . before. It wasn't this bad."

"This is the same . . . the right place?"

"Oh, yeah, I know exactly where I am. I grew up here." He veers slightly left, avoiding a cluster of children fighting over the unidentifiable contents of a bloodied sack. One of them looks up, and Paia recoils at the feral greed in its stare. N'Doch adjust his grip on the tire iron. "See? Here's the road into town."

The road is a potholed swath of dry red dirt that swirls up with the hot gusts off the beach and sticks at the back of the throat like a thousand tiny pinpricks. Like the dust off the plateau behind the Citadel. For the first time since falling through the portal, Paia feels uncomfortably right at home. This dry landscape is one she would know exactly how to paint, but the familiarity is unwelcome. Ahead, the palm trunks thin out onto a flat orange plain, the hard blue sky like a painted ceiling. The red road disappears into heat shimmer, where low rectangles dance in and out of visibility and a wide, dark smudge rises above the bright horizon.

N'Doch shades his eyes from the glare, squinting into the mirage. A strangled moan escapes him. Without warning, he takes off at a dead run.

"N'Doch!" Paia bolts after him. A vision of wandering alone in a strange time, strange place lends her speed, but she cannot catch up. She's forced to halt in the middle of the road and holler like a lost child. N'Doch turns, his arms beating a mad rhythm of frustration. He'd like to lose her. It's as plain as if he's said it out loud. But the image of the murderous soldier must linger in his mind, for he races back, grabs her hand without a word, and drags her stumbling behind him.

The mirage steadies as they approach, into the shapes and structures of a town. The red road passes through a formal opening in the stout stucco walls, but the tall metal gates hang twisted away to either side and the walls have been breached in several places by something large enough to crush stone. Columns of smoke rise from the taller buildings. People are climbing through the ragged gaps and streaming out between the gates, limping, coughing, weeping, with their possessions stuffed into whatever was handy, or strapped to their backs. The broken walls echo with shouts and sporadic gunfire. The town is in ruins.

Before the bent gates, the road is choked with refugees and rubble. N'Doch grips Paia's elbow and uses his body as a ram to shove them both upstream through the milling and confusion. He breaks the tightest clots with a threatening gesture of his tire iron.

Startled by a close-by burst of shooting, Paia shrinks against him. "Are we going in there?"

"Have to. That's where Fâtime is."

His cool determination is a surprise to her. He didn't seem like the implacable type. Paia has a thousand questions but asks him none of them. Her memory is hard at work again, this time assailing her with an image House showed her just before she left the Citadel. It was a live feed from a local farmstead that had been unable to pay its monthly tithe to the Temple. She saw a woman with her fist raised at the sky, tears of grief and outrage streaking her sooty cheeks. Behind, a landscape of smoking wreckage.

He's burning villages, House had said.

It's like a blow to the belly. Tears of a different sort of grief and outrage start in Paia's own eyes. She fears that she recognizes her dragon's signature.

"I have to find a way . . ." she mutters.

"What's that?" N'Doch glances back, notes her dampened face. "What's up? You crapping out on me?"

Paia reaches for the more resilient pose that will make him feel comfortable. "No, I just love strolling through a war zone when I know my dragon's responsible for all the mess."

"Don't say that."

"But I think it's true."

"Then that means he's been here before us."

With renewed vigor, N'Doch shoulders them to the edge of the throng and turns off the main thoroughfare, into a rubble-strewn side street where the crowd is thinner and no one pays them much attention. They're just one more empty-handed couple fleeing for their lives. "Of course, he's only encouraging the bad shit that was going on already."

"Or maybe he began it in the first place."

"What? The whole damn cycle of human violence? C'mon!"

"Why not?"

N'Doch slows at an intersection to scan the narrow crossing alleys. Smoke obscures the distance in both directions. Two young men race by with their arms full. An old woman shrieks curses from an archway. Three sweating men struggle to topple some kind of machinery onto a half-burned cart, blocking most of the street. N'Doch edges Paia past them.

"Looters," he snarls. "As if all this wasn't bad enough already."

"Why not?" asks Paia again, but so softly that only she hears the question. Why should N'Doch believe her? He doesn't know Fire like she does.

Several blocks farther, a wrecked van burns in the street. The driver is dead at the wheel. Another body lies half in, half out of an open door. Paia veers toward them in sympathy.

"No! There's nothing you can do!" N'Doch grabs her arm. Just past the van, two green jeeps are parked crossways in the road. Half a dozen armed men are stopping all passersby. Before N'Doch swerves aside, dragging her into the nearest alley, Paia sees a tall youth spread-eagled against a wall. The men are jabbing at him with the butts of their rifles. The youth looks a lot like N'Doch.

In the alley, shade brings some relief from the heat. Screams follow them as the buildings close in, and a racket of gunfire, ricocheting along bare, pockmarked walls of faded pink and orange. The barred windows are set high, out of reach. A rectangle of smoky bright light yawns ahead, an obstacle rather than a goal. At the edge of the narrow concealing darkness, N'Doch peers cautiously around the corner, then ducks back, pressing himself and Paia against the wall. A huge six-wheeled armored truck thunders past, grinding up clouds of dust and grit. Already breathless, Paia inhales enough to set her coughing convulsively. N'Doch is panting, too, but will not let her rest. When the vehicle roar fades, he leads her into the searing light.

A big square spreads to their right, lined with shuttered, ruined shops. All across the open space, wood and canvas canopies are collapsed and burning, stalls shattered or overthrown.

"This was the market."

It's the first local information N'Doch has offered. Paia guesses they are nearing his home territory. The devastation has become more personal to him. Bodies lie among the flames and ruins. It looks as if a fiery hurricane has descended without warning into a busy, crowded square. Just how it would look, Paia muses, if that hurricane was a fire-breathing dragon. Furtive shapes dart through the smoke, snatching up whatever's left to be scavenged.

N'Doch's luxurious mouth thins to a grim line. He scans the burned-out square but does not linger. "This way," he orders.

A soot-faced girl with an armload of charred electronics pushes off from the wall she's been lounging against, into their path. She suggests several things in seductive tones in a language Paia does not recognize.

N'Doch brandishes his tire iron. "Scram."

They see no one else but the dead for several blocks and several connecting shadowed alleyways. Just when this sector of town appears to be empty and N'Doch is moving ahead less cautiously, they nearly run into a second, sudden roadblock. More green jeeps, more men with assault rifles. N'Doch turns aside in the nick of time, sprints down a long passage barely wide enough to be called an alley, and they are out in the light again, carrying the reek of garbage on their clothing.

"Those bastards are sure looking for someone," N'Doch observes angrily.

"Maybe it's us."

He scowls at her over his shoulder. "Girl, you are paranoid. I did a lot of stuff I'm not so proud of a while back, but I was never Public Enemy Number One. Besides, how would anyone know we're . . . Oh. I see. The Fire dude."

Paia nods.

"But how would he get men mobilized so fast?"

"If he knew, somehow, that we'd be coming . . ."

"Phew," breathes N'Doch. "Now you're really scaring me."

They hurry past rows of small houses, squatter and more widely spaced than the buildings in the center of town. Tiny plots of tilled ground shelter the desiccated remains of kitchen gardens. There is less destruction here, and N'Doch is walking faster, muttering in hopeful distraction. On the other side of a building with its roof caved in, a row of cinder-block structures fronts an unpaved road. Windowless boxes with open doorways, hardly houses at all. A few look burned out, but all are still standing. At the far end of the row, a man slumps on a stoop with his head in his hands.

N'Doch makes eagerly for the fourth house down the line. Instinct holds Paia back as they reach the door. It's pitch-black inside, despite the white glare of the sun.

"Fâtime?" N'Doch eases into the darkness. "Ma? You there?"

Alone on the dirt street with the pop of distant gunfire, Paia's terror suddenly blossoms. Only the need to keep moving has kept it at bay. She's sure she hears a jeep approaching, or the tramp of running feet, or the swoop of giant wings. A dull metallic clatter echoes inside the house.

"N'Doch?" Paia backs into the doorway, tripping over the tire iron, which lies just inside the door. It's not as dark in the house as she's expected. A shaft of light from a high side window cuts across the interior. N'Doch stands in the middle of the room, backlit by the narrow dusty beam. He's gazing at a woman sitting in a chair against the opposite wall. His shadow obscures the woman's face but for a glimmer in her eyes. Paia wonders if the woman is weeping. She sees no damage anywhere in the room. A few battered pots and pans sit in logical places. An ancient television rests on a rickety metal table. So, it must be relief that sags N'Doch's shoulders, his whole slim straight back letting go into a slump.

But the only sound is the buzzing of insects and N'Doch's soft keening, not a sound of relief at all.

"N'Doch?" Paia goes to him quickly and takes his arm.

He turns his head away, out of the light, and the woman's face is lit instead. She's an older woman, with dark skin and graying hair, thin with starvation and fatigue. Her eyes are open, but Paia sees no tears, only a neat, dark hole in the center of her forehead. The wall behind her is crawling with flies.

"Ohhh." Paia leans into N'Doch's side. "Is it . . . ?"

"Yes."

After a moment, she says, "He did this, somehow. I'm sure of it."

"Yeah, probably. It sure was no accident." He eases out of Paia's grip. As deliberately as a sleepwalker, he crosses the room to close his mother's eyes. His fingers linger on her thin shoulder. "My fault, Ma. My fault."

"No," insists Paia. "No. How can you say that?"

"Because I was never there when she needed me before, and I wasn't there now."

She understands his muddled syntax. But must the child take care of the parent? This is a new concept for Paia. Were there things she could have been or done for her father that would have kept him from descending into drink and despair?

"What should we do?"

His sigh is more like a shudder. "Go find Papa Dja, ASAP."

"I mean, with the . . . with her?"

"Nothing much we can do. She's gone. No place nearby to bury her."

Paia imagines digging a grave as the bullets sing above their heads. If Fire keeps doing things like this, it will be easy to hate him.

"I mean, Papa Dja might still be okay. We gotta warn him if we can."

"So we just . . . leave her?"

"She's in her house. That's where she liked to be." N'Doch lifts his hands to his face and scrubs his forehead, then drags his palms hard along his cheeks. He paces away from his mother's body, then back to touch her shoulder again. "Hey, Ma. This is me leaving. Like always, hunh? Might not be smart to stick around here right now."

"I will know if he's approaching," Paia says quietly.

"Yeah, but will you know the hand that actually pulled the trigger?"

"Ah. Right." In dragon-form, Fire could neither have managed a gun or fit inside this tiny house. And his man-form is an illusion born of manipulated energies. It can be whatever size or shape he wants, but an illusion cannot hold an actual gun or press an actual trigger. "Someone else was here with him."

"To do the deed. Yes. Had to be." N'Doch moves away from the body and around the room, picking things up and putting them down, as if taking inventory of his mother's scant possessions. He stares for a moment into a small, blackened pot. When he sets it aside, his eyes are full and moist.

"Someone from the Temple?" Paia can't really believe it. She says it mainly to distract him.

It works. "Can he do that? Haul people around, like Earth can?"

"I'm not sure. He'd always threaten that if I didn't behave, he'd fly me off to a foreign land and abandon me. But he never took me anywhere."

N'Doch stops short. He bends over abruptly. When he straightens again, each fist is grasping one end of the tire iron. "Baraga!"

"Who?" Paia whirls, certain that someone is in the doorway.

"That's it! Sonofabitch!" N'Doch slashes the air, right, left, right, left. "Fire doesn't need to bring anyone from anywhere. He's got his own big toady right here!" He takes another swipe at nothing, and another. "Just the sorta guy who can get his thug into a burning town to do the job, and get him out again. Damn! Sonofabitch!"

It would be easy and obvious for N'Doch to spend his grief trashing his mother's home. Paia is glad when he lowers the tire iron, and chooses not to.

Within the next heartbeat, the room fills with a rich blue radiance. The old-fashioned video set has flicked on of its own accord. N'Doch's fighting stance collapses. They both turn to stare into the sudden glow.

Paia shivers. It's like the aged monitor that appeared so suddenly in her studio, dust-caked and battered as if it had been there forever. It showed this same empty blue screen. Foolishly, she ventures, "House? Is that you?"

But there's no answering crawl of white letters across the bottom of the screen. Just blank blue, and then, abruptly, an image.

"Hunh," says N'Doch.

"What is that?"

"Looks like a city of some kind."

Paia nods. She's never actually been in a city, but she's seen them on the vid and in her history books. This city looks brand new, as white and clean as if it had been finished yesterday. As if it has no history. Broad, smooth, empty boulevards. Terraced buildings topped with pale, shining towers that rise against a sky of the same blank blue that had filled the screen a moment ago.

N'Doch leans forward. "Where's all the people?"

As suddenly as it came, the white city vanishes, and is replaced with blue, as if the sky behind has swallowed every trace of street or tower. And now a message does appear, in big unadorned white lettering.

It says: HURRY.

Chapter Five

Silence in the crowded com room, awed and uneasy. The girl and Luther have vanished right in front of their eyes, without even the illusion of a place to have fallen into.

Next, a burst of querulous chatter. The Librarian glances up from his console, beginning to comprehend impatience. He has no time for wonder. Humans ask for miracles, then are upset and disbelieving when they get one. He could offer them a rational explanation, as rational as it gets with dragons, but it would take him too long to articulate it. Time he can't afford right now. He clicks his teeth irritably and bends back to his work.

Hurry, hurry, insists the imperative in his brain.

Hurry how? Hurry at what? He's doing all he knows how to do, what he's always done: search for the source. Where is this farther future, where his dragon is waiting, as desperate as he is to make contact? Desperate. He longs for it with every molecule of his being.

If only she'd send him an image of the place, or a

signal coherent enough for him to pinpoint its source location, temporal as well as geographical. But she does not send coherent signals, and he is besieged at his console. Too much noise. Too many people. Too many demands. Constanze wants to know what's going on inside the Citadel. Leif and the soldier require updated military data. House is in a fit of anxiety about Paia's disappearance and will not stop distracting him with suggestions and queries. The rebellion is crucial. The Librarian has aided and abetted it, but it is not his True Work. He'd like them all to get on with it, and leave him to his task: locating his dragon. If Air is not found, the rebellion—won or lost—will matter little.

But because he's so ruled by compassion and temperance, because so many of his lives have been given over to the service of causes—whatever cause . . . in the end, they were all the same: the survival of the planet—because he doesn't know how to make the demands go away, the Librarian grants them his attention for a while longer.

He transfers House to the private channel plugged into his ear, and convinces him to try a power-up of the deactivated surveillance cameras trained on the Citadel's front entrance. After a few false starts and some creative rerouting, two front-on views of the imposing Temple facade appear on the screen. A cheer goes up among the watchers. The Librarian takes a look himself. He's not seen the Citadel's exterior since the Fire-breather took over. The elaborate, overscaled columns and friezes, so sharply delineated by the harsh sunlight, are the dragon's addition. The Librarian notes an echo of styles affected by other, human, dictators in times gone by. Human, but not humane. What a difference a single letter can make.

The Librarian smiles, drifting again, content in a celebration of the power of language.

But soon Leif Cauldwell is back at his elbow. "See
what he's got on the Grand Stair. There's a camera
still working there, I'm sure of it."

The Librarian keys in the request. To accede is
much easier. Refusal would require a considered explanation. The Citadel's Grand Stair flashes up on
the wall. Meanwhile, House is murmuring anxiously
in his right ear.

"But how did this happen, Gerrasch? How *could*
it? Why didn't anyone *stop* her?"

"Accident."

"No such thing!"

Taking the very long view, the Librarian is inclined
to agree. There are no random events. In the short
term, however, humans are definitely subject to
them, mostly due to the thoughtlessness of their own
actions. "Accident."

"Will she be safe?"

"Will any?" counters the Librarian, as Leif looms
over him again.

"House, can you give us floor plans, level by
level?"

"Original or revised?" House is more terse on the
public channel. "Leif, how could you let this happen?
You promised to keep an eye on her!"

"Revised. Don't fret, House. We'll have her back
in no time."

The Librarian is not so sure. He has an uneasy
feeling about how quickly their united force has been
divided. If he was the Fire-breather, that's exactly
how he would begin his final conquest.

A row of neatly drawn plans marches across the
wall just at eye level.

"Thanks, House. That's perfect!" Leif beckons the soldier to the screen, and Stoksie wanders over for a closer look. "Here's what makes the place so hard to break into. You've never been in the Citadel, have you, Stokes?"

"Nevah bin close, even," the little Tinker replies gravely. "Das Scroon Crew's territory, y'know? But dey ain' bin too close, lately, cuza da Monsta."

Köthen traces out potential patterns of access to the Citadel from the surrounding countryside. Each route leads his finger to the same spot: the stone staircase leading up to the Temple's high outer courtyard.

"Five hundred very tall steps," Leif tells him.

"The only entrance?" Köthen asks.

"The only. In my family's day, there was an elevator, but the Beast is technophobic. He replaced it with something he could understand, something that looks more intimidating."

"Elevator. The room that moves?"

Leif nods approvingly, then taps the image of the Stair. "A perfect bottleneck. If we take it, they lose the advantage. This big gateway here leads to the Inner Court, and then directly into the Temple. And from there, into the complex."

Köthen studies the long view of the Temple facade. The Librarian marvels at how quickly this tenth-century man has mastered the concept of a live video feed. "For how long did your family rule this stronghold?"

"Rule it?" Leif chuckles. "Not rulers in name, not by your definition, but I guess it was sort of the Cauldwells' little kingdom. Our great grandfather saw the handwriting on the wall while most people were still in total denial. Entire governments, in fact.

He sold off the other family holdings and added to his land in the Adirondacks. Bought up a big chunk when the country went bankrupt. Moved his wife and kids up. Other relatives followed. The Citadel began as an out-of-the-way vacation compound, then a family retreat. My father's generation was forced to turn it into a fortress."

"It was a bad time, then," Köthen remarks.

Leif's laugh is a bitter retort. "You could say that, yeah." But there is recognition and empathy in Köthen's tone, not a lack of understanding. "You've had some hard times of your own, I gather."

"So I imagined, until I came here." Köthen turns back to the screen. He lays his palm on the long view of the cliff face as if to measure it in handspans. "This is . . . high. Is the courtyard within range from the top?"

"Not with the weapons we have."

"What do you have?"

Cauldwell makes a sour face.

"Wait, nah, Leif," Stoksie says. "Betcha we cud come up wit sumpin."

"What sort of something?"

"Doan look so doubty, nah. Yu bin buried up in da palace a long time. Der's stuff bin goin' on yu don' know 'bout. Stuff comin' up frum da Sout'."

"Stokes, we need serious, working ammo."

"Yu kin git it, if yu got trade enuff."

"Huh." Leif runs a hand through his long auburn hair. "Well, that's news." To Köthen, he says, "We have a big cave full of long-range weapons, you see, and nothing to put in them, not for years."

"Long-range. How long?"

"Plenny long, Doff," says Stoksie.

The Librarian sighs as the past rears up and ricochets around his head. So many years, so many pasts, so many of them dominated by guns, large and small. He knew when he set this rebellion in motion, that there'd be fighting, there'd be deaths. So why is the idea suddenly so exhausting? His other revolution, the reshaping of the people's hearts and minds with a new idea of how to live . . . it's taking so long, oh, so long. Longer, he fears, than the world has time left. The data and the computer models have been in sync for a century, since the climate change became irreversible. Worse still, recent sensor readings indicate that the final decline is accelerating. His new idea came too late. Only the One can save them now. His dragon. Air. He must hurry. *Hurry.*

"Gerrasch? You all right?"

Leif bends over him solicitously. The Librarian blinks, lifts his head from the keypad, where it seems to have fallen. In his earphone, House is complaining about incomprehensible commands. The Librarian rubs his eyes and murmurs an apology.

"Time you took a break, G."

"Later." Mere sleep will not cure this particular exhaustion.

"You know best." Briefly, Leif massages his shoulders. "Can you get me a print-out of the floor plans, small enough for Dolph to keep on him until he's got it memorized? And print out the area map, too."

The Librarian nods. Leif strides away, head high, back straight. The group at the wall screen watches him approach, moves aside to make room. It makes the Librarian smile. Leif Cauldwell has waited for this moment for over a decade. He is thrumming with strategy and resolve, and his ardor translates into those who look to him for guidance. The Librarian can smell their anticipation. Even Köthen, the outsider, has caught a whiff of it. He sets himself apart from the group, but is not in contention with it or with Cauldwell, its obvious leader. Separate but equal, and ready to fight.

The Librarian sighs. Perhaps now they will leave him alone for a while. And he'll give House a really challenging task to perform, so the computer will stop its whining. He requests a trace on the source of the portal image of N'Doch's Africa. It came up on his screens, so it must start as a signal somewhere. Just as his visions are signals, his dragon's mad sendings propagated through time and space. He can feel their minute physicality as they enter his brain, lapping like waves on a lake shore. No magic, and not just his imagination. Rather, some unknown physics. The Librarian sets his electronic trackers to work.

Hurry, hurry. But he needs time. Time to think. To analyze. Where is this new future? What's the exact nature of the change in him? His dragon touched him and left him altered, but how?

He imagines the Fire-breather, racing up and down the centuries, covering all his bases, making good on all his threats. Even for a power like Fire, this will be a strain on his resources. Good. He'll be distracted. The perfect time to move on the Citadel, but also the perfect time to find and rescue Air. Is this what he's meant to understand? That he must reassemble the four dragon guides, as soon as possible. Strength in unity. Only together will they find Air.

He sees Stoksie beside him, watching blunt fingers

play the keypad like a piano. How long has he been there? The Librarian cannot remember seeing him approach. The little man looks pensive, uncomfortable, like he's been standing too long on his bad hip.

The Librarian gestures. "Chair?"

"Nah." Stoksie props his elbow against the side of the console and leans his chin into his cupped palm. "Kin I ask yu sumpin?"

"Ask."

"Dat place dey wen', das like sumkinda time masheen?"

"Sumkinda." The Librarian slips unconsciously into the Tinker dialect.

"Luta, he be okay, nah?"

"Hope he will." Does even Stoksie believe he has some mystic power over life and death? To his right, the plotter spits out the printed plan and map. The Librarian passes the stiff rolls to an outstretched hand, without noticing whose, and hears the crinkle of paper being spread across a nearby table. He worries that the stockpiled reams will be too dry to use long before his supply is exhausted.

"Yu cud go anyweah, den?" Stoksie pursues.

"Theoretically." The Librarian takes a breath. So many syllables all at once. "With control."

Stoksie grunts. "But we doan have dat. How cud we git dat, dya t'ink?"

"Working on it," the Librarian mutters. Wait. What is that? There's a new humming in his earpiece, something that isn't coming from House. What is it? Too much noise in the room to be sure. Too much noise and too much busyness. He can't focus. He can't hear himself think. He waves his arms distractedly. "Quiet! QUIET!"

No one hears him except Stoksie. "Yu gotta raise yer volume sum, G."

The Librarian frowns. Wasn't he yelling at the top of his lungs?

"Heah. Lemme do it."

Stoksie limps away, moving from caucus to caucus, debate to debate. The Librarian doesn't pick up what he says, but the hubbub dies back a bit, and groups begin to drift toward the door. Soon the room is empty, but for the cluster of warriors around the printout.

". . . four days' direct march, if the dragons can't take us." Leif delineates a route across the area map, between spidery contour lines and the broken traces of old roadways.

"With how many men?" asks Köthen.

"People," says Constanze.

"Meaning?"

"Meaning the force won't be all men. The women will fight, too."

"Ah." Köthen's shrug suggests that if all the women are as staunch as Constanze, he has no objection. He straightens away from the map and turns to study the screen again. "*Herr* Stokes," he calls out, waiting for the translator to catch up. "Are those mules of yours saddle-broken?"

"Mebbe. Why yu askin'?"

Köthen seems to take this ambiguity for an assent. He nods. "Give me ten men of my choosing, Leif Cauldwell, armed with these wondrous weapons you speak of. I will take the heights, and clear the courtyards."

"Hmm, it's a good idea, but you'll be totally exposed up there when the Beast returns. And he will return, no doubt of it."

"The risk is no worse than that of an ambush in the lightless bowels of these unfamiliar warrens."

"Not entirely lightless."

"But well-known to you. In there, I would be a hazard to my men."

"I see your point." Leif nods. "Okay, you're on. The heights are your job."

So the soldier prefers to fight his battles in the open air, the Librarian muses. Better him than me. Hours later, his cave-adapted lungs still feel the dry sear of the mountaintop.

"When can we expect our dragons back, Gerrasch?" Leif asks.

"Unsure." The Librarian is not well-versed in the issues of real-time relative to dragon travel. It's not the sort of information you can easily find in books or data banks. He suspects that elapsed time in the past is not exactly equivalent to elapsed time in the present. Besides, time, as in a specific chronological goal, is not Earth's main parameter. It's *place* that draws him. The fact that places have their associated times is apparently coincidental. But standard time paradox should dictate that the physical dragon can't be in two places at once. So his return can be expected at any time *after* the moment he left. Could be seconds, could be days or weeks.

"Well, say, an hour or two, maybe?"

"Maybe. Yes." What will be, will be. The Librarian doesn't want to burden Leif Cauldwell with worries he can do nothing about.

"Let's say an hour, then. Time enough to talk to the folks upstairs."

"We do need a head count," notes Constanze.

"Let's get on it, then." Leif rolls up the printout and hands it to his wife for safekeeping. "Stoksie, can you stick around down here and keep G company? Anything important comes through from the Citadel, you can let us know."

"Betcha," the Tinker agrees.

And at last the room is truly empty. Silence settles in like a gentle rain. The Librarian remembers rain. He allows himself a moment to savor the precious memory, not wanting to waste it. Stoksie noses about for a comfortable seat, then drags a battered swivel chair up to the desk nearest the console. He props his feet on an open drawer and leans back into the cracked plastic with a sigh.

"Ain' slept sinze yestiddy."

The Librarian nods sympathetically. He feels like he hasn't slept in years. Centuries, maybe. How will any of them get rest enough to fight this war? He peers at the readouts stacked to the left of his keypad. The tracking routines are in their third loop, still without a result. He plants his elbows on the cushioned wrist pad and rests his head in his palms. Just for a moment, he tells himself. Just long enough to clear his head of the residue from the morning's noise and crisis . . . but that humming is back again. He can hear it clearly now, in his ears, in his mind. He can feel it in his gut. Is it . . . physical? Is something going on out on the mountainside?

The Librarian stirs, lifts his head. His neck muscles are cramped. His eyelids seem fastened together. He has no feeling at all in his hands. He's been asleep, and the humming has woken him. There's something different about the light. For a moment, before he is fully awake, he imagines that the sun has risen. But the sun does not rise when you're a mile underground.

The Librarian shakes himself upright.

The room is bathed in a pure white radiance. Every corner, every detail is softly delineated. In memory of his former animal self, every hair on the Librarian's body rises to attention. He lifts his dazzled eyes to the wall screen. Instantly he understands. The portal has opened again.

The darker walls and ceiling frame the bright vista beyond. Light spills in a long rectangle onto the scuffed flooring of the com room. A glowing path, leading right to his console. He is inside, looking out onto a shaded terrace, bounded by delicate columns and a railing of translucent stone. Like alabaster, the Librarian decides, but without alabaster's depth. This stone is as smooth and white as the paper from the plotter. Past the railing is a blue void, neither sea nor sky, but a seamless both. The white terrace continues out of sight to left and right, its hidden spaces beckoning.

What does it mean? It's not a place he knows or has ever been, or has ever seen. Yet it seems . . . familiar. How can this be? He's a librarian, after all. His memory is encyclopedic. If this was a place from any of his many pasts, he'd remember it. And he doubts it could be an unknown from his current present, unless there still exists some impossibly sheltered corner of the world, where such a terrace could show no sign of destruction or wear.

But he knows . . . he *knows* that a city lies concealed below the white horizon of the terrace railing. Images flood the space behind his eyes: tall glass towers reflecting the unchanging white light. Wide boulevards and open plazas. An empty city that calls to him. Is this to be the next phase of his search?

He has only to walk the width of the terrace to find out. It isn't far. Not far at all.

The Librarian lurches to his feet. Refusing to let

the image out of his sight, he fumbles over to Stoksie's chair and wakes him with a clumsy, flailing arm.

"Easy, nah! Easy!"

"Stokes! Look!"

Stoksie's eyes flick open. "Whatsit?"

"What do . . . wachu see deah, Stokes?"

"Weah?"

"On da screen."

The Tinker sets both feet carefully on the floor and squints into the light. "Dunno, G. Wachu t'ink it iz?"

The Librarian is wary of admitting what he thinks. It's too impossible, too crazy, that after so long, the moment could have actually arrived, so suddenly and without fanfare. He hopes Stoksie's determined skepticism will help him think past the exultant hammering of his heart. "I t'ink . . . think it's *her* place. Why else would it come to me? She's in there somewhere."

But Stoksie seems less inclined to doubt him since the other dragons appeared. He levers himself out of his chair and takes a few stiff steps forward. "Her? Yu mean, da One?"

"Yes."

"It's da portal opin agin, den?"

"Think so. Yes. Sure of it."

Stoksie rubs his stubbled chin, runs a hand over his bald head, then limps into the shaft of surreal light, right up to the edge of the opening. The Librarian follows, a long step behind. There is a faint line across the floor, a subtle change of tonality, like a borderline between here and there. Slowly, Stoksie extends his arm, up to and past where the screen should be. He waves his hand up and down, meeting no resistance. "It's da portal, all ri'. Wachu wanna do, G?"

The Librarian swallows. Physical courage has not been much required of him during his eternal waiting period. Endurance, persistence, patience, resourcefulness, and intelligence, yes. Those are his major qualities. But his body is thick and slow, his hands agile but not particularly strong. "Gotta go deah, Stokes," he whispers hoarsely.

"Nah. Bad ideah. Stoopid."

"Got to." What if the portal closes, and she can't open it again? What if it's only Fire's current distraction that's allowed her to do it? "Got to, Stokes. Can't miss the chance."

"Now? Ri' now, yu got to?"

The Librarian nods.

"Den lemme run tell Leif an' da othas."

"No. Please. They'll try to stop me."

"Shur dey will, an' gud fer dem!"

"No. Not good. Got to do this." The Librarian shakes his head. He takes a half step forward, until the change in the light falls across the middle of his toes. Is this the difference, then? That he can actually walk off into the unknown without quailing in panic?

Stoskie moves up beside him. "Den I gotta go wichu."

"No."

"Oh, yeah. Betcha."

The Librarian shudders. His last chance to refuse the summons has just crumbled. Now he has to go. But he doesn't have to go alone. Often he's convinced that the Tinker crews are the treasure-house of all that was once admirable in humanity. "Thank you," he gasps.

Stoksie laughs, a reckless sort of cackle. "Da lame an' da halt, nah? Fine peah we make ta go aventurin'!"

No random events, the Librarian reminds himself, a litany to bolster his courage. "Let's go, then."

He rests his hand on the Tinker's shoulder and, together, they step into the light.

PART TWO

The Journey
into Peril

Chapter Six

After only an instant in the snowy yard at Deep Moor, Erde knows that her Seeing has been a true one.

The white ground is churned up and stained with frozen mud. Acrid odors pinch her throat and nostrils, not the warm scent of cozy fireplaces, but the stench of burning. Black smoke billows beyond the surrounding pines, toward the barns, toward the house.

"Oh, no! Oh, no!" Erde flings the sack of woolens into Luther's arms and races across the ragged snow in her sandals and leggings. The path through the trees to the house is ashy and trampled. At the base of the stone steps, she collapses with an anguished wail.

The house is a ruin. Scorched stone. Charred timbers. No sign of life.

She can hardly catch breath enough to cry out her grief and horror. The dragons, appalled as always by humankind's potential for disaster, offer what little comfort they can.

Luther rushes up, shrugging into the last of his

winter layers. "Watsit, gal? Watsda matta?" He stops short at the sight of the ravaged house. Gently, he hauls Erde to her feet and presses her boots and sheepskin cloak into her arms. She throws them down, wailing.

"We're too late! How can we be too late?"

Patiently, Luther retrieves the clothing from the dirty snow. "Put dese on, nah. Yu'll freeze ta deat'."

"I don't care! How could we let this happen!"

The dragons are exploring the rest of the farmstead. Lady Water's tone is tight and furious.

THE BARNS ARE BURNED OUT AS WELL. THE ASHES ARE STILL HOT.

Earth's outrage is quieter. HE HAS BEEN HERE, OUR BROTHER.

HE, OR HIS AGENTS.

The hell-priest's armies! It must have been!

Away from the aura of the dragon's heat, Erde is soon shivering as much from cold as from horror and outrage. Guillemo's men in Deep Moor! It's sacrilege! A desecration! She lets Luther help her into her boots and heavy cloak. She notes his wary sidelong glances, at the mounded snow, the tall and blistered pines, the grim lowering sky—the habit of a man used to hidden dangers.

"Git yer stuff on," he urges. "Den we'll take a look 'roun'."

Erde forces her numbed fingers to tie up icy bootlaces. She must get hold of herself. She owes it to Luther and the dragons. "Is anyone here? Do you see any . . ." She can't bring herself to say it, so Lady Water does instead.

NO BODIES. SOME DEAD LIVESTOCK, BUT FEWER THAN MIGHT BE EXPECTED, GIVEN HOW TOTAL THE DESTRUCTION IS.

Luther climbs the terrace steps to peer into the smoking ruin. "Doan see anyone . . . yu know . . . leas' not heah."

"Then where is everyone?"

Water offers an answer almost worse than death. NO DOUBT HE HAS TAKEN THEM.

"No! Maybe they escaped. We'll search till we find out what's happened!" Erde's tears are freezing on her cheeks. She fights back a hiccuping sob and musters a more determined expression. "Look at me, weeping over an old house, when Raven and Rose and the others need our help!"

But, oh, how she did love that old house! Nestled in the leaves like a bird's nest, low and cozy and so full of life! Now her little bedroom among the eaves is gone and the massive stone chimney stands alone amidst the smoking embers of the roof. Rose's beautiful garden courtyard is a tumble of blackened sticks. The kitchen's long, sturdy, well-used table, the center of the women's lives and fellowship, is reduced to a heap of cinders clogging the charred stone sink.

Erde had come to think of this house as home, as if it had been her true home all along, and her earlier life in her father's castle was only a waiting time until she found Deep Moor. To keep herself from bursting into sobs again, she turns her back on the wreckage and her face into the frigid wind.

"Howya doin?" Luther asks.

"I'm all right now. Let's go see what we can find out."

She leads him back to the churned yard and across it, following Earth's wide, slushy trail through the pines and past the burned-out barns.

"These were big and warm and beautiful once, Luther."

The Tinker nods. "Yu kin always builda house back, y'know, gal."

"Yes, I know. Yes, of course you can." But it will never be the way it was, Erde mourns. It will never seem so perfect and protected, so . . . invulnerable. Perhaps that is the most devastating thing of all, that destruction came so quickly and so easily.

They find the dragons in the big farmyard, where it opens out into the flat meadows of the valley. Both are nosing among the smaller outbuildings that have escaped the flames. The yard is a chaos of mud and ice, trampled and refrozen, with a confusion of tracks leading off in all directions. Earth crouches at the center, the snow melting around him. He's reluctant to move his great horned bulk about and disturb the scents and signs he is taking such careful inventory of. Water has assumed a smoothly furred pragmatic shape. The dull late light glimmers in the velvet of her coat. Erde sees this particular shape has hands of a sort, for the dragon is clearing aside the remains of the henhouse. Luther hurries over to help.

Erde takes stock hastily. The duck pen is more or less intact. The hog sty sags and a burned tree has fallen on the goat hut. All the doors have apparently been flung wide. She's relieved to discover no dead animals inside. The rabbit hutch lies turned over. Luther nudges it with his foot.

Erde moans. "Did they steal *everything*?"

Earth's gaze is steady and sad. THERE IS FAMINE IN THE LAND, REMEMBER.

"I know." She relays the dragon's words to Luther, and for his sake, speaks her reply out loud. "But I hate to think of Fra Guill's men eating up all of Deep Moor!"

"Dey's all sortsa tracks heah," Luther's dark face is intent. "Like heah—dat's da rabbits runnin' away." He points across the snowy field, then straightens out of his habitual stoop to take in the long valley and the tall, pine-shrouded hills.

"You think so?" Erde squints to follow the trace until it vanishes behind a distant pile of brambles. She finds this small mercy enormously comforting.

"Betcha. We raiz'em at Blin' Rachel. Still had 'em wild, wen I wuza boy." Luther studies the ground again. "An' dis heah, das a mule."

"A mule!" Hope against hope! "Dragons, did you hear? Maybe it's Sir Hal's mule!"

OR IT COULD BE A HORSE. Lady Water noses at the tracks.

I don't recall any horses at Deep Moor.

SOMEONE ELSE'S HORSES, THEN.

Erde shudders, recalling the thick-limbed white chargers favored by the hell-priest's monkish body-guards, trained to maul and trample. "She says it could be a horse."

"Mebbe so. Ain' nevah seen a horse. Yu gottim heah?"

"Oh, yes. The knights ride horses to battle."

Luther frowns, turning back to stare into the distant surrounding hills. "Yeah? Wonda if dey's gone yit."

What if it was not just his men, but the hell-priest himself? That might account for the rampant and needless destruction. Fear and horror rise like gall, so physical a sensation that she clamps both hands to her mouth to keep the material glob of terror from spewing out of her gut.

IF HE WAS HERE, YOU WOULD KNOW IT.

She takes a breath, swallows, and lowers her hands. "Yes, dragon. I would. I always do." But it's hard to have faith in the face of such catastrophe.

WAIT! Lady Water's sleek head shoots up. LISTEN!

"What? What is it?" To Erde, the cold air seems as still as a tomb.

DOGS.

"Dogs barking?"

RUNNING.

"Yu heah dogs? Weah? I saw wona dem onct. He wuzza mean one!"

"What dogs, dragons? Can you tell?"

But because neither of these dragons' preternatural sense is sight over distance, it's Luther who spots them first. "Lookit! Look deah!"

Dogs. Even while she sees Luther casting about for a stout stick, even though she knows that hunting hounds travel with the hell-priest's armies, hope stirs again in Erde's heart. She can see the dogs herself now, half a dozen dark ovals flying silently toward them over the snow. She wonders what Lady Water could possibly have heard.

Luther brandishes his weapon. "Yu git behin' me nah, gal!"

"Wait, it might be . . . there are dogs who live here at Deep Moor. At least, there were . . ."

"Dey doan call a bad man a dog fer nuttin!"

"No, Luther, not all . . ."

IT IS THEM.

Leaping over rubble piles and snowbanks, the dogs are suddenly among them, long-legged, bristle-haired dogs, tall and gray, with amber eyes. They race around the farmyard in tightening circles, panting, dancing, still without making a sound. Then, abruptly, as if on command, they tumble into a ragged phalanx and drop to their bellies in front of Earth's foreclaws. Only now does Erde see that they are badly battered and beaten. Their lop-ears are torn and their bearded muzzles scarred and bloodied. Despite the energy of their arrival, several seem about to collapse from exhaustion and loss of blood. One, she sees, is missing a paw.

Luther lowers his cudgel. "Dey bin fightin' sum."

Fresh tears warm Erde's cheeks. *Oh dragon, help them!*

THEY WISH US TO GO WITH THEM FIRST.

Lady Water crouches among them. JUST LIKE A DOG. IS IT FAR?

DISTANCE IS NOT PART OF THEIR VOCABULARY. ONLY DIRECTION AND URGENCY.

"What do they want?"

FOR US TO HURRY. I HAVE TOLD THE WORST TO COME TO ME. THE OTHERS I WILL HELP LATER.

The dragon lowers his huge head. A dog with rough gashes on her hips and ribcage stumbles over to lean against a claw taller than she is. The dog with the icy, bloody stump struggles to get up, then falls back. His belly, too, is bleeding. A whine escapes him, and he rolls his eyes apologetically.

"Luther, help me!" Together, Erde and Luther lift the suffering dog and lay him beside Earth, who goes to work on him first, nearly wrapping him entirely in his vast, soft tongue. The other dogs watch expectantly.

"Lookit dat, nah!" The wounds close and heal before Luther's very eyes. He lowers himself to one knee in the damp snow. "Da One be praised!"

The dog shudders with relief and gratitude. He lies panting for a moment, then struggles up and shakes himself weakly. The dragon moves on to the next. Erde presses herself into the dragon's side to send him messages of love and appreciation. Here, even in the midst of horror, there are miracles.

As soon as the second dog is on her feet, the rest of the pack spring up, quivering with mission. The least battered of them sprint ahead into the meadow, then circle back expectantly.

Luther rises from his knees, dusting away snow and ash. "Dat way, dey're sayin'? Der's a big trail leadin' owt dere, seeit?"

"Let's go, then!"

"Slow, nah. Mebbe da bad guys wen' dere! Yu know wat's down dat way?"

Erde squints along the wide, roughed-up track leading out of the farmyard, then across the meadow and down along the valley. "Just fields and . . . wait! I know! The Grove is that way! Do you remember, dragon?"

OF COURSE. A GOOD DESTINATION. AND THE DOGS AGREE. I WILL TELL THEM TO MEET US THERE.

"We're going dragon-back again, Luther. Are you ready?" Erde shoulders her pack and conjures the entrance to the Grove in her mind, revising her image with the several feet of snow fallen since she'd been there last.

Her next breath fills her lungs with biting cold. They're in the middle of the valley with the tall oaks of the Grove rising before them. A sharp wind has been reshaping the drifts around the trees, but a recent disturbance is still visible The snow is deeper here than in the farmstead, but it's been trampled in a wide area in front of two massive trunks that mark the path into the Grove. Erde sees blood and hoof-prints, paw prints, bootheels.

"Ben sum fightin' heah, fer shur," Luther shrugs his woolens closer. He looks miserable, warmed only by courage and his righteous outrage. "Intrestin' how da trail goes 'roun' da sides, but not much goes in."

Erde is too cold and anxious to speak. It feels dangerously exposed out here in the open valley. She's uneasy past any rational assessment. The dog pack can be heard behind them now, no barks or howling, just their breathy scudding across the snow.

HERE'S HOW I READ IT. Lady Water turns back from a quick inspection of the trail curving off to the right. TWO GROUPS CAME HERE, ONE PURSUING THE OTHER. ONE OF THEM ESCAPED INTO THE TREES.

THE TREES TAKE CARE OF THEIR OWN. Earth sounds a note of optimism.

"Yes, that's it!" Erde exclaims in relief. "The Grove is a refuge! Gerrasch took shelter there, remember?"

Lady Water is not so certain. SHELTER FROM HUMAN ENEMIES, PERHAPS, BUT FROM OUR BROTHER FIRE?

WE SHALL SEE.

The dogs catch up, circle the big dragon once, then charge in among the trees and disappear. Now a great baying can be heard.

Luther peers after them, frowning. "Why're dey singin' nah?"

"To let our friends know that help is on the way?" Erde recalls her own confusion upon first encountering the magic of the Grove. The thick-trunked oaks look comfortably spaced. Room enough for even a dragon to pass between. Yet the dogs have vanished, within the first few ranks of trees.

"Shudn't jest walk in der, nah. Cud be a nambush."

"The dogs would know. They would warn us somehow."

WELL, LET'S NOT JUST STAND AROUND IN THE COLD, EVERYONE . . .

Lady Water takes the path between the trees. She'd sounded so exactly like N'Doch that Erde feels a sharp pang at having abandoned her fellow dragon guide for so long. And Paia, too. She'd nearly forgotten about the priestess. Thoughts of Baron Köthen inevitably follow, and Erde hastily shoves them away. There's nothing to be done about any of it until the present emergency is dealt with. She plunges anxiously after the blue dragon. She might find the women of Deep Moor, and still find disaster.

Inside the Grove, her uneasiness increases. The light is dim under the spreading branches. The air has gone oddly still. The leaves have shriveled, but have clung stubbornly to their perches. They make a softly ominous rattling, directionless and steady like the sound of water over stones. Scattered signs of flight appear along the path: a shawl dropped in haste, a basket emptied and tossed aside. Erde swerves, gasping, around the remains of a brown duck, trampled into the snow. Thoughts tangle in her head. The women would never be so careless . . . even though they were in the greatest haste, running for their lives . . . still, they would never have . . .

Dragon, could the soldiers have intruded into the Grove?

Erde hears the dogs ahead, and the snap of

branches behind that describes Earth's much slower progress. When she and the dragon first arrived at Deep Moor, he fit easily beneath the branches of the Grove. Clearly, his increasing size will not always be an advantage. For instance, it's harder now for him to feed himself adequately. Lady Water, her size conveniently under her control, trots easily along the path far ahead, thoughtlessly urging her brother to hurry.

At last there's brighter light ahead. Between the dark oak boles lies the pale reflective oval of the central pond, the pool that never freezes. No touch of wind disturbs its surface. Erde knows she will find green shards of grass springing up around its verge. The Grove's magic is gathered here. Here's where the women would have come. But no one's there. Erde spies Gerrasch's little hovel, mounded with snow. The sight of it unmoors her further. Such confusions of then and now. Gerrasch's rough shelter always looked more like a pile of sticks than a home, but now all sense of dwelling has gone out of it. The pile has been torn apart and scattered. Where was Gerrasch when this violation occurred? Here, or thirteen hundred years from now? Would the dragons have an answer? Or do they feel as she does, like a tiny leaf whirling on the tides of Time?

Erde stops beside the pile to catch her breath and let her brain stop spinning. Lady Water wades into the pool as if entering her own bedchamber. She takes a long drink, then plunges her head into the crystalline water. In an instant, she has flung up a large silver fish and snatched it neatly out of the air.

Luther pulls up beside Erde, panting. "Ain' usta all dis walkin'!" His grin is rueful and bright, but his eyes are busy scanning the dark trees and the wide stretch of snowy meadow beyond the curve of the pond. His grin fades. "Dere's bin fightin' heah, too."

"No! Not here!" Only her intent denial has kept her from seeing it. But the drifts around Gerrasch's shelter are as torn up as the farmyard. The damp leaf litter lies exposed in great russet swaths like clots of frozen blood. Erde fears suddenly that the dogs have brought them to be witnesses to death, not to prevent it.

"Rose?" she cries out. "Raven? Is anybody here?"

Luther hushes her. "Der's plenny yu doan wan' hearin' yu, gal."

"But they must be here somewhere! Where else could they be?"

"If dey ain' shown demselves yet, der's probly a reason."

The big Tinker chews his lip and looks away. Erde knows he fears the worst and doesn't want to say so. But never having met Brother Guillemo, Luther doesn't know that death is not the worst that could happen to any woman of Deep Moor who falls into the hell-priest's clutches. Just the thought brings on the old chills, the sensation that Fra Guill is nearby, watching her. Erde shudders. Then she notices the dogs.

"Look. What are they doing?"

The dog pack has gathered at the very far end of the clearing, a cluster of gray blurs against the roiled snow.

Lady Water swallows another fish, then flips a huge one to her brother as he halts just at the water's edge. THEY SEEM VERY BUSY ABOUT SOMETHING.

WE ARE TO FOLLOW THEM. BUT I WILL EAT

FIRST. WHO KNOWS WHEN THE NEXT CHANCE
WILL BE.

Erde is torn between the dogs' urgency and her
dragon's hunger. Certainly, he will need all his
strength. But peering ahead, she sees that the pack
has split to form two rows, facing one another. A
single large dog runs back and forth in the space
between, baying for attention. "Look!" she insists.
"They want us to hurry!"

The two rows lean toward each other, like the sides
of an arrow. At the arrow's point, two giant oaks wind
their upper branches together to form a natural archway. To Erde's distant eye, the inside of the arch seems
darker than the surrounding forest. Since the dragons
refuse to listen, she shakes Luther's arm and points.

"See that?"

"Eyah. Dey shur tryin' ta show us sumpin."

"Oh, I pray our friends are still alive! Dragon!
Please! Or shall I go without you?"

PATIENCE. WE ARE THERE.

And instantly, they are. Across the long meadow in
a blink. The dogs cry with delight and crowd around
Earth again, as if their job is done at last and all they
wish for by way of thanks is a swipe of his healing
tongue. He goes to work on them while Lady Water
investigates the darkness between the twining trees.

THE DOGS ARE COMPLAINING ABOUT BEING
LEFT BEHIND.

Left behind? Then, everyone's gone somewhere?

WAIT . . .

Erde gasps as light blooms within the archway, as
soft and colorless as the snowy meadow. The blue
dragon gleams like silver in its glow.

WHEREVER THIS IS, IT'S PROBABLY WHERE
THEY ARE.

Erde peers around Water's silky side. She blinks, then looks again. The space between the ancient trunks is . . . somewhere else. No doubt about it. To left and right, the trees march off in unbroken ranks, but between these two mossy giants, a city lies.

A city?

THAT'S WHAT IT LOOKS LIKE, ALL RIGHT.

A city between the trees. Nearest to them, a shaded overhang. Beyond, a view past delicate, translucent columns, out onto a broad white plaza dotted with fountains and stone benches. No snow, no wind. As if there was no weather there at all. Only the soft white glow. Across the pale plaza, entry porticoes lead into tall white towers that rise up beyond the range of view. Between their perfect sides, as sharp as sword blades, Erde glimpses slim blue shards of sky.

THIS HAS TO BE WHERE THEY WENT. Lady Water steps up to the opening. Snow and dead leaves scatter across the seamless white marble just past her toes. WHAT DO YOU THINK, BROTHER?

Earth lifts his head from his healing work. He has waited until he's finished with the last dog. His response nearly blasts Erde senseless.

AH! THE MAGE CITY! AT LAST!

Water regards him primly over her velvet shoulder. I THOUGHT WE'D DECIDED THERE WAS NO SUCH THING.

YOU INSISTED THERE WASN'T, SO I AGREED. BUT THERE IT IS! RIGHT THERE! THE CITY I DREAMED OF AS I SLUMBERED, AND AFTER I AWOKE.

"It does look like the city we dreamed of." Erde frowns gently. "Is it another portal?"

NO DOUBT.

NOT JUST ANOTHER PORTAL! THIS IS THE
PORTAL WE'VE BEEN SEARCHING FOR!

The big dragon edges into the path of the light, as
close as he can get without tangling his horns in the
branches overhead. The dogs pace about behind him,
grown anxious again.

WE MUST ENTER THIS PLACE. WE'LL FIND
ANSWERS HERE.

HOLD ON! WHAT ABOUT . . .

"What about N'Doch? We can't just desert him!
What if Fire's there?"

NO DOUBT HE IS, BUT HE CAME HERE FIRST,
SO THERE'S STILL TIME.

THERE ARE ANSWERS HERE! WHY ELSE
WOULD I HAVE DREAMED THIS PLACE? THE
DREAMS WERE A MESSAGE FROM THE SUM-
MONER WHO AWAKENED US, AND NOW, HERE
WE ARE. WE CANNOT LOSE THE CHANCE!

"Dey wanna go in deah?" Luther asks.

"Yes, but . . ."

"Well, gud, cuz it's eidah dat or da trees, an' bes'
be quick aboudit! Dere's summun commin'. Yu
heah?"

"Where?"

"Lissen!"

The dog pack has gone stiff-legged and still. Water
puts her debate with her brother aside, and listens
with them.

HORSES. A LOT OF THEM.

Though Erde hears nothing, a helpless whimper
blooms in her throat. "Maybe it's Sir Hal! He's got
word that Deep Moor has been sacked! He's brought
his own army!" But the familiar choking chill has
returned in force. Her uneasiness was no mere reflex.
The hell-priest has found them.

Oh, dragon! He's here!

She will not say his name out loud. She is the beacon the priest has homed in on, she knows it. It's just as before. She can see his avid, evil face in her mind's eye.

Earth rumbles his outrage. The dogs throw in their support with a chorus of snarls and growling. Lady Water's aspect is suddenly edgier and harder.

PAWN! MISBEGOTTEN TOADY! SHALL WE TAKE HIM, BROTHER?

WITH WHAT? THE ONLY WEAPONS WE HAVE WOULD WRECK THIS HALLOWED GROVE. AND TO WHAT END?

REVENGE, OF COURSE—FOR THE RUIN OF DEEP MOOR, AND FOR WHATEVER HE'S DONE TO OUR FRIENDS!

A DISTRACTION, A DIVERGENCE. PROBABLY INTENDED AS SUCH BY OUR BROTHER FIRE. RE-VENGE IS PETTY. OUR DUTY IS TO FIND OUR SISTER AND PROSPER OUR PURPOSE.

Water snorts. Erde notes the predatory gleam in the blue dragon's eyes.

PETTY PERHAPS, BUT SATISFYING.

WE HAVEN'T TIME! WE MUST FIND OUR SIS-TER FIRST!

"Waddevah we're doin', we oughta do it fas'!"

The approach is undeniable now, a thudding and crashing among the trees. The dogs fall silent and alert, like a small gray army awaiting orders.

Erde reaches for dragon reassurance. Lady Water is nearest. She buries a fist in the blue dragon's velvet hide. "What if he tries to follow us through the portal?"

PROBABLY THAT'S WHAT HE'S BEEN HOPING,

FOR SOMEONE TO COME ALONG AND OPEN IT
FOR HIM.

THAT WOULD NOT BE GOOD.

"When N'Doch went, the portal closed up right
after him."

"Dere's da ansa, den! Hurry on up!" Luther urges
dragon and girl toward the archway.

"Wait! The dogs!"

A gust of wind screams through the clearing, rousing the drifts into billows. The first horse thunders
out of the forest through an unnatural wall of white.
The dog pack scatters and streaks across the meadow
to charge at the horse's heels under cover of the
blowing snow. Another horse appears, white on
white, and then another. Erde recognizes the heavy
war steeds of the hell-priest's retinue. More come behind them. The dogs race and nip, duck away and
charge in again. The horses shy and startle. Their
white-cloaked riders yank hard at their mouths and
dig in with iron-pronged heels. Erde looks for Guillemo among them, but the snow curtain conceals
their faces. The dogs circle out and close in again.
One of the riders draws his sword.

"They'll all be killed!" Erde shrieks. "Dragon, call
them back!"

WE MUST NOT REVEAL OURSELVES. OUR
BROTHER MUST NOT KNOW WE'VE FOUND THE
MAGE CITY.

The big dragon has gone immobile, and vanished
against the tree line. Water stomps at Erde's side in
a convincingly horselike shape and gait. The meadow
is a swirl of white: snow, horses, men.

But surely the hell-priest has seen us already!

THEY FOLLOWED TRACKS. THEY MAY NOT

KNOW   WHOSE.   HURRY!   THROUGH   THE
PORTAL!

"We can't leave the dogs!" Fra Guill knows who
he pursues. Erde is sure of it. She can see his mad
eyes, feel him bearing down on her, and she's frozen
to the spot, like a mouse before a viper.

'Heah. Lemme try." Luther whistles, high and
clear, as he would to his mules. The dog pack hesitates. They fall back, gather, and charge in once more.
Then, as a horse stumbles and goes down, they peel
away victoriously and fly back across the snow to
rally, leaping and baying, around the tall Tinker.

Erde gathers them all into the image in her mind.
NOW?

Now, dear dragon, and quickly!

The transport is barely a flicker, a bird shadow
across the sun. But Erde feels like she's been flung
hard against a wall and been left to lie there several
days. Luther is sprawled facedown on the polished
white stone. As she watches, he stirs. He pulls his
knees up to his chest, clutching his stomach, and
groans. The dogs stagger to their feet and wobble
over to lick his face and hands.

Dragon?

HERE.

Are we safe?

WE ARE. AT LEAST FOR THE MOMENT.

She sits up slowly. She needs both arms to keep
herself upright.

*I think, Dragon, that we've traveled a very long way
this time.*

Chapter Seven

"**Y**eah? Same to you!" N'Doch's gesture is the worst one he can come up with on the spur of the moment, as the ancient bush taxi rattles past, full throttle. Teeners and old men are perched on the bumpers and clinging to the dented sides of the bus with their arms hooked around the window dividers. The children and older women are mashed together inside with all the family possessions they could carry. "Glad someone's getting a ride the hell out of here!"

He drops his arm and lets it swing loose, as if he couldn't care less. Truth is, he'd been thinking about Baraga as he'd raised his fist. If the Media King is after him again, he should be scared, good and scared, given what the man did to him last time. But he's too angry to be scared.

From the sound of it, the fighting's heavier now, toward the center of town. N'Doch heads for the perimeter, along the dusty, rutted street, gesturing Paia to follow. He's glad she hasn't asked him who's fighting who, 'cause he hasn't a clue. Never did, half the time, even when he lived here. "Might as well start walking."

"But you said it's thirty kilometers!"

"Might be a bit less. I ain't not going, okay?"

"Okay," she says meekly, and N'Doch realizes he's yelled at her.

"Sorry. Don't worry. We'll catch a ride before we go that far."

But the truth is, he's not so sure. He was a fool to come without the dragons. Used to be, any driver with an inch of room would stop, 'cause the rider would always pay. Not much, but something. Now, no one's even slowing down. Plenty of folks on foot, hurrying out of town weighed down with kids and chickens and their favorite lamp or prayer rug. There's traffic on the road, but a lot of it's military. N'Doch pulls Paia behind whatever's available when he sees them coming. Mostly they're heading back toward the center, where the action is—muffled explosions, bursts of gunfire and now, the sharp quick report of the sniper's rifle. Another palace coup, or something worse? The stuff coming from intown— trucks, bush taxis, an occasional private car—is already overloaded and moving as fast as it can. He wonders what those guys are saying to get past the roadblocks.

"You doin' okay, then?" he asks Paia. He's trying to be business-as-usual, but this hard lump of rage in his gut is as indigestible as spoiled lard. Things don't usually get the best of him, but this is real brand new, knowing your mama's been murdered and there ain't jackshit you can do about it. "Never thought I'd be *wishing* for dragon transport," he grumbles.

Paia takes two steps for each of his long ones, sticking close beside him. No dawdling now. "Are you surprised the dragons haven't come to find us?"

"Yeah, a little. You'd think Dolph would've made 'em come, for your sake."

"Something might be keeping them. Something might have gone wrong up there."

"Don't even think about it, girl." He doesn't mention the anxious emptiness he feels, in the inside places that grew to make room for the dragon. She probably feels exactly the same.

A vehicle approaches from intown. N'Doch turns, his thumb already out. A battered pickup roars past, churning up a moving envelope of dust. He turns forward again, blinking away grit. A huge explosion rattles the shutters along the wall beside them. Maybe they're bringing in the artillery. He tries to set a slick pace, but it's hot as blazes and they've got a long way to go. He can't afford to use Paia up within the first five klicks. He should've thought to bring water from his mama's house, if there was any. Should've looked around, at least, if he'd been thinking straight. He knows where water used to be, along the way to Papa Dja's, the shops and water-sellers' carts. But that was then. Who knows where he could find it now. Lots more has changed than the beachside *bidonville*. He'd like to get a look at a newsfax or just a calendar, to tell him what month it is, what year? Some very serious shit has obviously gone down here, stuff that'd take a lot longer than the two weeks that have passed for him, real-time. Two weeks! He can't fathom it. It feels like half his life.

Or is it just that he never noticed how bad it was, when he was living here day to day, intent on his own gigs and his own survival? He never saw how played out the people are, abject and sick, and stuck in a landscape that no longer supports them.

Doesn't matter, really. N'Doch knows now what it's all leading up to. He's seen the result, been there in person at endgame. Maybe it was too late already, by his time. But what if the right world leaders had seen what he's seen, had really faced the truth— could they, *would* they take the right steps to stop the downward spiral toward the end? If they'd known the truth, if they'd *believed* it, would they still have let the planet die?

You could test it, he muses, if the rules of dragon travel were more flexible. If only the big dragon could go anywhere in Time, not just to places he can see or that can be immaculately imaged in the mind of a dragon guide. It wouldn't be too hard to figure out when the irreversible decline began, then just go there and warn them. Snatch the key people forward, like he was snatched, and shove their noses in the inevitable results of their greed and shortsightedness.

But it ain't gonna work that way, is it. That would take hope, and in this part of the world at least, hope is obviously dead. Besides, we'd rather have every-thing we want, now, now, now, and to hell with future generations!

"What?" Paia asks gently, walking beside him.

N'Doch realizes he's been muttering. His fists are clenched again, so tightly that his wrists ache and his fingernails are boring holes in his palms. He shakes his head. When did he get to be such a raging bleeding heart?

"Nothing. Sorry." One day, he'll write a big angry song about it, for all the good it'll do. Make him feel better, maybe, but that's for later. Right now, he doesn't feel much like singing.

She peers up at him compassionately. He can see this priestess woman has a talent for empathy. Probably she needed it in the Temple, for dealing with her flock.

"I'm fine," he says, trying to sound less irritable. He considers turning back for the water, back to his mama's house, but then he'd have to look at her dead face again, so full of reproach. Instead, he speeds up, paying more attention to the rubble on the street than to what street he's on. He glances up finally to check his bearings, and sees he's nearly run them into yet another roadblock.

Idiot! He's been thinking about Baraga again.

This checkpoint's at the edge of town. Luckily, there's a line waiting in front of it. N'Doch yanks Paia behind a trio of anxious women whose heavily loaded baskets are balanced neatly on their heads. Should he try to bluster his way through? He wishes Paia was better dressed to blend in. Her plain, pale clothing stands out among the bright and busy patterns worn by the women ahead of them. The soldiers have a big APC blocking the street. They're checking papers, and matching faces against data relayed on their handhelds. The old people and kids, he notices, are being waved right through.

"C'mon," he mutters. "This ain't gonna work."

Turning aside, he hurries Paia through another maze of back streets, his stomping grounds from his bad old days. Who knew his sneak thief's knowledge would come in so handy? But the next road out of town is also guarded, and the houses and walled courtyards form a solid barrier in between. Just as it's occurring to N'Doch that they might be trapped, he hears the one sound he's been listening for all along, the one he truly fears: the thwock, thwock of 'copter blades. Paia hears it, too. She glances up, then quickly at him. He nods, and instinctively, they both shrink against the nearest wall.

"Coming in low and slow," he says. "Observational speed."

So it's not a troop transport. He could tell that by the sound of it anyway. In times past when he was chased by police 'copters, N'Doch would head for the market, to lose himself under the cover of the stall canopies. But the market is a burned-out mess.

He urges Paia into one doorway and he takes the next, as the bird makes its pass. He risks an upward glance as it glides by. It's small and sleek and white, not the olive drab of the military 'copters. Its engine noise fades a bit, then N'Doch hears it turn and head back in their direction. He gestures Paia to stay in her doorway for the second pass, which is slightly more toward the center of town. When it's gone, he waves Paia forward.

"He's gridding," he explains, pointing upward. "Search pattern."

"For us," she remarks quietly.

This time, N'Doch doesn't tell her she's paranoid. He vows silently to listen harder when she talks about Fire. "We'll go doorway to doorway. It's our only chance, till we find a way outa town."

The 'copter thwocks past on a third run, low enough for its rotors to stir up the dust in the gutters. N'Doch can just make out the insignia on its side: MediaRex Enterprises. He glares after it as if his furious stare was weapon enough to bring it crashing to the ground.

Paia tugs at his sleeve. "If we stay in the alleys, there'll never be a place big enough for it to land."

"Yeah, but if it spots us, it can radio the ground troops to close off whatever street we're in. C'mon, let's move."

They've just turned the next corner when the 'copter heads back their way again. But this alley has no doorways, not even a window, just tall, faceless walls all the way to the end, where it empties into a little square. N'Doch listens to the approach, and decides to make a run for it. But the 'copter swoops past sooner than he's expected. By the way it pulls up sharp and wheels around, he knows it's seen something interesting enough to investigate. Suddenly the sky between the walls seems very close.

"Quick! We gotta get outa this slot!"

He's tried not to drag Paia around too much, so he doesn't have to get physical. But now he's got no choice. He grabs her arm and sprints for the little square, praying for some sort of rabbit hole they can dive into. As they streak past the first few houses fronting the square, N'Doch's head swivels. He pounds to an abrupt halt. Paia slams into him. He's got to catch her in his arms to keep her from sprawling flat on the pavement. Her body feels great, pressed against his, but he hasn't time for that right now. He's just seen the weirdest thing.

The 'copter is nearing. N'Doch lets Paia go and backs up several steps. She watches in confusion. The square is lined with the older-style houses, with little high-walled courtyards out in front, entered through tall wrought-iron gates. A few of these gates are still fastened tight. Most have been beaten in or wrenched entirely off their hinges. But one orange stucco archway is closed with a pair of wooden doors, old paneled doors with flaking blue paint. It's amazing that the wood is still intact, and that's what caught his eye, but it's not what stopped him cold. One more back step, and he's in front of it.

One of the doors is slightly ajar. The courtyard inside must be catching some rogue patch of sun, because hot light streams outward through the crack like water from a bilge leak.

"What is it?" Paia glances from the noisy sky to his face and back again. "What?"

N'Doch puts the end of his tire iron to the un-latched door and shoves it open. "Omigod."

"What?"

"Omigod," he says again.

Paia hurries up beside him to stare through the doorway. "Ohh . . . !"

"Someone's sure got us on their radar, and it ain't only that 'copter."

Just past the doorway, the dry bush country stretches to the horizon and the blue, blue sky in all directions. A dry yellow landscape dotted with scrub, pursued by dust devils, hammered by the sun. They're at the edge of an abandoned peanut field, scattered brown weeds still marking out the rows. To the left, a faint red trace of a road leads off and behind a distant straggle of brush, crowned by an unlikely stand of trees. Tucked in its shade is a patch of mustard-colored stucco.

N'Doch has to shout over the scream of the rotors as the 'copter settles in to hover right over their heads. "See that, under that taller bunch of trees? That's Papa Dja's homestead." He wonders what the 'copter sees.

Paia pushes the other door wide, flat against the inside wall. Except there isn't any inside of the wall.

Her hair is blowing loose from her thick braid in the 'copter's downdraft. "We're going in, right?"

"Oh, yeah. This is gonna save our asses!" N'Doch has given up resisting the bizarre things that keep happening to him, but he can't give up being amazed. Could the old man have done this himself? Or the dragons? Maybe they're in there, waiting in Papa Dja's courtyard.

A bullhorn blares intimidations at them from over-head. N'Doch quick-scans the sky inside the door-way. Baraga could have his birds out looking here, too. Once they're in, the portal will close behind them and they'll be stuck in the middle of an open field until they reach the scrub around Djawara's house.

It must be something about being home. He's seeing himself as a vid character again. Like where the hero takes the beautiful girl by the hand and steps calmly out the door into certain danger. Or in this case, from one danger to another, and this hero doesn't feel anything like calm. Conjuring a ghost of his old rakish grin, N'Doch glances up and waves to the 'copter pilot. "See ya 'round!"

The rust-hued bush wind slaps them full in the face as they duck through the archway. Curious, N'Doch holds on to the doorjamb, and looks back. The wooden doors and their framing arch are there, and through them, the rubbled square whirling with flying grit and rotor roar. Elsewhere, for 360 degrees, nothing but red dirt and scrub, and the windy silence of the bush.

He lets go of the door. The portal vanishes. He and Paia stand breathless for a moment, absorbing the sudden change in their surroundings. N'Doch waits for that filling up of the empty spaces inside him that'll tell him the blue dragon's around. But the ache remains. He swears softly and strikes out across the empty peanut field. "Better not hang here in the open for too long."

He sees nothing moving around the distant compound or in the fields around. Not surprising, as it is pretty much midday, when anyone with a brain in his head gets out of the sun. Probably some of the mutts will be lying around the gate, though, just keeping an eye on things.

But no mangy critters leap up to confront them as they round the corner of the yellow wall. No flocks of blackbirds explode from the trees.

"Look," says Paia. "The gate is wide open."

"He always leaves it like that." But this is not strictly accurate. Papa Dja leaves it *unlocked*, not all bent askew and off its hinges, just like the big gates back in town. The tire iron hits the dry roadway with a dull clatter. N'Doch bolts for the opening, then sags against the gatepost, clutching the bent ironwork. He shuts his eyes, murmuring a prayer he didn't even know he knew.

When he looks again, the trees are still there, gathered in a green and inviting corner of the yard. And there's the neat little garden plot. But his grandfather's house is a pile of rubble. It looks like giants have stomped it into chalk and gravel. N'Doch feels like howling, madly, inarticulately, but even in the grip of fury, he's aware this might alert pursuers. He wishes he could just puke up the bile and blind rage tearing his gut apart like a school of sharks. His distant third choice is to push off the gatepost and slam his fist against the peeling stucco. Pound, pound. Loose paint and plaster fly like shrapnel. Pound. Pound. Again. Again. Where is the damn dragon when he really needs her?

Paia wraps both hands around his forearm. "Stop that! Stop that right now!"

The momentum of his strike swings her around and smacks her against the wall. N'Doch doesn't notice. "I fucked up again!"

"It's not your fault!"

"I should've been here!"

"You didn't know!"

"I did! We all did! The bastard told us what he was gonna do, and he went and did it while we stood around and fucking *talked* about it!" He lifts his fist for another pound, but she's on him again, grabbing at his arms. N'Doch shoves her aside and tears into the ruined compound.

Paia chases after him. She catches up as he stops to stare at the rows of wilting tomatoes. This time, she keeps her hands to herself.

"Papa Dja used to water his 'maters twice a day."

"I know, I know," she murmurs. "N'Doch, listen to me, please! You know why Fire's done this! Not because your mother or your grandfather were any danger to him. It's all about you. He's done it to disable *you*!" She reaches up to lay her palm against his wet cheek. "Don't let him do that, okay?"

N'Doch shakes her off and walks away. He doesn't want her seeing his tears. Halfway between the garden and the rubble pile, he's stopped by the sight of Papa Dja's metal garden chair, flung over on its side under the lemon tree. "The mutts must've all run off," he notes bitterly. "Cowards."

Fallen lemons roll around his feet as he stalks over and sets the chair upright. Then he sees the plastic water jug sitting at the base of the tree. His own old water jug, that he'd brought when he arrived with the dragons and got Papa Dja mixed up in this business. No, that's not exactly true. Djawara claimed to have been waiting for the dragons all along. To hear him tell it, he'd been mixed up in it before N'Doch was even thought of.

N'Doch feels the chill even before he picks up the jug. It's full of clear, cold water.

"Paia!" It may be the first time he's said her name, at least to her face.

"I'm here," she says, from right behind him.

He shoves the jug at her. "This was just sitting here."

She cradles it, sniffs at the open top. "Smells okay."

"It's *cold*. How could it be cold, sitting out here in the sun? I mean, long enough for the tomatoes to wilt."

She glances about. "Is someone still here? Hiding?"

"Hiding?" N'Doch bellows. He gestures furiously around the tiny walled enclosure and at the flattened house at its center, turning, turning, with his arms spread wide. "Where the fuck could anyone be hiding?"

"Under those trees?" she suggests, wary of his sudden raving.

N'Doch rolls his eyes. Can't she see? The trees are nothing. It's only because the landscape's so flat and the scrub so stunted that these trees look like anything at all. There aren't more than five or six of them. Okay, so their branches bend low. Even Paia couldn't walk under them without getting a face full of leaves. But the ground past their slim gray trunks is visible all the way to the wall behind, except for that little patch of shade way back in the corner.

And then he recalls the night when two dragons

vanished into that patch of shade. Completely vanished. They'd even invited him in, but N'Doch was too creeped out to venture in there. This was before he'd accepted the fact that the dragon biz wasn't going to go away any time real soon.

"Maybe the trees . . ." He's amazed to see Paia holding out the rusty tire iron. She must have picked it up outside the gate. He takes it with a brusque nod. Maybe it's not such a bad thing she's come along.

He takes a long, delaying-action swig from the jug, then approaches the little grove. He can't picture Baraga's business-suited thugs hanging out in the brush. Why would they bother? They're armed to the teeth with a lot more than tire irons. And it's just as hard to imagine the Fire-breather soiling his shiny golden scales with all that leaf litter. Still . . .

He ducks under the outermost branches. He sees no one—and nothing. But it's much cooler among the leaves than he'd expected, and he has to admit that it is unusually dark in that way-back corner. Not just dark . . . indistinct. As if a tiny black fog has settled there.

A sudden flapping nearly stops his heart. He recoils with a string of muttered curses.

"N'Doch?" Paia calls from the sunlit yard.

"A . . . bird. It's only a bird." He hates being startled. It's embarrassing.

"A real bird?"

"Of course a real bird! What'd you think?"

He ought to feel ashamed. He ought to apologize. He knows she's probably never seen a live bird before, but this lump of outrage he's carrying just under his skin keeps popping up, raw as a blister. It won't let him be easy and reasonable right now.

The bird has dropped out of the upper branches and is boldly stalking about right at his feet. It's an ugly, scrawny black critter with one wing half-cocked, not much of a bird at all. It peers at him brightly, and then it opens its beak to utter a sound so musical, so lovely, that it halts N'Doch in his tracks. It's like the sound pure silver might make if it could pour like water.

"What?" For a moment, the ache in him eases. He forgets his rage. "Say that again?"

And the bird does. Then it walks off into the deeper shade, turns around and comes back, fixing N'Doch with first one amber eye and then the other. It warbles at him again, repeating itself several times.

N'Doch calls out softly, so as not to spook the bird. He's grateful to it for showing him how to speak more gently. "Hey, Paia? You oughta come in here. Kinda slowlike."

She slips in behind him. She's got the water jug tight in her hand. Sensible woman. She knows to leave nothing useful behind. The bird doesn't spook. It studies Paia briefly, as if to say, what kept you? Then it treats her to a particularly passionate chorus of its lyrical song. Paia clasps the water jug to her breast like it was a child. "Oh! How wonderful!"

This time, the bird hops to the edge of the shadow and stays there, regarding them both expectantly.

"Is it a raven?" Paia asks.

"Damned if I know. Why?"

"In this book I read in my father's library, ravens are often the bearers of messages and omens."

"Messages from who?"

"Someone with the power to compel a raven."

"Well, if it's telling me a message, I don't speak its language."

"But you do," Paia murmurs. She kneels in front of the bird and holds out her hand. The bird shakes its head and warbles. "Its language is music.

"Huh," says N'Doch. He is thinking of another Raven, much more beautiful than this one.

"Wouldn't you say that it wants us to follow it?"

"I'd, um . . . yeah, I'd say that."

Together they peer into the oddly shifting darkness.

"We should hurry up, then, shouldn't we?" says Paia. "Remember the screen in your . . ." Her voice drops. "In your mother's house,"

Who's leading this expedition, N'Doch asks himself. "What about Papa Dja?"

"It seems clear, don't you think, that he isn't here . . . ?"

N'Doch grits his teeth, and looks away. "No. He sure isn't."

"Could he have gone someplace safe, and left this bird as a message?"

"Some place like . . ." He jerks his chin toward the foggy shadow. "In there? Does that look safe to you?"

Paia shrugs, sitting back on her heels with her hands folded in her lap, the very picture of acquiescence.

N'Doch sighs and rubs his eyes. Nothing in the world is less likely than anything else, he decides. "You win," he says. "You and the bird."

Chapter Eight

"It's a strange place," Paia observes later. "But not too scary so far."

When they arrived at the dead end, N'Doch stayed quiet for a while, watchful and waiting. But when the place just went on being what it was, with no visible way in, or even back out, he began to pace and mutter.

"I'm just as happy to rest a little," Paia offers agreeably, mostly to invite a more useful conversation.

"You rest. I'm looking for a way out."

Paia tries a smile, since smiles seem to render him more tractable. But the gesture is so mechanical that even she finds it irritating. Instead, she sets the water jug down on the nearest raised surface and drops beside it with a sigh. Who wouldn't want a moment or two to recover after being chased halfway across Africa by a demon helicopter? Besides, N'Doch is the problem solver. He's used to being able to figure his way out of things.

As for me, I'm just used to letting other people do the figuring for me.

Not particularly cheered by this admission, Paia wets the hem of her shirt with the tiniest slosh of water and dabs at her face. The pale fabric comes away ruddy with dust. "You want some water?"

N'Doch paces over, grabs up the jug for a long and noisy swig, plops it down again, and paces away. "It's a trap," he growls. "Now the dragons'll never find us!"

"It won't help if you wear yourself out storming about."

"I'm walking. I'm thinking on my feet."

"Well, I'm thinking, too. And all that useless motion is distracting!"

"Oh, great. Just when I'd decided it wasn't a total drag having you along!" He jams his hands on his hips. "You must've got real used to telling people what to do in that Temple of yours."

"Why do you say that?"

"Because you keep trying it on me. Except you're always pretending you're not. So, quit it, okay? I don't like it."

"But I was only . . ." Perhaps she had sounded a bit bossy. She hadn't meant to. And he does deserve some extra patience and compassion, after the shock of losing his mother. "Sorry."

N'Doch kicks at the thing she's sitting on. "What are these, anyway?"

There are two of them, set opposite each other: pale, smooth rectangles exactly the height of a chair. "Benches? They look like benches."

"They look like gravestones. What are they doing here?"

Paia flares. "How should I know?"

"Maybe you should give it some thought." He stalks away, unrepentant.

The bird, who has been hiding from N'Doch since narrowly avoiding a well-aimed kick in its direction, hops up beside Paia with its eye fixed on the water jug. She feels responsible for it now, as if she's acquired a pet. She looks around for a way to give it some and there, at the end of the bench, is a shallow, round container about the size of her palm.

"Well, bird, look at that." Paia slides over to pick it up, but it's either glued to or a part of the otherwise unbroken surface. Odd that she hadn't noticed it before. She shrugs and pours an inch of water into the odd little cup. The bird warbles, and moves in for a drink.

"I'm not sure you deserve it," she scolds, watching it dip and swallow, dip and swallow. "Look what you got us into."

But it had been her idea, after all, that she and N'Doch should follow the black bird into the fog at the back of the tree shadow. The fuzzy blinding darkness went on a lot longer than it should, given the high wall enclosing the compound. Perhaps they'd descended without being aware of it, and somehow tunneled under the wall. Whatever the explanation, they met no wall, just an enveloping darkness, which lightened gradually through several shades of luminous gray. When the last of it dissipated, they were in this very peculiar place.

It's a big, open-ended room, smooth-floored, high-ceilinged, and as featureless as a blank sheet of paper, but for the two white slabs in the middle. Looked at more closely, they're not like gravestones at all. They're obviously benches. Paia can't imagine why she thought otherwise. They have cylindrical legs and a thick polished top, subtly veined like white marble. There is one thing odd about them. Stone in the shade is usually cool, even at the Citadel, where almost nothing is cool. These benches match Paia's body temperature, as if someone has just gotten up from where she's sitting.

"Creepy," she says to the bird. "Some sort of plastic?"

And what about the walls? They're not so blank as she'd thought at first. A faint tracery of tall windowlike shapes angles away in sharp perspective toward the dark opening at the far end of the room. And there, where there should be a way out, Paia's study stalls. Here's the really peculiar thing about this place. There's nothing there. Not night or darkness, but *nothing*. Void.

N'Doch stands halfway between Paia and the void, staring into it as if willing it to explain itself. Paia doesn't blame him for letting sorrow and frustration make him so irritable. Her father'd had that way of dealing with his feelings sometimes. And surely, once N'Doch agreed to follow the bird, he'd really let himself hope he'd find his grandfather waiting for him.

The bird finishes drinking and waddles along the bench to hop up on Paia's knee. She's entranced by its bright glance and forthright manner, and by its obvious if alien intelligence. She forgives it for looking so much the worse for wear. After all, it's her first real live bird, and if it's not as lovely as all the pictures she's seen, it's certainly much more interesting. She used to know the date when the last bird died, at least in North America. Her father often reminded her of it. She regrets that she's forgotten it, and even more that she did not grow up with such interesting creatures in her world.

She extends a hand to the bird, experimentally. It lets her stroke its dusty feathers until a bit of sheen reappears. Then it crooks one scrawny yellow leg and grasps her forefinger firmly. Paia gasps, then giggles nervously. "Hello, bird," she says, wiggling the leg gently up and down. She's relieved when it releases her and stands back. She'd like it better if its feet weren't so reminiscent of dragon's claws.

N'Doch slouches over and slumps down on the far end of the bench, sending the bird scurrying to Paia's side.

"Look out . . ." she begins, but the container of water is no longer there.

"What? What?"

"Nothing. It was . . . I thought you might sit on the bird." But she almost orders him up again, so she can see the spot where the little cup fit so neatly back into the benchtop. Pressed down by his weight? She'd like to know. But she doesn't want him to think she's telling him what to do.

"I don't get it." He fists one hand restlessly inside the other. "All the other portals went somewhere. How come there's no there here?"

"It's like a waiting room." Like the benches in the halls outside her father's offices at the Citadel, where people seemed to wait forever.

"Waiting for what?"

"For an idea. For a way out. For something to happen. Like we are." Paia wishes he wouldn't glare at her so accusingly, as if she's said something unpardonably stupid. She's not stupid. She's just more accepting of their situation. In fact, she feels curiously numb, as if she's repressed her anxiety all the way to affectlessness. How totally sheltered she was in her family fortress! As long as she remained inside, she had nothing and no one to fear—except, of course, the God. In the outside world, apparently everything is a threat. Just as her father—and the God—had always warned her.

"Except you, bird," she murmurs. "Isn't that right?"

The bird regards her expectantly, as if it, too, is bored with waiting.

"Sorry. Not much I can do." Paia turns away to study the windows along the opposite wall. If only she could see through all that cut glass and heavy drapery! There might be a light behind. She's not sure, but the beveled patterns in the glass seem to sparkle with a different sort of light than the cool, even glow of the room they're sitting in. They could knock on a window, perhaps, even open it, or . . .

"What's over the railing?" she asks N'Doch.

"What railing?"

"The balcony railing."

He gives her that same accusing glare.

"Well, look." She points. "Down at the far end."

He turns toward the void. The railing is a waist-high band of white stone, supported by cylindrical balusters. "That wasn't there before."

"Yes, it . . . wait, no. You're right. It wasn't. Why did I . . . ?" Paia suffers a moment of vertigo. Because the bench wasn't a bench either. Not at first. She can picture it clearly: a plain white block. It's like waking up when you're not even aware you've been asleep and dreaming. "What about those windows?" The detail of their casing and mullions seems richer than a moment ago. "Those weren't there either, were they?"

"No. They weren't." N'Doch stands up. "Something's happening."

At least he didn't say, "What windows?" "Are we asleep?"

The accusing glare is slightly milder this time.

"Well, we might be. How would we know?" There's another possibility that Paia doesn't even want to mention.

" 'Cause I know, that's how."

The bird suddenly emits its musical cry and takes off in a dusty flurry. It soars once around the room, then flies straight out into the void, its call fading with distance.

"Hey, look at that!" N'Doch sprints after it. "If it got out, we can!"

Paia hurries to join him at the edge, and finds him gripping the balcony railing as if it might try to escape.

"Okay," he says. "This is weird."

To the left and right of the opening, long flights of stairs have materialized. The broad white railing leads downward like an arrow into darkness. But shapes are coalescing out of the void, a landscape rising from the fog. Or rather, a cityscape. As they watch, tall straight-sided towers appear, bathed in a cool, even light. Puffs of storybook cloud obscure their heights. Their feet are planted within an infinitely receding grid of wide, clean streets.

"Now where have we got ourselves to?" N'Doch murmurs.

"It's beautiful," Paia breathes, mourning the drowned and ruined cities of her own time. "It's huge. Are we supposed to go down there?"

"Where else?" N'Doch slides his hand along the railing, testing its solidity.

From high above its pale streets, the city looks motionless and deserted.

"Which way should we go?"

"If I had a coin, I'd toss it."

"The bird flew that way." Paia points vaguely toward the left. The sky between the towers is now a clear, flat blue. The puffy clouds seem permanently moored to their tips.

"As good a guess as any. Ready?" With a hint of returning bravado, N'Doch squares his shoulders and starts down the left-hand staircase. She can tell he's glad just to be moving again.

The first part of the descent is more like mountain climbing than walking. The steps are dangerously high and deep, and the stair goes straight down without a turn or landing, as if built for giants. Paia is reminded of the Grand Stair leading up to the Citadel, specifically designed to be difficult, in order to repel invading armies, but also to provide the worshiper approaching the Temple with an opportunity for penance. She doesn't question the oddness of such a stair until, after several minutes of perilous stumbling and a lot of awkwardness, the going gets easier and the steps are not so tall or wide. The farther they descend, the easier it gets, until the steps are the perfect height and width for speeding downward. N'Doch slows his pace voluntarily, to keep them both from tumbling headlong to the city streets.

The staircase spills them out at the edge of a vast, paved square. Paia glances back up the long run of steps, climbing the side of a windowless building as sheer as the face of a cliff. Who would build such a precipitous stair on the structure's exterior? The balcony is a vague smudge, a mere brushstroke in the upper distance, wreathed like the tower tops in clouds that to her painter's eye look as if they've been laid on top of an existing canvas.

"Are you sure we're not dreaming this?" she asks plaintively.

"Sure, I'm sure," replies N'Doch, with the intensity of one trying hard to convince himself. "What's your problem, anyway?"

"Look at this place!"

"What's the last city you were ever in?"

"I've seen pictures. Lots of them. Cities have people, but this place is empty. There's no one here!"

"We don't know that yet." He stands with his arms akimbo, gazing ahead down a wide street that vanishes into the distance without a crook or bend. His dark, mobile silhouette rests uneasily against the pale background of faceless buildings and streets, as if cut out with scissors and pasted on. "Wonder where the damn bird went."

Rather than striking out across the open square, N'Doch chooses the long way, around its perimeter. The pavement is as smooth and white as polished tile. The facades of the buildings are peculiarly blank, with tall arched niches wrapping curls of thin shadow around opaque windows and doors. Rather as an Impressionist might paint them, Paia notes. No detail, just the effects of light. But a painter's surfaces would never be so flat and lifeless. It's like there's an entire dimension missing from everything she sees.

"If there are people here," she asks, "how do they get in and out of these buildings?"

"What d'you mean, if? Who ever heard of a city with no people?"

"There's lots of them. Most of them, in my time."

N'Doch shakes his head impatiently. "Concealed entrances, probably. For security reasons."

As he says this, there's a shivering in the ground. A buildup of static in the air raises the hair on Paia's arms. N'Doch has moved off toward the nearest doorway for a closer look.

"You feel that?" she calls.

He steps up on a sidewalk she hadn't noticed before and peers into the archway. "Feel what?"

The sensation passes. Paia hurries to catch up with him. "You didn't feel that little . . . quivering?"

"Nope. Not a thing." He runs his palm across the blank space where the door should be. "You'd think maybe there'd be a sign or something. You know, like: dragon guides, ring here."

Paia is relieved to see his humor resurfacing. Her laugh echoes thinly, as if the buildings have absorbed most of its wavelengths. N'Doch moves on to the next entryway, which is flanked by a pair of white columns, but offers the same lack of access.

"I'd feel better if there was someone around," Paia ventures.

"Ha. Be careful what you wish for. Who says that someone would want us around?"

"But wouldn't you prefer an enemy we know about to one we can't even see?"

"I'd prefer no enemies at all. Enemies do things like blow you to pieces and murder your ma."

"Oh, N'Doch. . . ." Paia slips her hand around the crook of his elbow. His tensed muscles are more honest about his state of mind than his face is. She squeezes him gently. "I'm so sorry."

"Yeah. Me, too."

She's glad he can finally admit it aloud. They walk arm in arm to the end of the block, where a side street enters the square. But N'Doch disengages himself uneasily when they reach the curb. He looks out across the broad expanse of open pavement. "Y'know, the folks who made this city didn't have much of an imagination. Those buildings on that side are exactly the same as these here."

Paia allows his escape to safer subject matter. "And the other two sides match each other, too. An advanced appreciation of symmetry, perhaps?"

"Symmetry is boring."

"Always?" She glances up at him, risking a smile. "You'd look very odd without matching arms and legs. Or eyes."

N'Doch snorts. "Maybe. But I knew a guy once with one brown eye and one blue one. Made a shit-load of money on it, 'cause people thought he was a big magic man." His grin is sour, but Paia is happy to see it. "Point is," he continues, "I wouldn't want to meet the people that live here. They'd be the people who gotta do things a certain way. I wouldn't likely fit into their mold. Maybe if we got off the main drag a bit . . ."

He turns to peer hopefully down the little side street. The ground shivers again, a tremor like a tiny earthquake. Paia's vision blurs momentarily. Either that, or something odd is happening to the surfaces of the buildings. And then, it's as if nothing had occurred.

"There! Did you feel that?"

"Was that it before? I thought it was me phasing out for a nanosec."

"No, it . . . look! Ask, and ye shall receive!"

On the corner of the building across the side street, a little above headheight, is a sign—the first they've seen, the first detail of any sort. Paia's eyes fall upon it hungrily. It's a bright sky-blue rectangle with a neat white border and white block lettering. Familiar looking, but she can't quite place it.

" 'As the crow flies . . .' " N'Doch reads with a puckered brow. "Huh. I guess it could have been a crow."

"What's a crow?"

"A bird. Like the one that got us into this mess in the first place."

"Ah." Paia stares at the sign, trying to tease out further meaning. Of course! It reminds her of a monitor screen. Amazing, she muses, the significance letters can assume when they're the only ones around. There are very few signs in the Citadel, and no books at all, save the antiques in her father's library. There's no one to publish them anymore. The God requires literacy for the Temple priesthood, but only to enable them to carry out the day-to-day administration and to keep track of the tithing and finances. She wonders how many of the children in the villages that pay duty to the Temple are being taught to read and write. Why bother, if there's nothing for them to read? On the other hand, how will there ever be anything to read again, if no one is taught how to write?

Paia realizes that N'Doch is staring at her.

"You gonna read that sign right off the wall, girl?"

"I was thinking about books."

"Books? I've read one or two." He shakes his head. "You're weird. C'mon. This way. This little street looks promising."

At first, Paia is not sure she agrees, and she's glad when he chooses a cautious pace and sticks to the middle of the pavement. The street is narrow, and shaded rather abruptly into dimness by the tall buildings on either side—all the horizontal confinement of a cave without the vertical comfort of a roof. But, in the distance, several vague projecting shapes promise a change in the monotony of the facades. They gain specificity as the distance shortens, and are finally resolved into objects familiar to Paia only through pictures. In colors and stripes, they hang out over the sidewalk, which is less well-maintained on this back street than out in the main square. Long cracks spiderweb the concrete, and the curbstones are worn and broken.

N'Doch points. "See those awnings? Must be a little business district."

Awnings. That's what they're called. Paia thinks they look very cheerful, especially after a long trudge through a dull gray city. Urged along faster, she can soon see little tables under the nearest one, covered with red-checkered cloths. The black metal chairs have rounded, filigreed backs. Paia feels a sudden urge to sit down.

But N'Doch's eager pace has slackened. Abruptly he stops, in the middle of the street. "Oh, boy."

"What is it?"

"You wouldn't understand."

"I might, if you give me a chance."

"I know this place."

"What do you mean?"

"I *know* it. I've been there. Bunch of times, when I was a boy."

Paia has met many strange notions in her life, but for some reason, this one gives her a chill. "Oh, N'Doch, it just *looks* like some place you've been."

"No. It is." He jabs a finger at the scrawl of lettering on the green-and-white striped canopy. "See what it says? *La Rive Gauche.* That's what the place was called. It was Papa Dja's favorite hangout when he was still living in town. Okay. I'll reconsider the possibility that I'm dreaming . . . !"

"*We're* dreaming."

"We can't both be . . ."

There's movement among the tables. A large brown animal rises from the shadows and stands at attention, looking their way. Paia encounters her second extinct creature in less than a day. It's a dog, and the sight invokes a sharp twinge of nostalgia. Her father had tried to breed dogs in the early days of the Collapse, but feeding them became too difficult when the humans around them were starving. The feudal system of tribute-in-kind that keeps the Temple denizens so healthy and well fed wasn't put in place until the dragon arrived. This dog does not look well fed at all. Even at a distance, Paia can see that its raggedy coat is patched with the matted darkness of dried blood. But it looks alert and capable of being threatening. Paia doesn't know if she should be afraid of it or not.

"It's one of the mutts!" N'Doch waves at the dog, then whistles. "Damn! It's one of Papa Dja's old mutts!" He whistles again, but the dog stays right where it is, dancing from paw to paw and panting foolishly. "Okay, boy, wait there and we'll come to you." N'Doch breaks into a trot.

And is flung to the ground by a sudden shifting of the pavement. Paia stumbles as the street jerks sideways, left, then right, and left again, as if meaning to keep her tumbling. Scrambling to her feet, she hears a crackling and roaring, rolling down the canyon of buildings behind them. Grit swirls in the air, blinding her. Where did it come from? The streets are spotless. N'Doch is yelling over the roar. He grabs her under her arms, yanking her to her feet.

The grit is sharper now, biting at her skin like a swarm of insects. The gusts tear at her hair and clothing.

"Inside!" N'Doch screams in her ear. "We've got to get inside!"

They race toward the café, the street bucking beneath them, the wind like a giant's vicious sidearm punch. The crackling is behind them, approaching, nearing, deafening.

"Faster!" N'Doch bellows. "It's after us!"

Paia can't think about what "it" is. She can only run, as fast as she can, a frantic mouse scurrying for the baseboard. They gain the shadow of the canopy. The scalloped edges of the awning snap in the wind like the repeating crack of pistol shots. Empty coffee cups and butter plates are sliding, crashing to the pavement. The dog has vanished. N'Doch hauls Paia through the shifting maze of tables and chairs toward the door, shattered glass crunching beneath their feet. Paia fights off a flying tablecloth that's wrapped itself around her face and breathes a little prayer of thanks, because there is a door here and it's opening, just in time to receive them as they stagger blindly through. It slams abruptly shut behind them.

The silence is almost as deafening as the roaring had been outside. The floor is steady and level. The air is still. Paia inhales the long-forgotten dark scent of coffee and the earthy sweetness of fresh bread. The dimly lit room is full of dogs, scattered about on the black-and-white tiles. Several of them thump their tails in greeting.

"There you are! Took your own sweet time as usual."

An old man is standing behind them, silhouetted against the wall of windows fronting the café. His hand is on the doorknob. Paia cannot see his face. On the other side of the glass, tables and chairs are skidding and colliding in space like elementary particles.

N'Doch whirls. "Papa Dja!" He starts toward the man, then stops. "Damn, you're a sight for sore eyes!"

"Glad you made it in one piece."

Paia wonders if a penchant for understatement could be hereditary.

"A close thing, too," N'Doch exclaims. "You oughta stand clear of all that glass."

"We're safe in here. It can't come in."

"It?"

The old man glances behind him as a wind-borne chair crashes twice against the door, like a giant's knock. He lifts both arms in a gesture of resignation. "There is great evil abroad in this city, my boy." He moves away from the door as if exhausted, and lowers himself into a chair by the window. A tiny white cup and saucer rest on the marble-topped table beside it.

"Man, it was . . ."

"I know. I don't go out."

N'Doch drops to a crouch beside the chair and grasps his grandfather's knees, giving them a little shake. "Damn, when I got there and saw . . . I was sure you were . . . !"

The old man pats his grandson's hands awkwardly, and then the head that drops to press itself against him. "So was I, for a while there."

He is slight but elegant of manner, what Paia's father would have called an old-world gentleman. His hair has grayed in tight curls like a woolly skullcap pulled back from his high forehead. He's wearing white, a floor-length tunic with full sleeves and gold embroidery around the open neck. Paia takes to him immediately, especially when he offers her a warm and intelligent smile, and his dark, slender hand in greeting.

"Who's this, now? You're showing off with a different woman every time I see you."

"Not *my* woman, Papa." N'Doch sits back on his heels with a damp and weary grin, one hand still resting on the old man's knee. "This is Paia. She's a dragon guide, too. Paia, this is my grandfather Djawara. Pay no attention to anything he says."

N'Doch's grandfather peers at Paia without a trace of myopia. "Hmmm. The Fire-breather's, is it?"

"Yes, sir." Paia doesn't ask how he knows. She can see that this family likes to spring their knowledge on you sideways, to see if you'll startle. She hasn't called anyone "sir" since her father's diplomatic colleagues stopped coming to the Citadel, but the old gesture of respect comes back automatically with this man. She returns his handshake firmly. "We're so glad to find you alive!"

Djawara raises an eyebrow at his crouching grandson. "Nice girl. Beautiful, too. Why isn't she yours?"

N'Doch shoots a glance at Paia. " 'Cause somebody else got there first."

"And you're honoring that? Good lad. Your manners have improved."

"Funny. I'd have said I was losing my touch." N'Doch's hands are working patterns on Djawara's bony knees, soft musical rhythms of distress. "Papa. Papa. I got some bad news to tell you. Real bad. Fâtime's gone."

"Gone?"

"She's . . . um, she's dead, Papa."

Djawara's smile drains away like the color going out of a sunset. His chin lifts. He turns his face away to gaze through the dusty window. Outside, the windstorm has passed, leaving behind a rubble of broken furniture. "How?"

"Shot. Murdered."

"Murdered? Why? What for? For the house? For that ancient black-and-white TV? She had nothing worth killing her for!"

Paia pulls a chair over beside Djawara. She sits down and takes his hand. His skin is darker than hers, but just as soft.

N'Doch stands, walks in an aimless little circle, then goes to the door and leans his forehead against the glass. "Not a thief, Papa. It was too clean . . . like a hit. I think it was Baraga."

"It was the dragon," Paia says. "It was Fire. He's the one to blame."

"Who came after you, Papa? Your house is a pancake."

Djawara nods. "My lovely, loyal house. Men, for sure. There was a lot of shooting. Maybe the dragon as well. It all happened so fast. But I saved the dogs, or I should say, they saved me. Dragged me into the trees, and poof! Here I am. I always knew there was something lurking beneath those boughs. Just couldn't ever find it before."

"There was a bird," Paia murmurs.

"Oh, yes. He's around somewhere. They all are."

"But, Papa, why are we here in the Rive? No, strike that. Why is the Rive here?"

Djawara shrugs. "You don't know?"

"Not a clue."

"I thought maybe the dragons might . . . where are they, anyway?"

"On the way, I hope. We sort of got started without them." N'Doch turns away from the door to regard the café in all its richness of detail: the cracked plaster walls hung with faded posters advertising travel to cities that Paia knows were under water long ago; the dark polished oak bar with its glimmering mirrors behind shelves stocked with bottles and glassware; the towering espresso machine in the corner, surrounded by stacks of white china. He spreads his arms wide. "But why are we here? Is it . . . an illusion?"

"I worried about that," Djawara concedes. "I wandered for what seemed like days in this faceless city and suddenly, there it was, with a fresh cup of espresso sitting right there on the table, and the old horse trough full of water for the dogs."

"Suddenly? You mean, like it hadn't been there before?"

"Well, I don't know that, do I? Every street in this city looks alike. But when I spotted that old familiar awning, I'd just been thinking of how restorative a good shot of espresso would be. I walked in and everything, the whole room, was like the Rive, but not quite. Like a sort of sketch. Except for the steaming cup of espresso. That was so real, I burned my tongue." Djawara pauses to moisten his lips as if testing for lingering tenderness. "That was several days ago, and I haven't been hungry or thirsty since. And the place gets more like the Rive every day. If it's an illusion, I doubt it could feed me so convincingly. The dogs are so pampered, they're getting positively lazy." He sighs, leans forward and sips at his cup. "Sometimes I think tea would be nice for a change, and there it is. If it's an illusion, it's not your ordinary kind."

N'Doch walks to the bar, pats it, then leans against it and looks back at Paia. "This couldn't all be Fire's doing?"

She considers this nervously. But *La Rive Gauche* just does not seem to be Fire's sort of place. It's too pleasant and understated, too . . . democratic, and she says so.

"But," counters N'Doch, "the weather can be a real bitch."

"That was no simple windstorm," Djawara says. "There are monsters roaming the streets, make no mistake about it. I don't go out. Neither do the dogs. Not since we lost three of them. That's why I sent the bird. For some reason, they can get through."

"But, Papa, we gotta go out sometime. Can't just sit in here for the rest of our lives. Much as I love the Rive, and all. Remember, when I was little, you always gave me one of . . ." N'Doch looks around, then strides to a table to grab up a glistening brown lump from a white porcelain bowl. He holds it up, triumphantly pincered between thumb and forefinger. ". . . one of these! And sent me home to Ma." His grin fades. He returns the lump to the bowl. "Papa, I couldn't even bury her or anything. The whole town's a war zone."

"It was more important to find you," Paia adds softly. "Alive."

"We're all the family we have now, boy."

"You got it, Papa."

In the silence that visits uninvited, Paia's relief and exhaustion draws up around her like a warm blanket. She yawns, wishing for a more comfortable seat than the rickety metal chairs around the tables.

"Can I get you anything, my dear?" the old man asks.

There is a pitcher of water on the table now, with three glasses beside it. Lemon slices float among the ice cubes. Paia lets Djawara fill a glass for her. She's too tired to eat. N'Doch wanders about the little café, poking into cabinets and corners, lifting lids and un-corking bottles. Djawara sips his coffee silently and lets his grandson wear out his restless energy. Finally, N'Doch comes back to the table and drops heavily into the third chair.

He pours himself a glass of water and drains it. "Okay. Now, let me get this straight. You think real hard about what you want, and it appears. It does this right in front of you?"

"No." Djawara sets down his cup. "I always come upon it, as if it's been there all along. And asking for silly things doesn't work. Apparently, it has to be something I really need."

"Like coffee?"

"Well, need is evidently relative in this situation."

Paia yawns again, laying her head on her propped-up palm. "Maybe you just need to think you need it."

"What happens if I do it?" N'Doch asks.

"I don't know. Try."

N'Doch closes his eyes. In her sleepy stupor, Paia finds this comical. She giggles. N'Doch's eyes pop open in a glare, which makes her giggle again. "Why don't you try it?" he growls.

"I'm too tired."

He closes his eyes again. "I'm imagining a big plate of steak and *pommes frites*." After a moment, he opens his eyes. All three survey the room. Nothing has magically appeared on any surface. N'Doch tries again. Nothing.

"What the hell? What am I doing wrong?"

"Maybe it's like making a wish," Paia offers. "You shouldn't tell us what you're asking for."

N'Doch makes a rude noise. "What does it care if I tell you or not?"

"Interesting," Djawara says. "That you say 'it.' I also find myself personifying these appearances, as if they are a gift from some entity, rather than an inherent reflex of the landscape."

"Perhaps *you* must make the request," Paia suggests.

"Go for it, then, Papa. I'm getting hungrier just thinking about it."

"Or perhaps," Paia amends, not sure what has made her think of this, "N'doch should sing it."

"Hey, off my back, huh?"

"I'm serious!"

"It's not such a bad idea," Djawara adds.

"What, sing about food? Oh . . . you mean like . . . oh, man, I gotta make up a song about steak, *pommes frites*?"

N'Doch shifts his chair irritably, allowing Paia a new angle of view that reveals an informal seating area in a far corner, with sofas and easy chairs arranged like her mother's reading parlor in the Citadel. While N'Doch fulminates about singing for his supper, Paia gets up and drifts across the room to the nearest sofa. A worn patchwork quilt like the one from her childhood lies folded over one pillowy arm. The cushions receive her softly as she throws herself among them, sinking gratefully toward sleep. The last thing she hears is N'Doch's musical mutterings resolving into a melodic hum. But what ushers her into delicious slumber is the homey odor of potatoes frying.

Chapter Nine

The white-tiled terrace holds his weight as he
steps out onto it. The Librarian had been worried about that. The surface looks insubstantial, transparent, like the reflection on a still pond at dawn. He
remembers such a pond, from his earlier days. But
that pond was sanctuary. This is . . . something else.

Stoksie appears beside him, apparently untroubled
by issues of solidity. He assesses the situation with
quick Tinker pragmatism. "Dull sorta spot, G."

"Humming. Hear it?"

"Doan heah a t'ing. Watsit?"

It's a background noise, not the soundless imperative that's been urging him to speed for so many
hours. It's like static or the steady breathing of circuitry. The Librarian shrugs. Maybe his ears have
carried the sounds of the com room with him out of
mere habit. He peers around. Stoksie's right. It is a
dull sort of spot. The walls and roof enclosing the
terrace are plain enough to suit the most rigid mini-
malist, a Bauhaus patio before the decorators arrive.
The Librarian sighs. All his metaphors are archaic

lately. Minimalism is no longer a choice. It's all that's left. He is unsurprised when he looks back at the portal, and encounters a blank gray wall.

Stoksie follows his gaze. "Heh. Guez we're heah fer a while, den."

The Librarian nods. Was it foolish to let himself be drawn so easily through that opening, and his good friend with him? Did he really have a choice? The hum is louder. He shakes his head. It doesn't vary or go away. But he's sure it's not his imagination. Just in a frequency the Tinker can't hear.

Stoksie ambles up to the terrace railing, with its expanse of blue beyond. The Librarian notes that the little man favors his bad hip all the time now. He wonders if the dragon Earth could fix that for him, in a spare moment, if any of them are to have any spare moments, ever again. At the railing, Stoksie leans out and looks down. "Weeeooo! C'mon an' lookit dis, G!"

The Librarian quails. Something about the light glinting off Stoksie's bald brown head as he leans over the edge. Something inexorable in its cool white glow. He knows suddenly that he'll never see his console again. Another refuge has served its purpose and become obsolete. His own evolution could be charted by the dens he's made over the centuries, and then outgrown. He suspects this is why he feels so different since the morning's confrontation on the mountaintop. Time for the next step forward. Maybe the final step.

"C'mon! Yu gotta see dis!"

As always, the Librarian's first instinct is to resist. He'd flee back to the familiar shelter of that console if he had half a chance. But his Destiny knows him well enough to make sure he doesn't—by the destruction of a home, by the pursuit of enemies, by an outbreak of war, by the slamming of a door. Always impelling him onward. Resigned, the Librarian shuffles across the terrace. The pale insubstantial tiles still hold him up. Isn't this why he came, after all? To confront the inevitable, whatever it may be? The humming, constant in his ears, suggests that the inevitable is near. But then, he's often thought that in the past, only to see the distance to his goal again become elastic, stretched toward infinity. Long practiced in the exertion of will over reluctance, the Librarian gains the railing and gazes out over the white city he'd known would be there since the moment the portal opened.

The terrace perch is astonishingly high off the ground. Even in the old days of the skyscrapers, the Librarian was never so high, except in an airplane. And this city is a forest of such towers. Clouds gather around them like luminous, upside-down shrubbery. The expanse of blue is not empty sky, but endless ranks of towers fading into blue distance. An artificial Himalaya. The Librarian's knees go weak, partly in fear, partly in admiration. It is a magnificent creation, an urban architect's wet dream.

"Yu t'ink da One is down deah?" Stoksie asks.

"Hoping. Hoping."

"How we gonna git down?"

"Elevator," murmurs the Librarian, knowing they'll find one. It doesn't take long: a rectangular outline on the nearest wall, like a box drawn on a blueprint. The Librarian approaches it, and it opens with a willing hush. He's confused for a moment, for the cab is identical to the elevator back at the Refuge. Has he misunderstood? Is Destiny leading him back to the com room, his journey over before it's begun?

The Librarian shrugs, renewing his commitment to inevitability, and steps inside. Stoksie hurries to join him, and the doors whisk shut. There is a brass placket on the wall right where it should be, but no buttons to press. Time passes, without any sensation of movement. Stoksie whistles absently under his breath.

"Itsa long way down, aftah all," he remarks finally.

The Librarian chuckles. He'd love to be as firmly moored to reason as this staunch little man.

Without a warning tone or chime, the doors whisper open. It's like stepping through the portal all over again. It requires the same resolve. The Librarian's agoraphobia assails him. The space beyond the doors is so vast, so bright, so white. So empty.

"C'mon, G." Stoksie takes his arm.

Grateful, the Librarian lets himself be led.

He's expected a lobby, or an atrium at least, not this abrupt delivery out into the open. It's unsettling, architecturally, to be dropped without transition at the brink of this enormous and light-drenched plaza. Light, not sun. It's too white for sunlight. The Librarian recalls Tien-an-men, in the ancient city long destroyed. But the buildings surrounding this square are infinitely taller. To his agoraphobe's eye, the towers seem to be falling inward, toward the ground. But the Librarian is used to compensating for this old deficiency. He steps bravely forward. What brings him to his knees on the blank white pavement is not terror. It's the sound of that sunless light.

The sound!

Deafening, breath-shaking, a steady excruciating pounding on his head, his back, his ears.

"Whatsit, G? What?" Stoksie wheels back, struggles to help him up.

"The light . . . out of the light." He fumbles the speaking. He's barely able to complete the thought. He stumbles backward, blinded by noise. "Must get out of the light."

But there's no shade to back into, no retreat, no shelter. The elevator door has closed behind them and vanished into a gray wall as flat as painted granite.

"Okay, yu gottit. C'mon dis way!"

The Tinker is stronger than he looks. He guides the Librarian into the shadow of a tall, arched doorway. The hum still vibrates in his ears, but the pain subsides to a bearable level, and the Librarian can catch his breath. He tries to explain his predicament.

Stoksie sucks his crooked teeth. "Yeah? What kinda soun' duz da light make?"

The Librarian has not tried to identify it. He's been too focused on resisting it. His hands flutter. Words seem more elusive than ever.

"Izzit, y'know, like muzik?"

The Librarian shakes his head. He almost expects to hear loose parts rattling around. "Hum. Growl. Snap. Whine."

"Nice kinda soun', dat," Stoksie retorts disapprovingly. "Soun's 'lectric, like."

The Librarian has taken this for granted. But what's the source? And how will he manage to go about this huge city, searching for his dragon, if he's disabled from the start by the very daylight?

As if reading his thoughts, Stoksie says, "Y'know, G, if we go along in da shade a da bildins, mebbe yu'll be okay."

It's not a perfect solution. The flat facades fronting the square don't offer much shade, just the occasional recessed doorway. And none of the recesses have actual doors in them. No chance of retreating inside. But it will get him moving. The Librarian suffers through regular sound-beatings as Stoksie leads him from recess to recess. He tries plugging his ears, but the screaming, growling light invades his body, storming up and down his nerves. It drowns out all other voices, all other thought. Finally, they reach an intersection, where the height of the buildings lays a strip of deeper shadow along both sides of a narrow cross street. The Librarian is too relieved to question this directionless anomaly. He wishes he could sit down, just for a minute. Even at only bearable, the cacophonous light tires him out.

"Heah, G. Take a load off yer feet." Stoksie drags up a stout wooden crate. The Librarian notices there's only one. Otherwise, the streets are entirely empty, and clean as if newly made. The Tinker leans against the flat gray wall, shifting the weight off his bad hip. "I suspected da One wud be ina greener sorta place."

"Greener?" He's amazed to hear that Stoksie has thought about the One at all. He was never a professed believer.

"Yah, like yu say da wurld'll be agin, wen she come. Y'know, ta fixit."

"Patience," he says, hating his inadequacy with words. But how can he say 'have faith' to a man who's always insisted he had none? Does Stoksie's question indicate some sort of conversion, based perhaps on the arrival of dragons? Or is he still humoring his mad old friend, as he always has?

"Mebbe wen we find'er, it'll be green dere."

"Mebbe." He hopes so. He can't imagine a less green place than the one they're in, unless it's the desiccated world of 2213.

"So howyu wanna do dis serch, sizdammaddic-like, or as da win' take us?"

The Librarian is at a loss. He had no plan when he stepped through the portal. If he'd waited for a plan to occur to him, he might not have gone. Perhaps he'd assumed that the dragon would find him, once they were both in the same place. This is still theoretically possible, if indeed she is here. But will she know he's arrived? Is his mere presence a sufficient announcement? The task ahead is not as simple as he'd imagined when he stepped through the portal. Any search should be systematic, of course, but how to accomplish it in a strange and inexplicable city, away from all his equipment, his electronic eyes and ears and brain?

"Systematic," he says anyway.

"Den we gotta mark as we go, so we'll know weah we bin."

Leave it to a Tinker to come up with a plan. "How?"

Stoskie pulls a small jackknife from a hidden pocket. He unfolds a blunted metal spike and tries a few experimental scratches on the wall beside him. The awl leaves a clean line as bright as chalk. Stoksie grunts in surprise. He rubs his palm across the scratches and they disappear as if erased. "Mus' be sumkinda soff stone, dis."

"Convenient," the Librarian agrees dryly.

"Betcha." Stoksie draws three short parallel lines with a circle to the right of them, then stands back, grinning. "Dat's Tinka fer *'we wen' dattaway.'*"

The Librarian grins back. "Yer a gud man, Stokes."

They set off down the side street. He's tempted to haul the crate along with him, but he's slow enough already. He'll sit on the sidewalk if he has to, or maybe another perfect crate will appear when he needs it, as this one did, apparently out of nowhere.

"Big, emptee place," Stoksie observes, when they've walked several blocks and seen exactly the same rows of opaque windows, punctuated by the same doorless doorways, repeated over and over and over.

"Big, empty, boring place." The Librarian worries that the hum is getting louder again, though he's made sure to keep to the deepest shadow.

At the next intersection, the boredom is finally broken. Around the corner, in the middle of the wide street, sits an enormous hunk of machinery. Though it does not look rusted or broken, the Librarian knows right off that it's derelict—it has no working 'aura.' Stoksie would prefer to avoid it, as a large and alien device of unknown purpose, but the Librarian approaches it without scruple and lays his hands on its smooth surfaces, offering it solace for its untimely end. It's an awkward, ugly machine. He feels an instant kinship, grateful that he's not yet been cannibalized for parts, as this machine has. He can see the raw gaps and vacant connectors, empty housings for circuit boards and sensors. Clamps and cables have been ripped out. Its wheels have been removed, along with all their mounting hardware. He details the destruction to Stoksie at great length until curiosity overcomes the Tinker's scruples and he moves in closer.

"Mebbe gud salvage heah," he jokes. "Gud trade, huh?"

"If there was anyone to trade with."

Stoksie's shrug suggests there's always someone to

trade with. "So wadda we know so fah? One, dere's masheens heah. Two, we know dey break doun. An' t'ree, we know dere's no endlis supply a parts."

Three useful observations, the Librarian agrees.

"But watsit fer, G? Yu know?"

The Librarian shakes his head. It had wheels, so it was mobile, probably under its own steam instead of being driven by an operator. It has no structure to support working arms of any kind. It has no decorative or protective carapace. With all its parts exposed, what's left of them, it looks complex. Yet it could have been something as simple as a street cleaner. With that thought, he glances at the street. What need could there be to clean such already pristine streets? But because he's looked, he spots something his sharp nose would have alerted him to, if he'd been paying proper attention. He jogs Stoksie's elbow and points.

Along the gutter behind the machine is what appears to be a trail of animal manure, spread out as if the creature dropping it was still moving forward. Its organic nature is a screaming anomaly against the faceless pavement. The Librarian can't believe he'd missed it until now.

"Da first sine a life!" Stoksie crows delightedly. He hurries over to scoop up a drying lump. He sniffs it studiously, then crumbles a small bit between thumb and forefinger. "Not long sinze. Mebbe a day, mebbe less. Funny kinda mule, seems."

"Cow. Cattle. Some kind of." The Librarian has dealt with all kinds of domestic animals in his time.

"A cow?" Stoksie's world-weary eyes go as eager as a child's. "I'd likta see dat!"

"Follow it?"

"Betcha!" He looks off in the direction of the trail

of droppings. "Yu go fust, G. Yu da one wit' da killah nose."

A machine and a cow intersect, puzzles the Librarian. Maybe this pile of salvage really was a street cleaner. He wonders if whatever cannibalized the machine had its way with the cow, too. Animal scents are pungent. Easy to follow. This rich spoor is all the more articulate for being laid down in an otherwise odorless environment. The Librarian applies his nasal analysis.

"Cow. Cows, yes. Goat also. Sheep, maybe."

"Sheep! A 'hole farm, den? Wadda 'bout sum peeble?"

"Some also. Yes." The human scents are several, and they tickle the back of his brain with a feathery familiarity. An older knowing. It'll take him a while to search through the centuries of records archived in his head. Forgetting is never the problem, just locating the appropriate layer. In a few more blocks, he'll probably remember whose scents these remind him of.

The trail leads them in a path as random as the route they've already taken, a few blocks in one direction, a few in another.

"Dese folk doan know weah dey goin' needer," Stoksie decides. "Explorin'. Lookin' fer sumpin."

"Like us."

Stoksie nods. "Dey woan hab no ansers, den."

"Answers?"

"Aboud weah ta find da One."

"Guess not." Still, following a living trace seems more purposeful than wandering about at a total loss. The Librarian stays on the scent, down the next block, around the next corner, down several more blocks. More abandoned machinery turns up along the way, some as big as the street cleaner, most of it smaller, but all of it as unidentifiable as the first. Other than their dismantled state, the machines look out-of-the-box new and spotlessly clean. Stoksie shakes his head, disapproving of the waste.

"Not wasted. Recycled," the Librarian offers, to humor him. But really, in a city where the buildings or pavements show no sign of age or wear, why should its machinery be any different? *It's as if there's no weather here.* The idea stops the Librarian short. He stumbles, halfway into his next step. No weather. Of course!

"Yu alri', G?"

"Artificial," he mumbles.

"Wat iz?" Stoksie has on his humoring tone again.

"All this." It has to be. He does a full turn with his arms spread, and is proud of not tripping over his own amazement. "All."

Stoksie frowns, struggling to take in his meaning. "Da hole ciddy, yu mean?" He cranes his neck toward the narrow slice of blue between the surrounding towers. "My da tole me onct 'bout dis ciddy undah a reel big dome, like on da moon. He nevah seenit, bud he heerd aboudit. Das wat yu mean?"

The Librarian nods. Maybe a dome is what he means. He isn't sure. The insight came to him as they often do, without all its attendant evidence and explanations. He has learned to accept such understanding as visitors from elsewhere, from his dragon perhaps. At least, he's always hoped she was the source.

The hum in his head is getting louder again, except this time, it seems to be outside his head as well.

"Yu heer dat?" Stoksie asks.

"Betcha. You, too?" The Librarian is ecstatic to have the vagaries of his unruly senses for once confirmed.

"Frum 'roun' da nex cornah, sounds like."

They steal up to the mouth of the intersection. The crossing street is wider than usual. To the left, it travels for a short block, then passes through an open square. The external hum is coming from that direction. They forsake the livestock track in order to investigate.

"Git aginst da wall, nah," Stoksie advises.

When they're halfway down the block, the strong black-and-white design of the square's paving stones comes into focus. The Librarian squints at it eagerly. At last, a bit of visual interest! He fondly recalls the transformational geometrics of the twentieth century artist M. C. Escher, which this very much resembles.

In the middle of the pattern, two sprawling machines move in perfect tandem across the square. The exact nature of their work is not immediately apparent, mainly because what they're doing, while obvious to any eye, defies normal logic.

"Dey doin' wat it look like der doin'?"

It looks like one machine is pulling up the intricately laid tiles and piling them behind it according to shape and color. The other is taking up the neat piles and laying the tiles right back down again, in the same exact pattern.

"Routine maintenance?" suggests the Librarian, only half seriously.

"Das preddy weerd."

"Indeed." He listens for some hint of malfunction in the hum, but hears only smoothly functioning components. As with the derelict street cleaner, the Librarian is drawn to these devices. At least these are still functional. His inner hum is less chaotic now, he notices. He can detect patterns, a few more coherent lines among the general noise and static. While Stoksie hangs back, he moves out into the bright, hard light. The volume is deafening. He suffers it, like a man in a hailstorm, for the sake of curiosity. Hunched against the aural hammering, he totters up to the nearest machine and around it. It pays him no mind, but out of the agonizing clangor, two signals gradually resolve. This bit of ordering lessens the Librarian's pain. The signals coalesce into digital mutterings. Machine mutterings, about process and pattern and instruction. He senses no consciousness, no awareness. Less than in a barn he'd once had, where he would listen to the nighttime animal music, the murmurings and munchings, and learn entire histories of the day just past. He watches the mechanical pavers pick up tiles and put them back again, pondering their inchoate mysteries, until Stoksie edges up beside him.

"Yu bearin' up, G?"

"Not so bad, now."

"Wat nex?"

These machines have given up all their answers, if indeed they ever had any to offer the likes of Reuben Stokes, hardened rationalist. The Librarian turns away, regretful to leave them but glad to slink back into shadow, away from the discordant light. They retrace their steps to pick up the livestock trace. It moves straight ahead, block after block without turning. They pass no more machinery, abandoned or functional, for a long while. Then the quality of the trail changes. The Librarian slows to analyze the difference. Does adrenaline have an odor? He's sure he can smell it, just as he can smell fear.

"Running now." He points ahead, along the trace.

"Runnin'?"

"Running *away*."

Stoksie peers at the ground as if it might show footprints. "Wat frum?"

The Librarian is tempted to remind his friend that he's not clairvoyant. How different many things would be if he was. He's saved by the view at the next intersection: another black-and-white square, another audible hum. Here, the machine is stationed at a corner of the pattern, slowing and meticulously cleaning invisible dirt from the grout lines between the tiles.

"Wudn't be dat one, I guez."

The Librarian grunts his agreement.

"No wondah dis town's so clean!"

"Disapproving again, Stokes?"

"Me? Yah! Watta waste, yu know? Cud be doin' sumpin useful."

"Like what?"

Stoksie scowls at the slow, oblivious machine. "Doan know, G. Jes' sumpin beddah dan dat!"

The next square has a machine in it also, but this time, no new hum has announced its presence. It sits in the center of yet another elaborate *trompe l'oeil* pavement, intact and shining, and seems to be doing absolutely nothing at all.

They study it from the shade at the perimeter of the square.

"Das a big one, nah."

The Librarian nods. Bigger than any they've seen so far.

"Nobuddy bin stealin' dis one's parts. Yu t'ink its workin'?"

He shuffles to the edge of the shadow. "No sound from it."

Stoksie plucks at his sleeve. "Less leevit, G. Doan like dis one."

"Why? Arachnoid?"

"Waddevah. Jes' creepy."

The Librarian waves him back and ventures out into the light alone. Actually, the machine has only four supports, not eight. But its peculiar crouched-up position makes it look like a spider ready to pounce. Unlike the others they've encountered, this design is definitely based on an organic model, differentiating body parts to form a torso, legs, a head, even several protuberances that call to mind mouth parts, like jaws and teeth.

The Librarian pads across the pavement, once again braving the pounding light for the sake of his heedless curiosity. He's standing within four meters of the machine when he hears it switch on.

A click, a hum. The sighing of hydraulics.

Some miraculous instinct fires his usually somnolent reflexes and he's stepping backward and sideways before the crouching machine has fully raised itself, first on four legs, then on two. The front and smaller pair lift as arms, equipped with pincers jointed as precisely as dragon's claws.

"Run!" he yells at Stoksie.

The machine's head swivels. It aims itself directly at him, moving slowly. He doesn't hear its processing, as he'd heard the others'. It seems to be warming up. For the Librarian, who has never met a machine he didn't like, this one's aggressive stance has yet to be interpreted. He's not afraid. Not yet. Backing away at the same deliberate speed with which the machine is waking, he studies it with inadvertent delight. Several of his later boyhoods involved a fascination with dinosaurs. The organic model for this device just had to be *Tyrannosaurus Rex*. What is it for, he wonders? Who would build such a thing? If it decides to speed up, there's no way he can outrun it. It stands about six meters tall. Its powerful rear legs are streamlined for rapid travel. He's dimly aware that Stoksie is shouting at him. Why is the man still here?

"Run!" he bellows again.

"*Yu* run!" Stoksie bellows back.

He can't imagine himself running. Besides, in a city without doors, where could he run to that would shelter him from such a monster? The four facades fronting this little square are each as blank as a sheet of paper. On the other hand, if he did try to run, he could lead it away from Stoksie who, with a bad hip, stands as little chance of escaping as he does.

Step by step, the Librarian eases backward, spiraling toward the far side of the square. The *machina rex* turns with him, keeping him within range of its small but beady visual sensors. It's taking in his data, reading his every detail. He's surprised that it doesn't attack. Perhaps it thinks it can just frighten him to death. Perhaps it doesn't think at all. It saddens him that someone might create such a magnificent folly, and withhold from it the means of self-determination. The Librarian opens his hand to it, a gesture of sympathy.

He's almost to the edge of the building shadow, directly across the square from where Stoksie dances in helpless horror. For a moment, he fears the Tinker will do something suicidal and heroic, like charge in among the machine's hind legs to distract it. But Stoksie has found the limits to his courage. He fears both the saurian form and the machine nature of this monster. It's too much like a dragon. His pleading stare demands that the Librarian produce a miracle that will save them both. The Librarian rues anything he's ever said or done that's given rise to such unrealistic expectations. He backs up a few more steps. He's in the shade now. He can think more clearly, but he still has no idea what to do. The *machina rex* advances, servos whining.

Away from the punishing light, the Librarian becomes aware of another coherency emerging from the ubiquitous noise. This one's directional, like the signals from the paving machines, and it sounds like a summons. All other options gone, he backs toward it. Soon, he's flat up against the side of a building. His palms brush a surface as hard and granular as stone. The *machina* takes a long step forward, then another. Now it's looming over him. The sharp light glitters on its rows of metallic teeth. It eyes him with articulate intent, then throws up its silvery head to roar in convincing imitation of its ancient prototype.

The Librarian focuses on the new signal. He's certain it's calling him. Or at least offering direction. It's behind him. In the wall. No, in the building. Inside the building. The building *has* an inside. The Librarian imagines the signal as a path. It draws him sideways. A little more to the right. There.

The *machina rex* snaps its jaws like a cartoon predator and lunges for him. The Librarian retreats another step backward, where a step should not be possible. He backs into an open doorway. The metal jaws clash in front of his nose. Two more steps back. He's in a dim space, undefined except by the wall in front of him and the door opening where the hard light pours in. It silhouettes the machine as it rakes its steel claws against the stonework and tries to force its bulk through the narrow opening.

The Librarian breathes again, amazed to be still among the living.

Now, that's what I call a proper fire wall.

The door slams shut, enveloping him in darkness.

Chapter Ten

When she can stand without wobbling, Erde hurries to help Luther sit up. "Oh, I'm so sorry! It's all my fault!"

IT IS NOT YOUR FAULT.

Earth's great head looms over them. The dogs look on with concern.

"I mean, it's my fault he came at all!"

Luther's eyes flutter open. "We dere yet?"

"Yes, yes, we are. Somewhere." Kneeling beside him, Erde gazes around at the Mage City. The portal has winked out of existence without admitting a single white rider. She cherishes the thought of Brother Guillemo gnashing his teeth in frustration in the snows of 913.

Just try to find me here, you filthy man!

DO NOT MAKE RECKLESS INVITATIONS. IF HE IS FIRE'S CREATURE, HE WILL KNOW WHERE YOU ARE. ALWAYS.

But how? I don't even know where I am.

REMEMBER THAT YOUR SENDINGS ARE OFTEN STRONGER THAN YOU INTEND.

Her Sendings. Yes, she had forgotten. Or perhaps willed herself to forget what she'd done on the hill at Deep Moor.

But it was just that once, and never again!

NOT BECAUSE YOU COULDN'T . . . BECAUSE YOU WOULDN'T.

Yes. She'd hated how it felt, and the pain it caused Rose, the most Sensitive of the Deep Moor women. She likes even less the dragon's implication that her ability could betray her, nay, all of them, to the hell-priest. What if she was the cause of his coming to Deep Moor?

It's too much to think about. Too much worry and confusion. Erde glances up at the bronze mountain beside her and changes the subject. "Dragon, you've grown again!"

YES. I FEEL . . . I FEEL . . .

EXPANDED? Water has reappeared in her flock-of-butterflies incarnation, a glimmer of color and motion against the pale, static cityscape.

YES! AS IF ENLARGED BY EVERY BREATH. DO YOU FEEL DIFFERENT, SISTER?

The blue flutter of iridescence shivers and dances. NOT REALLY.

Erde is still contemplating the problem of Brother Guillemo. *Fire's creature.* It's a relief to think of the hell-priest that way. To explain her uncanny link to him, the way he can pick her out of a crowd, the way she always senses when he's near—all this is Fire's doing, and not some fault, or even evil, inherent in her own nature. She's glad to be rid of that guilty suspicion. She's been plagued by it for too long. If it's Fire's fault, she can deal with it.

She scrambles to her feet, flushed with new resolve. She plants her hands on her hips, like she's seen the men do in the practice yard, and gives the much-sought-after Mage City a long hard look. Its scale is daunting. Such topless towers could only be held up by magic. But what she finds most intimidating is the city's formal blandness, the total lack of welcome. If she were the Mages, she'd never choose to live in this hard, bright, silent place that seems entirely devoid of life.

"There aren't even any trees!" she exclaims to Luther, who is fending off the ministrations of two particularly earnest hounds. "Not even a blade of grass!"

Luther blinks, still gathering his senses. "Itsa neet cleen place, alri'."

"It's too clean, Luther! It looks like nobody lives here!"

"Leest it's warm agin." Luther peels off the first of his heavy layers. One of the dogs grabs his sleeve. "Git off me, yu mutt!"

Erde giggles. "She's trying to get your attention. Look, they've all gathered again."

THEY WISH US TO KEEP FOLLOWING THE TRAIL.

"Oh, my goodness, of course! Dragon, shall we?"

WE CAN LEARN LITTLE BY STANDING STILL.

As large as Earth has become, the wide white streets are larger still. It's a city made for giants. So where are those giants? Erde notes that the dog pack does not bound ahead on the scent as they had at Deep Moor. Though they seem confident about the direction of the trail, they are less bold, unwilling to lose sight of the dragons and humans, as if at each corner, they are fearful of what might be around it.

After several blocks for each of several changes of

direction, Erde realizes that the city is not just huge in vertical scale, its spread is enormous as well.

"A city as big as a kingdom," she complains to Luther. "The streets are so straight, like the squares on a chessboard. And not a bit of green anywhere! You'd think there'd be a weed or two at least!" She recalls the only other great city she's been in. "There were lots of weeds in Big Albin."

Luther rolls his eyes at the featureless walls rising to either side. "Nah, gal. Big Albin's a reel city."

"This is a real city. How else could we be walking in it?"

Mid-stride, he taps his foot on the smooth white pavement. "Well, I doan know 'bout dat. But first, it doan look like a reel city. An' two, doan it stand ta reezin dat if dis is a *magic* city, it otta be sumplace diffrint an' speshul?"

"Of course, but special can be real, can't it? Deep Moor was special, a secret, special place, until Fra Guill nosed it out, may he die a thousand deaths and rot in hell for what he's done!"

"Hey, nah," admonishes Luther gently. "Speekin' evil kin bring it to ya."

"I think my fear of him brings him to me. But you're right." Chastened, Erde studies the blank building facades rising like canyon walls about them. "I've never seen a really big city, except Big Albin, and it was all in ruins. This isn't the way a big city's supposed to look?"

The dog pack races ahead, then circles back to run ahead again. Luther watches them as they approach an intersection several blocks away. "I'm jes' sayin' it doan look like eny city I evah bin in. Okay, I ain' bin ina lotta dem, but lookit dese walls, nah. No doahs or windahs? How yu gonna git inside anya dese places?"

"It could be a fortified city." Erde's personal idea of a wall is tightly laid stone with only the smallest of openings, to hold in the heat and keep out the enemy. "I remember thinking in Big Albin that the dwellings were all full of holes. So many doors and windows! And such big ones. It seemed so . . . exposed, compared to what I'm used to. When you're from a different time and place, you arrive with all sorts of different definitions and assumptions, remember. I mean, this city is probably as real to the people that live here as Big Albin is to you."

Luther rakes a hand through the silver forelock that falls nearly to his nose. "Yu t'ink we'ah in sum odda time agin, den?"

"Oh, I should think so. Most assuredly. And a long way from my time, too. That's why we felt so bad when we got here. The distance."

"Long wich way? Inta da fuchah, or inta da past?"

Erde considers, then asks the dragons' opinions.

I CANNOT TRAVEL TO ANY TIME BEFORE MY AWAKENING. WHERE A PORTAL CAN TAKE US IS ANYONE'S GUESS. THE RULES MAY BE DIFFERENT.

Luther shakes his head when Erde relays this. "Dis kint be da past. I ain' no expert, but I seen pichurs."

"Then it's the future."

"Fuchah to wat?"

"To your time. And mine, too, of course."

"Dere ain' no fuchah afta my time, gal. We're in da lass days."

Now Erde must tread lightly. Among the Tinkers, Luther is one of the most devout believers in the faith that Gerrasch has been preaching. Her own and the dragons' understanding of the situation might not completely coincide with Luther's expectations for the world's salvation by "the One."

"Perhaps the very last days will come a bit later than you've feared."

"Wize dat?"

"Because we're here. So there must be some future at least, after yours." She doesn't ask the dragons to weigh in with their ideas on this issue. She's positive they'll agree with her, and she knows herself well enough to admit that if she's sure she's right, she'll want to push Luther until he accepts her version over his own. She really must learn to allow other people their opinions. Only a child, Erde reminds herself, assumes that its perception of the world is the only correct one.

Still . . .

No. Erde scolds herself and lets the subject drop.

The dogs have stopped at the intersection up ahead. They're milling about uncertainly while four of them search out the trail in each of the possible directions. Earth has been lagging behind as usual, so Erde welcomes the chance for him to catch up.

Lingering at the corner, she spots something down the side street: a flick of motion, a dark shape against the bright pavement? It's gone when she looks for it, leaving only an afterimage of memory.

"That's odd . . ."

Luther's looking in the opposite direction. "Watsit, gal?"

"I saw . . . like a person, maybe."

"Yeah? Weah?"

Erde points, down the pale, empty street. "It's gone now."

"Doan worry. I'll keep my eyes opin."

She lays a hand on the dragon's claw as he looms up behind her.

I'm sure I saw something. Someone.

Earth rumbles comfortingly. Water has hitched a ride between his ivory horns, so that he seems to be wearing a diaphanous crown of iridescence.

You are very quiet, dear dragon.

I AM TROUBLED.

WE BOTH ARE.

Erde is impressed that Water's voice can remain so present and coherent when her physical being is so ephemeral.

Why?

Earth answers reluctantly. SAY NOTHING TO LUTHER. DO YOU PROMISE?

Yes, of course. Why? What is it?

OUR SISTER IS HERE.

What? Really? Are you sure?

WE SENSE HER VERY STRONGLY.

How wonderful! Why didn't you say so? It's all we've hoped for!

YES.

But the dragons are not rejoicing as she would expect them to.

Well, where is she? Let's go find her!

Instinctively, she turns toward Luther.

SAY NOTHING!

But he'll want to help!

IT'S NOT THAT SIMPLE. WE KNOW SHE'S HERE, BUT WE DON'T KNOW WHERE.

WORSE THAN THAT. IT'S AS IF SHE'S . . . EVERYWHERE. SO . . . DIFFUSE.

But, Lady Water, so are you, and that doesn't seem to be a problem.

Water's dancing motes draw closer together. IN SHAPE PERHAPS, BUT NOT IN MIND.

Diffuse of mind. Erde tries to imagine it, but while her imagination might be far-ranging, her sense of self is very firmly rooted inside her head. Her thoughts all emanate from a central location. She watches Luther encouraging the dogs to settle on a single trail to follow.

Can you explain this another way?

Water's shape shifts slightly to reflect her words. HER PRESENCE IS VERY STRONG BUT IT'S NOT . . . ORGANIZED. LIKE THE PARTS OF HER CONSCIOUSNESS HAVE BEEN SPLIT AND SCATTERED.

Oh. Is that so dire? Dreams seem like that sometimes.

A VERY GOOD ANALOGY.

Down the street, Erde sees another flicker, the slightest bit of moving darkness. She decides to ignore it.

Could she be asleep and you're listening in on her dreams?

WE DO NOT KNOW.

Earth's great head sways side to side. He's unhappy with his own ignorance. But Lady Water, as always, has a plan.

WE'RE WASTING TIME WANDERING ABOUT HERE AT RANDOM. WE SHOULD GO BACK, GATHER THE REST OF OUR FORCES, AND PLAN OUT A LOGICAL SEARCH.

I DO NOT ENTIRELY AGREE, BUT NOW THAT WE'VE BEEN HERE ONCE, IT SHOULD BE EASY ENOUGH TO GET BACK AGAIN.

Erde judges this information safe enough to relay to Luther.

He nods, patting the dogs, who have gathered around him uneasily. "I wudn't mind sum reinforcemints. Dis place iz creepy."

"What about the hounds? We can't desert them."

"Bring 'em. Blin' Rachel cud use sum gud dogs like dese."

As if inspired by his praise, one of the scout dogs announces a trace worth investigating. Her sharp barks bring the rest of the pack racing to confirm her discovery.

"Look, they have the trail again!" Erde cries. "Oh, dragons, let's stay with them a while longer! Surely we'll find Rose and the others soon, and if anyone's hurt, Lord Earth can help them! I know N'Doch could get into trouble away from your sensible and steadying influence. But he's also quick and resourceful on his own."

IT'S PAIA THAT WE WORRY ABOUT. SHE IS THE MOST VULNERABLE.

Erde sees she will have to beg. "Please! Just a little while more?"

UNTIL THE NEXT TIME THEY LOSE THE SCENT.

The pack surges ahead, as if held back until the dragons relented. But despite their high excitement, the dogs do not risk getting out of sight. They double back expectantly in twos or threes, with long loping strides and lolling tongues. Erde hurries after them. Yes, the town is creepy, but most of her deepest fears involve darkness, so it's hard to be too afraid in the middle of an empty street in broad daylight. Still, like the dogs, she glances back. She's left Luther and the dragons farther behind than she'd intended. She slows to wait for them, and notices a difference in the facades just ahead. Slight, but a point of interest in this bland landscape. One section of wall is slightly recessed, creating a band of shadow and a shallow courtyard. The recess contains a bank of windows, five tall rectangles. Intrigued by the possibility of seeing inside one of these endlessly blank buildings, Erde drifts over. But she finds the windows entirely opaque, a mere outline scratched on the solid stone.

Except for the one in the middle.

Erde moves closer. Here, the featureless gray is less solid, less flat. Like a very dirty window. She rubs the smooth surface gently with her palm, and the view through it does sharpen, but less because she's cleaned it than as if her action has stirred something within, dissipating a shrouding fog. A shape appears, the hooded head and shoulders of a man. By the time she's recognized the silhouetted profile, the figure has turned to stare at her.

Erde shrieks.

It's the hell-priest. Smiling.

She whirls away blindly, crashing into Luther who has run up at the sound of her scream. She flails in his arms, then backs against him in panic.

"Look! Look! It's him!"

Luther looks. He sets her aside and goes up to the window to press his nose to the now opaque surface. "Ain' nobuddy deah, gal. Kin't see nuttin'. Yu say yu look'd inside heah?"

"Yes! Yes!"

But Luther sees nothing, and Erde begins to doubt herself. When the dragon arrives, she retreats into his shadow to find comfort in his warmth. "Am I imagining things?" But it persists, like a bad smell in the air around her, that horrid intruding presence that makes her feel dirty and violated.

YOU ARE, BUT THEY ARE TRUE THINGS.

"He's here? Brother Guillemo is here?"

NOT IN BODY, NOT YET. BUT YOU SENSE HIM WATCHING. AWAITING HIS CHANCE.

"Even in the Mage City, he can come after me?"

I AM RECONSIDERING MY ASSUMPTIONS ABOUT THIS PLACE.

The weight of his tone is unusual, even for a dragon somewhat given to gloom. Erde catches her breath. "How so?"

THIS IS CERTAINLY THE CITY THAT I SAW IN DREAMS. BUT IT MAY NOT BE WHAT I THOUGHT IT WAS. WHAT I HOPED FOR.

The dragon's voice in her mind is so disconsolate that Erde shoves her own terrors aside. *But you must not give up that hope, dear dragon! Never!*

PERHAPS WE MUST LEARN TO GO FORWARD EVEN WITHOUT HOPE.

There's always hope. Probably we haven't yet come to the part of the city where the Mages live.

Water's mote-cloud swells with sudden impatience, chittering like a swarm of disturbed insects.

THERE AREN'T GOING TO BE ANY MAGES! IT'S AS I'VE SAID ALL ALONG. YOU MISTOOK THAT PART OF YOUR VISION. BUT IT DOESN'T MATTER. IT'S ENOUGH THAT YOU DREAMED THIS CITY, SO YOU'D KNOW IT WHEN YOU SAW IT THROUGH THE PORTAL. THAT'S WHAT GOT US HERE. SO STOP WORRYING ABOUT MAGES. MAGES ARE A MYTH.

Leave him alone! Erde flings a quick glare at Water, then looks away, ashamed at having reprimanded a dragon.

NO, LISTEN! WE ARE THE MAGES. IF OUR SISTER IS HERE, AND I'M SURE SHE IS, WE ARE THE POWERS WHO MUST SEARCH HER OUT AND

FREE HER. WE CAN'T LOOK FOR ANY HELP OTHER THAN OURSELVES.

"Dese dogs're getting' antsy," Luther warns.

"In a moment, Luther!" Erde tastes her own irritation like a mouthful of bile. She's torn in too many directions, and feels Earth's hurt and indecision as if it was her own.

TIME TO MOVE. AS LONG AS WE STAY HERE, WE MUST KEEP FOCUSED AND ON THE SEARCH.

GO SEARCH BY YOURSELF!

BROTHER, LISTEN TO YOU!

The big brown dragon has hunkered down stubbornly. His plated hide has lost its bronzy sheen. Erde thinks he looks like a mountain of mud.

I NEED TIME TO CONSIDER!

LISTEN TO ALL OF US! HOW DID WE GET SO DISAGREEABLE ALL OF A SUDDEN?

"You mean, it's not just me?" Erde asks.

WE'RE PRACTICALLY DROWNING IN IT. IF IT WEREN'T FOR THE DOGS, WE'D HAVE BEEN BROUGHT TO A COMPLETE HALT WITH POINTLESS ARGUING.

Earth lifts his head to gaze around as if to locate the source of this contagion of despair. YOU'RE RIGHT. IT IS POINTLESS.

IT'S EXACTLY WHAT OUR BROTHER WOULD WANT—FOR US TO BE AT ODDS WITH EACH OTHER. DIVIDE AND CONQUER.

THEN WE SHALL DENY HIM SUCH SATISFACTION.

Earth rises out of his crouch with an alacrity that astonishes even Erde. He is a force again, a glimmering mountain rolling between the towering buildings, a crown of light between his horns. The dogs gain courage to range farther ahead, yipping and crying. Their chorus ricochets along the walls, back and forth, until the faceless blocks are alive with dog voices.

Luther shrugs uneasily, then moves after the dragons. "If dere's anyone about, dey shur know we're heah."

Sure enough, from far off along the canyons of stone, a whistle sounds. The dogs pull up to listen. The whistle comes again.

Luther nods. "Summun's callin' 'em."

"But who? Oh! It could only be . . ." Erde plunges forward as the dogs streak away after the call. "Wait! Don't run away! We'll never find you!"

As if they've understood every word, half the pack splits off and circles back, dancing and bounding with impatience at the glacial pace of the dragons and humans hurrying after them.

They are led down a long, straight roadway, discovering occasional evidence of the passage of other animals. Erde finds this soiling of the perfect streets very cheering. Signs of earth, signs of life, in a lifeless city. Hope warms her heart again. She'd been lacking it so desperately. How clever of Lady Water to recognize this dark disabling mood, and alert them in time.

The dog pack wheels right, into a district of narrower streets and rougher pavements. The trail grows crooked, evasive. It curves and crinks and cuts aside here and there at sharp angles, where buildings have been placed oddly, in the middle of a road. The light is dim, and the shadows deeper. Erde shivers. Is she belatedly feeling the effects of the transport, or is simple exhaustion confusing her perception? Several times, a street that has seemed clear and open is abruptly a dead end, with a hidden escape leading off at a sharp angle, barely wide enough for the dragon to pass.

"This is a mysterious sort of place," she murmurs. "it's like a maze or something."

Earth complains that he's scraping his hide against rough walls on both sides.

Luther drags his hand along the face of a building. "Dis look like old stone, nah. Da reel t'ing. Not like before."

Erde agrees. The city does feel more like a real place here, more rough-hewn, less impossibly perfect. More like the towns she knows from her own life. The doors and windows are smaller. Because they seem more real, they frighten her. Out of any one of them, after all, might spring the hell-priest. And in the confines of these torturous alleys, there'd be no escape.

What am I thinking? I have two dragons and a strong man beside me! The despair has crept back to wind itself around her like a rampant vine. Erde rips it loose, resolving to resist it. As she makes this promise, the twining streets seem to open out. The hard edge of the shadows eases. There is moisture in the air, where she had noticed none before. She can breathe again.

"Phew!" Luther mutters. "Das bettah!"

"You felt it, too?"

"Wat's dat, nah?"

"The despair again. Closing in."

"Guez I did, den," he replies thoughtfully. "Gotta keep da fait'."

"Yes. I shall have to be more vigilant."

WE MUST ALL BE.

UH-OH . . .

Erde wonders at Water's tone—half alarmed, half ironical—but not for long. Paying such alert attention to their emotional states has disabled their external awareness. They have come into a surprise cul-de-sac where the only way out seems to be the way they came in. They're surrounded by high curved walls, like the walls of a castle yard. Dark water drips from between the huge dry-laid blocks, striping the stone with moss and green slime. In the silence, Erde hears it flowing into the drainage well in the center of the courtyard. It seems to fall a very long way before it hits the surface of the water below.

"Outa heah, quick-like!" Luther turns, then freezes. The big knife he carries is already in his hand.

Blocking their escape are two scruffy, grim-faced archers and a pack of alert and snarling dogs. Erde is sure they've been betrayed. But she can't imagine how she could mistake the hell-priest's hounds for the dogs of Deep Moor. Then she feels Earth's dragon laugh gently rock the ground.

"Margit? Lily?" She barely knows them through the dirt and blood darkening their faces. She races to embrace them, but is stopped by their raised and loaded bows. "It's me, Erde!"

"Prove it," growls Margit, squint-eyed over the shaft of her arrow.

"What? Have I changed so much?"

"Not enough, is more like it," Lily calls. "We need to know it's really you!"

They're both much gaunter than Erde remembers, with a cruel angle of hardship and suffering in their shoulders that was not there before.

"Of course, it's me! Who else do you know who travels with dragons?"

"What dragons?"

Erde gapes at them. She can understand them not knowing Water for a dragon, but they'd have to be blind to miss Earth, with the size he's grown to. But when she turns to point him out, she sees he's stilled himself and gone invisible. No wonder.

I think you must show yourself, dragon, before these good women will believe me.

Earth agrees, and flicks back into visibility.

Lily lets out her breath and lowers her bow. "Erde? Is it really you?"

Margit looks Luther over carefully. "Who's this one? Another dragon?"

"This is Luther, who came along to help me."

At last, Margit eases back on her bowstring. This releases the dogs, who bound about in animal joy, untouched by whatever horror has darkened the lives of the two brave scouts. Their tunics and riding leathers are in tatters. Margit's gold-red braids, her glory, are dull and streaked with gray. Lily's head is bound with a stained linen bandage and a livid scar crawls down one side of her face.

"You both look awful!" Erde blurts.

"Well, thanks for that high compliment." A brief flash of tooth hints at Margit's old ironical grin. "We've seen some strange things since we've been in this demon-ridden hellhole. How did you get here?"

"We followed the dogs from the . . . oh, is everyone all right? Where is everyone?"

Lily purses her lips and looks down. Margit's grin fades behind the shadow of more recent sorrows. "You'd never believe it if I told you."

"What, is the news that bad? Oh, if only we'd come sooner!"

"It's bad, but what I mean is, you'll have to see for yourself."

"Now? Can we go now?"

The women exchange a glance. This time Margit looks away.

Lily says, "I'll take them."

She turns, beckoning toward a doorway in the wall behind her. Erde did not recall it being there before. Its rough stone arch is supported by more smoothly shaped pilasters topped with capitals in the form of leaves. Through the opening, Erde sees a stone walk crossing a surreally bright grass sward dotted with flowers. Warm sunlight shimmers through leaf shadow across the path.

I know this place. But it can't really be where I think it is. What new wonders await? What new terrors?

She eyes the narrow door. *Dragon, you will never fit.*

"Must Earth stay outside?"

Lily smiles wanly. "There's room enough for all."

Then I'll call for you when I get there, dragon.

Erde takes Luther's arm and escorts him through the archway, into the courtyard garden at Deep Moor.

Chapter Eleven

Alone. Alone in darkness. Not something he's ever minded. Likes it. Particularly the alone part. Or maybe it's just the relief of darkness. It feels like home.

But the Librarian knows he'd never have gotten this far alone. So he worries about Stoksie out there with his bad hip and a murderous machine on the loose. Perhaps the machine won't notice him. He hopes the little man has shown his good Tinker sense and gotten the hell out of there.

Darkness. Like a den. One of the many he's inhabited over the span of his years. Warm. Safe. At least in his later stages, once the body he wore had evolved to a size and strength that made threats not worth the trouble for most sorts of predators. The body heat of darkness underground. Later, the dim smoky fires of his hidden hearths, in caves and hovels and cottages. Eventually, the electric warmth of machine components stacked high in shuttered rooms he hardly went out of. He hated all those dying cities. The invention of the telephone was a godsend. Only a short leap, then, to ordering takeout.

Those were all his waiting places, where invisibility was a necessity. Now the waiting is over. So he mustn't slip back into the old passive modes. He must act. He must move.

But first, he listens to the darkness. Is it the same as the light outside, but with its volume turned near to zero? Sound no longer disables him. In the darkness, he can concentrate. He sits down and crosses his legs. He forgets about Stoksie and the *machina rex*. The smooth floor is the same temperature as the skin on his soft pink palms. He opens himself, tunes his array of inner sensors to the humming darkness, takes the tamed rush of signal into his mind as if gathering up a bundle of cables. Sort through the lot of them. What goes with what? What colors match? What frequencies? Some are obvious as code. Some have patterns that might be code. There are likenesses, pairings, sets, and subsets. But there are problems, too. Discontinuities. Dead ends. Nonsense loops. The Librarian grins and licks his lips. Familiar territory at last. He's doing something useful for the first time since he blundered through the portal. Something he's good at. Something he's trained for. With effort and luck, he'll make sense of it. He'll be able to map the city's ebb and flow of signal. If one of these webberies of current is his dragon's, he'll find it. Then all he'll have to do is follow it back to its source.

Alone in darkness, the Librarian chortles with anticipation.

Chapter Twelve

It's a clear and perfect summer morning in the garden at Deep Moor. And of course, that of all things is impossible.

Surrendering to the irrational, Erde follows Lily through the gray stone arch into a sonata of birdsong. She inhales the fragrance of sunlight on pine and sweet fern, and the flowering thyme creeping between the flat stones of the walk. Entering behind her, Luther stops short in amazement. Erde sets her anxieties aside long enough to stand with him and drink in the beauty, to gaze at the crisp blue sky and the grass so green it vibrates. Just a brief stolen moment to savor it all before her heart breaks again, thinking of what's been lost, and reality intervenes. Dozen of women are scattered like broken dolls across the shade-dappled grass: sitting, lying, sprawled on blankets, bloodied, bandaged, some stirring in pain, some not stirring at all.

She sees the healer, Linden, paler than the torn strips of muslin in her hands. She stumbles with exhaustion as she bends among the wounded. Against the central stone well, one of the redheaded twins, Margit's daughters, sits rocking the other in her lap, weeping silently. In the deeper shadow of an old maple tree, two frail shrouded bundles lie side by side.

"Oh, Lily," Erde whispers. "What has happened?"

But she already knows. She was there in the ruined farmstead. "Where's Rose? Where's Raven?"

"Raven is with Rose," says Lily. "Come, I'll take you."

"Yes. No, wait! Let me call in the dragon. He can help. Remember how he saved N'Doch."

Linden looks up in stunned relief as Earth's great bronzy bulk appears in an empty stretch of lawn. It hadn't looked nearly big enough to Erde before she sent him the image, but either her eye didn't measure well, or the space itself has expanded to suit. Erde hurries over and grasps Linden's hands. The healer's eyes are raw. She's thin to the point of wasting. Her grip is still firm, yet Erde feels as if she's holding the woman up by the strength of her own arms.

"Dear Linden, help has arrived. How long have you been without rest?"

"I hardly know anymore. This time, a few days, maybe more." Linden's voice is faint, as if she barely has breath to speak. Behind her, the weeping twin gently lays her sister down on the grass, and Erde understands the hard glint in Margit's eyes, and why she stayed outside.

"We'll hope it's not too late," she tells Linden. "It won't be too late! Lord Earth will do all he can!"

Luther watches silently from the dragon's side. Erde beckons him over. "This is Luther Williams. He's seen some hard times, too. He can help carry the wounded, but he doesn't speak our language. I'll help, too, after I've seen Rose."

"Yes. You must see Rose. I'm so glad you're back." Linden offers Luther her hand. His earnest and obvious compassion draws from her a wan smile of welcome. "Come with me, please."

Luther nods and follows the healer briskly across the grass. He picks up the limp redheaded girl easily, and carries her to the dragon.

Erde whispers, "Please let it not be too late!"

"Amen," murmurs Lily from beside her.

"Is Sir Hal with you, Lily?" The senior knight had been storm-bound at Deep Moor when she'd left it last. No, the time before last. Already her anguished brain is trying to deny the awful reality of her most recent visit. "And what about Captain Wender?"

"They were long gone, back to the war. Too bad, too. We could've used two more good fighters."

"Long gone?"

Lily looks back at her oddly, then away. "Of course. No point in Hal sticking around once you'd relieved him of the problem of Baron Köthen. Oh, Kurt would've stayed, but Hal piled on the pressure until he gave up and went with him."

"Kurt?"

"Captain Wender."

"Ah. Yes." Erde would swear she detects a blush in the other woman's wounded, weathered face. It seems, even in the midst of war and disaster, there is companionship to be found. *For everyone but me.* "Lily, how long has it been since I was last at Deep Moor?"

Lily frowns. "I don't know. Long time."

"No, really . . . how long would you say?"

"Months, at least. I'd say a whole winter, if we'd had anything but winter. You don't remember?"

"It's only been two weeks for me."

Lily stares at her, struggling with this notion.

"Can I see Rose now?"

She follows Lily around the impromptu field hospital and through a blossom-laden arbor into the paved inner courtyard nestled within the half-timbered arms of the house. The welcoming house that in reality was no more than a blackened ruin. How wonderful to find the thick thatch intact, and the stone chimney unstained. And she is relieved beyond measure to discover Raven and Rose at the stone table under the old apple tree, both upright and apparently unharmed. What a serene and pretty picture they make, sitting in the dappled sun: Rose's determined back and her short curls of russet and gray, Raven's more youthful lilt, her lovely face of high contrasts, bright and soft, dark and light. There are early apples scattered on the table, one of them neatly cored and sectioned. Raven is at work on a second. Hastily, Erde brushes away tears of joy.

Raven looks up. With a cry, she drops her knife and apple. She leaps up, hands and long hair flying. "Erde! How wonderful! Is it really you?"

Erde notes her hesitation, her quick and worried glance at Lily.

Lily nods. "Seems to be, all right. She's brought the dragon."

"It is me, Raven, truly!" Erde rushes to embrace her. "Oh, it's so dreadful what's happened! I'm so glad you're both alive!"

"If you call this being alive," mutters Lily, hurrying away again. "I'm due back on watch. See you all at supper."

Erde releases Raven and turns eagerly to greet Rose. But Rose is still sitting quietly. Her back is erect. Her strong gardener's hands rest on the worn stone table, her fingers spread as if braced to rise, the sectioned apple untouched in front of her. Her warm brown eyes are open, but fixed on some far more distant point than the mosaic of the garden wall she faces.

"Rose? Rose, it's me, Erde."

"She won't answer," says Raven quietly.

Unheeding, Erde crouches at Rose's side and takes one of her hands between both her own. She rubs it gently as if to relieve a chill. "Rose, I've brought the dragon. He'll heal everyone he can!"

"I'm not even sure she hears us," Raven says.

"But what's the problem? She looks . . . well, tired, but . . . fine."

"I know. But she isn't."

"Rose? Rose!" With a soft moan, Erde rises abruptly, spinning away in panic and despair. Raven catches her deftly and wraps her in a tight and calming embrace that lets her be a child again and sob out her great load of pent up sorrow and outrage.

"Oh, Raven, it's all so awful! Everything is!"

"I know, sweetling, I know. We've all cried our hearts out, every one."

Erde hasn't wept so hard in many weeks, and she feels much better when she's done with it and has caught her breath again. "So tell me, what's wrong with her? How did she get this way?"

"Come. Settle for a while. You look as played out as the rest of us. I'm sure you've had to be very brave." Raven hooks one arm about Erde's waist and steers her toward a high backed wooden bench in a slice of sun falling on the courtyard wall. Potted herbs scent the air as they brush past. Raven drops wearily onto the wide seat. Shoving back her cloud of dark hair as if it were the cause of all her troubles, she tilts her face to the sun with a sigh. "At least it isn't winter here. I'd forgotten what it felt like to be warm."

"Lily says it's been months since I saw you last." In the brighter light, Erde sees the bruises on Raven's cheek, and the tightness of the skin across her jaw.

"An eternity of winter, sweetling. Then Deep Moor was attacked. If that hadn't happened, we'd have all starved to death anyway."

"There are a lot more of you than there were."

"And fewer," nods Raven sadly. "Between the blizzards and the deep freezes, women would stagger into the valley from the surrounding farms and villages, and beg our protection. Or Lily and Margit would find them, half frozen, fugitive from the soldiers' foraging parties, and guide them to safety." She pauses, then sighs. "Or so we thought. Bringing so many in is probably what betrayed us. The valley's magic was spread too thin."

"Did you know he was coming? Did you have any warning at all?"

Raven's glance slides toward her, sideways. "You know, then. Did Lily tell you?"

"I was there. *He* was there. We went back to warn you . . . I told them we should . . . but we were too late. But, Raven, it's not just the hell-priest we're dealing with. The dragon Fire is behind him. That's who we're really fighting."

"The renegade you were worried about?"

"Yes." Later, she can explain how worry has escalated into terror.

"Ah. And then . . . ?"

"The dogs found us and led us here."

"Really?" Raven's finely arched brows contract, as if mere thought is an effort. It pains Erde to see her looking so drawn and tired. "And do you have any idea where 'here' is?"

Erde offers what little she understands about the portals and Time and the white city outside the walls.

Raven shakes her head. "Between one step and another? To the future, just like that? Doritt will be glad to hear it. She's convinced we've all died and gone to hell . . . or someplace like it. I said, don't be silly. Just because we haven't lived the way others do, doesn't mean we deserve that." She smiles faintly. For a moment, her eyes drift shut. Then she rouses herself with a cough. "But who could create these magic doorways?"

"I hadn't thought of them as being created. More that they just . . . were."

"Such devices are not the way of Nature, sweetling, as marvelous as she is. For one thing, there's too much purpose implied by a portal that opens just when it's needed."

"And closes, too, when needed. I'd say it was dragon magic, but the dragons claim to know nothing of them. But they do say their sister Air is here, somewhere."

"In this nightmare landscape? Then I'm sorry for her. But perhaps the portals are her work."

Erde clasps her hands. "Of course! That must be it!" Then her face clouds again. "No, it can't be. If she can make such portals, why didn't she make one for herself and escape Lord Fire's dungeon long ago?"

Raven gently brushes curls from Erde's furrowed

brow. "If she could, she would have, so we must accept that she can't, and hope to learn why."

Erde nods pensively. Gerrasch should be here instead. He'd understand it all so much better. "But now, please, tell me about Rose!"

"She's . . . well, I guess the best way to say it is . . . she's gone inside. As if she went into her room and locked the door."

"But how? Why?"

"Utter exhaustion, is my guess." Raven gazes sadly across the soft blooms of oregano and sage to where Rose sits unmoving at the table. "Let's see, where do I start? With the attack? We did have some warning of it. Both Rose and Doritt sensed that a great evil was headed our way. We'd already planned an escape route into the Grove, with all the animals. There wasn't much left to carry—our food stores were nearly gone and we'd shared out all our extra clothing with the refugees. But we were just so weak and tired . . . well, when the attack came, we didn't quite make it to the Grove in time. Margit and Lily and the dogs drove off the first thin wave—Fra Guill hadn't expected so stout a resistance from women! But we lost Esther then, very nearly lost Lily. We fled into the trees, and for a while, the trees kept the soldiers out. Then Guillemo himself turned up. He must have wanted us very badly."

Erde shivers. "For the stake."

"No doubt. The Grove's good and ancient wardings weren't strong enough to hold up against the dark determination of the hell-priest. So in he comes. It was Rose who discovered the portal, and urged us through it. Ordered us, I should say, in the end. There were some who'd have rather stood and fought than walk through that inexplicable door-way."

Raven lets her head loll against the carved bench back, and takes a deep ragged breath. A small, bright bird lights on a branch just past her reach and begins to sing. "And then we were in . . .that awful place out there."

"The City?"

"City? A lifeless, terrible place to bear such a noble name. More like death or bad dreams. We arrived cut and battered, totally spent. The half that could walk carried the other half. One of our new women bled to death before Linden could save her. No food or water to be found. And then we were stalked by roaring phantoms and clanking giants. Through it all, Rose kept us going, moving, insistent that a safe place could be found, certain that something—some*one*—was guiding her there. We took all our hope from her. Our two oldest ran out of their life-spark and died, within a day of each other. We wrapped them and carried them with us, loath to abandon their poor starved bodies without burial in such an ungiving, soulless place.

"Finally, Rose decided that a Seeing might help her know our path more clearly. None of us had the presence of mind to advise against it. Rose always said it was foolish to undertake a Seeing from a state of exhaustion or despair. We were, she was, both. She went into her trance, and never came out of it. But when the rest of us looked up from the Circle, we were in that grim castle yard outside the gate, and the doorway into the garden was before us."

"As if she . . ."

"Yes. Because it looks like Deep Moor, even feels

like Deep Moor, but it isn't." Raven pats the warm stucco wall behind them. "There's no house behind the facade. I think that, somehow, Rose made it happen, and the garden and courtyard were all she could manage before she gave out."

"The garden? Is there . . . ?"

"Food? Yes, and water—that's the wonder of it. Edible. Delicious. We're all getting well again, those of us who made it this far." Raven sighs deeply, guiltily, toying with the stained and shredded embroidery on her skirt. "Of course we were grateful. We can feed ourselves and the surviving animals, and nothing bothers us. But Rose . . . has been as you see her ever since. Occasionally her lips will move, as if she's talking with someone. But it's never with us. It's as if we weren't there. She won't eat or drink, or even sleep. She'll never get her strength back this way! I fear she'll just fade away."

"Rose, poor Rose!" Erde wraps her arms around her chest and rocks back and forth miserably. "The dragons will know what to do! We'll ask them immediately!"

But then a glad cry rings out on the other side of the garden wall. Raven sits up. "Oh, listen! What a lovely sound! I haven't heard laughter in a long, long while."

Lily runs up through the arbor. "Come quickly! Come see!"

Raven's eyes move to the still figure at the stone table.

"You go," Erde says. "I'll stay with Rose."

She follows Raven to the end of the arbor. From there, she can keep an eye on Rose and also have a clear view down the bright green lawn. She sees the women gathering near the dragon's crossed foreclaws, in the shadow of his huge head. As many as can walk or be assisted are huddled in excitement around Margit and her twins: three redheads, all three, alive and well, tearfully embracing.

A life saved! Well done, dear dragon.

THERE WERE OTHERS I COULD NOT SAVE.

May God rest their souls.

Erde repeats the usual benediction by habit, but she can't help but notice how empty it sounds, how inadequate. What kind of god would create a good and beautiful world, then let it be overrun by such evils as Fire and the hell-priest? She can't see the sense in that.

She'd much rather put her faith in dragons.

NOW THAT WE'VE FOUND OUR FRIENDS, MY SISTER SAYS WE MUST GO AFTER N'DOCH.

Yes, we must, of course. But first, there is one more rescue here to attempt, dear dragon.

Water has been listening in. AND AFTER THAT, THERE'LL BE ANOTHER DISTRACTION, THEN ANOTHER AND ANOTHER, UNTIL FIRE'S DONE HIS WORST EVERYWHERE! DON'T YOU SEE THE PATTERN? IT'S HIS MEDDLING, I TELL YOU!

BUT STILL, WE MUST DO WHAT WE CAN FOR LADY ROSE.

As if to prove Lady Water's prediction, a new and louder commotion breaks out at the stone arch leading to the city. Part of the dog pack streams in, howling an alarm. They sweep around and pile back out again, setting up such a racket in the outer castle yard that it echoes through the gate like the baying of a thousand dogs. Margit abandons her celebrating immediately. She kisses her daughters, grabs her bow, and sprints for the opening with Lily quick behind her. The other women pull back toward the house in a protective circle, shoving the weakest into the center.

What could cause the dogs to raise such a ruckus? Erde fears the worst. She shrinks against the arbor entrance, praying that Fra Guill hasn't found a way to bring his fiendish army through the portal in the Grove. For surely, then, all will be lost.

Chapter Thirteen

The sofa is soft and deep. Paia sinks into it as into warm bathwater, giving in to its soothing, enveloping suspension. But her sleep is restless. She'd hoped for oblivion, the luxury of not thinking. Instead, she gets dreams.

She dreams of all the baggage she's left behind, way too heavy to carry on this perilous journey. Her habits and life in the Temple fill several sets of matched leather luggage. The longings she's denied barely fit into a giant trunk. The fears she's buried, so as not to be a burden in this crisis to those around her fit neatly into a metal attaché case, but it's so leaden, she can't even lift it. Stepping around the mountainous pile, she's back in the closed safety of the Citadel, pacing its red-lined corridors, walking the cool stones of the Temple floor. She dreams of the routine of ritual, which she'd chafed at in boredom, and which now seems alluringly secure. She dreams of sheltering darkness, and of the rich comforts of her personal chambers. She dreams of being clean and fed and dressed and petted and cared for by a legion of servants and acolytes.

Her dream is a nostalgic review of her life with the God.

"You could have it all back again, my love. Exactly as it was before."

His voice purrs in her ear, rough velvet sliding over steel, the most intimate of whispers, as if he lay next to her. It thrills her to hear it again. Despite all, she has missed him. Paia tries to turn her head, to look at him. She can better gauge his true mood by what form he has taken. But this dream is the sort that prevents speech or movement. In her dream paralysis, she can only listen.

"You've had your little adventure now, my sweet. Youthful rebellion, and all that. I've kept you too close to home, I see that now. But I knew I must guard my most precious treasure. I feared for your safety, my darling."

My darling. He's never called her that before. *Treasure.* Paia can feel the warm stirrings of his breath on her ear, on the soft skin of her neck. Delicious. It distracts her from his casual dismissal of her soul-wrenching denial, from the accusations she should fling at him: liar, murderer, destroyer. How is he managing a true physical sensation?

"Yes, my love, I am here beside you. You've missed me, come now, admit it. You know where you truly belong, don't you?" His tone is endearingly unsteady, as if poised to say things he might regret, unguarded confessions of his need to have her back with him. "I won't speak of Duty or the Devotion that you owe me as your God. I'll speak of destiny. *Our* destiny, not the foolish plans of others. We are paired, you and I. Fated together. We have a kingdom to rule, once we defeat our enemies, and you shall rule it with me, not as my Priestess, but as my Queen."

Yes, but he talks to me as if I was still a child. And yet . . . *his Queen*. Images of pomp and splendor parade before her eyes. His lips enclose her earlobe. Paia cannot move away from or toward him. Her breath quickens.

His laugh is boyish, boastful with delight. "Ah, did I not tell you I'd thought of ways for us to become closer? So much closer, my darling."

The long weight of his body moves against her, fitting its nakedness to hers. Broad hands touch her, a man's hands, without scales. But she feels the delicate drag of curved fingernails across her skin. Poised between astonishment and delight, Paia wonders fleetingly if they're gilded, as his always are in man-form.

"It's so simple," he murmurs. "I can't imagine why I didn't think of it before. In life, I cannot manage substance in any form that would . . . ah . . . fit with yours. But in dreams, ah, in dreams I can provide any sort of satisfaction. Unimaginable pleasures, my darling."

He begins his sensual ministrations with his mouth and tongue. Still she cannot move or return his caress. She can only respond with the rising clangor of her body, as he wakens it to ecstasy.

How like him, she thinks, in the moment before delirium drowns out reason. How like my beloved, broken God, my Fire, to invent an idea of lovemaking that only works one way. In that moment, her most profound feeling for the great golden dragon, the scourge of the world, is pity.

Chapter Fourteen

Paia stirs, and N'Doch moves away hastily. He realizes he's been humming faintly, under his breath. She shouldn't know how close he's been watching. Watching and humming. What's that tune? He's lost it now. He glances toward Djawara, snoozing in his straight-backed chair by the window. Old people and babies, he marvels. They can fall asleep anywhere.

He folds himself into an overstuffed armchair. He doesn't recall there being any furniture like this at the Rive. The upholstery is a maroon cut-velvet, like some rich matron's boudoir. Big, soft cushions—supposed to be comfortable, but if you're as tall as N'Doch is, they make your arms and legs stick out all over the place. He plants his elbows on his knees, which feel too close to his chin. He feels gawky and aroused, a combination he's not at all happy with. He's humming again. Is this some new nervous tic? Paia's eyes open. She blinks at him, still sensuous with sleep. In the dim, shuttered light of the café, she is unbearably lovely.

"Musta been one hell of a dream you had," he says for openers. He adds an evil grin to hide his self-consciousness.

"Dream. Yes." She seems to be struggling to remember.

"Dreaming of Dolph, I bet."

She looks away, down, then back at him. Despite her moist aura of slaked desire, her regard is bleak. N'Doch might almost say, tragic. "It wasn't."

He laughs and wriggles his eyebrows, trying to cheer her. "Maybe it was me, then."

She smiles sadly, as if he's offered the sweetest sort of false compliment, and then the smile is gone. She sits up, brushing back her damp hair, straightening her clothes as if surprised to find them there at all.

"Okay, I give up. Who's the lucky man of the hour? Was it . . . Papa Dja?"

She will not be jollied. He can see there's a war going on in her head, and his questions are a distraction. But maybe not entirely unwelcome. "Not a man at all."

N'Doch takes about a half a second. Then he gets it. Uh-oh. No wonder her eyes looks so haunted. "You have dreams like that about *him*?" he blurts before he can stop himself.

Her glance slips toward Djawara. She's clearly relieved to find the old man sleeping. "Was it so obvious?"

"Oh, yeah." Now it's his turn to look away. "Oh, yeah. Phew. Complicated relationship."

Paia stares down at her hands, lacing and unlacing her slender fingers, soft and well cared for but no longer so clean. "It was his dream, really. He's trying to woo me back to him."

Again, it takes him a while. He's not usually so

slow on the uptake, but often Paia speaks as if, since her history has been revealed to him in the Meld, her moment-to-moment thought process will be equally apparent and understood. "You're saying the Fire dude sent this dream? Ordered it up and sent it?"

"I could never have invented it on my own," she murmurs.

He tries his grin again. "Lot of women have told me their dreams are way better than the real thing."

"But I know nothing of such things!" Her cry is raw with both shame and regret. Her hands wring themselves into tightening knots. "He never let me have *real* lovers. In this dream, I wasn't even allowed to participate! He just did things to me!"

"Hey, every once in a while, that's a nice way to go."

She glares at him. He sees his attempts at humor are coming off as insensitive. He tries to figure out how he could gracefully slide over onto the sofa next to her. But it's the wrong time to take advantage of a girl, when she's so worked up and vulnerable. He reaches over to untangle the furious maze of her fingers and ends up holding her hands instead. "Easy, now. At least it was only a dream."

"But that's just it!" She grasps his hands as if she could force a fuller understanding into him by the strength of her grip. "I don't know that. I could feel him . . . touching me. I could really feel it!"

"Dreams always seem real while you're dreaming 'em."

"No, at first it was like it always was. Like putting your hand in a flame. Heat, no substance. Then it seemed that the more I wanted him to touch me, the more real he became. In the end, he . . ."

N'Doch frees his hands, holds up both palms.

"Whoa, girl. I don't wanna hear the details. I'm no kinda saint, y'know."

"N'Doch, please, don't you hear what I'm saying?" She leans toward him as he pulls away. Beneath her soft shirt, her breasts mound invitingly between her hunched shoulders.

"Yeah," he retorts. "The Fire dude made love to you long-distance, and you feel bad 'cause you liked it."

"No! Well, not only. It's . . . what if it's my desire that makes him real?"

"Okay. Lemme think about that." N'Doch is struggling to master his own desire. He knows it's making him stupid. He wishes she'd sit back and leave him alone. "Why should it matter, as long as it's still a dream?"

"But what if it isn't?"

"Isn't what?"

"Just a dream." Not only does she not sit back, she slides to the floor in front of him with her hands on his knees. "What if my desire acts as another kind of . . . portal? Allowing him to physically manifest in human form? He's never been able to do that before."

N'Doch doesn't move a muscle. There's a song rising in the back of his brain, for the first time since he left his dragon behind. "So what you're saying is, Fire comes to you in a dream, transports you to the heavenly spheres, then when he's done, he gets out of bed and wanders over to the bar to have a beer with me." And all I get to do is watch, he thinks, but doesn't add.

"Except that having a beer is not what he's most likely to do with you!"

N'Doch remembers the gilt-scaled giant in his

cloak of fire up on the mountaintop, his scimitar claw aimed at Köthen's neck. "No, I suppose not."

"And he'd be able to do it this time. He wouldn't need a proxy hit man like your Kenzo Baraga."

Now there's an image that's a real turnoff. N'Doch feels his lust seeping away, allowing room in his brain for the fuller implications of what she's said. The inner music he's been hearing fades. He scrubs his face with his hands. "That might not be good."

"No." Paia slumps back against the base of the sofa as if she's spent herself in struggle. The bleakness is back in her eyes again. "Maybe you should make love to me. Then I won't be so lustful anymore."

N'Doch stares at her through the web of his fingers.

"I mean, of course it should be Dolph, but he's not here and . . ."

Her gaze lifts to meet his, veiled by shining hair and luxurious lashes, sultry with promise. N'Doch drops his hands, struck breathless by the hot flush of desire racing through him, searing away his will. Then he sees the bright tongues of flame leap in her eyes. He's not so stupid after all. He understands who he's really staring at. Like a dry wind in the desert, the presence resonates in all the hollow spaces his own dragon left behind.

"Whoa," he says. "No way."

Her face twists. The flames flare defiantly and die. He knows he's had a close call, but there's no struggle. N'Doch senses the shadow departing, like a whiff of smoke, and understands another, more puzzling thing. The bleakness in Paia is not her own. It's Fire's.

Paia shakes her head as if she's just dropped off to sleep again and waked with a start. "What?"

"You're asking me?" Suddenly he's glad that his friend, his hero the good baron, is a time warp away from this woman. She could eat the man alive. She carries a dragon within her. N'Doch should know. So does he. At least, he hopes to, soon again. But there's a difference. Paia's dragon feels he has nothing left to lose. "Didn't quite leave him behind, did you."

She flicks a wary glance around the café. She doesn't ask who. "Why? What happened?"

"An interesting little sleight of hand. Well, sleight of body's more like it. He tried to woo us both at once."

"He?"

"The Fire dude."

She starts, convincingly. "He was here?"

"Don't you remember?" He's sure she does, but he humors her, to spare her pride. "Seems he convinced you it might be a bright idea to seduce me." He sees her whole body recoil. With shame, he hopes, not with horror. Maybe she really doesn't remember. "Hey, don't worry. It didn't go far. He gave himself away too easily."

She looks like she's afraid to ask. "How?"

"He was in your eyes. Did you know he could do that? I mean, you know . . . use you that way?"

"I, ah . . . he never has before. At least, not that I . . ."

N'Doch watches what's left of her self-possession collapse. Body, face, her entire being goes limp. All her actions, past and present, are suddenly up for question.

"How . . . how will I ever know?"

How will any of us know, he wonders. Not just about Paia. About ourselves. Four people bonded to mythical creatures driven by alien agendas and protocols. He recalls the exact instant he let his dragon into his soul. The song he sang then wasn't an act of love or selflessness, though he did it to lend her his strength. It was more like surrendering to an inevitability. "You'll know 'cause I'll tell you," he says. "That's why there's four of us, I guess. So we can keep each other honest."

He's grasping at straws, but Paia seems grateful for the effort. She stops shuddering uncontrollably. "I can never be alone, then."

N'Doch has a leap of intuition that skews his take on things abruptly enough to leave him faintly dizzy. And hating it that once more he has to buy into all this mystical symmetry of events. "And that's why Dolph came along. So you don't have to be."

She smiles wanly. "I wish he was here now."

"He probably does, too." He says it to reassure her, but it makes him nervous again for Köthen, who has no dragon to protect him. Then he takes another leap. It's like a lyric writing itself in his head. Part of the epic he could sing about the dragon renegade and his beautiful priestess. Colorful. Dramatic. Even, in a perverse sort of way, romantic. Villains have been some of his most inspiring subjects. "He's not real happy, your man Fire." It sounds silly, now that he's said it, talking that way about a devious, inhuman, fire-breathing murderer. "I mean . . ."

"I know." Paia seems eager to talk about her dragon. She hasn't had much of a chance, N'Doch realizes, to download how she feels about all of this. "He's never been reasonable. He's angry all the time.

I just took it for granted." She looks up, caught in an insight of her own. Her tears reflect the gray daylight. "An angry god. I guess it just seemed fitting, after all the horrors of the Collapse. What other kind of god could you believe in, after that?"

"He's like the black sheep younger son, maybe?" A little like me, N'Doch admits privately. "The one who's sure the older ones got something he didn't get, so he figures he's got a right to go out and take what he wants to make up for it."

Paia tilts her head. "What an interesting notion." She grasps the fat arm of the sofa and levers herself up onto the seat. On a side table is a crystalline glass of iced water that N'Doch is sure wasn't there a moment ago. Neither was the table. Neither was the gleaming acoustic guitar that's leaning against it, like it's been listening in on the conversation. N'Doch stops breathing. Paia drinks deeply, collecting herself. When she sets aside the empty glass, N'Doch lets his lungs fill, and waits for it to vanish. He waits for the guitar to vanish, too. But both just sit there. This magic, he decides, won't happen while anyone's watching. So as long as I keep this baby in my sight . . .

He grasps the guitar casually by the neck, then drags it into his lap and thumbs the strings. It's real and sleek, and in perfect tune. He nearly hollers for joy, but he's wary of upsetting Paia's delicate state of balance.

But maybe she's not so delicate. She allows the sudden instrument into their universe without batting an eyelash. "You must think I live my life entirely at the whim of my handlers," she says.

"No, I . . ." But of course, this is exactly what he's thought. Petted, spoiled, but ultimately the dragon's and the Temple's tool. He picks out a quiet little riff to let himself off the hook. Cocktail music. He glances at the deserted bar. *Wonder if I could sing myself up a drink.*

"To some extent, that's been true. But I feel like I've been waiting for the moment when it didn't have to be."

"This could be it, girl," he says lightly, the same tone as his fingers on the singing strings. He hopes he'll never have to choose between holding a woman and holding a guitar. He's pretty sure he knows which way he'd go.

Paia's on her own sort of roll. "With all that's happened, so much and so fast, there's a lot I haven't had time to really take in. Like, the existence of the other . . . dragons." She laughs softly. "I was never allowed to say that word, you know. He was 'the God.' Only 'the God.' When he spoke of his enemies, he never hinted at them being his own kind, especially not his own . . ."

"Family."

"Yes. Do they have something he doesn't?"

Besides a sense of decency? N'Doch shrugs, damping the guitar with his palm. "Young Erde and her dragon would say he lacks belief in the rightness of their Destiny. He's sure made it clear he wants none of that, even if no one knows exactly what it is."

Paia says, "He's always given me the impression he knows what it is. Otherwise why would he be so against it?"

N'Doch peers at her. The café is growing shadowed, as if dusk has fallen. But on the other side of the windows, the light is as harsh and bright as ever. Best as he can, he replays the confrontation on the mountaintop in his mind. "Didn't he yell something about humans not being worth the sacrifice? What'd he mean by that? The way he's been living, it doesn't look to me like he's sacrificed much." He shifts his lanky body within the velvety grip of the chair. Not room enough in here for himself and the guitar, plus the song that's taking shape, even the first few bars. Or maybe it's the notion he's hatching that's making him so uncomfortable. "I think we gotta find out what's bugging him."

Paia laughs, eyeing him sidelong.

"No, really." The edge on her laugh surprises him. Bleak, like Fire. He hikes himself forward on the puffy cushion, elbows draped over the sinuous curves of the instrument. He's amazed to hear his own voice sounding so earnest. He has to keep himself from turning the words into a lyric right on the spot. "Whatever's this Big Fix the dragons are supposed to pull off, they're convinced they can't do it without Fire. So we got to bring him over to our side. And you know they're looking to you to do it."

Paia shakes her head hopelessly. He guesses she doesn't hear the music.

"Well, of course you can't do it alone. You're too close to him. Too much of an insider. The problem is, who else is there?" His fingers go to work on the accompaniment. "Gerrasch is too busy finding his own dragon, even though we gotta have him. Earth and Erde don't really give a shit about the whys. Their gig is doing what's right and proper according to the Big Rule Book. And we need that, too, I guess. But nobody's gonna get Fire to mend his ways by quoting him chapter and verse." The ending chord is harsher than he'd intended. "You agree with that?"

"Of course. His only real motive is self-interest."

"Right. So we find out what he wants, and if

there's any way we can give it to him, we do. At least enough so's he'll play ball."

"We."

"Yeah. You and me." Now the background line is ticklish. He's thrilled by the subtle complexities of his improvisations. "You're connected to him 'cause you're his guide. But I might be able to help figure him out. 'Cause of my own history, I mean. I had all these grandiose plans, like he does. And I haven't done so well by my family either, have I? Ever since that blue dragon showed up, I've asked myself, why'd she pick me? If it was just to bodyguard young Erde into the future, she'd have better chosen someone like Dolph, or your cousin Leif. So maybe this is why." N'Doch grins at her. " 'Your mission, if you choose to accept it . . .' "

She gazes at him blankly.

"From an old vid series." He tosses off a few notes of the theme song. "Way, way before your time. Before mine, even. Anyhow, what do you say?"

"I'd say what he wants is power, luxury, and me, probably in that order. It's not all that complicated."

"But you're back into whats, not whys. Even a dragon's got to have his whys. And when you know a person's whys, then you've got power over him." He stops, shakes his head, then throws both hands in the air and flops backward into the chair. The guitar lies prone on his stomach like a resting limb. "I can't fuckin' believe this! I'm talking about making deals with my mama's murderer."

Near the front, a chair leg rasps against the tile. "What sort of deals?"

N'Doch jerks upright, cradling the instrument. "Hey, Papa! Sleep well?"

"Not a chance." The old man walks toward them

stiffly and pulls up a straight chair from a nearby table. "There's too many voices in the air here to get any rest. What sort of deals?"

N'Doch just knows he means voices other than his and Paia's. But he'll elaborate when he's ready. There's never any rushing Papa Dja. "I'm telling Paia here how it's likely our job to try to turn Fire."

Djawara nods gravely, approving. "Was a time, lad, that I'd have had to point out that sort of duty to you. Then grab you before you had a chance to escape."

N'Doch cackles. Just like Papa Dja. Always knowing better. He plays the up-tempo intro to a traditional folk tune. "So how we gonna pull it off, O Great Shaman of the Tribe?"

Djawara crosses one knee over the other and nests his hands in front of him. "In my day, when two sides had irreconcilable differences, they met to discuss them in neutral territory, where neither could do harm to the other. Some place like the beach or the market square . . . or here."

"Here? How we gonna bring him here?"

Paia clears her throat delicately. "You just told me I did."

"Almost. Papa, why you so sure this is neutral territory?"

"Instinct, my boy. Intuition. Trust me."

The old man's gone woo-woo on him, just like the old days. To punish him, N'Doch turns away to Paia. "So you dream him here, and *afterward* . . ." He leans on the word and wishes it was light enough to see if she's blushing. The guitar is growing warm in his arms. "Afterward, I offer him that beer and say, hey, dude, just what is your problem?"

"I don't think I'd have to dream him here," Paia

replies steadily. "I think he would just come if I called him."

N'Doch looks to his grandfather. "Is this insane or what? I'd sort of had in mind sneaking up on him."

"And how were you planning to do that?"

He bends low over the strings, picking delicately. "Dunno. Hadn't got that far yet." He moves into a more familiar melody, his own this time.

"If nothing else," Paia adds, "we could keep him distracted while Cousin Leif takes back the Citadel."

"And the others go looking for Air. Oooh, he's just gonna love that idea." N'Doch can smell the Rive burning already. His thumb pats out the rhythm of the flames on the guitar's polished box.

"Negotiating with him was your idea in the first place," she reminds him.

"Hey, are we arguing? Ain't gonna get nowhere if we're arguing." But he's encouraged to see a flash of spirit out of her.

"Were you thinking of attempting this on your own, without the others?" Djawara asks.

N'Doch spreads his hands, balancing the guitar on his knee. "If we put them together with him, there'll just be another big fight. End of discussion. You know how families are." But it occurs to him how good it would be to have his brother Sedou at this debate. The old political hand. If the blue dragon were here, he could sing her into that uncanny transformation: half Water, half Sedou. A winning combination. N'Doch hums the tune wistfully. He can't believe he's about to do something this drastic without her pushing him into it. "Are you both really up for this gig?"

Dread and eager anticipation chase each other across Paia's face. She's wringing her hands again.

"There's a time and a place to be proactive." Dja-wara uncrosses his legs and places one hand care-fully on each knee. "And there's no time like the present, I suppose."

Paia says faintly, "This may take me a few moments."

N'Doch's hum grows into a song.

Chapter Fifteen

He's fine for a while, cross-legged on the smooth stone, caught up in the work. One bright line of signal attracts his eye: bits of silvery chain with intervals of silence, sequences iterating with progressive changes. Music, he guesses. He wishes he could hear it, but he can only see its patterning. It seems to be searching, but it keeps running into dead ends and flowing back along itself until its lyrical orderings eddy off into chaos.

The Librarian has often imagined code as the soft and tensile cotton twine that's best for handweaving and knotwork. In dreams, he has created magnificent tapestries of electronic macramé. So, because the place he is now feels like a waking dream, he attempts a few simple manipulations, just for the fun of it. He nudges the glimmering chain toward a less congested route. To his delight, it finds an open path and speeds along toward its destination unhampered.

By then, his pudgy body is complaining, longing for the comforts of his ergonomic desk chair, and for the back and elbow support of his streamlined, waist-level, black matte console. He can't concentrate. He can't fly along the retreating lines of code and signal when he's cramped by such a vivid awareness of the strained sinews and tense muscles that anchor him to physical reality.

The Librarian sighs. He's never had a superior body, but at least it was fit at one time, for quite a long time in fact, until he retreated into the sedentary life of a cyber-jockey. He understands this now as the careless relaxing of an appropriate if noisome discipline. He should have adopted a hobby that got him up and moving around.

In the womb-temperature darkness, the Librarian sticks his legs straight out and props himself from behind on his palms. He feels like an overgrown teddy bear, and just about as useful. Surely *somewhere* in this void-space, there's got to be something better to sit on than the floor.

Also, action is definitely more interesting than self-pity. The Librarian looks around. The darkness is very, well . . . dark. A particularly felty darkness, stippled with textures of Brownian motion and incipient light. His gaze is drawn to an area of the darkness more mobile than the rest. More transparent. He groans to his feet and shambles in that direction. The darkness seems to have substance, a dense granulation that gives way before him in a tubular passage. He can't put his hands on this substance. Nothing solid meets his outstretched arms. But he can feel the *idea* of it enclosing him. He senses the direction in which it's leading him.

Then his shin whacks something hard that rolls away from him with a sharp plastic chatter. The Librarian bellows in pain and irritated surprise. *What fool left that there?* He always shoves the chair well in under the desk, in case he has to find it in the dark, as happens so often in these days of brownouts and power outages. He moves forward, finds the desk first, then fumbles for the errant chair. And then he remembers there's no way he could be where he thinks he is.

He stands motionless for a long moment, searching out an explanation. He grips the back of the chair. It creaks under his pressure as he leans against it. Its smooth hand-worn metal frame and torn padding mended with peeling layers of duct tape are entirely familiar. Even though his hands haven't touched them for two hundred and twenty-three years. He sees the indicator lights on the surge protectors, just where he'd expect them, pin-point eyes in the velvet darkness. The Librarian takes a breath, reaches, and switches on the desk lamp.

The cool halogen glow illuminates a beige keyboard, a bulky monitor and system case, flanked by racks of extra memory, modem, speakers, printers, tape storage, all linked by a spaghetti mass of cable. Books and manuals to right, left, and below. Above, just inside the lamp's small circle of light, a weather radio, a row of world maps, a list of satellite flyovers. And more books, with declarative, earnest titles and stacks of *Nature* and the *JGR* as bookends. It's all there, even a half-filled cup of coffee, cold but not spoiled, as if he had left it yesterday.

The Librarian moves slowly around the chair without letting go of it. He's afraid he'll collapse if left without support. He sits, and hauls himself automatically up to the desk. He flattens his palms on it. The very desk, the very equipment that delivered up his first undisputed signal from the dragon.

What is going on?

He has never felt so rattled, so close to believing that he's finally slipped his moorings. But there's only one logical thing to do. Only one. His hand hovers, then flicks the toggle to power up the system.

Chapter Sixteen

Erde clings to the arbor post. Rose petals drift around her like fragrant snow. Voices are raised at the gate. Outside, more frantic barking. Whatever's out there is coming in. The dogs spill through the gate again and out across the lawn in a blur of teeth and hackles. Erde grips the post so tightly, her knuckles crack. She prays that the hell-priest and his white-robed minions will not be next.

Then Lily and Margit stride in, forcibly escorting a small, dark figure by both scrawny arms. They shove their prisoner roughly to the ground. The figure curls up defensively in the thick green grass and lies there, unresisting. Erde goes up on her toes for a better view. Some captured denizen of the city?

Margit's voice floats up from the lawn. "Caught this one skulking about!"

Erde squints to see more clearly. "Oh, my!"

She bolts across the lawn, forgetting Rose entirely, and arrives just as Luther has shoved his large body between the two snarling scouts and the hapless intruder.

"Leave 'im!" Luther shouts. The dogs mill about, barking.

"Lily! Margit! Wait!" Erde pleads. "He's a friend!"

The women back off only enough to give her room. Erde throws herself down beside the curled-up ball and pats it urgently. "It's all right, Stoksie. They won't hurt you!"

"Too late fer dat!" Stoksie uncoils warily, glancing about. "Hey! Wachu doin' heah?"

Luther bends to help his friend to his feet, gently brushing him off. "Yu okay, Stokes?"

Stoksie nods, shooting a grim look at Lily and Margit. "Yu prizners, too?"

"No, no. It's all a misunderstanding. You're with friends." Erde takes his arm. "This is Stoksie, everyone. He's one of Luther's countrymen."

Stoksie looks to Luther and gets his nod. "Well, den. Das diff'rent." He straightens his clothing, then bows around, as if calling on all assembled to notice how forgiving he's being.

Erde is seized with giggles, but swallows them. She knows how the plucky little Tinker dislikes being bested. "Stoksie, how did you get here?"

"Well, nah, I cud ask yu da same questchun."

"Margit says you were sneaking about out in the yard."

"I wuz lookin' fer help!" He claps his hand to his bald head as if suddenly recalling his errand. "Hey! Doan mattah how I got heah! We gotta run help G! Dere'sa monsta afta him!"

"A what?" She's heard this term before from the Tinkers. She beckons Raven and the scouts to listen. "You mean Fire? Is he out there?"

"Nah. Dis sum kinda vishus masheen!"

Machine. Erde pictures the elevator at the Refuge,

and the sleek humming furniture in Gerrasch's work-room. She knows these are machines, but it's hard to imagine them being vicious. Then she remembers the flying machines of N'Doch's time, and the wagons that rolled without horses. The one N'Doch called a *tank* truly was a monster. She saw it break down stone walls. "Is it coming here?"

"Doan know, but we gotta go afta G. Yu know how he kint run much."

"What's going on, sweetling?" asks Raven, less patiently than usual.

"Oh, forgive me!" Belatedly, Erde translates. She'd forgotten that none of the women would understand a word of the Tinker dialect. Nor do they know what a machine is, but they all recognize the description.

"We saw such horrors during our journey here," Raven agrees.

"But they didn't chase us," says Margit. "They hardly noticed us, but we had to be on our guard all the same. They'd flatten anything in their path."

"Often," Lily adds, "they were fighting each other."

"We gotta hurry!" Stoksie breaks in. "Kin yer frens help us?"

Erde passes the request to the women.

"Gerrasch?" exclaims Raven. "Our Gerrasch? Here?"

"Not quite as you remember him, but yes, it's our Gerrasch."

"Did he flee through the portal, too? I saw his house was destroyed, and I feared the worst!"

"I'll explain everything! After we've rescued him!"

Lily and Margit agree. Lily hurries off to recruit a few of the stronger refugee women.

Dragon, should we go with them?

I MUST SEE TO ROSE. BESIDES, I'D ONLY SLOW THEM DOWN. SISTER, WILL YOU GO?

PHYSICAL STRENGTH IS NOT MY GIFT, BROTHER. AS SOON AS YOU HAVE SEEN TO ROSE, WE MUST GO AFTER N'DOCH.

Then I'll go, and call you to come when we find him.

I WILL WANT YOUR HELP WITH ROSE.

I HEAR MUSIC. DOES ANYONE ELSE HEAR IT? MUSIC, I'M SURE OF IT!

Erde feels their attention languishing. *Dragons! Are we to desert Gerrasch? Your sister's dragon guide? Surely not!*

THESE STRONG WOMEN WILL BE HELP ENOUGH. WE MUST ALL USE OUR TALENTS ACCORDINGLY.

Guiltily, Erde relays all this to Margit, but the older woman seems unsurprised that the dragons are preoccupied with their own concerns. In fact, Erde decides, Margit is flattered that the great beasts trust her to get the job done. She nods tightly and whistles up the dog pack.

"The hounds won't be much use against a machine," Erde tells Stoksie. "But they know Gerrasch from the old days. They'll help you track him down."

Stoksie marvels over them, real living dogs that crowd around to lick his hands instead of attacking. "Dey wuz nicer ta me den doze two wimmen."

"Those women are good fighters, Stoksie."

"Fighters, all ri'," the little man grumbles.

Luther negotiates the loan of two stout pikes from Margit. Erde is relieved to note that the women of Deep Moor did not flee their burning homestead entirely unarmed. She smiles hopefully at the party assembling at the gate. "Bring him back safely!"

"Betcha!" Luther replies.

She watches them out of sight. Then, calling the dragons, she follows Raven back to the garden courtyard, assailed by the conviction that events are happening much too fast. Faster than usual, she's sure of it. She leaves Earth to hunker down outside the rose arbor. Water joins the women inside. Raven watches her flow in and out of the corners and niches, exploring the garden.

"Like a flock of butterflies this time. But humming, like bees."

Erde listens. The tune sounds vaguely familiar.

"Could she become Sedou again?" Raven asks. "Rose was very taken with Sedou."

"She would need N'Doch to sing her into that shape. His memory. His song, not hers."

"Ah." Raven nods soberly. "A pity."

Water completes her circuit of the garden and comes to hover over the table where Rose sits, exactly as she had been. As slowly as the petals falling from the arbor, Water settles onto the motionless woman until Rose is blanketed by a cloud of scintillating blue motes.

Erde queries the dragon. *What is she doing?*

MY SISTER GREETS THE LADY ROSE AND OFFERS HER OUR AFFECTION AND SUPPORT.

Does Rose respond?

SADLY, SHE DOES NOT.

Lady Water, can you tell what's wrong with her?

The blue motes withdraw from Rose and gather at the arbor entrance. THAT'S FOR MY BROTHER TO SAY. I ONLY WISHED TO PAY MY RESPECTS BEFORE I LEFT.

You're leaving?

N'DOCH IS SINGING.

But he's in Africa

THE MUSIC I'VE BEEN HEARING JUST NOW ORGANIZED INTO A SONG. HE'S SOMEWHERE NEARBY, HERE IN THE CITY.

But how could he be?

Erde blurts this in total disbelief. But on second thought, it makes perfect sense that N'Doch is in the city. Symmetry demands it because Gerrasch is also here, delivered by yet another portal, to judge from Stoksie's description. Erde believes in symmetry, especially as regards the destiny of dragon guides. Eventually, she'd have worried if N'Doch had *not* shown up.

Is Paia with him?

I'LL FIND OUT WHEN I GET THERE. I'LL KEEP IN TOUCH. CIAO.

Water doesn't wink out as the dragons do when Earth is providing instant transport. She flutters away under the blossom-laden arbor. Peering after her, Erde sees her flit across the outer lawn and through the stone gate into the city as if heading off on an afternoon stroll. Erde sighs. The scent of flowers and bruised grass and the warm softness of the breeze belie the dire realities they all are facing. And then Earth's deep rumble reclaims her wandering attention.

NOW LET US TURN OUR MINDS AND HEARTS TO HELPING LADY ROSE.

Chapter Seventeen

Paia listens to N'Doch's song, glad for the excuse to put off her summoning a bit longer. His voice is strong and pure, and the melody murmurs of loss and longing. By the second verse, in a happier vein, he's left off his guitar accompaniment, so that the song drifts entirely on its own through the thickening dusk. Paia imagines it like water, flowing into the darkened corners of the room. Where it's been, it leaves a new glimmer behind. Chandeliers flare softly overhead. Etched glass sconces glow to life. The darkness retreats a little.

N'Doch is still singing when the front door opens and shuts with the throaty rattle of thin glass in an aging wooden frame. N'Doch falls silent in the middle of a word. Paia fears to look. She's sure the God has somehow preempted her summons. But how has he managed the doorknob?

Djawara's back is to the door. He turns, then rises with a quick, stiff jolt and a gasp. His chair clatters to one side.

"Easy, Papa," says N'Doch quickly. "It's not who you think."

A tall black man stands in front of the closed door, reconnoitering. As tall as N'Doch, maybe taller, and more broad-shouldered. A big man. But Paia immediately sees the resemblance. It's in the smile, the great transformation from a glower to a grin.

N'Doch wrenches himself out of the overstuffed armchair. One fist shoots into the air angrily. The other clutches the neck of the miraculous guitar. "Whacha trying to do?" he yells at the man, "Give Papa Dja a heart attack?"

"Nice welcome." The newcomer frowns, and the heated air in the café chills noticeably. "Papa," he says gently. His voice is deep, like the roll of distant thunder. "I didn't know you were here."

Djawara finds his own voice, but barely. He looks so frail and overcome that Paia worries for him. She puts her hand out, and he grasps it gratefully. "Sedou? Sedou, my boy?"

N'Doch hugs the guitar against his chest. "Nah, Papa, it's her. It's the dragon. Will you please just sit down and take a breath?" To the big man, who hasn't moved from the door: "You oughta be ashamed of yourself!"

"Be cool, bro. I didn't know. You should have warned him before you sang me."

"I didn't . . ." N'Doch notices the guitar in his arms. "Did I? Shit, guess I did. What was I thinking?"

"I guess you weren't. Nothing new there."

"Glad to see you, too."

"The dragon?" murmurs Djawara.

Paia is amazed. Water in human form has none of

Fire's charged, holographic glitter. The dragon has simply become the man, the older brother that N'Doch was singing about. The *dead* older brother, she now recalls. No wonder Djawara is so distressed.

"The dragon?" the old man asks again.

N'Doch is busy squabbling with his pseudo-sibling. "How did you find me here?"

Paia sets Djawara's chair upright and urges him to sit. "His dragon. Water. She's a shape-shifter."

He knows this, but had for the moment forgotten. She sees comprehension return as if a mist has cleared from his eyes. "Ah, yes. Shape-shifter." He looks away from the apparition of his dead grandson, then back again. "Remarkable likeness, really." He smiles at Paia and pats her hand. "Remarkable. Though now that I look more closely, not exactly as I remember him. Sedou was not so . . ." Djawara's hands sketch out height and breadth. "Not such a giant."

"He's the Sedou that N'Doch remembers," Paia offers quietly.

"I am what he sings me." The big man moves gracefully among the empty tables, snatching up a chair as he passes. He sets it down in front of Djawara and sits, his eyes level with the old man's. They regard each other for a long moment, while N'Doch hovers uneasily in the background.

"Ever since she showed up," he mutters to Paia, "I always thought it should be Papa Dja she came for. He's been expecting dragons for years."

"I am very sorry for the loss of your daughter, good sage," says the dragon. "But happy that you are alive and well."

Djawara's round face crinkles, caught between joy and sorrow. "Had I never met a dragon before now, I'd never have thought to look for salvation in a grove of trees." He pauses. "What shall I call you?"

"Whatever makes you easy, Papa."

"Sedou, then. In honor of."

Paia tries to imagine Fire ever putting someone else's comfort before his own. She offers her hand, mostly for the chance of convincing herself of the dragon's material presence. "Sedou. I feel I should introduce myself."

N'Doch's fist descends on the big man's shoulder, beating out a soft repeating rhythm. "So, you're here. Did you leave the Big Guy outside?"

"Not here."

When the dragon has explained about Rose and the destruction of Deep Moor, N'Doch begins to pace. "We're all here, then, here in the city. Even Gerrasch. Damn, that's got to mean something."

"Still missing one," Paia reminds him.

N'Doch levels a knowing glance. "Not entirely missing, though."

Sedou sits back, swinging his arm over the curve of his chair. "Yeah, what about that? I'm picking up vibes about this little project you all have in mind. Seems like I got here just in time."

N'Doch frowns. "You mean, time to tell us to forget it, huh?"

"No. No." Sedou looks thoughtful. "Brother Earth certainly would. But I'd kinda like to hear what Fire has to say for himself when he's not trying to incinerate me." The man/dragon lets his eyes roam the shadowed length of the café. "Perhaps this civilized and casual setting will be more conducive to rational discourse than a barren mountaintop."

"He's often most deadly when he's rational," Paia warns.

"But in this zone of safety, his only available weapon will be his tongue," Djawara points out. "The only real power in words is what we give them ourselves."

Paia is surprised that this old man should be so willing to meet the dragon who has just murdered his only daughter. She's also surprised that Water is willing to go along with N'Doch's mad scheme. But she nods, accepting the inevitable. The idea seems less crazy with another dragon in the room.

"That's it, then?" N'Doch tightens his hold on the guitar. "We're still good to go?"

Sedou stands. "The sooner, the better. Before our less devious colleagues get wind of this."

"Come now." Djawara puts on a fey grin. "What's devious about a little negotiation?"

PART THREE

The Call to the Quest

Chapter Eighteen

The Librarian flicks the switch, and nothing happens. Despair surges through him, like the rush of a bad, cheap drug. His heart pounds. His fingers rattle against the noisy, antique keyboard. *Shame, Gerrasch!* He's too smart, too experienced to rest his entire future on the outcome of a single action. And yet, he did, he has. He's secretly hoped she'd just . . . be there.

Then the rising whine of the drives drowns out the blood roar in his ears. The flood of returning joy nearly knocks him flat.

What doesn't kill you makes you strong, the Librarian intones silently. He vows to settle down. Get a grip. He is unused to being tideswept by the force of his own emotions.

Okay. Where am I?

His tiny crash pad in Frankfort. His desk and chair. A few books. His battered ham radio. Other than that, there was just a mattress on the floor and a crate for his clothing. Is the mattress out there also, lumpy and dank, in the darkness that, now as then, surrounds his desk? He's sure that's its sour smell he detects, mixing with odors of boiled cabbage and crumbling plaster. The old-fashioned mechanical keys feel both strange and familiar. He cocks an ear for the sounds of traffic and footfalls outside the cracked basement window. A single monitor shivers to gray life at eye level, and coughs up the DOS prompt. The cursor flashes at him balefully. The Librarian never liked cursors. He knows already that this system will be inadequate to his uses. Can it even do as much as he's already doing (miraculously) on his own, without the aid of machinery? Unlikely. Meanwhile, it's here, so there must be a reason. The dragon's reason, he hopes. He'll have to scour his memory for all the tricks he used back then to tease power, speed, and flexibility out of third-hand equipment. In those days, his ingenuity was fueled by necessity as well as obsession. He's tickled by the image of his burly neck and shoulders as solidly built shelves of a library, the required architectural support for all the information he carries inside his head. He stares at the cursor, pondering his course of action.

He considers what he knows, what he's sure about: the dragon Air is somewhere about. Instinct tells him this, not hard evidence. But trusting instinct has won him through many situations where rationality proved dangerously misleading. Assume, then, that she's close by, but either cannot or will not speak to him directly. The Librarian opts for *cannot*, since he feels still and always the pull of the dragon's desire to communicate. It's the bright star by which he's navigated through his many lives. He can't believe, he *won't* believe, that it would fail him now, when he's so close to his goal.

So she's here, she can't speak to him, for whatever reason, but there's all this signal in the air, which his peculiar ear perceives as sound, and his particular brain as code. *There are no accidents.* He now recalls that, back when, he'd rigged this system to do primitive cryptography, once he'd given up asking his geek acquaintances about the mysterious binary sequences that kept showing up in his system. There'd been equivalent incursions during his ham radio years, even on his CB, but he rarely mentioned these, lacking the material evidence to back up his claim. It became a very private matter. Either his friends began to suspect his sanity, or they got much too interested and insisted on burdening him with reports of their own communications with space aliens. He had no desire to admit to being one of them, and yet, there were these "messages." Not sentences. Not even words. Only their elegant patterning indicated intent on the part of the sender. But the intent was mysterious, and the sender never identified. Looking back, the Librarian is proud that he kept the faith for so long, his faith in his preternatural senses, and never let himself be convinced that he was imagining things. Eventually, in desperation, he'd developed his own private array of listening devices, but none of them was ever a channel for the mystery signal. It didn't use his devices. It just . . . arrived. And, doggedly, the Librarian would attempt to decode it.

So now, reverting to the habit of the location he finds himself in, he calls up a menu of active frequencies and chooses one at random. He squints into the monitor as the numbers scroll past.

The keyboard feels different when he sets his hands back on it: sleeker, more compact. He glances down and recognizes yet another old friend, from a slightly later time when he began to wear out his keyboard every six months. More books, piled at his elbow, his single shelf having overflowed. The familiar bibles are there: *Silent Spring, Limits to Growth,* the report from Rio, mixed in with his deep ecology journals and action alerts from Greenpeace and Earth First. For a moment, he's distracted by the hopefulness of all these pages of horrifying statistics and earnest prose. *If only we can get the word out, the people will listen!* The Librarian sighs and rubs his eyes. He believed that, then. He looks up again to find a bank of three monitors, each showing the processing of a different line of code. On the right-hand screen, a familiarity in the sequencing catches his eye. It's the signal he'd monkeyed with in order to free up its logjam. He types briefly, then waits for what seems like a lifetime. *Too slow, too slow,* he fumes. At this rate, the world will be burned to a cinder before he gets through to his dragon. At last, the screen offers him several options. When he lowers his fingers, the keyboard has become a chunky but functional laptop. The Librarian taps in his choice, and music enters the void like a friend walking into the room. A single plaintive guitar, and a voice he's sure he recognizes, even though he's never heard it singing before. He doesn't ask why he's hearing N'Doch sing. It's a pleasant and appropriate accompaniment to his work. And when he finds *her,* she will explain it all.

He calls up the frequency list, marks this one as identified, and moves on to the next. He ceases worrying about the limitations of his equipment. Each time he complains of a particular shortcoming, the machinery evolves to compensate. More memory, more speed. The CD-ROM drive. The emergency fuel cells and storage batteries. The voice recognition capability. And none of it is an illusion. Nothing so simple. The Librarian shrugs. No common standard of credibility can be applied to this situation. He believes in the material reality of place and machinery, equally, in each succeeding incarnation. It occurs to him after the first few mutations that it might all be a metaphor for processes actually taking place in his head, a sort of visual aid to help ground him and move him forward. Otherwise, wonder and disbelief might bring him to a dead halt. The Librarian can't afford wonder or disbelief. Not right now. Time, he knows suddenly, is of the essence.

He's in his loft in New York by now. He recalls the big steel desk and the double banks of monitors. It still smells old, but not so decrepit. Better digs, more add-ons, now that computing skills can equal an income. He has the Internet, and a hacker's access to the databases. Software engineer by day, eco-terrorist by night. The decoder works faster, almost as fast as he can think. He checks off several more signals. One sends instructions to the street-cleaning machines, simply and traditionally written in a long loop, so that when each machine has completed its assigned task, it will begin the process all over again. Another resolves easily into a video image: an elderly black man drinking espresso in a quaint twentieth century café. *Must be an old movie clip.* The Librarian lets the illogic of this notion pass, along with his temptation to watch for a while and see what happens next. He marks the frequency and moves on. The next several signals seem to be associated with the city's air quality maintenance and power routing. Another is a more complex set of machine instructions, but appears to be somehow damaged or degraded. *Tampered with,* the Librarian amends, then wonders why this conclusion came to him so surely and suddenly. He cannot quite make sense of it. In the next signal, the tampering is more obvious, like a text broken up by commentary from a nonnative speaker.

He sits back, glowering at the screen. N'Doch's song has ended. The silence is hollow and unfriendly. So far, the Librarian has judged all the code he's looked at to be of human origin. The additions strike him as something quite different.

What now?

The Librarian rubs his eyes some more, a habit he never has been able to break. He feels incapable of thought. His back is stiff with cramp and his well-padded butt is nearly fused to the chair. How long has he been at this? It doesn't seem like . . . but then, how would he know. He works life into his lower limbs, then gets up for a stretch. There's a bit more light to see by than before. When he turns away from the desk, his breath catches in his throat and he grabs for the chair again. Which is lower than it was. He starts, and almost tumbles sideways from the force of memory.

The space around him has evolved along with the equipment. Compact fluorescents dangle from the crossbeams inches above his head. He's in the first real bunker he'd built for himself at his vacation home in the mountains, once he saw the way things were going. He'd hired a local excavator to dig it into a steep hillside, claiming a fancy for a really big root cellar. Small for a large person, however. Dank and claustrophobic, exactly like an oversized grave, once the door was closed. The Librarian's animal origins kept him from panic, but as it turned out, he wasn't in it long. It had been unwise to let anyone know about a facility whose proper functioning depends on secrecy, no matter how far in advance of actual need the location is prepared. The excavator's family apparently had a long memory. The Librarian squeaked out of that crisis alive enough—they hadn't expected the "tree hugger" to be armed—but he'd made damn sure to dig the next hole by himself, when no one was looking.

Inhaling the earth-damp scent of the remembered burrow, he glances uneasily over his shoulder. How far does this memory world extend? What will he see if he undoes the several locks and dead bolts, lifts the steel crossbar, and shoves open the heavy wooden door? Wood. That had been the Achilles' heel. He couldn't see how to explain to his neighbors the need for a reinforced steel door on a little old root cellar. Eventually, they'd burned him out.

Interesting, the Librarian muses, *how many of my life-threatening events have involved fire. Just how long has this sonofabitch been at this?*

He stumps over to the door and lays a hand on the thick, rough planks. He doesn't really want to open it and see those lovely, lost pines, those fresh-scented hills rolling green over green over blue into a misty horizon. Dead now. All dead. Chopped down, wind-torn, bulldozed, burned out, poisoned, drought-killed, worm-eaten, pest-chewed, disease-ridden. The evergreens were the first to go. The Librarian sucks in the breeze blowing in his mind: the springy perfume of the needles, the sweet fern carpet beneath, the faint crush of wintergreen, the trailing whiff of wild stock from the meadow's edge. He's not easily given to weeping, never has been, but he knows that if he opens the door and sees those trees, he will be unable to hold back his tears.

He decides to be hungry instead. He goes looking for the refrigerator.

He'd installed one in this first bunker, using a buried power line. Later, what should have been obvious before became all too clear: he'd need his own power source as well. By the next time, solar techology was available to the rich, and the Librarian's cleverness with his keyboard had made him a lot of money. But this first, optimistic bunker lost power after the first three hours.

A tall white rectangle hums up out of the darkness in front of him. He flips open the door and finds exactly what he'd shoved in there so hastily when the time came to pull inside like a tortoise into its shell and barricade the inadequate wooden door. He finds ham from his pigs, and cheese and butter from his cows. Two loaves of bread. A roasted chicken. Eggs. Several bins of greens from the garden. Optimistic, indeed. How long did he think this would last him? How long did he think it would *need* to last him? Could he have guessed then that no length of time he thought of would be long enough? He'd been so sure he was well prepared.

He closes the refrigerator quietly. There'll be bushels of carrots and cabbage and potatoes stored away somewhere, and a row of tomato vines heavy with fruit, ripped out of the furrows in the last moments of his pack up. He feels around in the darkness behind the fridge and knocks his head against the hanging root balls, still moist from the ground. Soil cascades around him in a fragrant shower. The sharp green smell of bruised tomato leaves accomplishes what the Librarian has hoped to avoid by not opening the outer door. He slumps against the humming refrigerator and buries his face in his hands.

The tragedy was so fresh to him in those days. He had nothing to offset his despair. He hadn't yet worked out the purpose of his dragon-haunted existence, of his miraculous many lives—which were a tragedy of sorts in themselves, in that they forced on him a very, very long sort of view, and the fullest realization of how much, how terribly much, has been lost . . .not the least of which was any remaining faith he might have had in humanity. Each generation carries forward a part of the experience of the generations before it, but these recollections fade and mutate with time, even among such experts at oral tradition as the Tinker crews. Stoksie, for instance, with all his tales of what his father and grandfather said and saw, has never known a century-old oak tree, a real winter, or a truly green spring. He has only a borrowed, mythic notion of the truth, the real, entire truth which assails the Librarian yet again as he inhales the odors of his vanished hilltop garden.

How could such a clever species be so stupid, so shortsighted? No sensible animal fouls and destroys its own nest! Only the human animal.

Cast up on the sharp rocks of despair as if for the first time, the Librarian gives in at last, and weeps. Each time he has wept, he has sworn to be strong and never weep again. But always, always, the loss is too devastating, the ache too profound.

And this time, he seems to have lost his ability to haul himself back from the brink. This time, along with despair, there is doubt. The doubt is sudden and spreading, like a fast-working virus, like the oxygen being sucked out of his lungs. He's drowning in salt water and snot. What if . . . what if there is no dragon, no purpose, no rescue? What if he's made it all up, all of it: a tall tale to defend himself against

his paralyzing grief and hopelessness? What if he
didn't really live all those past lives? The Librarian
hears a high-pitched mewing. He wishes it would
stop, but it's him making that pitiful noise. What if
he's met no other dragons, never actually confronted
one of them on a sun-bleached mountaintop?

Wait.

The Librarian halts in mid-motion, massaging his
taut brow. His damp hands drop to his sides. He
turns toward the door. He smells smoke.

Smoke?

Is that it, then? The portal was a trap after all, and
he's to be forced to relive the very nearest of his
many near-death experiences? Well, he didn't panic
the first time, so he refuses to panic now. He goes
back to the door. The hardware, he remembers, trans-
mitted the heat of the fire outside long before the
wood began to burn. He flattens his soft palm against
the strap of a hinge. The smooth metal is cool, room
temperature at most. And the scent of smoke is
fainter by the door. The Librarian pads back to the
refrigerator, sniffing studiously. Nothing. Just his
imagination, as it were, overheating? He believes his
nose is more reliable than that. He replays the moment in his head, calling up the odor again. Not the
smell of wood burning at all. More like molten metal,
or rock. Magma.

Ah. Him. The Librarian has managed for a long
time to keep below the Intemperate One's radar, or
so he'd thought. But now, those days are over. He
glances about, expecting to see a different kind of
glow in the darkness, but the acrid tang is gone from
the earthy air of the burrow.

He was here, I'm sure of it . . . if only for a moment!

What let him in? The vividness of the memory?

If simply the recollection of burning allows the Fire Dragon access, the Librarian swears to banish all such thoughts. He yanks open the refrigerator door and fumbles among the vegetables until he finds the object of his search, smooth and slim and chill. He hauls it out, trying to remember how many he'd stashed back there and how long he can hold out before going back for the next one. He hasn't had a real beer in decades. He twists it open as he walks, but waits until he's seated again at the desk before taking his first long swig. *Ah. Much better.* Until the return of the hops blight, he'd brewed his own. No wonder he was so fond of the stuff. Giddy with nostalgia, he swivels his chair a few times, working up speed, then shoves off with his toes to see how many rotations he can manage in free flight. As the chair spins him around, he spots a reflective glimmer in a direction he hasn't explored yet. He drops his feet, dragging himself to a halt. Oh, yes, there was an old television over there. As the memory sharpens, the object clarifies and brightens. Just like manipulating a digital image. The TV is a slim-lined table model. The Librarian sets his beer down. He goes over to the television and brushes dust off the screen. Wasn't it broken past all repair? He'd never used it much even then, but for the hell of it, he tabs it on.

To his astonishment, he gets a picture. Immediately. He's further astonished when he recognizes the location. It's the Citadel. Somehow, this broken-down television is broadcasting the feed from one of the Citadel's security cameras. He's looking at a long view down an interior corridor. A still image, or maybe the hallway is empty right now. No, here comes someone hurrying past, huge and close to the lens at first, then quickly diminishing down the dim tunnel. The Librarian sees only shoulders and a back, large and male and carrying a spear. He rocks back on his heels pensively, then stabs a finger at the channel selector. Obligingly, the image blanks and a different camera comes on-line.

"Hunh," grunts the Librarian, and is startled by the sound of his own voice. He backs up to where he can feel for his chair without taking his eyes off the screen, then hauls it over and plants himself in front of the television. He shifts through the channels, bringing up each of the functioning cameras in succession, with static or blue-screen for the dead units in between.

"Hunh," he says again. Has his subconscious been screaming to know what's going on back home? He sits up suddenly, then swiftly backpedals to the desk. No reason why it should work, but he tries it anyway. His laptop has become a touch pad. He taps in the address he uses to call House at the Citadel. He gets an error message. He tries a few more times and gives up, but on a whim, keys in his own address at the Refuge, adding the command for voice transmission. The call goes through.

"Hello? Hello?" A boy's desperate query.

The Librarian clears his throat. "Mattias?"

"Who's there? Who is this?"

"Gerrasch, Mattias. It's Gerrasch."

"G? *Where are you?*" The boy's yell seems to penetrate the darkness at the Librarian's back. "I come back, you're *gone*! Just gone! Where are you?"

"Pipe down. My ears." Illusion or reality? He can't believe this is happening.

"I bin waitin' ferever!" The boy's Tinker accent rises with his pitch. "Weah are yu?"

"Difficult to explain. Not where you are. What's 'ferever?' What's happening there?"

"Yu okay? Yu alri'?"

"Yes, yes. What's up? Is Leif there?"

"Nah, he's gone! Dey're all gone, 'cept da little'uns! T'ree days, nah. Wuldn't let me go wit' dem! Said I gotta stay an' wait fer yu!"

"And here I am. You say Leif left three days ago?" It doesn't seem possible that three days have passed since he walked through the portal.

"Leif an' da 'hole army! Day shud be 'bout dere by nah."

The Librarian glances sidelong at the television. No sign of any action yet. That is, if what he's seeing on that screen truthfully represents the facts. "Food and water, Mattias? All you need?"

"Yah, shur. Dey lef' us ev'ryt'ing. But dere's nutting ta do heah. Yu commin' back soon?"

"Hope so. Listen, Matt. Boring, yes. But stay, okay? More important than you know. Safer if I can reach you."

"Safer yu, or safer me?"

"Both. The world."

Mattias groans, but it's only for show. "I be heah, G."

"Good. Now, patch me through to House."

"House! Oh boy, kint do dat, G. House wen' offline yestiddy."

This news convinces the Librarian that he's talking in real time. "Why?"

"Doan know. He jess blanked."

The Librarian reviews the list of the Citadel's surveillance cameras. There are none in the library or in the computer room. How can he find out what's happened to House? Meanwhile, there's an avalanche of code waiting to be sorted through and analyzed. Can't let himself be distracted from his search. He must bend his mind to the issue of the differing interpolations. House will have to take care of himself.

"Mattias. Stay on station. Keep trying House. I'll get back to you soon."

"Wait, G. Tell me whachu bin doin'."

"Can't right now, Matt. Later, okay?"

"Okay," concedes the boy heavily. "I guess. See yu soon den?"

"Hope so." The Librarian cuts the connection with no real conviction that he'll be able to establish it again at will. But soon he should be able to witness Leif Cauldwell's assault on the Citadel, at least from certain points of view. He wheels back to the television and tabs through to the camera trained on the Grand Stair. The landscape is sere and barren. Dust swirls off the wide, steep steps and is lost in curtains of heat shimmer. At the head of the stair, two Temple guardsmen huddle in the slim shadow of the terrace railing, their eyes slitted against the glare and windborne grit, fixed on the distant pale gash where the mountain pass empties onto the valley floor. When something happens, he'll notice. The Librarian leaves the channel tuned to that view, and returns to his code analysis.

He misses the boy's eager, trusting voice the second it's no longer with him, warming the darkness. He wishes N'Doch had not stopped singing. He needs no more eruptions of despair putting him off his course. He decides to attempt to trace the song's origin. At its current stage of evolution, his equipment should be able to go back and pinpoint a sig-

nal's location anywhere in the world. Of course, the
difference in time-location may intervene. He runs
the inquiry anyway. A bloom of cool light draws
his glance upward. A window-sized wall screen has
succeeded the monitor bank. On it, a brightly colored
schematic: a vast and repetitious grid. A map, the
Librarian decides. Of this very city. But not a map
of streets. A map of power distribution. A flow chart
of signal. He studies it with the eager anticipation of
a lover who's discovered his beloved's diary, as if it
had secretly been written for him only.

Certain things are immediately obvious. A green
dot marks the origin of the signal he's inquired
about. A red dot marks his own position. According
to the map, they're only a few blocks away from
each other. This is convenient but inconceivable. The
Librarian knows N'Doch is in twenty-first-century
Africa.

*On the other hand, I don't know exactly where I am,
do I? Or when.*

He runs the inquiry again and gets the same result.
He sets this conundrum aside as currently unsolv-
able, and goes back to the flow chart. A deeper perusal tells him that even this trove of information
will provide no easy answers. Nowhere does he find
the central nexus he's hoped for, pointing to a master
control. If the dragon draws from or imparts energy
to this network, she is not currently announcing her
presence. The Librarian downloads his disappoint-
ment into three long, deep breaths, and returns to
his methodical analysis, signal by signal.

He chooses a random city block for closer study,
one of countless seemingly identical squares. He en-
larges the scale by a factor of ten, and discovers that
what he has taken to be mere digital texturing in the

image is actually an underlying layer in the grid: more power lines, myriad and tiny, almost too small to be seen as individual signals. He increases the magnification by another factor of ten, then sits staring at the screen, trying to make sense of what he sees. He zeroes in on one line and magnifies it until a pattern reveals itself. More code. Infinite and infinitesimal beams of instructions, blanketing the entire city. Every meter, every centimeter, every millimeter, every . . .

The Librarian shoves back his chair and lurches to his feet. He glares around wildly. Comprehension lurks like a treasure in the darkness. It awaits him, rich and gleaming, if he's willing to make the leap. But it's a big one, and he fears the chasm in between. He starts to pace.

The space is smaller now, walled in by maps and monitors and wall screens. The void beyond exists only as stripes of darkness between. It's the Refuge. Not as he's recently left it, but as it was when he first came to it, sixty years earlier: raw, freshly painted, still smelling of wet concrete. Paia's grandfather was renovating the Cauldwell family compound fifty miles farther west. "Hardening," as it was called in those days. The Librarian stalls his epiphany with a moment of nostalgic revisiting.

His office down on the fourth level monitored the sea level rise. Next door to the left were the ozone boys. To the right, the Storm King, the scowling head of Meteorology whose office was always on high alert. The Librarian and his fellow post-docs told themselves how lucky they were to have wrangled jobs on high ground and in a secure location, away from the chaos in the cities, the food riots, the epidemics, and with all the hardware they could want.

Let's watch the planet go into the toilet on a hundred different screens in gorgeous living color! But of course, they all assumed the need would be temporary. With the horrors of the final collapse yet to come, they still thought their work had meaning, that civilization could be saved if there was somebody out there doing good science. And it could have been saved, if anyone in power had cared to listen. But Power has a very, very short view, the Librarian learned. It's just down the block to the intersection of Profit and Job Security. Daily in his office at the Refuge, it was someone else's turn to shove open the door and exclaim, "You're not gonna believe what they've done now!"

The Librarian is sorry not to see those weary young faces around him again. Long dead, most of them, or vanished back into the maelstrom in desperate search of family and loved ones, or for a reason to continue living. The Librarian has hoped for one or another of them to resurface among the Tinker crews, but sadly, none ever has.

He pads up to the old map he'd pinned to the wall next to the door, a huge, laminated USGS composite of the Adirondack counties. His red-penciled scrawl spiders the contour lines, notating an inked-in overlay that detailed the successive backing up of the Hudson River into the floodplain of its tributaries, and after that, into the lower valleys. New York City had gone under around the turn of the last century. The Librarian sets his toes against the base of the wall and brings his face up to the map until the tip of his nose is nearly touching the surface. The pale green-and-beige shapes blur out of focus. The thin red letters waver like splashes of blood. In his mind, he sees the machines in the city square, tearing up the patterned pavement and setting it right back down again.

"I know what you're made of," he murmurs to the map, suddenly willing to admit it. Not a dream. Not his imagination.

Nanotech. It has to be.

Nanotech. Still science fiction in those early days at the Refuge, but close enough to being a reality, if the resources for R&D hadn't dried up entirely. After the Collapse, the Librarian just assumed that technological development had ceased, and it was all downhill from there. He must have been wrong.

Nanotech.

He feels a big, involuntary grin stretch his face, his body responding to the news before his brain has registered all its implications. His feet shuffle out a little two-step. He wraps his arms around his barrel chest and gives himself a hug. Somehow, somewhere, progress has continued. The reign of the God of the Temple of the Apocalypse is not the Last Days. There is a future after all.

And . . .

The Librarian stills as the last insight drops into place. There is a future, and he's probably in it. Now. Right here.

Nanotech. How long did it take to develop? No wonder each remembered place has looked, felt, and smelled so real to him. They *were* real, as real as matter ever truly is. Built, then rebuilt upon the instant. A numberless submicroscopic legion of machines, working at the molecular level. A whole city created and maintained by their constant labor. Worlds of memory, remade as reality. Just add water.

The Librarian lets out a slightly mad cackle. He staggers back to his high backed, high-tech chair and throws himself into it. It absorbs the force of his weight and rebounds gently. He feels it mold obediently to the curve of his back. Creepy, but astonishing. He tries not to shiver with awe.

Nanotech.

Now that he's sitting down again, he can ask himself the really scary question. The existence of nanotech is a minor miracle compared to the really big mystery: how do all the little nanomechs have access to his personal memories? From where or whom are they getting their building instructions?

The Librarian is fairly sure he knows.

Chapter Nineteen

Erde returns to the garden and slides into a seat at the stone table. Looking into Rose's distant stare, she is convinced that a terrifying darkness lurks within. Much more than exhaustion has driven Rose of Deep Moor into retreat from the world.

"Should we bring her to him?" Raven asks.

"He says it would be better not to move her," Erde replies.

"I'm glad to hear it. Linden thought a change of scene might help, but I've been resisting that."

There's a third chair at the stone table under the apple tree, directly opposite Rose. Erde can't recall it being there before, but Raven takes it without comment. Rose's uncanny stillness doesn't mar the compassion and intelligence in her features. She is not a beautiful woman, like Raven, but certainly the one you would turn to in a crisis. Now, the crisis is hers. Though Rose's face is suffused with calm, it's the calm of withdrawal, not of being alert and in command of one's self. Erde is sure that some terrifying darkness lurks within that distant stare. Much more than exhaustion would be needed to drive Rose of Deep Moor into retreat from the world.

Erde seats herself, then signals Raven to join her at the table.

"Are you sure?" Raven has been holding back in the fragrant leaf-shadow of the rose arbor. "I won't be in the way?"

"Of course not. The more support we offer, the better, wouldn't you think?" She wonders if Raven expects a grand gesture of some sort. Whatever healing the dragon can manage, it will be a very quiet event.

Now, dragon . . . how shall we proceed?

I WILL NEED SOME BODILY CONTACT WITH HER IN ORDER TO DETERMINE IF THERE IS ANYTHING PHYSICALLY WRONG.

Erde is utterly certain that Rose's healing will not be so easily accomplished, but she is equally certain that things done properly must be done as the dragon requests. So she takes Rose's strong, mute hands in her own and quiets her mind to give the dragon room to do his good work. She pictures Rose busy and smiling, and lets the music of the garden fill her awareness: the birdsong, the hum of passing insects, Raven's shallow, anxious breathing. But all too soon, Earth has completed his exploration.

THE DAMAGE TO HER BODY IS NOT THE CAUSE.

But there is damage?

I MADE A FEW . . . ADJUSTMENTS THAT MIGHT BETTER NOURISH HER HEART AND MIND. BUT I DARE GO NO FURTHER.

Erde sets Rose's hands back on the table, side by side.

"What does he say?" Raven whispers.

"That the problem is in her mind."

"Can he heal that?"

"Do you remember at the Seeing, when I first came to Deep Moor and was still mute, how Rose could hear the dragon in her head?"

"I remember it was very painful for her."

"Exactly so. He worries that he'll make matters worse if he intrudes upon her thoughts, whatever they may be."

"So . . . ?"

"It will require a human touch to help her."

"A human touch in her mind?"

Erde nods. She is reaching her own understandings seconds before she must convey them to Raven.

"Would that be . . . yours?"

Erde nods again, less confidently. "So he says."

Raven settles back a bit, throwing one arm over the back of her chair. "I also recall Rose commenting on the power you would come into, once you found your voice." She tilts her dark head playfully, though her tone is serious. "I assumed she meant the voice you speak with."

"So did I. And so when I could speak again, and I didn't feel very different, I guessed she had misjudged, and put the whole thing from my mind."

"And now?"

"And now, I think it was I who misjudged. If only I could ask her. I feel that I should know, that I *need* to know."

Raven smiles. "Why so worried? I'm sure she meant your self, when you find your self. There's nothing wrong with growing up, even if you have been forced into it a bit prematurely."

"There is if you're not sure you like what you're growing into."

The terror comes at her in a wave, not like the surf

of the African beach where she first faced an ocean, but as she's always dreamed of it, sudden, towering, inexorable, and cold. "Oh, Raven, I'm so frightened!"

Raven leans forward. "Sweetling! Why so?"

"I feel like there's something . . . coming. Something I have to do."

"Then power will be a useful attribute."

Erde takes a long, slow breath. She is inches from hysteria and has no idea how it's caught her so unawares. She loves Raven, but Raven is cheerfully fatalistic, rather like the dragon. What happens, happens . . . and then one copes as best one can. Rose's insight is the sort Erde needs to help interpret this lowering cloud of portent. "When have you ever seen power put to use where it didn't hurt someone?"

"Power is a good thing when it's properly employed."

"No. No, it isn't."

"When your dragon heals someone, that's power put to a good use."

Erde shakes her head. She needs to be unreasonably stubborn until this terror and confusion make sense to her. "No, that's his Gift. Something he gives. Power is something that's imposed on people, whether they like it or not. Like my father tried to impose his will on me. Like Fra Guill wants to on all of us. Like the dragon Fire . . ."

"Easy, child. You're working yourself up into a state." Raven pats her shoulder, rubs her arm. "Have better faith in your own good nature."

"Rose didn't say powerful, she said 'dangerously charismatic.' *Dangerously!*"

Raven laughs, a rueful tinkle entirely without mockery. "I think she was being poetical, sweetling."

"No, I wasn't," says Rose. "I meant exactly what I said."

The other two stare at her in astonishment. Raven finds her voice first.

"Rose? Are you back with us? Are you all right?"

The awful insight that Erde was just on the point of realizing flies from her mind. "Rose!" She leaps up to envelop the older woman in a hug. "We were so worried!"

"Whatever for? I've been right here all along. Did I doze off?" Rose smiles and shrugs, raking her fingers through her graying curls. "Well, perhaps I did. I feel quite refreshed. But a good thing you called me. It's the first sign of age, you know. You're in your garden, with a spare hour finally to devote to the pruning and weeding, and you sit down to take a moment's peace in the sun, and off you go! The Land of Nod." She laughs and plants both hands determinedly on her knees. "I'll have to delegate one of the twins to keep an eye on me so I don't start sleeping through supper." Her eyes light on the sectioned apple in front of her. The edges are browning already, but Rose doesn't seem to care or notice. She grabs one and shoves it into her mouth.

Erde's hands have lingered on Rose's shoulders, but she lets them slide away as she meets Raven's sober glance.

"Supper," says Raven hopefully. "You must be starving. You haven't eaten since . . ."

"I had lunch, just like everyone." Rose brandishes a second section of apple. "Don't fuss! Why are you both fussing so? All I did was doze off. Goodness, I think I'll survive."

"That's our Rosie. Get her going and you can't shut her up." Raven's laugh lacks her usual contagious glee. Rising, she fans herself elaborately. "How about something cool? Oh, this heat. I'll just run for a celebratory pitcher."

"Wonderful," agrees Rose. "What are we celebrating? The berry harvest? A new arrival in the barn? Is somebody pregnant? You both looked so somber a moment ago, I thought something awful had happened." Her face brightens. "Ah! Is it Heinrich? Is he coming? Is he back from the war? You should have woken me earlier!"

Raven reaches the end of her inspiration. Her arms float upward in a helpless shrug. "Rose, darling . . . we tried." To Erde, she says, "I'm going for food and to tell the others. You try to explain to her."

"What? Wait. Me?"

But Raven has whirled away through the arbor, leaving Erde alone with Rose, who calmly reaches for another section of apple and offers up her wisest, most sympathetic smile. "Explain, eh? Tch, tch. Sounds dire. What mischief have you been up to now? Has Lord Earth eaten one of Doritt's precious breeding ewes?"

Erde's eyes widen involuntarily. In an instant, she is a child again. "He'd never do that! Never! At least, not without asking!"

"I know, I know. I'm only joking. But you're up to something, I can see that much. Come on, out with it!"

Erde can see Rose preparing to be stern if necessary. She wonders what storybook day in her life at Deep Moor Rose believes she is living. She hates herself for being the one who must drag this smiling woman out of her dreamworld into a present where Deep Moor lies in smoking embers. "Raven wants me to explain where we are."

Rose blinks. Her shoulders lift and tighten, as if to ward off a blow. Then she slides back her chair, rising, leaning over the table to sweep apple cores and stems into the palm of one hand. "I'll just clear up a bit here, so Raven will have room for the tray."

"Please, Rose . . ."

"No, no, I must. You know how Raven hates a mess, especially when there's food around." Rose's hands are busy, busy at the tabletop. Her eyes dart everywhere, except at Erde.

Dragon, help me!

YOU KNOW I CANNOT. NOT WITH THIS.

Why has Raven left this awful task to me?

PERHAPS SHE BELIEVES YOU ARE BEST SUITED FOR IT.

No! Not me!

Erde longs for Raven's speedy return. If she won't help, she'll at least bring Linden, who'll know much better what to do. "Rose, please sit down and rest yourself."

Rose carries the apple cores to a corner of the garden. "Rest?" She uses the little paring knife to scratch up a section of dirt. "I've never felt more rested! I wasn't really napping just now. I was thinking, while you girls just chattered on and on." She buries the apple cores neatly and comes back to the table, dusting her palms and still refusing to meet Erde's gaze. "On and on."

"What were you thinking about?"

Rose's shoulders tighten again. She turns away, frowning. "I really must find more time to work in the garden. The weeds are positively taking over!"

Erde cannot spot even the trace of a weed. In Rose's reconstruction of Deep Moor, there wouldn't be any. "Tell me what you were thinking about."

Rose's hands weave patterns of warding in the air, but her reply is casual. "Oh, it was nothing. Just a dream I had."

"A dream?"

"A nightmare, if you really want to know." Rose bends to the flower pots clustered around the apple tree, deadheading barely spent blooms. "I have them all the time lately. Too much red meat, Linden tells me."

"I'm sure she's right," murmurs Erde, thinking exactly the opposite. How peculiar—she has become the elder, and Rose has become the child. She recalls what her beloved nurse Alla used to say when she woke up paralyzed by night terrors. "Maybe if you tell me about it, it won't bother you anymore."

Rose snorts. "Maybe if I tell you about it, that will remind me what it was. Can't really recall it now, so it can't have been too important."

"Are you sure? You can't remember anything about it?" Terror beats birdlike at the inside of her ribs, roused by the recollection of childhood. Which is ending, Erde understands. It can only mean that her destiny is close at hand. But why should the very thing she's looked forward to and fought to attain cause her such sudden palpitations? She looks up and catches Rose gazing at her. Before the older woman can glance away, their eyes meet and Erde is staring into the eyes of Death itself: raw, despairing, ravaged by horror and guilt.

"What is it?" she whispers hoarsely, but the moment is gone.

Rose turns away with a dismissive shrug. "No, can't recall a thing about it. I had a book out here a while ago. Have you seen it?"

"No. I haven't."

"Come into the library a moment while I look for it." Rose's hand is already on the latch.

"Rose, you can't . . . there isn't any . . ."

Rose unlatches the door and swings it wide. "Might as well let some fresh air in anyway. It's such a perfect day! Isn't it wonderful, after all the rain we've had?"

"Rain?"

But Rose has disappeared inside. Erde hurries after her, and finds herself in the cool, wood-paneled shade of the book room—which, according to Raven, should not be there. Leaf-scattered sunlight filters through the many-paned windows along the outside wall. Erde glimpses the rolling spread of the valley through the branches, a glint of silver water, and the green hills beyond. She sees she will have to be extra vigilant. There's no place she'd rather be than in this perfect vision of Deep Moor, existing first in Rose's mind, and now all around them as Rose reconstructs it. It will not help Rose or anybody if she is drawn into Rose's world, instead of the other way around.

Rose is at the end of the room, searching among the piles of leather-bound volumes scattered across the big reading table. *Piles* of them! Before arriving at Deep Moor, Erde had never seen so many books in one place that piles could be made of them. Big books, used so often that they were left lying about, instead of hidden away under lock and key. Her father's castle had no library. It would have been unseemly for Baron Josef von Alte to be seen indulging in unmanly pursuits such as reading and study.

Rose picks up a book and leafs through it, seemingly at random.

"Did you find it?" Erde tries to sound casual. "What were you reading?"

"Oh, something about . . . something . . . I forget."

BE FIRM, the dragon reminds silently.

Erde folds her arms and plants her shoulder resolutely against the doorpost. "Rose, doesn't it seem odd that you can't remember anything? You are not a forgetful person."

Rose flicks a wrist and reaches for another book. "Getting old, like I said." She sets the book aside and begins to rearrange the piles.

"But you're not. And it's even odder that you, the calmest person that I know, suddenly cannot sit still even for a minute!"

"Do you need me to sit still? There's so much to be done!"

"I need you to listen . . . and remember."

Rose sighs and rolls her eyes. "Remember what, dear girl?"

"Where you are. Where you *really* are."

Now Rose's protest is faintly irritable. "I'm here. Where else should I be?"

As a child, Erde wasn't known for her patience. Impetuous, impulsive, stubborn: these were the accusations commonly hurled at her by her chambermaid, who felt that little girls should sit in the corner and sew. But even this self-knowledge does not prepare Erde for the force of the impatience that boils up in her as she sees Rose turn back to her useless tidying and stacking.

"Rose!" Her summons fills the entire room, though she has hardly raised her voice. She almost steals a look behind to see who has spoken with such authority.

Rose goes as still as a startled deer. "What is it, child?"

As soon as she has Rose's attention, authority fails her.

Oh, dragon! Now what?

YOU'RE DOING FINE.

"Please, Rose, let's sit down."

Rose sidesteps obediently to the nearest chair and settles herself with her hands folded neatly on the table. "You're upset."

"I am, but only because I'm so worried about you."

Erde takes the chair beside her. Perhaps this will seem less confrontational. She detects a desperate sort of defiance in Rose's posture, uncharacteristic in a woman normally so confident in herself and in everything she believes in. It will be an unforgivable cruelty to force Rose to remember the terrible events that drove her into this state of forgetfulness. But it must be done, or Rose, the real Rose, wise and present, will be lost forever.

THE ROSE WHOSE GIFT IS SEEING THINGS AS THEY TRULY ARE.

Yes, dragon, I know. But it will be so painful to her.

IT WAS PAINFUL TO N'DOCH WHEN YOU DRAGGED HIM AWAY FROM THE LIFE HE KNEW AND FORCED HIM TO ACCEPT HIS ROLE IN THE QUEST.

I didn't . . . how did I force him? Surely Lady Water did that.

IT WAS PAINFUL TO THE WARRING BARON YOU KIDNAPPED TO FIGHT BATTLES NOT HIS OWN.

Because we needed him! And it saved his life!

TRUE, AND TRUE. BUT BOTH AGAINST HIS WILL.

This accusation she cannot deny, though Köthen might feel differently about his suicidal urges now. Erde is shaken by the realization that she's been bending others to her will all along, while excusing her actions as childish impetuosity. All she's done has been in the service of the dragons, always, but it's been willful nonetheless. Even though her understanding of the Quest has been imperfect, as it has several times proved to be.

THIS CURRENT DUTY IS PAINFUL TO YOU AS WELL, SO YOU RESIST IT. BETTER TO ADMIT TO THE NEED, THEN TAKE FULL RESPONSIBILITY FOR YOUR DEMANDS.

Full responsibility. The dragon's tone is mild, but it carries the power of a warning. Her willful actions were necessary, of course, but there'll be no more laying the blame on accident or the dragons or the forces of destiny. Destiny, presumably, is something that happens whether you act or not, but it takes no account of human feelings. Neither has she, because she's seen herself as Destiny's tool. Erde bows her head. Perhaps this explains her high failure rate at predicting human behavior.

I understand, dragon . . . I think.

When she looks up again, Rose is staring at her, trembling.

"He's here, isn't he?"

"He? Here?" Erde is sure she means the hell-priest.

"Earth."

"Oh. Yes. Of course. He's right outside. Why should that frighten you?"

Rose covers her face with her hands. "He'll make me See it again."

Erde slips an arm around Rose's shoulders. "He won't make you do anything, you know that. He's here to help you."

"He will require the truth."

"He will *ask* the truth, *expect* the truth, but only as you're able to give it."

"How can I say no to a dragon?"

Erde smiles, seeking some way to put Rose more at ease. "That's what I've always said. But you haven't met Lord Fire yet."

Instead of relaxing, Rose shudders, muttering into her hands. "Perhaps I have, or at least his handiwork."

The image of the smoldering, blackened farmstead hovers invisibly between them. Erde bites back her own outburst of grief and rage to allow Rose room to maneuver. "Is Deep Moor the truth you fear?" she murmurs. "The dragon knows it already. We were there, too late to warn you."

"Ah." Rose's hands slide away from her eyes, as if concealment is finally pointless. "Then let him be satisfied with that. Enough truth for any heart to bear, even a dragon's."

THERE IS MORE.

What more can there be? Can't we let her be for a while?

THERE IS MORE. YOU MUST PRESS HER FURTHER.

But it's like torturing her!

AND YET, YOU MUST ASK.

"Rose, dear, the dragon asks . . ." She's doing it again, blaming the dragon, but surely his requests will carry more weight.

"No." Rose twists her head away like a recalcitrant child. "No more. There is no more."

"He says there is."

"No no no no."

"Please, Rose. What further truth did your Seeing reveal?"

Rose flings both arms out and away toward the sunny window as if yelling for help. She struggles to rise. Erde holds her fast, and is surprised to learn that she is the stronger.

"Truth about what?"

"No no no nonono!"

"Rose! Whatever it is, running away will never change it!"

Rose cries out, the hoarse helpless wail of the lost, and collapses against the back of the chair, into Erde's encircling arm, grabbing at the edge of the table and hanging on as if she might fall or be dragged away. Shivering as if being flailed by an invisible hand, she gasps, "The truth about what I Saw!"

Look what we've done, dragon! Is there nothing you can do to help?

I CAN ONLY BE, BUT THAT MAY OFFER SOME COMFORT.

Erde feels his presence draw in around them, as the trees in a glade, or the tall grasses in a meadow. Gently, in a secret zone of safety and warmth and the sweet scents of summer, Erde rocks the quaking, sobbing woman, soothing her with whispered nonsense, until Rose has exhausted herself and at last lies quietly with only the occasional shiver. Erde contemplates the miraculous medicine of bodily contact, parent to child, friend to friend, lover to lover, the surest antidote for the loneliness of despair.

With a last shudder that rumbles through her like a small earthquake, Rose gets hold of herself and releases her death grip on the table. "Oh my oh my

oh my." She sits up, weakly brushing at her cheeks.
Erde offers the corner of her linen tunic. Rose waves
it away and gathers up the length of her skirt. When
she notes its stained folds and its frayed and dirty
hem, she laughs ruefully. "Oh, dear. I guess this
should be proof enough for me."

"Proof of what?"

"That I'm not where I'd like to pretend to be. Not
at Deep Moor, whole and safe. Isn't that what Raven
wanted you to explain to me?"

"Yes. Yes, it is. Oh, Rose, I'm so sorry!"

Rose nods, her lips tight. "Of course. But it's a war,
child, and we must keep at it, or evil will triumph."

"Never! And that's why *the dragon* needs you to
tell us what you Saw!"

"You are persistent, aren't you!"

Hope blooms like a sigh in Erde's chest. "And you
are at last the Rose that I remember. The Rose who
can face anything!"

"Apparently she can't, or you wouldn't be suffering through all of this."

"Dearest Rose, it's you who's been suffering."

Rose sighs, a great heaving release and giving in,
and wraps her arms around herself, rocking with
shuttered eyes, gathering resolve. Finally, she says
quietly, "It's more possible to speak of in recollection,
but even now, I . . . I can hardly believe . . . it doesn't
seem . . . it can't . . . yet I know the truth of what
I Saw!"

Erde settles her features into a facsimile of patience, though she feels Rose's barely restrained
dread seeping like ice into her own veins. "Maybe if
you begin at the beginning? At Deep Moor?"

"No. No, child. Even in the safety of tale-telling,
I've no heart to relive that awful journey. The flames,

the screams, my dear friends and companions felled and dying, Guillemo's death's-head grin . . . he'd reached his transcendent moment, and I . . . I had to take whatever escape was offered."

Erde wonders if she means the portal or her fantasy-trance of Deep Moor. "Of course, and you did right."

Rose shakes her head. "Death might have been more merciful."

"How can you say that! Fra Guill has no mercy! He'd have put you all to the stake!"

"No doubt. And yet . . ."

"Rose, Rose, what can be worse than the end of life?"

Rose's gaze is the bleaker for being so calm. "The end of *all* life."

"What?"

"I know you think me melodramatic, but that is what I Saw."

"I don't understand."

"Nor do I. I only know it was true. Is true." Rose sits up straighter, suddenly insistent, indomitable. "I Saw . . . that everything is gone. It's all an illusion."

Erde frowns, still missing the meaning. "What is?"

"This . . . this . . ." Rose's hands scribe airy circles. "This place."

"This house?"

"This house. That garden. That absurdly lush green lawn. And the awful city outside. All of it. All."

"The city is an illusion?" Luther, Erde recalls, had expressed a similar opinion of the city's clean and empty streets. "But we walked in it."

"Oh, yes." Rose gives the tabletop a trio of sharp raps. "It seems real enough. Or at least, solid and material. But it's not . . . true. I can't explain it. I did not See *how* the city is, I Saw what *is*, what the whole world is, behind the illusion."

Erde hesitates, appalled. Should she trust the word of a woman who's been sunk for a week in illusions of her own? "What . . . what is it?"

Rose plants her palms on the table, the same defiant pose she held for so long out in the garden, holding at bay the temptation to turn away again from her horrific vision. "The earth is . . . empty. Barren. Everywhere. Lifeless. Bare windswept rock. Oceans of sand. Desert. No sign left of the works of man, except for mountains of shattered stone, and the gaping pits left from the digging of it. Nature, too, has been defeated. There's not a tree, a blade of grass, not even a weed, anywhere. Only dust and dead rock and howling wind."

Rose squeezes her eyes shut, shivering with memory, then opens them and turns her gaze on her companion. If asked, Erde would have said that her eyes are a warm brown, but now they seem as vast and black as a starless sky.

"Perhaps this is Hell," Rose murmurs. "Perhaps that's where the hell-priest has driven us."

"I don't know. Can it be?"

Dragon, what do you say to this? What if this is not our future world after all, but some magical other place we've come to through that portal?

I SAY THAT THIS EXPLANATION AVOIDS THE TRUTH. THERE IS ONLY ONE REALITY, DESPITE APPEARANCES, AND WE ARE IN IT.

Erde shoves rising terror down with a mighty effort. No time for terror now. She must be adamantine, or else give up entirely. "The dragons think the city is our far future," she tells Rose, as if it was the most reasonable idea in the world.

"It could be our future, and still be Hell," Rose replies. "If Hell is any place without life or hope, then we are in it. Not the hell of the Church—you know I don't believe in that. I tried to pretend it was a nightmare or a vision of warning. But, limited as it is, my Gift has never failed to provide what it promises: knowledge of what is. So I had to believe it. Outside the illusion of these walls, that city, the world is a lifeless place."

Then I must believe it, too.

But if she does, what is left? The implications of Rose's Seeing are too vast and terrible for her to encompass in an instant. Erde has listened to N'Doch rail about the destruction men worked on the world. She's seen the results of that destruction in the devastated landscape where the Tinker crews struggle for survival. She's heard Luther's sermonizing about the coming of the Last Days of the Earth, but all of it seemed like a story, a cautionary tale that she could take to heart and move away from. Until now. She's abruptly aware of the silky wood beneath her damp and shaky palms, of the homey creak of her chair's leather seat. How can reality be both material and an illusion? And where does the illusion come from?

If it's the hell-priest's illusion, dragon, why would he give us back all that we've lost?

SO THAT WE MAY SUFFER ALL THE MORE IN THE KNOWLEDGE OF WHAT WE'VE LOST.

Ah. Yes.

No wonder Rose retreated from the knowledge, pulling the comfort of a lie over her head like a favorite quilt. Erde would do it, too, if she could be a child again, and crawl into Rose's lap to be comforted. But she will have to live without comfort, they all will, from now on.

Is it the end of the world, then, dragon? Have we come too late? Has our Quest failed?

I SAID THERE WAS ONE REALITY. I DID NOT SAY IT COULD NOT BE CHANGED.

But how?

THAT'S WHAT WE'VE COME TO THE END OF THE WORLD TO DISCOVER.

Of course! And while we live, there's hope. Is it not so, dragon?

IT IS SO. THE BATTLE IS NOT ENDED.

Erde slides her arm around Rose's slumped shoulders to offer a comforting hug. "Well, then, we shall just have to think of what to do next."

Chapter Twenty

"So . . . are we good to go?" N'Doch asks again. The guitar, he notices, has a colorful woven strap on it now. He slings the big instrument across his back, reminded of Köthen and his sword. Not such a big stretch. Music can be a weapon, too.

Now there's *something to write a song about.*

N'Doch grins. Tight and wide, stretching the muscles in his cheeks. It's what, in his gang days, he called his "fighting grin," almost involuntary, showing a lot of teeth and fueled by anticipation and adrenaline. "Are we ready set?"

Djawara nods. "As ready as we'll ever be."

They both look to Paia, who looks down and away, then quizzically to the only calm face in the room. "I can't believe I'm doing this."

Water-as-Sedou smiles, catlike. "We'll be safe here, for the time being."

N'Doch rolls his eyes. "Doesn't exactly inspire confidence. . . ."

"You'll be safe," says Paia, "but will I? Just as I

can summon him against his will, he has the same power to compel me."

Sedou nods. "That very connection is our greatest hope of winning him over. Be strong, and keep our true purpose in mind."

"Easy for you to say," mutters N'Doch.

"Not really. I'll retire to a corner to begin with. It's sure to be useful if he can be kept unaware of my presence at first." Sedou studies the long dim room for possible darkened corners, then his eye lights on the bar with its shelves of glimmering glassware and mirrors behind. "I'll be . . . the bartender." He moves away with a rapid blurring of profile and slips behind the counter. When he turns to face them, he's wearing a classic bartender's shirt and apron. He flips a towel over his shoulder and leans against the gleaming wood as if born to the trade. "What can I get you folks?"

"He'll nose you out soon enough," says Paia.

N'Doch is inclined to agree. "Just don't look him in the eye. Yours are a dead giveaway."

"Maybe so." Sedou turns to Paia. "But he won't be thinking about me at first. He'll be thinking about you." He drags the towel off his shoulder and polishes the top of the bar. "Something to drink?"

Djawara rises stiffly. "A little cordial might be fortifying."

"Hey, I thought you were kidding! You got a Spark Orange?" N'Doch strides over hopefully. "Girl, you want something?"

Paia shakes her head numbly.

"Gimme two of 'em!" He brings the sweet citrus concoction to her anyway. Paia turns the bottle in her hand like a foreign object. "Go on, try it! I bet you never had soda in a glass bottle before, right?

Guess what? Neither have I. But Papa Dja always used to tell me how it was much better in the bottle than in the box." He salutes his grandfather and lifts the bottle to his lips.

Paia watches dubiously. "I've never had a soda at all."

"Don't swill it down like he does." Djawara sips delicately at his slim-stemmed glass as if to underline his point.

N'Doch drains his soda and sets it aside with a satisfied belch. "Now, how do we go about this?"

Paia's tone is more collected than her body language. She fusses with her hair and straightens her clothing. "I just call him and we see if he comes."

"Shouldn't you be sitting down or something?"

His solicitude raises a wan laugh, which was exactly his purpose. If he has to play the clown in order to lighten things up a little, N'Doch doesn't mind. "All right, then. You go, girl."

She perches on the rounded arm of the sofa, more like a girl waiting for her date to show up than a woman about to conjure a fire-breathing killer. She takes a breath and seems to turn her awareness inward. The rest wait in silence for a minute, for two. Then Paia says, "Ah," and N'Doch is aware of a difference in the room, as if a wind has shifted or the temperature's risen very suddenly. He tenses, expecting smoke and fireworks of the sort he's seen up on the mountain. He wishes he had a more obvious weapon in hand than a guitar. Seconds later, there's a sharp rap on the front door.

"Oh, that's excellent," Djawara murmurs.

"What? The door's locked?"

"No. This one can't come in unless he's invited. A good sign. Remember? The other walked right in."

The rapping sounds again, louder, more preemptory. The shadow on the frosted glass is human-shaped but larger than human size.

"If I don't let him in, he'll be furious," says Paia, as if she wishes someone else would volunteer.

Interesting, N'Doch muses, that she looks to Djawara for permission, not Sedou or himself. "Can't we just yell at him through the door?"

The old man sets down his glass. "Allow me."

"Papa . . ." N'Doch starts forward, but Djawara, steely-eyed, waves him back. His first few steps are cramped and slow, but he's striding along briskly by the time he reaches the door. The flat daylight falls through the glass onto his dark face and erect back, making his grizzled head and white robe shine.

And the angel let in the devil. The lyric is already writing itself in N'Doch's head. He pulls the guitar around in front of him, fingers fitting themselves to the strings. *Now the devil said, open up, open up. So the angel let him in.*

Djawara opens the door and stands beside it. "Lord Fire. Please join us."

Fire fills the opening, shimmering gold and red, a haze of smoke behind him. Pale, questing tendrils approach the doorway and draw back. The man/dragon is forced to duck under the lintel, making it awkward for him to sweep through the doorway as he has obviously intended. Once inside, his glitter fades slightly, as if he's walked into shadow. Irritated, he pauses, squinting into the dim room beyond.

Djawara holds out his hand. "Welcome. I'm . . ."

"I know who you are." Fire brushes past him. "Where is she?"

At the bar, Sedou has turned his back to the door

and is busily wiping down the espresso machine until its chrome and copper gleam.

Paia steps into the pool of soft light from the nearest chandelier. "Here. I am here."

She and Fire stare at each other—rather hungrily, N'Doch thinks—across the scattering of empty chairs and tables.

"You are looking well, as always, beloved," Fire croons.

"You are looking . . . odd."

"Odd? Odd?" She has startled him. He preens defensively.

"I mean, why are you . . . aren't you . . . what are you wearing?"

What's really odd, N'Doch decides, is that she looks so disapproving. Having only seen the Firebreather buck-naked except for a sinuous cloak of flame, he assumes that full parade dress is the dragon's normal clothing in man-form. Besides, why should she care what he wears? Back in 2013, all the power brokers are in uniform. Except for Baraga, whose personal drag is silk, a designer business suit. Fire's uniform is close fitting and smoothly tailored in a rich blood red. Gold glints at his high collar and across his chest. With his half-scaled skin and his furious red-gold locks, he looks like a battle-weary alien commander stepping off his starship. Either that, or a rock star, whose faintly dimmed postconcert luster makes him seem more approachable. N'Doch wants to find the Fire-breather vile and grotesque, but instead, the bile he tastes is envy. He can't help thinking the dude looks absolutely splendid.

Fire tugs invisible wrinkles out of his sleeves. "My estates are under attack, may I remind you? And the

Temple is in a shambles. How devious of the traitorous Son Luco to neglect the training of a competent successor! I am at war wherever I turn, thanks to you."

Paia's chin lifts. "The Temple's command structure was loyal to their head priest, not to you. And my cousin seeks only to regain what belongs to us. Remember that the Citadel was mine before you seized control of it."

"Seized?" Fire snarls. "You welcomed me gladly! I brought order to chaos! Where would you and your ingrate cousin be now if I hadn't come along? Dead. Both of you. Starvation, disease, attack from squatters or war bands, you name it. You would owe your life to me even if you weren't bound to me by Destiny!"

"That debt was paid by our years of servitude in your temple! And how dare you invoke Destiny when you're so busy denying it?"

N'Doch feels like he's at a grudge match. Fire hasn't stirred from his position of power by the door, and Paia has refused to go toward him. Already they're yelling across the room at each other. He sees how it is with these two. Together much longer than the other dragons and their guides, their years of contention have compounded until every conversation starts at an inflated level, so weighted by emotional baggage that any possibility of amity is doomed from the start. His stance is aggressive, hers as sullen and passive as a child. They're like a married couple who don't get along, but just can't imagine divorce. The most archetypal of the dragons turns out to exhibit the most human failings? There's a lesson in this, N'Doch muses, as he risks a glance toward the bartender.

Maybe this wasn't such a useful idea.

NO TALK. HE MIGHT HEAR.

And Fire lifts his magnificent head, listening. N'Doch moves toward the bar. Hide in plain sight, he tells himself. He leans back against the fat ogee softening the counter's edge. He has to crane his neck upward to meet Fire's reptilian eyes. He knows he should feel driven to spit in his face, shout "murderer." Or ram his fists into actual flesh, spew venom, acid, flame, anything to destroy the dragon's awesome supercilious beauty. Instead, strumming the guitar flung across his chest, he says, "Can I get you a drink, general? What's your poison?"

The distraction works. Fire tosses off a sneer as sharp as a shuriken and returns his attention to Paia. "Why have you called me here?"

Paia says nothing. N'Doch is alarmed by how obviously shaken she is, how she can't keep her eyes off the glittering giant. But her silence seems to mean something else to Fire.

"I suppose you hope to lure me from the defense of my kingdom. But you'll be disappointed, beloved. Time is in my favor. I am able, no matter how long I am here, to return to the battle mere seconds after I left!"

N'Doch recognizes a vainglorious boast when he hears one. He's been guilty of enough of them himself, and a few times he's been caught out because of them, having given up too much information in the boast, thereby making himself more vulnerable. *So get him to brag and run his mouth,* he decides. Something useful is bound to turn up.

"I wasn't thinking about your battles," Paia replies.

Fire throws his weight back on one foot and crosses his arms satirically. "Then perhaps you've come to your senses and wish to be rescued. The company you're keeping since you left me gets less interesting each time we meet."

"I need to talk to you."

"Talk? *Talk?*" He flings his red-clad arms wide. "My Temple is burning, my Faithful are being slaughtered, and you need to *talk*?" He makes a great show of gathering up his patience. "All right, then. What is it? Shouldn't we go somewhere more private? I don't see your new concubine hanging about." He tilts his head, a lampoon of sadness. "Oh, is that it? He's ditched you already?"

"Is the Citadel really burning?" Paia stands up a little straighter.

The golden eyes narrow. N'Doch notes the quick calculation: which answer is more likely to rouse her sympathy and interest? Despicable as he is, his goal is to win her back. "Not yet, but every second that I am away from the line of defense brings that possibility closer. So state your business, and let me be on my way."

Shrugging off her pout at last, Paia mimics his stance. "I thought it didn't matter how long you're away."

"Impertinence is unbecoming in a woman, beloved. What do you wish to talk about?"

"Your sister Air."

Fire stares at her as if she's said the unpardonable, then looks away, out the window into the empty street. "I have no sister."

"A lie. You have two."

"My enemies feed you lies. I say I have no sister."

N'Doch thinks it's time to provide a little reinforcement. "Too late for that, general. You already admitted to it up on the mountaintop. How 'bout this: you have an enemy . . ."

Fire's glance at Paia is venomous. "I have many enemies."

"Well, we'd like to negotiate for the release of the one called Air."

It sounds right to N'Doch, like they do it in the vids: no beating around the bush, if you want to sound serious. Besides, what else can you say to the creep who's murdered your mother? Small talk just doesn't cut it. But Fire ignores him, driven at last into restless motion. He paces around the café, his knee-high boots clicking smartly on the little black-and-white tiles. He takes in its details and full measure, as if he was thinking of buying it. He studies the posters on the cracked walls. He pauses before the narrow door that says *monsieurs*. He stares up at the glass-and-brass chandelier just inches above his head until, apparently, curiosity gets the better of him. "What is this place?"

"My favorite café back home." Djawara accepts the diversion as if happy to share a pleasurable nostalgia. "An exact replica."

"I leveled your home."

"Indeed you did. I meant, in the city back home."

"Your favorite?"

"I spent many fond hours there."

"I shall seek it out and destroy it immediately."

The old man snorts gently. "No need. The politicians did the job for you long ago, when N'Doch was still a boy. One faction pulled down the old place to build themselves an expensive office building. As soon as it was finished, another faction blew it up. It's a pile of rubble now, like much of the city."

Fire looks interested, perhaps nosing out a weapon he hasn't yet considered. "How sad for you."

Djawara shrugs, nodding.

Fire wanders a bit more, smoothes a gilt-nailed hand along the length of the bar as if enjoying actual contact with its material surface. He gives the bartender's muscular back a long moment of consideration, then moves on. "And how does your café come to be here, in *my* city?"

"Is it your city? I wondered."

"It is, since the day I claimed it. This was not here until now."

"It was not here until I created it."

"Really? Aren't you clever?" Fire jerks his thumb at the bartender. "Did you create him, too?"

Djawara beams. "I did! Isn't he convincing? After all, can't have a bar without a bartender."

"Of course not."

N'Doch is sure the Fire-breather has a tactical reason for this satirical display. Is he hoping to catch us off guard with his willingness to banter and admit ignorance? Or hoping to figure out how much we know? Or both? N'Doch senses his grandfather mulling over how much ignorance to admit to in return.

Scowling, Fire begins a second circuit of the room, studiously avoiding Paia, too impatient to wait the old man out. "A dull sort of place, to spend the rest of your lives."

"I don't expect it will be that long," Djawara replies.

Fire grins at him, as if they were becoming fast friends. "How pleasantly ambiguous, old man. Should I take you for an optimist or a pessimist?"

"Take me for whichever you wish. And I will take you for a renegade and a murderer."

"Tch! Insults!"

"What are your terms for the release of the dragon Air?"

"Oh, that old song. I liked the quaint little café better."

"Your terms?"

"No terms. Prisoners do not negotiate."

"Be nice, general," says N'Doch. "You're in our space now."

"The instant you walk out that door, you're in mine, and you *know* what I will do to you. So . . . prisoners." Fire starts his third circuit, this time staring at Paia all the while. Paia tries to stare back at him, but soon gives up to gaze in confusion at the floor.

"But that's not entirely true, is it?" Djawara continues. N'Doch admires his grandfather's speculative tone. It's as if nothing more was at stake in this debate than a proper understanding of the argument. "This was just another blank city block until I created the Rive in its place. Or should I say, until something allowed it to be created from my memory. . . ."

Fire gestures grandly around the room. "You wish to disavow this charming bit of magic?"

"Not I. I have no magic. But magic there is. It appears that we have a protector."

"You put great stock in mere illusions, old man."

"Can an illusion keep me fed and safe? Was it mere illusion that required you to knock before entering? Perhaps when I walk out that door, I will create the Rue Senghor, further neutral territory, which will allow me safely to create the Marché, which will lead me safely to create the . . ."

Fire halts his circular pacing. "Try it, then!" He stabs a forefinger at the door. "I dare you! You escaped me once in your own territory. You think you can manage so well in mine?"

"As long as my protector is listening." Djawara moves toward the door.

N'Doch leaps to stop him. "Papa, no. You see what he's doing, right? Turning it into a pissing contest, just to get us off center!"

"I have no need to waste my energy," says Fire. "I am merely pointing out that there's no possibility of negotiation, as you have nothing to negotiate with. Life in here, or death out there. Those are your alternatives."

"No. There's me," says Paia.

All eyes turn to her, even the bartender's.

"There's me to negotiate with," Paia continues resolutely. "I offer myself in return for the release of your sister Air."

"No, girl, you don't. . . ."

Paia shakes her head. "I do. He's right. We have nothing else."

"It just seems that . . ."

"If we're to accomplish anything at all, we must work with what we're sure of."

Fire's languid gaze flares. Probably he's searching out the way he can take the offer without delivering the goods, which makes sense to N'Doch, since he's doing exactly the same. But meanwhile, he also sees how stirred up the big dude is, as revved as a lover. See him that way and he begins to make sense: as a proud, obsessive, jilted lover who can't imagine why any woman wouldn't want him, and who lives in the belief that it's only a matter of time or the right words before he has her back. So Paia's heated dreaming wasn't some one-way fantasy. N'Doch is ashamed he'd given this thought even a moment's notice. And it's faintly slimy to be hoping to use the bad guy's only good intention against him. Or if not exactly a good intention, then a true passion, at least. Like a junkie who craves his fix, Fire's need for Paia might render him willing to bargain.

At least that's what the dragon Water has in mind.

"Maybe you're right," N'Doch is unable, though Paia is a coconspirator, to quite look her in the eye. The apparently oblivious bartender has moved on to polishing glassware, but N'Doch senses Water's quick and absolute assent to Paia's offer. This spooks him as little else so far has. Not a moment's consideration for the sentimental gesture, now that the game is in the final innings. Not even the pretense that another solution should be sought. Even Papa Dja-wara does not speak up in protest.

Are we all expendable then?

HUSH, NOW! LATER!

Despite his initial resistance to his dragon destiny, whatever it may turn out to be, N'Doch has assumed since his miraculous resurrection that a protected status comes with being a dragon guide. But what if the dragons prove willing to sacrifice whomever it takes to achieve their Purpose? What if the only privilege of being a guide is being saved to be sacrificed last? Or maybe he's got it all wrong. Maybe Water is a better bluffer than he's realized.

"Of course," he continues, since no one else seems willing to, "we won't deliver Paia until you've given up Air."

Fire focuses on him directly, advancing a few steps in his direction as if just now noticing he's there. It's like being drilled with a laser. The dragon's gaze is contemptuous and bleak, the sort of look that says because you are such an idiot, there is no hope left for the world. "Not that it matters, really, but . . . why do you do their dirty work for them?"

"Who's what?" N'Doch blurts.

"My oh-so-innocent siblings. You've bought their entire line, haven't you. Surely your wise old shaman of a grandfather could have advised you otherwise."

"Hey, mother-killer, you're the one who's. . . ."

Fire glides another step closer, dropping his voice to a more intimate range. "I mean, you seem like a likely fellow. What's in it for you, being at their beck and call?"

N'Doch glances helplessly at Djawara. This is too close to his own former thinking for comfort.

"The satisfaction of a destiny fulfilled," offers the old man gracefully.

The man/dragon laughs.

Djawara crosses one knee over the other and peers up at the red-jacketed figure looming over him like the shadow of death. "If you have another idea, perhaps you might care to enlighten us."

"What?" Fire spins away with a toss of his head. "And spoil the fun?"

For once, N'Doch misses having Erde around to act as the mouthpiece for the dragons' Purpose. No one speaks of it as earnestly and eloquently as she does. The fact that the goal of the Quest is not yet entirely understood by human or dragon makes him queasy about trying to sell it to the main dude standing in its way. But what better way to pump the Fire-breather for his implied superior knowledge than to throw down a few cards he can't resist the pleasure of trumping?

Fire strolls among the chairs and tables, chuckling gleefully to himself, but N'Doch sees no real joy in him. His laugh is just a release of nervous energy. N'Doch looks for that vast underlying calm he's come to expect from dragons, even his own busy meddler, Water. He sees none of it in Fire's restless meandering, only frustration gathering like a storm. He should be more scared of the Fire-breather. He knows that out on the sidewalk, he'd be cooked mincemeat before he could even think to run. He knows that the situation in the Rive is artificial, and the dragon's man-form only a temporary limitation. Still . . .

STILL WHAT?

Is there something you haven't told us?

"You humans," Fire sneers. "Wave a few big words around, like Duty or Destiny, and you come running like sheep. You lose all common sense."

"What's sensible by your definition?" N'Doch retorts. "Murder and intimidation? Despotism?"

"Survival is sensible." Fire stops by the window, gazing outward again. "It's the only thing that does make sense."

Erde would have a heroic comeback for that remark, but N'Doch can't make his mouth say the words.

"But you're tired of mere survival, aren't you?" Paia asks suddenly. "And of the price you have to pay for it."

Fire laughs. "Price? What price? I've had everything I want."

"Except me."

A warning rises in N'Doch's throat, hovering stillborn. What is she up to? She moves toward the Firebreather, her gait slow and sensual. She's become the seductress. Is it to lure him into divulging information, or because she can't help herself? N'Doch thinks this is a very dangerous game to be playing here and now. He considers whether to intervene. Fire is still turned away at the window, but he senses Paia's approach and turns to meet her just as she stops in front of him. They stare at each other, and Paia crosses her arms beneath her breasts so that they are presented to him roundly, a sweet and teasing gift.

"Isn't that so, my lord?"

"Yes, beloved. Except you." Fire looks down at her. With a faint but knowing smile, he lifts one gilt-scaled hand and places it gently against her cheek. "Until now."

Paia gasps and recoils, her own hand flying to her face. "How did you . . . !"

Fire says nothing. He holds himself utterly still, his hand poised in the air where her cheek has been. By the bar, the others start up on instant alert.

"What'd he do?" demands N'Doch.

"He . . . *touched* me."

It takes him a moment, then he gets it. "You mean, actually touched?"

The bartender calmly lays aside his towel.

Paia stares at Fire. "How did you do that?"

"Because you wanted me to." Fire lets his hand drop slowly. "You did want it, do want it, don't you, beloved? You always have before."

"No!" Paia steps back, but wavers in mid-stride and stalls in confusion.

"Why are you frightened? You wish to speak of Destiny? Then admit we are bound by it. You and I. I only want what's best for us. All I've done has been for your sake." Fire holds out both hands to her, like a father to a child. "See? Let me show you."

Paia's body sways toward him, though her feet do not move.

"Come, a joining of hands at least. You owe me that much, after all these years."

Paia shakes her head, but her hand floats toward his.

"Don't do it, girl!" N'Doch is only guessing that touching will give the dragon power over her. But he can't bear the longing in her eyes, and in Fire's. They are a matched set of long-frustrated passion. Köthen should never have let this woman out of his sight. But, then, he didn't. He wouldn't have.

It's all my fault, even if it was by accident.

THERE ARE NO ACCIDENTS.

As Paia's hand lifts to meet Fire's, the bartender vaults up and over the bar. Chairs and tables whirl aside. In a dizzying blur and sprint, Sedou is a large black mountain between the Fire-breather and his guide.

"No!" He shoves Paia behind him. "You shall not take her from here!"

"You!" Fire's yearning gaze cracks into a mask of fury and hatred. His outstretched hand lashes back, then forward, his gilt nails lengthening into claws. Sedou grabs that wrist, and then the other, as it swings up to join the attack. Fire snarls, held by both arms. He doesn't struggle, but the tang of hot metal invades the rich coffee aroma of the café.

"Not too practiced at the hand-to-hand stuff yet, brother?" Sedou grins. "It's a man-thing, you know? Yet I congratulate you. This new manifesting must be exhausting. Careful, or you'll wear yourself out utterly."

"You cannot prevent her if she wishes to go!"

"If she wishes, and only if. Or else . . ."

Fire's snarl deepens. "I am as safe here from you as you are from me."

"True enough." Sedou releases him abruptly and steps back. "So, brother. Let's talk instead of fight."

"There is nothing to talk about."

"Oh, but there is." Sedou reaches behind him to draw two chairs out from the nearest table. "Shall we sit down? You can sit, right? A chair is a marvelous mechanism. You should try it."

"I have nothing to say to you."

N'Doch slides over to urge Paia away to the rear of the café. She shakes him off silently.

Sedou sits, kicking the second chair closer to Fire. "For instance, let's discuss these lies you accuse me of, or the information you claim your brother Earth and I are withholding."

Fire folds his arms across his broad red chest. "So confident of human loyalty? Very rash. It's not too late, you know, for them to see the wisdom of my way."

"Then tell us what your way is, as you see it."

"You know what it is."

"No. Truly. Tell me. It's what I came to hear."

Fire frowns, furious to have been trapped into any sort of discussion at all. "I have said it plainly enough: survival."

Sedou nods, easing back in his chair. "All right. None of us would take issue with that."

"Oh, come now."

"What? Why would we?"

Fire looks away contemptuously.

"Well, then I will amend that slightly. Given that anything worth doing inevitably bears some risk, I'll say we seek survival *as well as* the accomplishment of our Purpose. Which is yours also, since you are one of us. So, explain it to me again. Why have you set yourself against us?"

"Such endearing earnestness!" Fire bends a satirically pleading gaze toward Paia. "Release me, my priestess, I beg you. Don't ask me to sit still for this mawkish spectacle!"

"You are free to go any time, my lord, but without me."

"Why so impatient?" Sedou asks.

Fire flings both fists into the air. "Because this is so *boring*!" He paces away from the window, then stops, arms and fingers spread. "Do you really suppose that because Paia is here, I'll be a party to your lies and deceptions simply to spare her? Well, you suppose wrong! If I'm tired of anything, I'm tired of the hypocrisy that lurks at the heart of your so-called Quest! It's time she knew the truth. It's time they all knew!"

"Lies, brother? Deceptions? A dragon cannot lie."

"Ah, granted, a dragon cannot lie. But we can manipulate the truth to the same effect."

"I assume you are speaking from personal experience," retorts Sedou sharply.

"What truth?" asks Paia, and N'Doch is grateful. He senses a drawn-out dragon debate in the offing, and he'd rather they just got on with business. "What truth?" she asks again. "If I should know it, tell me."

Fire gives her a long, tragic look over his shoulder. N'Doch can't decide if it reflects the Fire-breather's true mood or the aura of high drama he prefers to surround himself with. "If I'd thought you should know it, beloved, I'd have told you long ago."

Whatever its intent, this performance brings Sedou angrily to his feet. "Oh, please! Has all this sabotage and destruction been merely for your own amusement, brother? You have a big secret, but you can't tell anyone what it is? It's a childish game, and a waste of your talents! I believe there is no secret at all!"

Fire smirks. "If it were our poor innocent brother Earth saying this to me, I could almost believe he doesn't know. But you? The clever, meddling one? No wonder you're so at ease in man-form. You should have been created human to begin with."

"Enough!" bellows Sedou. "What is it you have to tell us?"

"Whoa. Easy, bro," chides N'Doch. He sees his dragon/brother's shape wavering in the heat of rage. If both dragons take their own form in this confined space, the humans will be done for. "He's the one supposed to be the hothead, not you."

Sedou's eyes show green and golden against his ebony skin. He collects himself and subsides, but not before kicking one of the café chairs the full width of the room, sending it smashing against the wall. As the shattered pieces rattle across the tiles, N'Doch laughs softly, his heart aching. So much, so very much like his real brother.

In the impasse that follows, Djawara breaks his long silence and steps forward, hands clasped peaceably at his waist. "May I make a suggestion?"

Fire rolls his eyes. Sedou grunts and throws himself into the nearest chair.

"Go for it, Papa," says N'Doch, fed up with both dragons now.

"I propose that there is no deception. I propose that you both believe the truth of what you're saying."

"Huh," says Sedou sulkily.

Fire sighs theatrically, but his gaze drifts back to the big man slouched in a chair much too small for him. His stillness expresses his doubt better than any words could, or his constant avid reckoning of whether what he has to say will win him new friends or further enemies. "Proof, old man?"

"A dragon cannot lie."

"I told you what . . ."

"Listen to him, my lord," puts in Paia. "I beg you."

Fire laughs soundlessly. "Ah, beloved. You hope for me to redeem myself with reasonableness? Me?"

"In my eyes, if in no one else's."

"Then what choice have I?" He flashes her a sultry, resentful grin. "Let me then entertain the possibility that I silenced my sister Air before she was able to pass her knowledge on to my other siblings." He stalks to Sedou's table, pulls up a chair, and seats himself with elaborate formality. He rests his chin on steepled fingers, arch and condescending, and faces his fellow dragon. "Look into my eyes and swear you do not know."

"Know *what*?" Sedou growls.

"If you and our brother are truly ignorant of the final Destiny laid out for us, then your mindless pursuit of it is all the more tragic. But I suppose I must actually consider this possibility."

Sedou meets Fire's calculating regard. "Consider it well and quickly! Tell me what you know!"

Again, Fire glances back at Paia. Her return gaze is fervent and hopeful, so bright that even the Firebreather seems to shrink from its glare. *Guilt*, ventures N'Doch. Maybe even a trace of remorse?

Nah, can't be. Remember who we're dealing with here.

Fire sits back and rakes his gilded nails through his hair, which does nothing to tame its mobile energy. "Then I will tell you, because I must. Because my priestess requires me to." He looks nervous and intent, like a performer about to go on stage. His big moment, N'Doch realizes. The unloading of his secret weapon, his last hope to win Paia back to him, and perhaps even a sibling to his cause. "But don't hold me responsible for the results. Because I warn you, you with such faith in the rightness of Destiny . . . my news will destroy that faith, as it did mine."

In the waiting silence, N'Doch finally understands why the Fire dude has been so civilized, so tractable. Not just to please Paia, his priestess, though obviously that's what he'd like her to think. No, the guy thinks he's won, and he's just having fun jerking our chains.

Must be one hell of a piece of news he's about to lay on us.

Chapter Twenty-one

Hard thinking has always made him ravenous.

The Librarian piles rye bread and cheese, cold chicken and tomatoes and lettuce beside his keypad, and uses an obsolete mouse pad as a cutting board. Rye bread with caraway. And mustard. What a luxury! He lets himself concentrate entirely on the elaborate architecture of the sandwich, offering his brain a brief rest. But only the conscious part accepts the holiday. While he's slicing his precarious tower neatly in half, then in quarters, his mental subroutines are clipping away a meter per millisecond. *Per* nano*second*, he amends, filling his mouth with sensual distraction.

Nanotech. He still can't quite believe it. A whole city of it. Mind-boggling. But he figures it could work.

For instance: he's connected to the dragon in the way of dragon guides, even if the lines of communication are interrupted, and function randomly at best. So, sporadically, his memories are open to her. Assuming she has control of the city's infinite population of submicroscopic mechanisms—a big assumption, but it makes sense—and she's instructing them to re-create selected portions of his past in dimensional replicas.

How she does it is interesting enough, but the real question is, why? Why not just speak to him directly? The Librarian takes another huge bite of his sandwich. He's gone over this territory a million times. She doesn't because she can't. He has to be satisfied with a half-baked answer. But building memories around him is apparently something she *can* do. So maybe she's doing it in order to attract his attention. She's trying to communicate, and he should see each of these apparitions from the past as a sort of coded message. The dragon is telling him something general about the past, or about a specific aspect of his past . . . or maybe it's something about the nanomechs that can so easily re-create it.

The Librarian lets himself focus for a moment on the pure pleasure of Swiss cheese Like the beer, it's something he hasn't tasted in a very long time. A thing of the past in 2213. And the dragon has created it for him. So maybe it is the past she wants to talk about. But what about it? The nanomechs seem like a better bet. And at least he has an idea of how to proceed with them. He can look at their programming.

He sets the last quarter of his sandwich aside. Brushing crumbs from the desk and then his chin, he centers the keypad in front of him. Before he sets to work, he glances over at the old TV sitting at the edge of the darkness. The Grand Stair to the Citadel is as hard and bright on the screen as the Sahara at noon, and still just as empty, except for the two Temple guardsmen, who appear to be sleeping. Or perhaps they are just too heat dazed to move. The Librarian offers them his sympathy, then turns back to his search and forgets about them entirely.

It doesn't take him long to discover anomalies in the nanomech programming, the same sort he'd seen with the larger devices like the street-cleaning machines. Are they accidental corruptions, or intentional interpolations? The Librarian reverse engineers several of the modified nanomechs, and decides that their functions have been purposely altered, and then linked, so that they form a sort of broadband signaling device. Very broadband. He can't get the signal to play over his human-ear-specific speakers. But as soon as he activates the device, the signal is there, shouting in his head. And not just noise this time, but articulate with meaning.

AWAKE! COME! YOU ARE NEEDED!

The voice of the Summoner. The Librarian has been hearing this call all his lives, ever since . . . well, it began by the lake, didn't it, when the elder knight arrived with his squire in tow. Only the squire was a girl, disguised and on the run. And if that wasn't interesting enough, she traveled with a dragon. The knight, an old lore-hound, announced it proudly: *a dragon!* As if he was responsible.

The Librarian chuckles. Good old Hal, doing his preordained duty by jump-starting the Quest, considering it a minor part to play and consequently feeling sidelined, never realizing how crucial he'd been. For on that very day, the Librarian—or the creature he'd been then—took the young girl's hands in his own and saw Destiny written across her palms. Hers, yes, but his own as well.

The girl's dragon was following a mysterious inner "summons." The Librarian—not a librarian then, just

Gerrasch, half man, half beast—stared into her eyes and heard the Call himself for the first time, though it was several lives before he understood that it summoned him as well.

The Librarian blinks. He's been dragged into memory again, as irresistibly as if with a block and tackle. Some important message waits, abandoned in the past. Some understanding he should have recognized then and carried with him. What? *What?*

There were questions asked that day. He recalls that much. What were they? Hal paid him good king's silver for the answers. The Librarian retrieves the abandoned quarter of his sandwich and munches it pensively, searching for the mnemonic hook that will haul that memory out of the shadow of a millennium.

Bread and cheese. Hal had brought some of that as well.

The answers come to him stripped of their questions. They flare into his brain like bright meteors, inexplicable but sure.

The first answer: *The Purpose is to fix what's broken.*

Well, that's clear enough. The question was: What is the purpose of the Quest? And what's broken is obviously the Earth. The whole ecosystem is on the verge of collapse. But was it then? Who in 913 had any inkling of the horrors to come? The Summoner must have known, and therefore, the purpose of the urgent Call that woke the dragons.

The second answer: *The Summoner is not here.*

No, not there in 913. Because the Summoner was here, in . . . wherever here is. The Librarian has long assumed that the Summoner is Air, his dragon, but he'd never guessed the mechanism. A million nanotech voices calling down the centuries.

The third answer, for three was all he'd had time

for, with the girl's pursuers fast approaching: *Ask them about the City.*

He knows he meant the women of Deep Moor, but what was the question? Does it even matter?

For here we are in it, millennia later. The long-ago Gerrasch saw the City that day, this city, in the girl's frightened eyes. Which explains the déjà-vu he was assailed with the moment he stepped through the portal. The Librarian rubs his forehead vigorously. He needs his brain to work faster, deeper.

The Purpose is to fix what's broken.

Those few words could be said to describe the entire arc of his life, of all his lives. It's always been his purpose, and there's always something broken: a bird's wing, a man's spirit, an entire ecosystem. Or this city, for instance. He thinks of the crippled street-cleaning machines, and the mangled lines of code he'd repaired to let N'Doch's song take flight. So much of everything now is broken.

But why is the dragon directing his thoughts backward? What was there to fix in 913, except the hell-priest's wagon? Now, at least, there is no shortage of candidates.

The Librarian's strong thumbs are wearing bruises into the soft skin of his temples. He shifts to massaging his head, his fingers twisting in the salt-and-pepper thatch, as thick as an animal pelt. There's some connection he's not making, he's sure of it. Something so obvious that any child could see it, but not a full grown, super-educated, overcomplicated man. It's the reason the dragon has brought him here. Something he's meant to fix, might actually be *able* to fix, unlike the sad old broken planet. That's beyond his abilities. *She's* the one who's supposed to make that happen, but she's . . .

The Librarian goes still.

That's it. Of course. It's the dragon herself that's broken.

He has, since he was aware of her, conceived of Air as a storybook sort of prisoner: shut away, gagged and bound in some dank dungeon, perhaps physically, perhaps by magic. Whatever the mechanism, she's been denied the normal means of communication, has only occasionally been able to slip a message past the barricades. But her messages, when they arrive, are never whole and coherent. And besides, what are the *normal means* to a dragon? Now that the Librarian has met a few more of them, he realizes what an imperfect scenario he'd constructed. Just the sort of notion born of living with your nose stuck to a computer screen. Even if forcibly restrained, a dragon should be able to speak to her guide through barriers of any sort. The breakdown must be within.

What sort of breakdown? Is she mute, as Erde was when he first met her? That would make little difference to a supposedly telepathic dragon. Besides, dragons are not equipped for human speech, unless they're in man-form.

The Librarian releases his aching scalp. He swings up and out of his chair to pace, and sees that the confining details of his office in the Refuge have vanished. Only his console remains, an island in the void, its brushed chrome gleaming, its idiot lights shining like the eyes of forest creatures in the night.

He has to fix his dragon? Not just locate, free her, and do her bidding, but *fix* her?

How? How? How? His hands stray to his hair again. He has to repair her like some sort of machine? He's never felt more helpless.

Machine? Nanomech?

He has an unwelcome vision of the dragon as a benign version of the *machina rex* that chased him into this memory-haunted darkness. He sees her as a collection of parts spread out on the machinist's workbench, or as countless invisible specks of nanomech. A hateful notion. It makes the Librarian abruptly nauseous, which he recognizes as panic. Because if any of this is true, there'll be no eureka, no golden breakthrough of mutual recognition as he bursts through the walls of her prison to find her whole, waiting and material, ready to save the world. The Librarian swallows convulsively, banishing his panic to gnaw invisibly at his gut. Well, it was a silly romantic notion anyway.

Sudden peripheral motion distracts him. The old TV still lurks at the edge of the circle of light, its bright screen hovering like a window in the darkness. The somnolent view of the Grand Stair has erupted with frenzied preparations. Soldiers are racing to the parapet, taking up battle stations.

"Not now! Not now!" the Librarian pleads. He can't lose the many threads of his elusive and still-developing epiphany. But he throws a quick glance at the screen anyway. He has to. Leif Cauldwell's army has reached the Citadel. The security camera shows the view down the long final flight of steps from the midway landing to the ramshackle buildings clustered at the bottom. The long dry road is a pale scar down the middle of the village and out across the valley. But past the edge of the village, details blur with distance and heat shimmer. If he had House on-line, the Librarian could ask for a satellite close-up, maybe even sound. He gets up and shuffles nearer to the screen, but he can only squint and guess at how much of that broad dust cloud inching across the arid plain is actual and how much is mirage. Running a few numbers in his head, the Librarian estimates that even if Leif took with him every adult in the Refuge, he must have doubled that number in order to throw up a cloud that size. The Librarian is not surprised that the Temple-ruled towns and hamlets along the army's route have proved less loyal to the Fire-breather than they're sworn to be.

And where is Fire, while all this is going on? The Librarian sees no vast winged shadow gliding across the barren flatlands or sliding down along the parched swell of the hills. No sign of burning wagons, or men. At least not yet.

It'll be an hour or more before the rebel army reaches the foot of the Stair. He has to get back to work. Grunting with the effort, the Librarian manhandles the big television closer to his console. He's amused by its lack of a power cable. How convenient if we could edit reality as readily as we do our memories. He throws himself back into his chair. No more casual sorting. He'll have to scrutinize every signal, every line of code for hints of the dragon's presence, guessing at the outline of the whole by the shape of the parts.

Hands poised above the keypad, he hesitates. Should he try to contact Mattias again to let him know that Leif is at the Citadel? Maybe the boy has managed to raise House in the interim. As he ponders the wisdom of this further delay, the Librarian hears the oddest sound. It's so anomalous that he turns in his chair, expecting to find himself in some new memory place, a much older one this time, judging by the sound. But past his circle of light, there's only darkness.

And the baying of hounds.

Perhaps all hounds bay alike, but the Librarian is certain he knows those dog voices. The memory that goes with them includes a rough stick dwelling by a pond in a grove of ancient oaks, where the verges were always green and the water never froze, even in the deepest winter. The void ahead is thinning now, but it's not tree trunks the Librarian sees. It's a paneled door and a row of tall windows with sills as high as his chest. The walls have reappeared, and through the windows, the paved city square is visible past the looming shadow of the *machina rex*.

Damn! It's still there.

How much time has actually gone by while he was indulging himself along memory lane? No, not indulgence. Important information was gathered, passed on by the dragon, in the only way she can.

And the baying is not a memory. It's outside, filling the square.

He goes to the window farthest from where the *machina* is mindlessly raking the facade around the door with its claws. The jointed, meter-long spikes don't seem much the worse for wear, and neither does the building. But suddenly the squeal of metal on stone is deafening, perhaps because the dogs have fallen silent.

Certainly some time has passed, because Stoksie has managed to escape and return, somehow, with reinforcements. The Librarian spots the little Tinker at the entrance to the square, pointing at the Rex. Inexplicably, he's got Luther with him, two women and a pack of dogs. This is disorienting, and for a moment, the Librarian is forced to question what he sees. He doesn't recognize the women at first, but the dogs help jog his memory. It's the two scouts from Deep Moor, he's sure of it, though he can't retrieve their names. What are they doing here?

Looking for him. He can tell that much from Stoksie's wild gesticulating. And not finding him anywhere, they will assume that the Rex has eaten him, or pounded him into a red smear on the otherwise spotless black-and-white pavement.

The Librarian doesn't want the distraction of company just now. He needs to get on with the work. If they find nothing, will they go away? Or, not knowing he's alive and well, will they tangle with the *machina* to recover what's left of him?

Lily and Margit. That's what they're called. How did they get here, they and their dogs, so out of place in this high-tech city? And Luther here also, who'd left with Erde and the other dragons to warn . . .

Ah. The Librarian remembers N'Doch's song, and how the signal locator had placed him a few city blocks away. If N'Doch is in the city, very likely Paia is, too. If Luther's here, probably Erde and the other dragons aren't far away. All the players are here. Lily and Margit he'll figure out soon enough. The Librarian sees it now. The forces are gathering. He's always assumed that the Citadel would be the final battleground, but the campaign heating up there might be only the misdirection. Then who's the magician, Air or Fire?

Ask them about the City.

Perhaps he did know, even then in 913. Because the dragon told him. He just didn't take in the full meaning of her only partially coherent message.

Across the square, Lily and Margit assess the situation with the hard-eyed squints of seasoned warriors. Margit shakes her head while Stoksie argues and Luther attempts to run interference. The dog pack is gathered in tight formation, ears erect, all eyes fastened on the stupid clanking hunk of metal that's trying to tear down a building. It occurs to the Librarian that as fast as the Rex rips away layers of brick and stone, the dutiful little nanomechs are building it right back again, like the two machines that were unpaving and repaving the nearby square. Perhaps it's the best a machine consciousness can do by way of a metaphor for human birth and death. If any of these machines have a consciousness. The city as a whole has a kind of consciousness, perhaps. But certainly not the Rex. It clearly hasn't a thought in its titanium alloy head. It seems to be working on a single instruction: *get Gerrasch.*

This is brought home more forcefully when the Librarian, watching the increasingly heated debate across the square, steps sideways for a better view. He drifts into the Rex's line of sight through the window nearest the door. It spots him, and immediately shifts and redoubles its abuse in his direction. To the Librarian's horror, cracks appear in the featureless gray wall. Long snaking fissures etch the smoky glass with patterns of dead tree branches. But the cracks are knit up as soon as they're made, over and over, birth and death. He decides that the Rex will not get in. But neither will he be able to get out, definitely not through the door, and he sees no way to open any of the oversized window sashes, even if he could do it without drawing the Rex down on top of him. He's safe, but trapped. He tries jumping up and down at the farthest window, waving his arms to attract Stoksie's or the women's attention. The Rex is there instantly, battering away and blocking the Librarian's view of the preparations across the square.

Now he's worried. Because he's no longer sure who the Rex is answering to. Fire is the obvious answer, but the Librarian hasn't lived this long by assuming the obvious. What if Air has sent the Rex to keep him confined to the building and his console until he figures out a way to rescue her? Could she be that impatient, after all these years? The good news is that this could mean he's actually close to a solution. The bad news is that, though he wouldn't willingly sacrifice his friends' safety to the interests of the Quest, the dragon might not be so choosy. The Librarian has few illusions about the altruism of dragons where their Duty is concerned.

A handful of other women appear around Lily and Margit. Not Deep Moor women, at least none of the ones he knows. Margit issues instructions, her hands indicating positions to right and left around the square. Lily huddles with the dogs, as if coaching a football team. The *machina rex* has noticed none of this. The Librarian recalls that he walked within four meters of it before tripping its proximity alarm. Maybe its range really is that small. He offers it another moment of sympathy. It reminds him of athletes he's known, or career soldiers. It's a handsome, scary machine with no brain and one skill—intimidation—at which it excels. Sneaking up on it will not be difficult, but sooner or later, the women's activity will snag its dim awareness, and what they'll do then, the Librarian cannot imagine. He wishes he saw more weaponry spread among the eight women and two men sidling along the bright building facades. The sketched-in doors and windows offer scant refuge.

Only speed will save them if the Rex attacks, and the Librarian can neither warn them nor help them. He's always refused to carry a weapon, except his brain and his two clever hands.

He's gazing guiltily at his hands, pink-palmed and soft as a baby's bottom, when he gets his idea. It sends him stumbling back to his console. If only he can do it in time! Fingers pounding the keypad, he sets up a series of searches aimed at picking up signals from machines operating within the immediate vicinity. He asks for red locators on a map of the surrounding blocks. Outside in the square, the hounds are baying again. The Librarian glances toward the windows just as the Rex pulls away from its destruction of the facade and turns to face the new intruders. His fingers thrum against the console. The search is taking longer than he'd hoped. When he looks up at his map, the entire screen is hazed in red.

He whacks his forehead. He's forgotten to exempt the gazillion building and maintenance nanos from the search. Or maybe there are two gazillion. Whatever. He taps in new instructions, and the map clears. A dozen possibilities remain, six of them on his side of the square. What could they be, smart street lights and sewage drains? He'd seen nothing in the square but the Rex.

A crash outside nearly catapults him from his chair. The dogs are barking now, their high-pitched, got'im-cornered bark. The Librarian hears a yelp, and a soft, wet thud against the window glass. He groans, and lines the six signals up, one below the other, looking for hints.

He picks it out right away, so quickly that he double-checks himself. It shouldn't be so easy. But it's the only constant signal. The others are intermittent: loops of regularly scheduled basic instructions. The Rex, or what he hopes is the Rex, has to go back to base every time it changes its direction or its target. The Librarian needs to follow the signal back to the Rex and capture enough of its code to be able to create a new instruction to send along to the machine. What he wants to do is turn the damn thing off. Fast. Soon. Quickly.

He thinks he hears Lily whistling off the dog pack, but maybe she's actually urging them forward. He can't worry about the skirmish outside. He closes his ears, and bends his fingers to the chase. Once he locks onto his target, he's inside the Rex soon enough. It's like breaking into a big, empty, and echoing warehouse, with a few crucial items left prominently in the middle of the floor. The Librarian is delighted to find its programming so simple. It'll make it much easier to mess with.

Now that he's doing a block by block analysis, the Librarian is struck by how similar the big machine's code is to the tiny nanomechs. As if the Rex is the giant sibling to the nanos, somehow grown up way out of proportion and scale. He shoves this insight aside for future analysis. No time for it now. He's on a mission of life and death. Still, in his frantic search for an on/off button, he can't help noticing that the places in the Rex where its code differs the most radically look like the same sort of later interpolations that converted a big batch of nanomechs into the voice of the Summoner. He slows the rapid scrolling of ones and zeros. No, in this case, it looks like repair work. Rather artless repair work, at that, like a tapestry that's been worn, then rewoven. The transition from original to restored is not entirely smooth. The

reweaving looks to have been done by an unimagina-
tive student, one who only knows how to go by
the book.

Like it's been done by another machine.

The instant the notion comes to him, the Librarian
knows it's right. Machines repairing machines, just
like they constantly make and unmake the city. Because there's nothing else for them to do, and no one
else to do it? There'll be no human population to
look for, then, except those the dragon has managed
to import. Was there ever, or was the city made for
as well as by machines? The dragon will be able to
tell him, when he finds her.

He studies the repaired sectors again. The damage
was extremely random. This may have confounded
the logic-driven nanomechs, and made their reweaving awkward. Which introduced anomalies, which
affected the broken device's development, as if a fun-
gus had invaded its originally clean and functional
structure. Essentially, the repair nanos created a mutant, a machine mutant that grew into the *machina
rex*.

So the Rex isn't his dragon's creature, at least not
intentionally. He'd like to know what caused this
odd kind of damage. It's not what he'd find if someone had gone into the programming and purpose-
fully taken stuff out. The breaks aren't that clean. It's
more like the result of physical damage, to the actual
hardware. Like smashing the processor, or cooking a
memory unit.

Cooking. Fire damage? The fire *dragon's* damage,
that is? Could be. It's widespread enough throughout
the code he's been looking at to be due to one
major incident.

The Librarian chews his lip. How would Fire, a

proven technophobe, go after a sibling who's so at home in the ether? Would he smash her electronic toys? Burn everything in sight? He's dealt with all his other problems with flame and violence. It would explain why Air can't communicate using normal electronic means. But not why her *dragon* means aren't functioning. Unless . . .

Circular thinking brings the Librarian back to his vision of the dragon as a machine. He doesn't, he *won't,* believe it. It's too . . . inelegant. But it's certainly possible that the Fire-breather went on a rampage at some point, among the city's machinery. One reason he might do it is to contain or disable Air.

A shout, a scream, and another crash from outside penetrate the Librarian's haze. The Rex! He's forgotten it entirely, with its code still staring balefully at him from the screen. He'd prefer to shut down the machine rather than wreck it, that is, write the instruction that will tell the Rex to turn itself off. But he hasn't time now for the clean solution. His friends are out there being murdered. He flexes his fingers and starts deleting entire blocks of code, whole hog, grimacing as he does so. When he's done what he hopes is enough, he sends it along and waits, hands lifted scant millimeters above the keypad. He doesn't race to the window. He just listens. Soon there is a horrid grinding as the Rex tries to execute two conflicting motions at once. Joints squeal. Pistons bind. The Rex shudders to a halt. The Librarian hears a wan cheer from the forces in the square. He relaxes. Probably they think it's something they've done that stopped the monster. So what. At least they're safe.

Or are they? Motion on the screen draws the Librarian's gaze upward. In the spaces where he has deleted code, lines are reappearing one after the other, as the nanomechs rebuild the *machina*. No telling how long before it goes on-line again, but at least he's bought his friends some time to escape. Which they'll only do, he fears, if he can manage to let them know he's still among the living.

They're doing something out there. The Librarian hears a slow muffled banging, like wood on metal. The rhythm is too irregular for the Rex. He shoves back his chair and goes to peer out the high windows. The rescue party is standing about glum and bloodied, inspecting the stilled Rex. All but Stoksie, who is beating furiously at its huge foreleg with the shaft of a pike while Luther attempts to reason with him.

A pike? Where did he get a pike?

Time slippage is making the Librarian dizzy. Several dogs lie dead or dying beneath the Rex's belly. One woman is down and another is nursing a limp arm. Luther tries to draw Stoksie away from his raging and is abruptly shaken off. Voices resonate through the glass, not clearly enough for words, but the Librarian can tell they all think he's dead. He pounds on the window, and again jumps up and down, waving his arms. He bellows at Stoksie and Luther until he's hoarse. No response on the other side of the glass. He might as well be watching them on television.

He decides that if he can't open the window, he'll smash his way through it. He whirls toward his console for a suitable weapon, a book, a chair, anything portable. But his console has vanished. No desk, no chair, no circle of light. Nothing but darkness. He turns back to the window, and it, too, has disappeared.

A small animal moan escapes him. He wraps his

arms around his chest and stands swaying in the void. He's emptied of conviction. How can he not question the reality of all he's just seen? Did Stoksie really return with the Deep Moor scouts? Did he really manage to subdue the Rex? Is he being played with, tested, tortured? Or is he just living through the city's version of daily random event?

He rotates slowly, arms outstretched. One full three-sixty. No sound, no break anywhere in the velvet black. The only sure and solid thing is the floor beneath his feet. And perhaps he shouldn't be so sure about that. Yet the darkness is somehow full of meaning, of *intent*. The Librarian stands listening, waiting for it to speak to him.

And it does. *Hurry! Hurry!*

Chapter Twenty-two

The women gather murmuring at the library door.
How odd, Erde reflects, that they don't just come
piling in. She imagines a charged aura of magic in
the room that keeps them at bay, awestruck by Rose's
marvelous restoration. Or perhaps it's the wonder of
the room itself, appearing so suddenly and in all its
details where it hadn't been before, a room they all
know lies in ashes in their home time. She looks
down the long narrow space, past the shelves full of
old books and the dark, low-slung beams and the
bright slashes of sunlight from the windows. She realizes with a shock that it's not Rose they're staring
at so searchingly.

Do I look strange to them? Erde's hand strays up to
rake at her dark scrawl of curls. She smiles at the
women self-consciously.

"May we come in?" Raven asks.

"Certainly!" Erde turns to Rose. "I mean, if . . ."

But there's a rush through the door already. The
chorus of joy and welcome overwhelms Erde's hesitation. The women surround Rose to hug and pet

her, and proclaim their vast relief until Rose laughingly shrugs them off. Raven stands aside with Erde, and gives her shoulder an encouraging squeeze.

"Well done, sweetling."

"But I did nothing . . ."

Raven arches an eyebrow.

". . . much."

"Whatever it was, it was enough, and more than any of us had managed so far."

"It was the knowledge Rose carries that broke her spirit. But she found her strength again and came back to us renewed." Erde grips Raven's arm. "Oh, such tidings, Raven! So terrible! But Rose must tell it in her own way."

Raven smiles and ruffles Erde's hair. "Do you know how lovely you've grown? I just realized it, standing there at the door. All this racing about dragon-back must be good for you."

Erde blushes, confused by how delighted this compliment makes her, as it comes from the most beautiful woman she knows. Yet her delight stirs the ache beneath it. What good is being beautiful if the one she loves has already given himself to another? Köthen's face fills her mind's eye until she has to shake her head and blink it away.

"Sweetling? Erde?"

"Forgive me, I was just . . ."

"Thinking?"

"Yes." She hasn't thought about Köthen for several hours at least. Perhaps that's a good sign.

"Such sad eyes! Must be very deep thoughts you're having."

Erde shrugs shyly. What a relief it would be to tell Raven everything, to be able to talk with another, more experienced woman about her unrequited passion. "It's just . . ." She can't make herself continue. There are so many more important things to worry about.

"There, there," Raven soothes. "If Rose brings bad tidings, it won't be the first time. We've lived through disaster before, and we can do it again. It isn't the end of the world."

Except that it is.

Erde chokes back a very N'Doch-like laugh. His smart-mouth graveyard humor must be contagious. Instead, she nods. These women have a true reason to celebrate. She will not dampen their joy until Rose herself decides that the moment has come.

Standing in darkness, the Librarian wonders if he should trust his senses.

HURRY! HURRY!

Is it an actual voice whispering through the void this time, from a source outside himself, or is it the old neurons firing, sparked by some inner signal?

Or does it matter?

It's like the bet he took once, several centuries ago. For the winner's choice of pizza and beer, he proposed to outlast a colleague in the psych lab's sensory deprivation chamber. The Librarian won handily, understanding beforehand that the contest was essentially rigged. Who's more comfortable with the infinite, after all, than a man who's lived many lives? The void is not so disorienting, so soul-swallowing, if you're willing to just sit still and listen to the universe. The music of the spheres, the ancient conceit that claims that inaudible, holy music surrounds us all our lives. It's a lie, of course. It's not inaudible at all. The Librarian is hearing it now.

Hurry! Hurry!

In the sensory dep box, after the first few hours, the Librarian had felt himself growing, expanding outward. Not in a defined way, like the swelling shell of a balloon, but like a dissipating gas. Space flowed into him, easing all his molecules apart. An equal opportunity expansion. Remarkably, he lost no sense of self. He did not "become one with the universe." He had no religious epiphanies. He just lay there listening, growing and listening. And he remembers feeling—even after he climbed out of the box and toweled off, even as he wolfed down the victor's super-large with mushrooms and extra cheese and went about his life—he recalls that he experienced no contraction. The added space remained inside him, like the air that never leaves your lungs. He was, still is, expanded matter masquerading as ordinary flesh.

And he's never been more aware of the extra space than he is right now. Because Nature abhors a vacuum, and inevitably that space will want to be filled.

Hurry! Hurry!

He's been listening to this appeal for hours, who knows, maybe days, and he's not yet asked himself the obvious question: hurry up and do what? *Fool, Gerrasch!* It's not hurry up and get *somewhere*. That's much too simple. Or that may have been the idea once. But now the entity—the dragon, he believes—appears to have him exactly where it wants him, and is keeping him there. Hurry up and do what? Get me out of here? Hurry up and . . . understand what I'm telling you?

And suddenly, he is not alone.

If the void was to clear, and the Librarian were to find himself in the center of an arena filled with thousands avidly watching, he would not be surprised, so profound and pressing is the sense of presence in the darkness surrounding him. So insistent the anticipation. Crowding him, demanding . . .

There's an idea in the air. He hears it spoken.

Entrance.

Demanding entrance? The Librarian throws his head back with a gasp as understanding comes, and the panic that never touched him in the dep tank takes hold with iron fists. Entrance. In order to fill the space inside him. *She, inside me.* The Librarian's integrity of self seems suddenly precious to him. The dragon is knocking at his door.

Hurry! Hurry!

This is the crucial detail he's never intuited, never reasoned out. Has she kept it from him intentionally? It's the explanation for his many lives, for the peculiar way his brain works, for the mystical expansion of his matter. It's his particular destiny.

He is to be the dragon's vessel.

And lose his self in the process? If he lets the dragon in, will she erase him? Will Gerrasch cease to be anything more than the name pinned to a carcass inhabited by another?

The Librarian has waited all his lives for this moment. And yet . . . and yet. . . .

"Your only faith is in yourself, and that seems as intact as always." Paia's quiet scoff shocks even her. It's the closest thing to a snarl she's ever let out of her mouth. Fire's lip curls, but he only looks away.

N'Doch nudges her. "Maybe we need to hear what he has to say."

"Oh, yes," Fire returns. "I think you do. After all, why perish in ignorance?" He adjusts his chair to put his back to Paia, facing his fellow dragon. "My tale begins with our wakening. Or mine, I should say. I was waked earlier than you or Earth, due to my den's chance proximity to the chronological end of humankind. Or perhaps it was . . ." he grins slyly, ". . . because I was always Air's favorite."

Water-as-Sedou sniffs. "Certainly our sister would have trusted you to aid with whatever crisis awakened her. A trust you then betrayed."

"Define the nature of the betrayal."

"Subversion of our ancient duty."

"By your terms. By mine, I've chosen the much wiser path. My intention was to save her, to save us all."

Sedou crosses his arms and leans back, as if weary with incredulity. "So you locked her up?"

"Yes!" Fire bolts out of his chair. The chair teeters and topples against its neighbor as he stalks away from the table. "You're always so sure you're right! I see no reason to proceed with this charade!"

Paia moves after him. She's sure Fire will slam out the door. If he can move a chair about in his newly material form, he can open a door. But N'Doch grabs her arm, and Fire's not ready to leave quite yet. He plants himself by the window, hands on hips, gazing outward with an air of wounded dignity. The flat daylight limns his golden profile with an icy edge.

The dragon-as-Sedou rocks his chair gently. "Then why do you stay?"

Djawara clucks his tongue. He walks over to stand beside Fire as if he's been invited to enjoy the view. "It's the shape she's taken, you understand. My grandson Sedou . . . you never met him, but . . ."

Fire casts a knowing eye at the old man, and Paia shivers. Either the dragon can't bear to admit to any sort of ignorance, or he's been interfering fatally with N'Doch's family for longer than any of them have guessed. She's glad that Djawara's gaze is fixed on the street outside.

". . . he was a magnificent man. Bravehearted. A dragon of a man. But impulsive. Rash. Headstrong. A bit like you." Djawara clears his throat gently. "So perhaps you will pardon . . ."

"She is neither rash nor impulsive. She's merely insufferable, and always has been. She gets no pardon from me."

"Nor needs one," Sedou interjects.

"Tell *me* your story. I'd like to hear it." Djawara clasps his hands behind his back, his slight, erect form so vulnerable-seeming beside Fire's towering bulk. "You were saying that you waked early . . ."

Fire sighs, not the satirical exhalation that Paia is familiar with, but a long hissing release. "I find myself in need of someone to run my temple, old man. Are you available?"

Djawara chuckles politely.

"I take that as a 'no.' Pity. Perhaps you'll reconsider when you hear what I have to say."

"Please do continue."

But Fire is growing restless with human interaction. Paia knows the signs. At home, in this mood, he would bellow at a subordinate or two, resume dragon-form and swoop off to terrify a few villages. In a rage, he'd do much worse. He's not in a rage, not yet, but she can see the darkness gathering in him. He turns away abruptly from the window and his moment of quasi-intimacy with Djawara, and announces flatly to the room at large, "It's very simple, really. Our Destiny requires our death. That's the short explanation. Air, of course, gave it to me in endless painful detail at the time, but I . . ."

"Come now," says Sedou. "There is always risk with . . ."

"Listen to me! I said, *requires*. The concept of accident is not involved. But I wasn't having any of it then, and the same goes for now."

"But what . . ."

Fire whirls back to the table to loom over his sibling with his palms planted to either side of Sedou's elbows. "Shut up and listen!"

Sedou's chin juts and his nostrils flare, but he stays seated and quiet.

"Fortunately for all of us," Fire continues tightly, "the final fulfillment of this absurd plan demands the presence and more crucially, the cooperation of all—four dragons, four guides—within a certain time frame. Which, of course, will not be revealed by me, and is otherwise known only to the missing fourth of our number, who you have been unsuccessful at locating."

"So far," Sedou hisses.

"Perhaps." Fire looks down, flicking a trace of ash from the gold braid circling his cuffs. "But the point is, like it or not, I'm saving your lives. Now tell me how that constitutes betrayal?"

. . . and yet, he must.

His genes decree it. Every atom spiraling in his cells is arranged to obtain precisely this result. His will, even if he wills otherwise, is secondary.

She, immaterial, an ephemeral impulse, a *signal*. He, physical. She has need of his voice, his hands, to move in the world of men. To move at all. And she is the One. There is work that must be done, and quickly. If there is hope yet for the planet, it's her. The dragon. Air.

Hurry! Hurry!

The Librarian tells himself that he's had more lives than any ten men could hope for. Perhaps that's what his recent trip down Memory Lane was intended for—to remind him of that. Now it's time to let the dragon live . . . if only he can find the courage. So hard to let go. Never once, down along the centuries, has the Librarian ever contemplated suicide.

But now he searches his overstocked data banks for images of his most beloved places. A difficult choice. He's had so many. Though his physical body will continue without him—former occupant moved, left no forwarding address—he imagines it enshrined in earth, a final resting place, at each favorite site. He chooses one.

It's the mirrored, dark-rimmed lake where he first met a fellow dragon guide, and got his first whiff of Destiny. He sees his stick hovel deserted, the worn plank door thrown wide, the chimney clear of smoke. He see the oblong pile of smooth lake stones that marks his grave. He lets the clear orange sun sink past the far shore, toothed by spruce and pine, and just as the moon is rising behind him, the Librarian says . . .

Yes.

Chapter Twenty-three

He doesn't . . . *cease*, as he's expected, as he's prepared himself for. But very soon, the Librarian suspects that oblivion might have been easier.

His mind is eclectic, wide-ranging. It has made for him, over the centuries, a commodious and varied inner space. But the dragon is vast. Like a mighty ocean tide, she rushes in through the opened locks of his consciousness, into every bay and inlet, every nook and cranny, until there's little room left for his smaller, more finite, self. Pressed flat against the curve of his skull, he's near to suffocation. The dragon is unpracticed at sharing even an ephemeral geography. She has no sense of how to keep her mental feet and elbows and breath and volume to herself. Crushed, jabbed, stomped on, deafened, the Librarian quails.

He could blank on her. Overstretched, overwhelmed, he could choose a painless voluntary oblivion. Put his besieged brain to sleep. But he worries that the dragon has no idea what to do with this physical body she's so abruptly claimed. He can sense her testing its mechanisms, without any concept of its limits. She's playing with his heart rate, speeding it up, slowing it down, dilating his pupils, stimulating his muscles into spasm, inflating his lungs past comfort or reason. Stretching him like an elastic band. Deep, primal agony. Lightning bolts of pain. The Librarian imagines a teenager climbing into his first car. The dragon could kill him out of sheer ignorance, before she has a chance to make use of his body. His miraculous serial lifetimes, wasted in a moment of clumsiness.

Stop! Stop!

But begging for mercy has no effect. The dragon isn't listening, or can't. Or rather, she's listening at such a cosmic tuning that the Librarian's faint human pleadings go unheard. Suffering, helpless as a laboratory rat, he knows he must, somehow must, resume his task of calibrating the lines of communication. But this will take time, time he may not have if he can't wrest control of his limbs and metabolism from the dragon before she carelessly tweaks him into cardiac arrest. And this means giving himself to life again, after having made his quietus. It means rejoining the fray.

Life. Okay, perhaps. But can he do it?

His fists open and close. His fingers and elbows stretch and recoil. His legs twitch. He's stumbling about in involuntary dizzying circles while his features twist through a series of grotesque grins and grimaces. What does a dragon know about human expression, after all? Or human balance? The Librarian's ankles tangle. He goes down hard, shuddering, breathing in gasps, and still the dragon, in her perilous curiosity, seems intent on jerking his strings like some demon puppet master until every last one of them snaps.

Writhing in the dark on the smooth, chill floor, the Librarian fights for a hairbreadth of elbowroom in his beleaguered consciousness. Grasping at straws, he sends out a fervent SOS. A bit of signal snatched at random, its code rewritten and released, like a messenger pigeon taking wing from the walls of a besieged castle. A demand for recognition, a request for dialogue. He thinks of it as a dove. For clarity's sake, he images its diagonal, white flight in his mind. The bird flies home, from one sector of his brain to another.

This is insane, the Librarian muses. It's like pleading with myself. But it works. The puppet master eases off abruptly, leaving him limp and panting on the invisible floor. But the Librarian is wary. The dragon's urgency has not faded. She's still there crowding him into the farthest, tightest corner of his self. He can see that a simple giving in, giving over, is not how this is going to work. A more active partnership will be required if they, man and dragon, are to accomplish anything at all. He dispatches another dove, requesting a parley.

The dove returns. He can see it this time, a pale, faintly glowing, fully dimensional bird. It lands silently on the floor beside him. He takes it into his hands, astonished, and gently picks the slim curl of paper from the capsule banded to its leg. He unrolls the tiny scrap. It's thin, almost translucent, and totally blank, but its message comes to him loud and clear.

SORRY.

The Librarian chuckles, half amused, half for joy.

Well, now, that's better. A bit awkward, birds and paper bits and all, but who cares, if it works? It seems he doesn't have to actually write out the minute print with his big, soft hands and lack of any sort of writing implement. He has only to think his words, and there they are.

A second dove lands beside him, announcing itself with a soft salvo of flapping. The Librarian extracts its message.

NOW? HURRY!

Ah. Back in familiar territory at last. He's relieved, but no more enlightened. Hurry, yes, of course, but where and how, not to mention why? What exactly are we meant to do? He has so many questions. Too many to fit on a tiny scrap of onionskin.

Perhaps a larger messenger? The Librarian pictures the big crow he'd once rescued from a trap. After it healed, it stuck around, apparently because the life he offered it was more interesting than the one it had known before. He smiles at the thought of it, and out of the darkness ambles the very bird, its bright eye fixed on the pile of raisins that have appeared in the Librarian's palm. By now, the Librarian is incapable of surprise. He greets the bird, then lays half the raisins on the floor and nibbles the rest himself, pondering his next message. What questions will win him the most information in return? Meanwhile, a shorter query goes out with the dove. He doesn't really care if she answers, but he'd kind of like to know.

Why me?
HAS ALWAYS BEEN.
What is my part in all of this?
HANDS. EARS. EYES. FEET.
I know! I know all that! Though to tell the truth, he

hasn't thought of being her feet before. *What am I supposed to DO?*

HURRY!!

The Librarian takes a breath. Perhaps he can inhale a measure of patience from the very air. Finding a common language is not always the same as finding a common basis for reasoning. The dragon is as circular as ever. Random access. Well, fine. He knows how to deal with that. He sends the crow out into the ether, its tightly rolled scroll black with printed code.

And so, painstakingly, and strained by the effort of staving off the dragon's single-minded urgency, the Librarian extracts the outlines of the history he's lived, but has never understood. Finally, it's no longer a mystery why he's felt the need to live so many of his centuries in hiding.

In the beginning, he and Air were one. She, a discorporate entity, deaf, dumb, and blind to the material world. He, an animal body, canny, clever, and secretive, willing but hardly self-aware. The perfect physical vehicle for an ephemeral power. He existed while she slept, keeping himself alive and ready, should the need arise for the dragon to walk in the world.

But when the call came, the aeons of separation proved a desperate disadvantage. Air woke still wrapped in vast and cosmic dreaming. In her waking confusion, her sibling Fire saw an opportunity. He stole her physical vessel and stashed it away down the timeline, far from the forward point in the world's history that Air had chosen for her den. And so her den became her prison. A prison not of walls but of silence. Marooned far forward in time with no way to communicate either her dilemma or her whereabouts, except by the faintest of beacons, as likely to reach their goal as signals from another galaxy. No way, that is, until her kidnapped guide had lived long enough to evolve a brain capable of recognizing her distant transmissions, and figuring out how to reestablish their connection.

Kidnapped! The Librarian lets the memory surface, so long buried beneath the sediments of time and terror. The sharp grip of the golden dragon's claws, the fury and heat of his presence. The horror of abandonment in a cold, wet world full of unfamiliar threats and vicious two-legged predators. Why didn't the Fire-breather murder him right then and there?

Either he couldn't, or he . . . wouldn't.

The Librarian decides that an answer to this particular mystery could prove a crucial key in dealing with the renegade. Perhaps Fire was simply being lazy. Probably he believed the vast gulf of years between Air and her guide would be enough to suit his hedonistic purpose. But how ironic that the technophobic Fire should resort to such a high-tech prison. He may not even have recognized it as such. Considering it further, the Librarian is sure he did not. Certainly, Fire could never have predicted the development of an electronic means by which his imprisoned sister could amplify her calls for help.

The Librarian formulates another bird: *What is this place, this city? Why did you choose it for your den?*

Instead of birds, an abrupt and shocking downloading of images. The Librarian reels, clutching his temples. The entire history of the White City in pictures, neatly packaged in sequential files for storage in his capacious memory.

FOR LATER STUDY. LATER.

This last message comes through strong and clear. The dragon has no time now for education.

Basic information! Necessary!

Hastily, the Librarian opens the first file. A holographic video of the city streets, full of sunlight and green trees and living people. Immediately, his hands and legs spasm with involuntary motion. While he wrestles with his rebellious limbs, a peculiar sensation, an entire flock of white-and-gray pigeons settles down around him, feathers flying like snow.

HURRY! HURRY!

The Librarian knows he's gotten all the information he's likely to for a while. But he's learned that once, humans did inhabit the White City. Pondering their fate, he hoists himself awkwardly to his feet and tests his legs for control. He sends several of the birds back expressing his total willingness to serve but pointing out in no uncertain terms the absolute requirement for a physical body such as himself to follow a linear plan of action.

First one foot, and then the other. He images himself walking. *Get it?*

Air images her other siblings, and the Librarian is briefly distracted by how aware he is of her accessing his personal data banks for the necessary visual information. Item: one large bronzy-plated dragon called Earth. Ivory horns. Stubby tail. And so on. She pictures the four dragons coming together, the fourth image being himself. A gathering of dragons. He's always suspected that would be the plan. But Air seems unaware of all that Fire's been up to since she saw him last. After he stole her guide and left, he's apparently managed to avoid the temptation of coming back to gloat. But does Air suppose that her guide has been missing for centuries by accident? The Librarian explains. A single goldfinch delivers a minuscule reply.

OH, THAT.

Even behavior as unforgivable as the Fire-breather's is not vast enough to register on Air's cosmic scale. The dragon seems sure that her wayward brother will show up, once the other three have gathered. The Librarian is a whole lot less convinced, but for now, it seems pointless to argue.

Where should we gather?

This time, letters appear in the air in front of him: ANYWHERE. FOR NOW.

He understands that she does mean *anywhere*, in time or space. And he knows that it's his own brain supplying the alphabet. But, good, excellent. Further progress. The birds were getting very cumbersome.

WHEN ALL HAVE GATHERED, THE RIGHT PLACE WILL BE KNOWN.

Practically a paragraph. And there will be a right place.

Now we're getting somewhere. Except . . . how do we get there? How do we get out of here? And how do we contact the others?

He hopes she will confirm his guess that Earth and Water are in the city, somewhere nearby. Perhaps she will even explain how they got there. Instead, he gets confusion and impatience and a storm of grackles wheeling and arguing overhead. Not a one of them bothers to land. The Librarian gets the idea that locomotion and communication are solely his territory. He feels stolid and clumsy. He's tempted for a moment by exhaustion and despair. He hates taking action based on so little knowledge, so imperfect an understanding of the whole picture. But, after all, he's come up with the necessary solutions so far. One problem at a time. He must trust his dragon and get . . .

Of course! The Librarian enacts the cliché. He slaps his forehead.

Escaping this darkness isn't about bashing his way out. He'll just program a few nanomechs to build him an exit. He glances behind him, for the vanished windows looking out on the square. He's sure a faint towering shadow of the Rex lingers there, like an afterimage burned into the inside of his eyelids. The *machina* will be reviving soon. Better make his exit on the opposite side of the building. Then he'll rescue Stoksie and find out how the Deep Moor trackers got there, and then . . .

Already the darkness is thinning, and the door is forming in front of him, a pale rectangular outline floating in the void like chalk on a blackboard. He waits for the knob to complete, then grasps it and gives it an experimental twist. The door cracks open and flat, bright light spills in, the light of the city. But when he hauls the door fully open, eager for air and space, he's not where he expects to be. He's on the edge of the huge empty plaza where the elevator left him when he first arrived, with Stoksie, after coming through the portal. He's stymied, but only briefly. Perhaps the dragon has sent him this new insight, or perhaps he's figured it out on his own. No matter, he understands now that the city, like the dragon, cannot be counted upon to be linear. It has a random access geography. He remembers his schematic map of the power lines, and how he'd marked the source of the signal carrying N'Doch's song. He'll start there, with an address he knows. He shuts the door on the empty plaza, calls up the map, and reprograms his door to open across the street from that source location. He opens the door again.

There is a street this time, narrow and cluttered.

The potholes surprise him, a hint of the texture of real life. If he had any doubt of his data, he'd wonder if he was still in the city. Across the cracked pavement sits an old-fashioned café, complete with a worn striped awning and metal tables and chairs. The furniture looks like it's been recently thrown around. The tall windows are fogged with grit and condensation, but the Librarian detects light and the motion of bodies inside. If he's guessed correctly, one of them will be N'Doch.

He's about to venture out across the street, when inexplicable paralysis assails him. A weight in his chest, like a boulder crushing his heart. Panic first, then realization: it's the dragon, holding him back.

What? Why? You were in such a rush before.

He spots a flock of bright blue finches perched along the sagging rim of the café awning. Though he's never thought of birds as having expressions, these little critters look distinctly reluctant.

NOT YET. NOT ONE BY ONE.

The Librarian is reminded of other long-sentenced prisoners who, when released, find it difficult to walk through the open door into freedom. The weight on his heart eases but does not go away.

ALL MUST GATHER. ALL AT ONCE.

It's something about the news she bears, the Librarian senses. She wants everyone to hear it at the same time. He doesn't ask why again. She will simply turn vague and prod him to get on with his part of the job, collecting their allies, simultaneously, in one place.

As the Librarian ponders this new logistical challenge, another understanding blooms inside him, like a flower captured by time-lapse photography. Inspired, perhaps, by the tired but insistent reality of the café across the way, he asks himself: *If I can program a door that leads anywhere in the city, could I not also program the place it leads to?* If the initial gathering can be *anywhere,* he can create, or better still, re-create a site of his choosing. A place of safety and comfort from which to plan the rescue of the planet.

The Librarian deliberates issues of security and size, even familiarity. Urged to quick decision by his dragon's implacable impatience, he settles on a place he recalls most fondly: the Grove at Deep Moor. And since he can set his own parameters, he'll tweak it a little. He'll make it an Ur-grove, a haven of peace and beauty. The Grove the way it was before the dawn of man.

That accomplished, he will set about providing transportation. The Librarian takes a last, hungry look at *La Rive Gauche,* certain he detects the sharp fragrances of espresso and fresh-baked *brioches.* He sighs, shuts the door, and gets down to work.

Chapter Twenty-four

N'Doch thinks maybe it's time to pour himself a *real* drink. Normally, he's not much for alcohol, but the mood in the café is beyond tense. The very air has darkened, humming like a plucked string. Or maybe it's the guitar he's got clutched in his arms, responding on its own in some kind of celestial angst. *Our destiny requires our death.* N'Doch's sure he's not the only one who'd like to know exactly what the Fire-breather means by that.

Water-as-Sedou has taken a dragon's own time to consider his reply. He's holding very still while Fire leans over him. N'Doch can see the effort in it, both for the dragon and for the man whose identity she's borrowed. "I repeat," Sedou says at last, "betrayal is the subversion of your given duty."

Fire drops his head between his outstretched arms, the very picture of exasperation. "Have you even been listening?"

Sedou nods, a new and scary resignation deep in his eyes.

Fire snorts. He gives the metal table a rough shake

and shoves himself upright, folding his arms. "I did not volunteer for that duty, and made no promises to it."

"Betrayal is also doing harm to those who've accepted the responsibility you seek to avoid."

"I've hurt no one."

Sedou's eyes widen. He turns half away in his chair. "Brother! Please! We all know better!"

"Things! I've destroyed things!" Fire snaps. "Stuff."

"People's homes and livelihoods!"

"What about my mother?" N'Doch finds himself suddenly nose-to-nose with the Fire-breather instead of challenging him, as he'd intended, from the comparative safety of the bar. The guitar vibrates in dissonant sympathy from the countertop. "You threaten her up on the mountaintop, and next thing, she turns up dead! I call that hurting. I call that murder! What do you call it?"

If it's possible to look bored and furious simultaneously, Fire has managed it. "A regrettable accident."

"*Accident?*" N'Doch can feel the dragon's heat, standing so close. A human this hot would be dead of spontaneous combustion, but it matches the heat in N'Doch's heart. "You called in your hit man! Remember your man Baraga? Remember what he did to me?"

"Kenzo Baraga is very much his own man," Fire replies, without taking his glare from Sedou's. "I only offered him what he craved already. Besides, you look alive and well enough. Are you a ghost?"

"Woulda been, if it weren't for the big guy Earth. Shot to pieces. You don't call that hurting?" N'Doch almost grabs the Fire dude's gold-braided lapels, but a quick hard NO! slams through his brain. He backs off like he's been hit. The dragon can pack a wallop when she wants to.

Paia has worked her way around to stand beside Sedou. She lays a very visible hand on the man dragon's broad shoulder. "You can lie to others if you must, my Fire, but don't try to tell me I haven't seen you burn men to cinders before the altar of your own Temple!"

Fire watches Sedou lean back into the curl of Paia's arm. "I am not lying! As my sister has agreed, a dragon is incapable of lying."

"Dissembling," Djawara murmurs from the side, like a helpful referee.

"No! Take an honest count! I've hurt no one who wasn't in harm's way already, or who didn't willingly put themselves there to honor me, or for fanatical reasons of their own."

"Fanaticism that you created and encouraged," Paia pursues.

"For your sake, beloved! Always for your sake, to have servants around me to help keep you safe!"

"An elaborate and delusional denial, brother," growls Sedou.

"I can't be expected to answer for the bloody deeds of humans, suicidal or otherwise!"

"I doubt my daughter Fâtime understood herself to be 'in harm's way,'" Djawara observes quietly.

"Really, old man?" Fire gazes at Djawara sideways, framing his incredulity in theatrical scale. "Though she lived in a dying town in a dying country on a collision course with the end of the world? Though she suffered in poverty and lost all but one of her sons to the greed and violence and corruption of the time? Not in harm's way? Really? Could a sage like yourself have birthed a fool?"

"Enough!" Sedou rises, taking Paia gently by the shoulders and setting her down in the chair he has just vacated. "Give us something more creative than a coward's whine of denial! You are steeped in blood, my brother, be it by your own hand or otherwise. Not a one of us doubts it. The only question is *why*, and you haven't yet made that fully clear."

"I told you . . ."

"But you didn't *convince* me."

Fire watches Water-as-Sedou place both hands on Paia's shoulders. Longing and reluctance shine through the veil of irritation shading his golden eyes. "Must I?"

"Do you mean, must you, with the humans present?"

Fire's jaw hardens. "And you consider me heartless."

"It's only reasonable that all of us know the fate all will share."

Fire's lip twitches in an unborn snarl. He says, slowly, deliberately, "All right. If you insist. Does the phrase 'mutual annihilation' bring anything to mind?"

N'Doch thinks it brings a lot of things to mind, and none of them good. But his repeated subliminal calls to the dragon for an explanation go unanswered. The sense of foreboding he's been shoving aside for a while comes flooding back big-time. His grandfather takes a half step forward, as if unsure he's heard correctly. Paia shifts slightly in her chair, maybe because Sedou's grip has tightened. Protection or restraint? N'Doch can't be sure, for the big man's outward manner is completely calm.

"How? Why?"

"Ask our sister Air, if you can find her. Which you

never will. A shame really, since she appears to be in possession of all the facts which have been hidden from the rest of us."

"But some of which she shared with you."

"When she sent me off to collect you and our brother."

"Perhaps you misunderstood. She's not the clearest . . ."

"No. It was unequivocal." After this suddenly reasonable and direct exchange, like actual conversation among siblings, Fire seems uneasy under Paia's expectant stare. He turns away. "So I took other steps . . ."

"Ah," says Sedou. "Ah."

A moment follows that's so still, so lacking in purpose, so much as if the entire world has stopped, that N'Doch wonders if it means a stalemate. The two dragons have reached some sort of understanding, that much is obvious. But the light seems different, and there's a new rigidity in Fire's red-clad back as he lifts one clawed hand to the misted glass. Thin curls of steam rise as he swirls his palm against it to clear his view. N'Doch would swear he's seen Fire shudder. Quick and hard, like he's gotten a bad shock but mastered it instantly. His hand drops like dead weight to his side as he moves back from the window, one step, then two, and turns on his heel.

"Well, I think it's time I left. A delightful diversion, but I really must get home. I have a war to fight."

N'Doch is disappointed. Is the Fire dude really giving up so easily? Sidestepping the central issue? N'Doch has expected him to be bigger, badder than that.

Fire's glance slews sideways toward Djawara, but slides on past to rest intently on Paia the whole time he's talking. "Are you sure you won't reconsider my offer, old man? The religious life can be very rewarding, I assure you. A measure of comfort and luxury to ease your old age? I know my priestess would appreciate your company. Far more stimulating than any she's had up till now. Myself excepted, of course."

Something's happened. N'Doch feels the change blow through the room, as palpable as a storm gust off the Atlantic, but he's got no sense of what it means. He glances at Sedou, sees him straighten, watches his attention move outward, past the café walls, into the street and beyond.

"And of course," Fire continues, "I can promise a bevy of lovely ladies to decorate your days and nights."

Paia shakes her head, her tone almost as mocking as Fire's. "Shame, shame! How do you ever expect to win any credibility if you go on like that?"

A long look passes between them. Then the satirical light blooms as wildly as hope in Fire's eyes. He lifts his sculpted chin and pounds his chest like a cartoon despot. "Because I am the God."

Paia smiles sadly. "But you're not. You're only a dragon."

"Yes, and you are my guide."

N'Doch's glance swivels from one to the other. *What is it? What's happened?* They could be errant lovers, reconciling.

Sedou shakes his head, listening, but not for any sound audible to human ears.

Paia sighs, rising from the table, politely disengaging Sedou's grip. "If only you'd let yourself be guided by me."

"We could work on that," says Fire agreeably.

She laughs, as if he's made a frivolous joke.

He returns a charming, deprecatory smile. "Of course, I'm not making any promises."

"No. For then, you might be forced to make good on them."

"I see you understand me now." Fire holds out his hand. His gilded nails gleam in the light from the window, which seems warmer than before, as if the sun has risen. "It's time, isn't it?"

N'Doch sees the tide turn in the priestess' eyes. It spooks him badly.

What the hell is going on?

LISTEN!

To what? I don't hear a thing!

"Unless you mean that humming," he says aloud. Getting no response, he turns to his grandfather. "You hear anything weird, Papa Dja?"

Djawara is grinning like an old fool. "I believe the 'never' has just become a 'now.' I wonder how that happened."

"What are you talking . . . oh."

And now he hears it, too. Voices. A flurry of voices on the dragon internet. New voices. *What does it mean?*

HUSH!

Fire says, more urgently, "Are you coming, beloved?"

"It seems that I have no choice." She looks to Djawara.

Djawara nods. "You are our only chance."

Fire barks a laugh, a desperate, uneasy guffaw. "Ha, old man! You're convinced she'll convert me?"

Djawara smiles up at the towering man dragon, then very decorously lays a hand on his glittering cuff. N'Doch tenses, ready to spring to the rescue, but smoke does not rise, and there's no stink of burning flesh.

"Here is my hope, lad," says the old man earnestly. "That she will help you to see reason and accept the inevitable. And if more can be expected, that she will lead you to find that deep place in your dragon's heart where compassion and honor lie waiting in chains, and convince you to set them free."

Paia nods, and places her pale hand in the dragon's red-and-gilt palm.

"No!" N'Doch cries out, but too late. The pair has vanished before the protest leaves his mouth. "No!" He spreads his arms to his grandfather in fear and loss and frustration. "Why? How could she? Why did she go with him?"

Djawara's face is solemn and shining. "She knows it's only a matter of time."

Chapter Twenty-five

The carved wooden beams of the library at Deep Moor resound with the glad laughter of unsuspecting women. Though warmed by Raven's cheerful affection and the women's awed and grateful smiles, Erde is sure that she's never felt lonelier. Deep Moor is not the home she hoped it would be, and tried so hard to make it. Even if the real Deep Moor did not lie in ruins, it could never be.

Not now. Now that I've been where I've been, seen what I've seen, know what I know.

Deep Moor stands for all that's good and right about humanity. But her life has become—*she* has become—something not quite human. Something only her fellow dragon guides can comprehend.

My home, my fate, whatever it is to be, is with them.

As she is contemplating all this and feeling sorry for herself, which she admits is one of her least favorable characteristics, a sudden imperative from the dragon outside banishes all other thoughts.

WE MUST GO.

What? Where?

A NEW SUMMONS. FROM THE GROVE.

A trill of fear roughens Erde's reply. *No, dragon, surely not there!*

YES! WE MUST LEAVE IMMEDIATELY!

For the Grove? But Fra Guill is in the Grove! And all his minions! Have you forgotten?

MY SISTER AIR IS THERE.

Erde is so astounded that her mind blanks momentarily, like a mill gear slipping its cog. *Impossible! We would . . . you would have known!*

I DIDN'T SAY SHE WAS THERE BEFORE. I SAID SHE IS THERE NOW. I HAVE JUST RECEIVED THE SUMMONS. WE ARE ALL TO GATHER THERE.

Surely there is some mistake! Did she say the Grove, exactly?

OF COURSE NOT. HER SUMMONSES DON'T COME IN WORDS. BUT I KNOW THE GROVE WHEN I SEE IT.

We can't go back there, thinks Erde desperately. We just can't!

"Erde? Sweeting? Are you all right?" Raven laughs. "You really have become the most distracted child!"

"I'm sorry, I . . . I was just talking with the dragon. He . . ." Erde knows she cannot share this news with Raven. She might insist on coming along. "Will you excuse me for a moment? I think I'll go speak to him in person."

"By all means. Give him my best."

Erde puts on her best calm face as she eases casually through the throng of celebrating women, receiving their thanks and congratulations as she goes. So many of them now! What a refuge Deep Moor had become in her absence, for the battered, mistreated, and misunderstood. Erde wishes she better comprehended the nature of the illusory Deep Moor that the City has created here. It would do her heart good to be able to promise these women a permanent place of safety, though surely even an illusion is better than the horrors they fled from.

Erde's heart pounds as she imagines those horrors: starvation and servitude, beatings and witch burnings. It could have been her own life, but for the coming of the dragon. She gains the library door, hurries across the dappled garden courtyard and through the shaded arbor, wrapped in the heavy fragrance of roses.

She finds the dragon lumbering up and down the open lawn, the closest thing he can manage to pacing impatiently.

"Look at that, dragon!" she scolds, hoping to lighten his urgent mood at least a little. "You're wearing a great mud track in that tender green grass!" But she also notices, to her amazement, that the bruised grass at the farthest extent of his pacing has healed itself completely by the time he returns to it.

ARE YOU READY?

Ready?

TO LEAVE. WE MUST GO IMMEDIATELY.

Dragon, please. We must think this one over carefully.

She has never refused him before, never withheld from him the mental image he needs to guide his transport, or as N'Doch would say, his "homing device." She can sense his surprise.

WHY ARE WE LINGERING? MY SISTER CALLS!

But Fra Guill . . .

PERHAPS SHE HAS VANQUISHED HIM.

But are you sure it's her? How do you know?

Earth halts in his tracks and pulls his massive

bronze body up to its full monumental height. HOW CAN YOU ASK SUCH A THING!

He towers over Erde like a rugged cliff face. His scimitar horns could almost tangle with the clouds and brush the dome of the sky.

That is, she muses, if it was the *real* sky . . .

He lowers his great head, letting his horns sweep through the sunlit air like the vanes of an ivory windmill. His plated snout swoops toward the ground and settles inches from Erde's toes with a hearty snort. The warm gale of his breath tousles her hair like an unseen hand.

"Dragon!" she exclaims fondly. "You did everything but roar! Are you trying to intimidate me?"

Earth's fierce demeanor wilts. AM I NOT SUCCEEDING?

Of course not! Now, let's discuss this new summons of yours.

"A matter of time, sure, but after all the trouble we went to, getting her away from him? I can't believe this!" N'Doch scrubs his face with both palms like a sleeper waking. Surely he *must* be dreaming. "What's Dolph gonna say? What am I gonna tell him?"

Sedou stands at the window with his back to them, as the Fire-breather had done before. "The knight has already played his role. It's endgame now."

"Endgame, huh?" N'Doch laughs nervously. "Sounds a little too much like 'mutual annihilation' for me."

"I mean that it's time for the major pieces to do their part."

"Easy for you to say, bro. It's not your head the good baron's gonna be after."

"Hush, boy!" Djawara hisses. "It's no time now to be playing the fool!"

"I'm not. I was only . . ."

"You are. I know it's only your apprehension babbling away, but now's not the time for it."

"Yeah?" N'Doch glares sullenly at his grandfather, who always manages to hold a man's face to the mirror just when he's least interested in looking at himself. "What time is it, then?"

"Time to meet my sister." Sedou turns back to them with an elated grin. "We've been summoned!"

"Just now? You heard . . . ?" Djawara clasps both hands as if in prayer.

"Air? She got out? She's free?" N'Doch exclaims. "Wow! How?"

"Unclear," Sedou admits. "But we'll find out soon enough!"

N'Doch puts two and two together. "So that's why the Fire dude split so suddenly." He rounds on Djawara. "How'd you know?"

"It seemed the only logical explanation."

"Nah. C'mon!" N'Doch doesn't want it to be so simple. Truth is, he doesn't want it to be so at all. If it's so, if the last dragon is out of the hatch, it means they're on to the next stage of the Quest, the stage Fire's been working so hard to prevent. It means finally finding out what he means by "mutual annihilation." "You got some kind of magic, right, Papa?"

Djawara ignores him. "To where are we summoned?"

Sedou gazes at the far wall, as if the message was

printed there. "Now, there's the problem. No words, only images, and it *looks* like . . . the Grove at Deep Moor."

N'Doch offers his grandfather a brief explanation, then shrugs, hoping his relief isn't too obvious. "Well, that's a no-go until we hook up with the Big Guy again. He's our only mode of transportation."

"Easily done. He's only a few blocks away." Sedou heads for the door. But the instant his hand touches the knob, the gale starts up again outside, as if it had been lying in wait until someone ventured into the street. Violent gusts lift and tip the café tables, and slam the chairs against the base of the facade. Then, louder than the wind, a roaring and pummeling sound. The door and the windows vibrate in their frames. Sedou clears a circle of condensation and peers through the glass.

"Hunh. Not so easily."

Djawara quickly joins him. "Oh, my."

And then there's nothing left for N'Doch to do but follow. Besides, he'd like to know what all the noise is about. He clears his own little view port, and looks out on a hail of stones. Not hailstones, which he's only seen once in his life anyway. These are actual stones. Rocks the size of chicken eggs, falling from the sky in a steady downpour, like petrified rain. More than just falling, each stone seems to have been flung downward by force, so that when they hit the street, they bounce. N'Doch sees there are two hazards out there: the stones coming down hard on your head, and the stones careening back up in your face. The quaint old striped awning that had led him down the street in the first place is already in shreds and tatters.

"That'd lay us all flat in a second," he observes

with as much neutrality as he can muster. So they won't be leaving the safe haven of the Rive for a while yet. He strolls back to the bar and picks up the guitar. He'll want to take it with him anyway, when the time comes. "It'll stop, probably. Let's just kick back till it does."

"I can go, and come back for you." The outline of Sedou's body shimmers as the dragon contemplates a shape change.

"But is that wise?" Djawara asks. "From what you've said, separating us seems to have been his most successful delaying strategy."

Sedou scowls, shimmers again, then retreats from the window and flings himself disconsolately into a chair. "What, then? We can't just sit here! Earth will be summoned, too, but will he think to search us out before he goes?"

Djawara settles beside him quietly, as if keeping vigil over an ailing relative. "We'll think of something."

Suddenly, a knock at the door. N'Doch nearly drops the guitar. Three evenly spaced raps, neither demanding nor impatient. Formal, N'Doch decides. "Who's it gonna be this time?" he wonders unnecessarily.

Nobody moves, as if all of them expect the door to burst open of its own accord. Finally, Djawara nods and rises to answer it. "Seems I'm the Gatekeeper here . . ."

An ordinary looking man in a plain gray uniform, neatly pressed, waits beneath the shredded awning, his billed cap in his hands. The stones are still falling, but none of them seem to be falling on him. "Your car, sir," says the man helpfully.

Djawara's impeccable poise finally wavers. "My . . . car?"

"Yes, sir." The man glances down at a slip of paper tucked inside his hat. "Says here, two passengers for the Grove, sir."

"Did you say, the Grove?"

"Yes, sir." He skins a look past Djawara's shoulder at the two staring faces inside. "Will that be three, sir?"

N'Doch comes up behind his grandfather. Out in the narrow street, a long, gleaming, sky-blue limo waits with its engine running. The stones aren't hitting it either. N'Doch shivers.

Djawara rolls marveling eyes toward Sedou. "Will we be three?"

Sedou nods.

Djawara turns back to the man with a courtly nod. "Three. Yes." He gestures casually at the rain of stones, as if stones fell every day of his life. "Would you care to come inside while we gather ourselves for the journey?"

"Oh, no, sir. Thank you, sir. I'll just wait right here, sir. No rush. Take your time."

No rush. Yeah, right. N'Doch can hear the urgent imperative hidden in the man's implacable courtesy. "She sent him, hunh? Hey, you didn't tell me your sister had style! And we're going?"

"Oh, yes." Sedou laughs. "I would say so."

N'Doch looks back at the sleek blue car. Its unblemished finish shines as if with its own light. It's the perfect embodiment of all he'd ever thought he wanted out of life. *But that was then.*

He sighs. *Hey, I've died once. How bad could it be a second time?*

He wraps grateful arms around the foundling guitar, puts his ear to the box to hear it hum its quiet, consoling song. It appeared just when he needed it. Like magic. Now, he's as ready as he'll ever be.

Chapter Twenty-six

Paia cannot say clearly what makes her grasp the hand of the intemperate, murdering bully she had denied with such conviction not twelve hours ago. Or was it twelve days? It could have been weeks, for all she knows, she's so entirely lost track in this place where time seems somehow irrelevant. What she does know is that she's exhausted, dirty, hungry, and overwhelmed by a longing to be home again, no matter what the situation there might be.

I can do nothing useful here, she tells herself, reaching to lay her hand in Fire's palm. *At the Citadel, perhaps I still can.*

Paia has had little experience of life outside the narrow sociology of the Temple and the Citadel, but she's consumed enough of the House Computer's large stock of classic novels to understand at least secondhand that a young woman's first taste of freedom can result in a reckless plunge overboard. In the safety of Djawara's quaint café, as her dragon defiantly justifies his bloody deeds and flagrant dereliction of duty, Paia suddenly sees his actions as mirrored by her own. At that moment, her connection to him has never seemed more real or poignant. For what was leaving the Citadel if not a dereliction of duty? Or a denial of her proper destiny? Fire is her dragon. She is his guide. Her responsibility, her life's duty is to him, not to some stranger lord from a distant past. Nor even to the other dragons or their guides. If both she and Fire do owe allegiance to some larger Purpose, her best way to serve that Purpose is to fulfill her duty to her own dragon, in her own place in the continuum of time. Ironically, Fire would agree, the only difference being how that duty is defined. And it's a major difference, she realizes, now that she's clear about it, but not so much in its particulars of behavior as in its intended result.

I had to come all this way to figure it out.

Paia consoles herself that her little rebellion was not entirely pointless. Of course, she fears what might happen should she meet Adolphus of Köthen again, face-to-face. Or even see him from a distance. Perhaps she gave in to her attraction to him with girlish abandon, but the attraction was real enough and certainly mutual. This is probably on her dragon's mind as well, which will make Köthen either a prime target, or someone to be avoided at all costs. It's a shame, Paia muses, that they must be rivals. For wasn't it Köthen's dragonlike qualities that made him so desirable? The perfect stand-in for the dragon lover she dreamed of but couldn't have. But now . . .

Paia recalls the heat of Fire's fingertips against her cheek. Now everything is different. Now she might actually have some power over him.

She lays her hand in his outstretched palm.

The sensation of falling goes on forever, falling not toward or into, but away from, falling until fall becomes flight, without up or down. The rush and lift of the wind beneath her wings is so thrilling that she soars deliriously for more endless moments, drifting in the thermals that rise off the dry, red cliffs. Then self-awareness stirs, and exhilaration gives way to fear.

!!

Her flight falters. Speed fading, altitude lost. A spinning plummet into a dive. Confusion and terror. Then amazement and gratitude as the great dragon body—hollow bones lighter than air, vast and glittering wingspread—turns back into the wind, catches a strong updraft and rises, exultant, laughing.

I SEE YOU'LL NEED SOME FLYING LESSONS.

It's as if he's right beside her. Not inside her head, but as if this scaled and gilded frame is a vehicle they both are driving. He's just taken over the wheel to save them from disaster.

!!

Speechless still, even inside herself. Sorting out identities, separating the physical entities. Words are useless until she's sure whose self they've come from. Is she the dragon, or merely resident inside the dragon's body? Is this a temporary manifestation, Fire's own mode of dragon transport, which he's never invited her to experience before, except as a threat of deportation and abandonment? Or is it some more permanent arrangement that she's unwittingly agreed to by placing herself, literally, in his hands?

As she struggles to form the question, Fire distracts her with a breathtaking surge of speed, wings billowing and snapping like the sails of an ancient galleon. Her heart fills with air and sky and freedom. Joy gives her back the words.

Could we have done this before?

ALWAYS.
Why not, then?
I DIDN'T TRUST YOU.
And now you do?
NOW IT DOESN'T MATTER.

Paia has had this thought also, without knowing where it came from, or exactly what it means. It wasn't just the dragon's touch. In the café, something changed, and now all things are different.

Why doesn't it matter? What happened?
DON'T THINK ABOUT IT NOW. THINK OF ME. ONLY OF ME.

The great wings pump. Higher, higher, past the soft mist of clouds into the darker blue of the sky, and then into a spiraling roll, as if tunneling through the air itself, or swimming, in water the temperature of blood. At once aware of wings and claws and scales and flight, and of two more human bodies within, rolling together, skin slick and hot, rolling entwined, pillowed by the wind, his forked tongue in her mouth, his gilded arms cradling her hips. Paia sighs and takes him inside her as they roll and soar and rock in ecstasy.

"It's all an illusion, of course," says Fire later, as the dragon body rests on an isolated windblown crag.

"My body doesn't think so."

His murmur suggests a self-congratulatory smirk. "Your body is an illusion. As is all matter."

Paia recalls her physics lessons only vaguely. "Some more so than other, then."

The illusion now is of their human bodies lying in the softest of beds, limbs entangled, slack with release. No sight, only sensation. Damp skin and whispers. And desire, so intense. Already, she wants him again.

"I mean our lovemaking is an illusion."

"I know." It's like receiving his thoughts, Paia notes, rather than sharing them. He still holds part of himself aloof.

"And yet, it's not. My energies have absorbed yours. Therefore, we are joined more fully than any normal lovers could be."

"Hush," she whispers, stroking him. "Don't talk."

"But I could as well have been describing this outer body. That, too, is an illusion, its design derived not from some magical genetics but from the darkest corner of human imaginings. Shaped to rule the souls of men."

The outer body lifts its reptilian head to arch and preen. Paia is the dragon again, showing off her sleek and sinuous neck, her magnificent form, proud of her powerful legs and tail. She stretches gilded wings and extends curved claws to whet their razor tips on a handy rock. Then the dragon settles down again and closes its eyes. Paia is released to a single consciousness. She doesn't mention how she prefers the shape of the man-body beneath her hands, the one she feels but cannot see. "You're trying to tell me something."

"My siblings and I are made of elemental energies. Our physical form is determined by the genetics and evolution of the human mind. We have no DNA of our own. So which came first, the dragon or its myth?"

"Is it a riddle?"

He pulls away slightly. "A basic truth."

"Does it matter? You are here." Now she's sure he's working his way around some bit of information he doesn't want to come right out and deliver. What now? She'd thought he'd told her the worst already.

"It matters to some. But in the long run, well . . ."

"Your siblings have different shapes." She had been about to say "kinder."

"No accounting for taste," he quips, but she senses an attempt to redirect her line of questioning.

"Why take any shape at all? I mean, why does it matter what shape you take? You could be one shape today, another tomorrow, like some people change their clothing. Water does it."

"No." He stirs brusquely, as if recalling some old grudge. "It's not my gift. Water *actually* changes. Her power is over matter. Mine is over minds. I had a choice and I made it, and that was that. Because . . . no, never mind. We have better things to do with our time."

"Because? Because?" She pushes his hands and mouth away with mock severity. "You can't leave me hanging!"

"Better for you if I do."

"I am you now, or so it would appear."

"Beloved, you always were."

"Then I should know what you know." She stretches against him like a cat. "You were saying, because . . . ?"

He rumbles his irritation, reminding Paia how very recently she feared doing anything that might displease him. Now what's left to fear? He's dissolved her already, and her consciousness appears intact and fully capable of sensation. Yes, fully indeed, she muses, as another tsunami of desire sweeps over her, rolling her against him. Astonishing, how desire can animate a body all of its own accord. Astonishing and wonderful. Still, she wishes she could see his eyes. They were always the surest gauge of his true mood. But his eyes are now her eyes, those great golden orbs lidded against the scouring winds of the heights. To test the extent of her control over the dragon body, she focuses her awareness of it and lifts one lid, thinking of it as a kind of giant window shade. The flood of light is blinding. The cold air sears. Fire growls in protest, and Paia closes the eye. Some control, then. But whose eye is it really? A perplexing dilemma.

"Am I to have my own body back, my own . . . self?"

"Is that what you wish?"

Just like him to twist a question into a complaint. "Whose choice is it?"

He shifts again. Another flare of silent irritation. Finally his voice comes muffled, as if from the depths of pillows. "Yours."

"Ah. You didn't want me to know that, did you? Among other things."

Silence. Yet, in their old days together, she got nothing at all from him if he didn't want to tell her. So even this little is progress. Wishing she knew more about the art of seduction, Paia puts her hands to work, and when it seems she has him pliant beneath her, she murmurs, "It's a lovely shape. It fits just right. But explain to me: why take any shape at all?"

He is a creature with a long habit of illusion, so bedsprings creak faintly as he twists away from her and up, to pace invisibly. Only the air moving across her cheek marks his passage. "Because," he says in a voice she recognizes, his angry voice, the voice of the God. "Because men need to be controlled! Because men are Nature's suicidal impulse! Because the

history of the world would be so much shorter than
it is to be already if terror and awe had never been
given form and articulation!"

"And you did that?" she asks meekly.

"I am that!" His voice booms as if he's grown to
fit the scale of his rage. "I am the terrible image of
Nature uncontrolled and uncontrollable! The hint of
awesome Powers beyond their ken! The threat of the
dire consequences of misbehavior! A deterrent
against greed and selfishness, against mankind's
wanton thirst for power and taste for destruction!
Terror and awe! Before there were gods, there were
dragons!"

Now Paia is glad for the unnatural darkness
around them, for how could she possibly conceal her
utter dismay and disbelief? He cannot be unaware
that most others, human and dragon, would level at
him exactly the same accusations he's just thrown at
mankind. Is this some new strategy of self-
justification, an art she knows he's already well-
practiced in?

"But what about the innocent humans? Not all can
be blamed! All those innocent lives you've . . ."

"There are no innocents! All humanity is complicit
in the death of the Earth, by inaction as much as by
intent!" His volume dims, as if he's turned his back.
"Besides, intimidation is not the same as murder.
How often must I make this point? Count the dead,
I tell you! You'll find that either their lives were willingly offered here in my own time where I can physically manifest, or they died in other times at the hand
of some human gone out of control! If human nature
is weak and corruptible, am I to blame?"

"But surely there are other myths you could have

personified!" Part of her curses and accuses him, but another part accepts the tragic truth of all he says. "More . . . hopeful ones."

"That was my brother's theory, and Water's, too. And you see how successful they've been at keeping mankind in check. If it weren't for me . . . !"

Paia waits, for what seems an abnormal length of time. Perhaps there's a part of him that's lost faith in his pitiless rhetoric. "What?" she asks finally, and hears him sigh, long and dry, like a wind off a wasteland.

"Well, no method is perfect, when you're working with such fallible material as the hearts and minds of men. Sooner or later, some human or other wants his own piece of the terror and awe. And then there's no controlling them. They lose all respect for the natural order of the world, and the long doomward spiral has begun."

Paia thinks of the girl Erde, able at the direst moments to find an optimistic angle of view, or an excuse for positive action. *I am not that girl,* she decides. *I have seen too much of the destruction men have brought about. I have lost my family to it, and the life I once knew. What convincing arguments can I pull together to counter his, when the evidence in his favor lies all around the Citadel, in the greedy hearts of its merchants and in the scheming minds of the Temple's priests and priestesses?*

"I always wondered, even as a little girl, when you first arrived . . . I always wondered why the God was so angry all the time."

"Not *all* the time." His growl from the darkness is half-denial, half acknowledgment.

"Yes, all. All the time. Even in your most generous

or frivolous moods, it was always there, that underground simmer of rage. I thought you were just mean."

"I am mean. I am the . . ."

"I know. The God." An uncomfortable pressure is building in Paia's chest. She reaches for a sheet to pull up around her shoulders, and finds it right there beneath her hand. Silk. "So you came to the Citadel to punish mankind for all they'd done?"

Fire laughs bleakly. "The world they've made seems punishment enough. Let them suffer in it. I came to the Citadel to enjoy myself while the planet still lives. And because you were there, dragon guide. You might say I had no choice. Perhaps a bit of revenge seemed excusable, under the circumstances, and since there was nothing better to do with my time . . ."

"But you became all and everything that you despise men for!" she cries out suddenly, and bursts into tears.

"Don't do that. Don't *do* that!"

"I can't help it! It's so . . . such a terrible waste!"

"Maybe I became what humanity deserves!" he shouts. "It's too late to change things now. Stop crying!"

Does she detect some faint stirrings of regret? Or does he simply mean it's too late for *him* to change? Paia hiccups and swallows a sob. "Earth and Water tell a different story."

"And I have told them, and you, the truth of that story. And a dragon cannot lie." He sits down beside her and draws the sheet aside. "Come, beloved, why concern ourselves with the fate of undeserving men? My siblings are fools to do so. I refuse to join them. My clever ingenuity has made a way for us to be together, at least for a while. Shouldn't we enjoy it while we can?"

A new concern saps Paia's resistance: wouldn't a dragon guide inevitably share her dragon's weaknesses as well as his strengths? "I suppose a little while longer can't make any difference. But do you think, my Fire," she adds only half playfully, "that you will be able to accept the responsibility of an actual relationship?"

He kisses her in reply, then fills her again, and again, and somewhere in their endless excess of orgasm, Paia realizes that they've had the argument he was willing to have, but meanwhile strayed completely from the questions she most wants an answer to: *Why now? What made me know to come to you so willingly? What's happened? What has changed?*

Chapter Twenty-seven

The Librarian programs a tiny window through the blankness around him to watch the sky-blue limo glide away along the narrow, pitted street. He's programmed a longer journey than necessary for its passengers, a guided tour of the White City while he takes the time to rescue Stoksie and the others from the *machina rex*, and discover what Luther knows about Earth's whereabouts.

Now that he has a method, he works quickly and efficiently. He'll gather up the next ones in a group. He calls up the power grid diagram to trace out the Rex's location. He hunts up the nearest paver machine, and sends it a long set of radical instructions. Just before leaving, he remembers his video feed to the Citadel. He turns to find the old TV waiting behind him, like a patient family retainer. The screen frames a bright view of the Grand Stair and a great deal of commotion. The Librarian reflexively reaches for the volume control, then recalls that this signal has no sound. In the dust and pitiless sun, armed men are pouring up the steps toward the Temple.

The Librarian can't even think of staying to watch, but he lingers long enough to observe that the vanguard of resistance has already crumbled. The soldiers guarding the stair have thrown down their weapons. Some seem to be greeting Leif Cauldwell's army as if they were old friends. It's possible, the Librarian muses. As if famine and epidemic weren't enough, the Fire-breather's tyranny split families, estranged neighbors, destroyed the fabric of entire communities. There is a sporadic hail of arrows from the walls of the upper plaza, but perhaps Leif will have less of a battle than he was prepared for. All for the best . . . and still no flash of gold from above, no vast dragon wing darkening the sky. What can be keeping Fire, the Librarian wonders?

HURRY! HURRY!

Yes, yes, I will. I am.

When he opens the door this time, he's around the corner from the Rex's square. His transportation and rescue vehicle is already waiting for him.

It's tall, gleaming, and yellow. Yellow like daylilies, or the sun before global warming. It makes the Librarian smile, something he's felt the need of for a while. It's a replica of Luther's Tinker wagon, as accurately as he could remember it, having only seen it in the lantern-lit darkness of the great central cavern at the Refuge. Of course, he's taken a few liberties. He's enlarged it substantially, to have room inside the cargo box for a crowd. He's also beefed up its armor to withstand potential Rex attacks. And if the nanomechs had any real grasp of organic forms, they'd never have produced a nasty looking mutant like the Rex. So the Librarian has avoided replicating Luther's sturdy mules. Instead, he's restored the old truck's propulsion system, substituting clean nanopower for its original filthy-dirty internal combustion engine.

He shuts the door behind him and walks around his creation admiringly. Even the chipped paint and faded signage is bright and new: *Schwann's Ice Cream*. The Librarian licks his lips. He remembers ice cream.

HURRY! HURRY!

He's never been one to rush about. How did he get matched with such an impatient dragon? He sighs, and climbs up into the cab. It's been half a century since he's driven a vehicle of any sort, but since the last one was an armored personnel carrier, he figures an ice cream truck should be a piece of cake. It'll come back to him quickly enough. There's a key in the ignition, not bright and new, but a match to the one Luther wears around his neck as personal amulet and talisman. The Librarian grasps it boldly and fires up the engine. Its nearly silent nano-hum is so different from what he's expected that for a minute, he's sure nothing's working. Then he feels the soft and steady vibration. He slips into gear, gingerly presses the accelerator, and the old/new truck rolls obediently forward. Down the length of the street, the Librarian gains confidence . . . and speed. Enough to come careening into the square with some doubt still in his mind that he'll find the Tinkers there with the women and dogs. But he's proved to himself that N'Doch's song was not imagined, so probably the women and dogs are real, and Luther, too. As real as anything can be said to be in the white nano-city.

And there they are. The Rex has rebuilt enough of its damaged circuits to begin a random, self-protective flailing of knife-edged limbs. The women have wisely drawn back, hauling their dead and wounded to the square's perimeter. He counts two bodies at least. Stoksie and Luther turn at the approaching squeal of tires as if sure it's a new attack from the rear, then stare dumbfounded as the Librarian screeches to a halt in front of them. He tumbles out of the cab, pointing madly without explanation. The Rex is waking, waking!

"Get in! Get in!" he shouts. Later, he'll tell them all that's happened, if he can find the words.

Stoksie is stunned to immobility. "Weah'd yu cum frum, G? I t'ought yu wuz . . ."

"No! Not dead! Quick! Hurry! Get the women!" He grabs Luther, who stands entranced by this altered vision of his beloved and familiar wagon, and hauls him around to the rear. "Open it! You know how!"

No strangers to wonder or emergency, the Tinkers spring into action. As the Rex rediscovers coordination by gnashing its jaws and retracting and extending its claws, Stoksie enlists Lily and Margit with nod and gesture to help him herd the others toward the big yellow vehicle. They're willing to trust the dark little stranger, whom they've lately seen bashing the metal monster with a pike. The dogs are less willing, however, and Lily, burdened with one of their wounded, is forced to be stern with them before they'll leap blindly into the dark cave of the rear cargo box. The Rex finishes testing its systems. Its sensor-laden head swivels toward the source of sound and motion.

"Hurry!" the Librarian calls. Or is it his dragon's urgency he's giving voice to? The borderlines are blurring.

Luther and Margit insist on delaying long enough to load the dead.

"Mebbe he'll fix 'em," Luther says. "He did sum al'reddy."

He means Earth, the Librarian realizes. "Yes! Hurry!" The Rex is moving toward them, gaining speed fast. He leaves them to finish up, and stumbles for the cab. He's just started the engine when he hears the rear doors slam. Luther vaults into the passenger seat, just ahead of the Rex's vicious sidearm slash. He ducks, grabs for the door, and pulls it tight. Steel claws rake the window, screech across the armored side. The truck sways wildly.

"Go!" Luther yells.

The Librarian floors it.

The Rex pursues them for a while, swift on the straightaway, but tending to madly overshoot its turns. Taking evasive action, the Librarian gets lost several times, with the Tinkers hotly debating the route and Margit and Lily swearing up and down that the streets have changed since the trip out. The Librarian offers them the minor consolation that they're probably right. No knowledge is permanent here, and nothing is to be trusted. Also, he's noticed something else. The city's machined perfection seems to be breaking down. Entire townhouses disintegrating. High-rises developing gaping holes in their upper reaches. And, here and there, as they've sped past, he's seen places where the nano repair machines are not replicating the bland building facades as they were before. Instead, the new portions reflect a much more alien geometry, as if the nanos' memory of buildings designed by and for humans has failed, or stranger still, been jettisoned intentionally. The Librarian wonders if he needs to start worrying about the city's life-support systems.

"Yu gottit! Lost 'im, I t'ink." Luther hangs out the side window, searching for signs of the Rex.

Stoksie pokes his head through the hatch between front and back. "Yu gotta turn back leff, nah."

The Librarian accesses the grid map to locate a concentration of nano power lines in the general direction that all describe. Eventually this guides them to the dank courtyard and the stone archway that all agree leads to Deep Moor. Here, too, in the fabric of this nano re-creation, the Librarian sees anomalies: blank spots in the drystone masonry, or patches of circuitry mingling with mossy cobbles in the court.

He pulls up in front of the iron gate. Luther jumps down to open the cargo doors. Lily and Margit pile out and through the arch, calling for help. But Margit is back soon, too soon, and Raven is with her, her lovely face tense with worry that eases with surprise and delight when she sees who's come.

"Gerrasch! Oh, it's you! I mean, it's you and yet it isn't. Just look at you! What a marvel!" She smiles, holding out both hands. "Quite the figure of a man you've become!"

The Librarian presses her fingers between his soft palms, and blushes.

Margit says, "He's not here!"

"He's not?"

"Gone!" exclaims Margit desperately.

Raven grasps the scout's sleeve. "Shhh! Don't tell them. Don't worry! Linden will do all she can."

"She can't bring back the dead!"

"Shhh! Shhh, dear!"

"You should have kept him here!" Margit jerks her arm free and stalks away to help unload.

"Had I known, I . . ."

"Where is he?" The Librarian has definitely planned on Earth being here.

Raven's eyes follow the wounded being carried through the gateway. "Gone again. Both of them. Without a word to any of us."

"Why? Why?" His demand is more to the dragon inside him than to poor, distraught Raven, who looks further stricken anyway.

"Why, indeed! I can't fathom it! Especially when they knew the rescue party had been sent out after you!"

Should have acted sooner! Should have got here faster! The Librarian knows his reaction time is down, way down. But it's hard, after so many millennia of waiting, of living in slow motion. He vows to work on it.

"I'll find them," he promises, to whomever's still listening.

"And odd things are happening here, too," Raven continues. "I mean, the whole place is odd to begin with. At first, we were constantly finding more and more of Deep Moor. You'd go through a gate or a door and discover a garden or a room that hadn't been there moments before. But now, parts of it are disappearing. There's less and less of it. What do you think it means?"

"I don't know," the Librarian lies. Then he climbs back into the yellow truck to concentrate on programming a new sort of search.

Chapter Twenty-eight

With enormous misgivings, Erde pictures the Grove in her mind, paying proper attention to its most telling details. She has failed to talk the dragon out of answering this latest summons, though she tells herself she shouldn't call it failure, since that would imply that she'd had some vague chance of succeeding. As gentle and diffident as Earth appears at most times, when decided on something, he's as stubborn as a rock and cannot be dissuaded, however foolish she might consider his chosen course.

Erde's final warning concerns the stretch of years from this far future to her far-away past, and the risk of arriving in the midst of a dangerous situation already half-felled by weakness and nausea from the long journey. The dragon promises he will protect her, and how can she insult him by questioning his ability to do so? It's a shame that the law of dragon transport does not permit her to travel any farther back in her own time than she has already lived in it. She cannot, for instance, send the dragon to the Grove as it was when she first saw it. It must be to

the Grove of snow and ice and cold, and the black
ashes of Deep Moor. At least she has thought of a
backup plan.

So, sensing doom in every nerve ending, Erde tells
the dragon she's ready, then offers up her image of
the Grove: solemn, majestic and, even in the smothering snow, heartbreakingly lovely.

She has chosen a smaller side clearing as their specific destination, away from the central pond and the
broad, open meadow where the portal to the city had
opened. Given his ever expanding size, the dragon
will just barely fit under the arch of the great spreading limbs, but there they might manage to arrive un-
detected if Fra Guill and his forces are still about, at
least for long enough that she might recover her balance. But when they arrive, though Erde's travel ill-
ness is mild this time, the trees are much thinner
than she's remembered. She barely has a moment to
catch her breath and stand steadily on both feet,
when a cry goes up from the meadow.

Dragon! We are discovered!

Hastily, she tells him her backup plan.

NO. NOT YET. WE MUST WAIT FOR THE
OTHERS.

*But surely you can see! There's no one here but white-
robes and soldiers!*

Brother Guillemo's army is encamped across the
meadow, and all around the sacred pond. Their
equipment and personal kits are strewn across the
snow like garbage. Their heavy-footed warhorses
have trampled the once-flowering verge of the pond
into mud. Their boots and tents and lumbering supply wagons have crushed the delicate forest grasses
and flattened the meadow into a field of rutted ice.

And now Erde sees why the thick lattice of branches did not conceal them. Raw stumps protrude through the dirty snow where several vast and ancient giants have fallen to the ax. Cook fires and campfires dot the clearings, blackening the tender earth and sending up dark billows of smoke to blur the air.

Oh, the trees! They're killing the trees! Oh, dragon, what are we to do?

The dragon, too, is stunned.

How could such sacrilege have been allowed to happen? Could not the Grove protect itself? Is the hell-priest's power so very great?

In her grief and horror, Erde for a moment forgets her own peril. The alert soldiers who'd spotted them spring up and reach for their weapons. They kick dozing neighbors awake and send word of intruders down the line. Messengers race toward the cluster of tents, blindingly white, taking up the center of the meadow. The nearest men brandish their pikes and glower, but they do not advance. They glance behind, awaiting reinforcements.

They fear you, dragon, but you'll see. Once their numbers give them courage, they'll be on us like a swarm!

OR THEY WILL WAIT FOR THEIR LEADER TO APPROACH.

Their leader. Erde can feel him there, sniffing her out. She could point directly to the tent he hides in, not the biggest—the decoy—but that scruffier one off to the side.

No! We can't wait for him! We can do nothing here without the others. Let's go! We must wait until they come!

The first reinforcements have come up. At a shouted signal, the soldiers lockstep toward them, pikes and lances leveled. The dragon is hemmed in by trees. There is no possibility of retreat. For once, Earth is sensible, and relents.

An instant later, they are on a wide stone ledge high above the valley, overlooking the old downward trail. Once this was a faint and secret track that kept Deep Moor hidden from the world of men. Now, it's trampled raw and wide, obvious even to the unskilled eye. An icy wind scours the ledge, but Erde has her old woolen clothes and the dragon for warmth. She leans against him disconsolately and knuckles away tears she can't control. From this ledge, she'd beheld Deep Moor for the very first time. She wonders if she can bear any more sadness, any further loss.

Ah, dragon, I feel as if nothing good will ever happen again!

Earth lifts his horned head from a perusal of the battered trail. THEN LOOK OUT THERE, AND BE GLAD!

Far out in the middle of the valley, where the snow-flecked trees nestle in a bend of a silver ribbon of river, a further army spreads in a closed circle around the Grove. A protective circle, Erde assumes, the overflow of Fra Guill's numberless legions. She cannot imagine why the sight of more tents and men and wagons littering her beloved valley should make her anything but horrified, and tells the dragon so between her sobs.

THEN LOOK CLOSER.

She does so, if only to please him, then sags against his foreclaw with a gasp. *Do I see it right? Is that the king's standard flying above that red and gold pavilion?*

The dragon assents gravely, as if this joy might be too fleeting to admit to.

Oh! And do you see . . . ?

A LITTLE TO THE LEFT. He helps direct her gaze, not so keen as his over distances.

"I see it!" she cries aloud, grasping Earth's claw to keep from pitching wildly over the ledge. The red dragon crest of Baron Weisstrasse flutters bravely among a cluster of smaller tents. "Hal! Sir Hal! Oh, listen to me! As if he could hear me! You see? I told you he would come to rescue Deep Moor!" She says nothing of him arriving too late, after Deep Moor is already in ashes and its women fled. That he is here is enough to lift her spirits. "Let's go to him immediately!"

THESE SOLDIERS WILL FEAR ME MUCH AS THE OTHERS DID.

Then take me partway, and I'll walk in alone to find him. We'll let Sir Hal introduce you to his men. Imagine how proud he'll be!

PERHAPS.

Now it's Earth's turn to be dubious, but he sets her down along the icy road, a decent distance from the encampment, then instantly stills himself to invisibility. The wind cuts cruelly across the valley floor, but Erde gathers her woolen layers about her, and with as much grandeur as she can muster, marches toward camp.

The outermost pickets are too cold and battle-weary to offer more than a halfhearted challenge, plus a few perfunctory leers. Erde does not offer her name. When last she was here, her father was the king's enemy. But when she asks, with the grace and dignity learned from her grandmother the baroness, to be directed to the compound of Baron Weisstrasse, the three guards are intimidated into silence and pointing.

Only when she is walking away does one sneer, "'*Compound.*' Get her, willya?"

"Likes 'em old, I guess," mutters another.

"And crazy," adds his friend.

"You'd be better off with me," the third calls, now that her back is to them.

Erde lets it be that way. She can't blame these broken soldiers for their lewd assumptions. No lady of her station would travel on foot in such weather, never mind without her lady's maid and several stout retainers for escort. No lady would dress as she is dressed, with her short curls unbound to the wind beneath her sheepskin hood. She tries to see herself as those men had seen her. She's grown quite tall, she realizes, measuring her height against the soldiers, who'd seemed dwarfish by comparison, battered and underfed. She has forgotten her lady's mincing steps, and now strides like a boy. No wonder they jump to the only conclusions they have definitions for. To them, she must be a camp follower. She's an exotic, a freak. If she looks them in the eye, and doesn't smile coquettishly or flinch, perhaps she is even a witch.

But the surprise is, she's beautiful. At least, to battle-weary soldiers, she is. She can see it in their eyes. It makes her stand straighter and walk along with a more confident step, if only not to disappoint their expectations, as their stares follow her down the road.

The second round of sentries have a tent and a sputtering fire built in its lee to huddle about. These have strength enough to stop her and question her more fully about her business. There are also more of them, and they leer with more serious intent. One tries to rub his hands on her, under the pretext of searching for weapons.

"I do have a weapon," she declares, revealing but not unsheathing the heavy dagger she's worn since she traded her ancestral brooch for Sir Hal's sword in a dusty market town far in the future. Köthen now carries the dragon-hilted sword. In its place, she got the dagger, which had belonged to his captain, a man called Wender. Erde thinks of Köthen now, as she says sternly, "And I will use it, in the king's name, if you do not stand aside and let me pass!"

The soldiers laugh uproariously. Her defiance only whets their appetite. Four of them form a ring around her and smack their lips over all the "favors" they'll extract from her, which they describe in lingering detail. She should be terrified, but she knows she can call a dragon down on them in seconds flat. She stands still, waiting with exaggerated patience while the men argue, with increasing heat and distraction, over which of them will "have" her first. Finally, she sees her opportunity. She shoves hard at the shoulders of the two loudest and shocks them into momentary recoil. In a breath, she's past them and drawing her dagger, rounding on them threateningly. As soon as she's done it, she's amazed at herself. Little Erde, throwing her weight around. For the second time that day, she tells herself: *Won't Hal be pleased!*

"The king shall hear of this," she rebukes them haughtily, though she has never met her infirm and elderly liege, who might have little sympathy for the daughter of his enemy, Josef von Alte. "Or Baron Weisstrasse," she adds. "If you will direct me in his way now, nothing more shall be said of this."

A couple of the soldiers snicker.

"Yeah?" says one beefy guard, "And what's that crazy old coot gonna do to me?"

But his smaller neighbor elbows him warningly. "Wender," he mutters. "He'll do it to you, and you won't forget it."

Some of the others nod their agreement. Erde is delighted to hear Captain Wender mentioned. It must be the same man, she's sure of it. She can see their enthusiasm for her has dimmed. She's looking like too much trouble to be further bothered with, and so, she presses the advantage. "Well, then, if you haven't the decency to direct me to Baron Weisstrasse, will you tell me at least where I can find Captain Wender?"

The smaller man steps forward, but only to send her farther along the road. "You'll want to go on down that way, milady, and take the first right."

Erde thanks him graciously, as if no unseemly incident has passed between them. She leaves him smiling, quizzically and much against his better judgment, and continues onward, trying not to rush. There are tents and wagons rising to either side by now, and soon she is passing the taller canopies of the minor nobles, more spacious and artfully decorated, with clusters of warhorses tethered alongside. But these finer tents are as stained and many-times mended as the lesser ones, and the poor horses are hunched together against the cold and look as starved as all the men.

She takes the turn as directed, narrowly avoiding being run down by a young man on horseback whose armor looks much too big for him. Finally, in the distance, above a row of shorter canvas shelters, Erde sees Hal's silken banner stretching boldly in the hard north wind. Now she can't help but quicken her step, with her gaze downcast as much for seeming modesty as to keep her balance among the icy wagon ruts, which are wide and treacherously full of half-frozen mud. Surely there must be a few women of virtue among this spread of apparently lawless men! Who else, she wonders, will care for the sick and wounded? Who will say prayers for the dying?

With this mournful thought, Erde glances up to be sure of her path. Ahead of her, a tall man is flinging orders at a scurrying group of unwilling boys, squires, perhaps, or scullery lads. She is reminding herself that there is no scullery to be had for leagues about, when she realizes with a shock that the faded tunic that the big man wears over his battered mail was once the sky blue and gold of Castle Köthen. Quickly, her memory sorts out the man's broad back and burly frame.

"Captain Wender!" she calls, though she knows it's hardly ladylike. "Captain Wender!"

The man has been shouting at the boys. His scowl lingers as he turns, then evaporates abruptly as he recognizes her. To Erde's surprise, an even fiercer expression replaces it, a sudden and desperate bloom of hope.

Erde quails before its brilliance. *Oh, dear. He thinks I've brought his baron back.*

"Milady!" Wender banishes the boys to their errands, then hurries toward her. His frown has returned. "Milady! Alone, and on foot?"

She gazes up at him for a long and helpless moment. "Alone. Yes."

Wender's mouth sets in something like despair. "Then how came you . . . ?"

"I came. . . ." Then it comes to her. It's the *dragon*

he's hoping for. "I left Lord Earth a ways away, so as not to frighten the soldiers."

Wender sags as if every breath has gone out of him. "Then he is with you? The . . . the dragon?" When she nods, puzzled by his vehemence, he rushes on with little of his usual deference. "Then you must bring him, milady! Quickly! The knight has need of him!"

"Sir Hal? What? Why?"

"Cut near to death a day ago, milady, and won't lie still! If there's even hope of his mending, he won't give it a chance! I beg you, milady, call in your creature!"

"I doubt even Lord Earth could convince Hal to lie still if he doesn't wish to," Erde says.

"I mean to heal him! Please! Quickly! He's dying!"

"Dying?" Finally, she takes in Wender's haggard look. She's been so wrapped up in anticipation of a fond reunion with her elder knight that she hasn't properly listened. "*Dying?* Oh, sweet Mother, help us! Take me to him, and we'll summon the dragon immediately!"

Chapter Twenty-nine

The limo's ride is the smoothest he's ever known . . . not that he's actually been inside one before, so okay, it's smoother than he's ever imagined. N'Doch tunes the interior lights up and down on their dimmer just for the hell of it, then lounges back on the soft, dark blue leather, so real you can smell it. Room enough for his whole body, plus the guitar. Room enough between the seats for the full stretch of his legs. He grins at his grandfather, perched opposite him.

"Okay, now, Papa, why don't you just pop open that cooler beside you and see what's inside?"

Djawara is still regarding his tall grandson as if he's not sure they're related. He glances at Sedou next to him, for support. But the man/dragon is gazing out the window, frowning in thought.

"C'mon, Papa! Maybe there's nothing. You oughta look, at least!"

"There'll be water," Sedou murmurs from the depths of his brown study, as Djawara bends disapprovingly to search the compartment between their seats. And there is, but only water. Three chill blue bottles bright with tiny bubbles. Djawara passes them around. N'Doch takes his and inspects the label.

"You were expecting something stronger?"

"Nah, Papa, you know me. Not much of a drinker." He doesn't jump to the bait like usual. Feels like he's done arguing over small stuff. Can't see the point anymore.

The car purrs forward though identical streets, and the men sip their water in silence. The driver's head never moves. N'Doch knows this 'cause he has the forward facing seat, and he's been watching. The dude's as still as glass. Like he's a robot or something. N'Doch strums the guitar absently, picking out a mournful little tune. Finally he says, "So, I'm waiting, bro."

Sedou stirs. "Waiting?"

"For that explanation I figure you owe me." N'Doch shifts his gaze, which he hopes looks accusing enough to win him an answer. "Or maybe you can tell me, Papa, since you seem so tuned in on the dragon hot line."

"Hardly, my boy. I just pay attention."

This time the bait is hard to ignore. N'Doch shoots a look back at Sedou. "Is he in on this 'mutual annihilation' gig, too? 'Cause if he's not, I think he oughta just . . ."

"Look!" Sedou leans forward, his attention caught by something outside the window.

It might be a diversionary tactic, but N'Doch checks it out anyway. Between two faceless building facades, he sees a flash of rock and darkness. Then the limo has rolled on past, and it's just the usual bit of boredom out there.

"What was that?"

Sedou is frowning again.

"You notice how it's never night here?" The uncanny blackness between the buildings lingers in N'Doch's mind. "I mean, we got to have been here long enough for it to get dark out, doncha think?"

"I suspect," says Djawara, "that if you asked for night in the right way, you would get it. If you actually *needed* night, for instance."

Sedou nods silently.

"Like you needed your espresso?" N'Doch laughs, though none of this seems particularly funny right now. "It's like a big hologram, isn't it? Like, y'know, the holodeck." He's remembering the old vids.

"More material than that." Sedou turns the blue bottle in his hand. "More *actual*. But my real concern is, why is it breaking apart?"

"Is it?" Djawara asks.

Sedou gestures at the buildings gliding past. "That . . . space we saw. An anomaly. Like a hole in the fabric of this particular reality."

"A hole?" N'Doch looking hard, now, to find another one. "Where does the hole go to?"

Sedou shrugs. "To another layer of the illusion? Or, I suppose, it could be to . . . actual reality."

"I challenge you to define that satisfactorily," Djawara chuckles.

"You mean the world outside?" N'Doch goes for a more literal interpretation. "It looked awful . . . y'know, empty."

"Barren. Airless, you might almost say."

"What's airless?"

"Lacking an atmosphere," Sedou supplies patiently.

"I know that! I mean, why?"

"Look!"

They all stare as another 'hole' slides by. This one is taller and wider, exposing a brief but definitive glimpse of a raw, red landscape, dust and rock, illuminated by a hard white light. Not a single speck of relieving green.

"Sky's a weird color," N'Doch observes. "Not black, exactly, but . . ." He thinks of the old photos of lunar landings, ancient history in his day. "That's what you mean by airless, huh?"

"That's what I mean."

The weirdest thing, N'Doch decides, is that right after the facade bordering the hole, there's a crossing street, which extends away from the intersection as if the city had turned a corner around this "anomaly," as the dragon called it. The contrast blows his whole perception of three-dimensional space.

No, wait, that's not the weirdest thing . . .

N'Doch's head slews around, trying to stay level with the view down the next intersection, where he's just seen, or thinks he's seen . . .

Nah. Can't be. A Tyrannosaurus Rex? *Now I'm really losing it!*

It was remembering those vids, that's what did it. Like when he first laid eyes on Water and was so sure she was a special effect. He decides not to mention this, to her or his grandfather.

The glass panel between the driver's seat and the rear compartment whispers aside. The driver leans sideways to speak through the opening. "I beg your pardon, sirs, but I thought you'd like to know: there's been a destination change."

"Really?" asks Sedou. "Who says?"

"My principal, sir. Straight from headquarters."

N'Doch rolls his eyes at his grandfather.

"And our new destination?" Sedou pursues.

"Says here, 'Deep Moor,' sir."

"That'll be fine. Thank you."

"Thank you, sir. You're welcome."

"Robot!" mutters N'Doch, as the glass panel slides shut.

"Quite possibly," Sedou agrees.

N'Doch stretches back against his seat and regards the man/dragon owlishly. "Well, going back to Deep Moor's all right with me. Might get some answers there. Those witchy ladies know a thing or two. 'Course, we gotta worry about them being okay. Wasn't only my people the Fire dude was after." He says it lightly to ward off his shiver. He'd really rather not find any more good women with holes in their foreheads.

"I'd give you answers if I had any," Sedou growls.

"And you don't."

"Don't sound so dubious."

"Something passed between you and Fire back at the Rive. And don't be telling me you were just catching up on old times."

"It was my sister . . . when we both sensed she was free. It blew his mind, and he couldn't quite keep it from me. Beyond that, I have innuendo, half-truth, implication, and guesswork. But answers? No."

"Never mind." N'Doch slumps back and draws the guitar across his chest like a shield. He's thinking how like Sedou the dragon's become, how . . . human. Like the taking on of a human biology has changed her more than just physically. She didn't used to hold back on him for the sake of his feelings.

"Hey, bro," he calls softly across the chasm between the seat banks. "You gonna need a song any time soon, you think?"

Sedou gives him a long, deep look, the dragon gazing at him through the man's dark eyes. "Might be, bro. Might be."

"Now here is an interesting neighborhood," remarks Djawara suddenly.

N'Doch feels the car slowing. They're into another district of narrow streets. Narrow and twisty, with twin ruts worn into the paving stones, and dirty water flowing in the gutters. And animal signs: the occasional manure pile, though none of it looks very recent. N'Doch tries to lower the window beside him, and runs into the first thing about his dream car that doesn't work. Broken? He somehow doubts it. Probably if he tried the door, he'd get the same result. Is it a trap, or just a safety precaution? He's just about to air this latest anxiety when the car rounds a particularly tight corner and turns into a circular courtyard, dark and dank, and bounded by high stone walls. At least most of it's stone. Here and there, N'Doch sees odd patches of what looks like electronic microcircuitry, enlarged a billion times. He squints as the car sweeps past a nearby one. It's big, taller than he is. Maybe it's some kind of art, set into the walls.

He's distracted as the driver pulls around and stops beside the only other vehicle N'Doch has seen since setting foot in the city. He lets out a snort of recognition. The thing is twice the size he remembers, and a whole lot brighter, but he knows what he's looking at, sure enough.

"This sure ain't Deep Moor, but hey, check it out!

There's Luther's old caravan. Looks like he got him-self a new paint job!"

When he tries the car door, it works just fine. The driver's already popped out of his seat to open the door on Sedou's side. N'Doch wonders idly if the robot will expect a tip. But as soon as they're all out and standing expectantly on the broad, wet stones paving the yard, the driver tips his cap neatly, climbs back into the limo, and drives off. N'Doch stares after it. He misses the blue leather seats and the soft ride already.

"This way," Sedou calls. "She's this way."

Making a quick inspection tour around the big yel-low caravan, N'Doch sees the man/dragon vanishing through a tall stone arch. Its nasty-looking iron grille is partially ajar. Djawara waits at the opening, his calm eyes not entirely able to contain their amaze-ment. Is it what's inside, or what's outside, or the contrast between? N'Doch cups the old man's elbow and escorts him through the gate. He's getting more than used to walking through strange doorways into unexpected places. This time, he finds a rich green lawn and a cluster of old trees, half-concealing a low-slung dwelling. The house he recognizes, with its big stone chimney, and some of the outbuildings and barns. But others seem to be missing, and it had been deep winter at Deep Moor when he was there: bleak, leafless, and monochromatic. This symphony of green and bloom and fragrance stops him in his tracks by the gate. He liked the place enough before, but now . . . ! All his senses go on overdrive—eyes, ears, nose, bathed in lusciousness. The air is sweet in his lungs, and the touch of the sun on his cheeks is gentle, like a caress. It's all he can do to keep himself from racing off and rolling in the grass. No wonder the girl always talked like this place was paradise!

Djawara gently jogs him out of his daze. "We're waited on, I believe."

There's a big crowd up by the house, full of people N'Doch recalls, and some he doesn't. He's relieved to see Raven and Rose, and most of the women he'd known there, alive and well. He sees Luther and Stoksie and heads their way, not even bothering to ask himself how the hell they got here. He looks for Erde and the Big Guy, but they don't seem to be around. The real surprise is Gerrasch, who N'Doch thought would never willingly leave his techno-haven in the Refuge. He's got mirrorshades on, and he and Sedou seem to be having some sort of re-union, which is interesting, since N'Doch can't recall Gerrasch ever having met Water in his brother's shape before. What's more interesting, everybody else is watching, with near-breathless anticipation.

"Whazzup?" He eases in between Stoksie and Luther, short and tall, as if he's left them only yesterday. Fact is, it *could* have been yesterday, for all he can tell.

"Itz her! Itz da One!" Luther is beaming.

"The one? You mean, Air? Where?"

Stoksie nods at Sedou and Gerrasch. "Itz G. He's gotter in 'im. Or so he sez."

"In him?" N'Doch knows he can test the truth of this. He can ask Water on the old dragon internet. He can ask Gerrasch, for that matter, guide to guide. But they both look pretty busy, plus he's even more reluctant than usual. If it's true, Air will be there, too. A whole new dragon voice to contend with, a whole new variety of invasion. And this one's the one they've gone through all this to find, the one who has, everyone keeps assuring him, all the answers. He tells himself he oughta let the dragons do their catching up in private anyway.

"How'd she get loose?"

"G diddit. Sumhow."

Luther's sigh is soft with admiration and awe. "He tuk her spirit wit'in 'im."

N'Doch can't think of anything worse, but he respects Luther enough to keep that irreverence to himself. Besides, Gerrasch is different from the other guides. He's already half dragon, so maybe it doesn't bother him as much. "But he's still . . . he's still, y'know . . . still Gerrasch?"

"Yah," Stoksie marvels. "Seems like it."

"Huh. So where's Erde and the Big Guy? Looks like everyone else is here, and I wouldn't think they'd want to be missing this."

"Gone." Stoksie shakes his head, then scrapes his hand over its shining baldness. "Gone. G's not reel happy 'bout dat."

"You mean they were, but . . . gone where?"

"Doan know fer shur. Dat lady . . ." Stoksie points out Raven, N'Doch's fantasy woman, who looks more worn and anxious than he's ever seen her. "She t'inks dey wenta . . . weah izzit, Luta?"

"Da Grove," Luther intones solemnly.

"Makes sense. The summons. That's where we were headed." N'Doch would love to spin out the tale of the sky-blue limo, but he senses this just ain't the time for it.

"Da reel Grove," says Luther, grimmer than before.

"So? What's the problem?"

"Dat wacko preechur iz dere. An' heeza bad'un, all ri'. I saw 'im."

"Didja? Fra Guill?" N'Doch is curious. "I ain't had the pleasure yet."

"Well," drawls Stoksie darkly, "I t'ink yu gonna gettit reel soon."

Chapter Thirty

It seems a very long and languid time before the novelty of actual lovemaking wears off, and Fire recalls that he has a war to fight. But though his mind returns to the subject increasingly, he is still easily distracted by a caress or a heated glance. In between, he is content to expound at length about his superior strength and winning strategy, more willing to boast of the dedication and ferocity of his loyal followers than to rush to join them on the field. Paia is bemused by how easily she has conquered. It cannot be her shapely body and her loving alone. She's not that good at it yet. Observing Fire from as clear-eyed an angle as she can manage, she would swear she detects signs of exhaustion in the slow way he gathers himself at last to return to the fray.

"Well, they will be looking for me to claim the victory. Make a few decorative passes over the battle-field. Incinerate a few prisoners."

"You won't!"

"Why not? Think how much it will cheer the priestlings to see their old chief go up in flames."

She pulls away from him, wrapping the sheet around her shoulders. "Do you plan to carry me with you to this battle?"

"I can hardly leave you here on this barren mountaintop."

He draws suggestively on the sheet, but Paia holds it fast. "You cannot expect me to war against my own cousin!"

"You won't be fighting him, I will."

"But it will be as if I was fighting him." Perhaps an argument can be her next delaying tactic.

Fire lifts an arm over her shoulder and draws his sharp nails lightly down her back. "You would not fight him to reclaim your exalted status as my priestess? To regain your ancestral home?"

"I hate being a priestess." She tries to sound prim and disapproving, when all she wants is to press herself against him. "And Leif wants the Citadel for all the Cauldwells, myself included. From there, he can provide help and shelter for all who come to him in need."

"Very noble," murmurs Fire into the small of her back. The heat of his breath traces the curve of her hip. "But a waste of valuable and vanishing resources. With so little time left to us, I have no intention of allowing my hard-won luxuries to be shared out among the worthless and inept who can't find a way to take care of themselves. Death to the weak," he says, taking her nipple in his mouth.

"But fighting wastes resources, too."

"Ah, but it results in fewer mouths to feed."

Paia summons a vastness of will and pushes him away. "Listen, my Fire. Couldn't you work out some sort of truce? That way bloodshed could be prevented and the resources be conserved. If you swore on your honor as a dragon not to harm anyone . . ."

Fire falls backward on the bed, spread-eagled in a cascade of helpless guffaws. "On my honor?"

"But I'm serious. I could ask my cousin. I'm sure he . . ."

"No." He looks up at her, his laughter fading. "Come now, beloved. You're not actually suggesting that I share my palace with a legion of dregs and riffraff? That I live at the sufferance of my former slave?"

"Not a slave! He . . ."

"Subordinate, then! Servant! Stop splitting hairs!"

"The Temple ran smoothly due to my cousin's inspired management! You'd never have been able to carry it off without him. You should be more grateful!"

"GRATEFUL?" Fire is on his feet and pacing before Paia can blink. "But for me, he'd have starved with the rest of the riffraff! He's the foulest of traitors! He destroyed the Temple! He betrayed me and all who believed in me!"

She can offer him no denial on that count, and the usual excuses and explanations will only enrage him further. But Fire seems to have lost his relish for impassioned debate, as if even he senses that his accusations are growing repetitive and stale. Instead of heating up his diatribe against the ex-priest, higher and higher to the point of threats and invective, he slumps and turns away with a hiss of frustration. "Besides, even if Cauldwell did let us live in peace until the end comes, my siblings will be after me soon enough. With the end so near, they'll never let me rest."

"They're well occupied with the search for Air, my Fire." Paia has seen for herself the other dragons' capacity for obsession. Though its focus differs radically, it is the match to his own.

But Fire, wandering in the shadows, shakes his head. "Not anymore."

"What? Why not?"

He turns away again, waiting so long to answer that his reluctance is finally obvious. "My clever sister has found her own way to freedom."

"You didn't tell me."

"No. I didn't."

Because you're ashamed, guesses Paia. *Because now there's a real possibility you've failed. It's three against one now.* That's *what's changed.*

"How did she get out?"

He flicks an impatient hand. "What does it matter?"

And Paia thinks, *His real shame is that he doesn't know. She's outwitted him.* "So, then . . ."

"So there'll be no deals. No truces. What's the point? It's all or nothing now."

"But why?"

"Because!"

"Really, my Fire. You sound like . . ." She can't find a stinging enough comparison. "Well, you're being completely unreasonable."

"And this surprises you?"

"I thought perhaps . . ." She falters, knowing the words will sound foolish.

"Perhaps what?' He stalks out of the shadows to loom over her with his hair wild and his arms folded across his chest. He is looking less . . . *human*, she notes. More like his familiar scaled and gilded man-form. "You thought I would give in? Give up? You thought you'd *tamed* me? You and that sage old fool back in the café: you expect me to wax suddenly reasonable for the good of humanity? Humanity doesn't deserve my charity. Besides, what's the point of reason at the end of the world? Beloved, you forget who you're dealing with!"

Paia droops. She smooths the silky bedsheet with her hand. She is not disappointed. She has done the best she could. She only hopes it will be enough. "No, my Fire. I do not forget."

"Good. See that you don't! Enough of this. I'm bored. We're off to war! My faithful are waiting!"

And she is aloft again, instantly, her protest swept away by the wonder of flight. Again she is the great winged beast gliding over the ragged hills, where the only color is the red and yellow and gray of stone and the dust-thick windblown sky. Having now walked a landscape softened by trees, even one as sparse and dry as N'Doch's Africa, Paia looks for green and feels a lack she never did before. The endless barren rock seems unfinished, lonely, somehow . . . tragic.

She hasn't seen the Citadel from the air since she was small. Besides, things look different through the eyes of a dragon than they did from the passenger seat of her father's hover. Or maybe things are different: drier, more scrubbed, more beaten down by heat and scouring winds. Either way, they are nearly on top of it before she recognizes the wide sweep of valley, cut by the straight bright line of road. And there, in the shadowed curl of the upthrust cliff face, the walled courtyards climb like stacked boxes to the gilded facade of the Temple.

Paia would prefer to swoop and glide though the hot gusts of the heights, aloof from the struggles of

priests and warriors, exulting in the glory of wings.
She could observe the interesting dynamic of human
geometry imposed upon the more random pat-
ternings of rock and sand. A juxtaposition once
strong, now fading with the weakening of man's
hold over the Earth. Paia often tried to capture it in
her paintings. She could learn the newer patterns,
like the intruding fingers of blue, not as distant as
she'd thought, and beyond and around, the infinite
spread of ocean.

Perhaps she could exert some control over this
magnificent body not her own, through sheer delight
with its speed and agility, with its gleaming skin and
taut muscle. She knows how the dragon responds to
flattery. But Fire, having avoided the battle for so
long, is now impatient to be at it. He banks and
drops, chasing his own broad shadow across the
wasted valley floor, toward the Grand Stair where
dust and smoke rise and mix in an unnatural cloud.
Clots of figures appear as the cloud thins or shifts,
then vanish again behind a thickening billow. Running to and fro, the figures look like scurrying ants,
dark against the red dirt but indistinguishable as to
sex or age, or loyalty. Fire stoops out of the pale hot
sky to wheel over the courtyards, his shadow scudding across the cliff face like a cloud crossing the
sun. The ants are resolved into soldiers and priests
and villagers, mingling in a common melee. Many
halt as the dragon passes, to stare upward. Their gesticulating could be fearful or defiant. Paia cannot tell
for sure. Even if she tries to deflect the dragon's attack, which way should she turn him? She sees no
neat and comprehensible battle lines. Apart from the
occasional red flash of an Honor Guard's tunic, it's

impossible to tell the sides apart or determine the course of the fighting. Leif Cauldwell's army marched to war in the same clothes they farmed in or cared for their livestock, and the villagers loyal to the Temple would be no better equipped. They could be fighting a wildfire down there, instead of each other. The dragon offers no comment, but she senses his victorious mood plummeting like the pressure before a storm. His silence speaks his dismay and disbelief. He circles out over the valley and heads back for a second pass, lower this time, his roar crashing like wild surf along the cliff. He's searching for patterns, too, a direction in the movement of bodies, a focal point, a leader. Some sign that his forces are rallying. They're close enough now to see actual fighting, sprawled bodies here and there, the wounded being dragged to safety. But it seems that the motion is mostly toward the Temple, a steady inward flow meeting only sporadic resistance, passing eddies of stillness formed by groups of guarded prisoners, sullen in the heat or relieved to be out of the fighting. One large group near the top of the Grand Stair is entirely uniformed in Temple red. Several of them are chatting amiably with their peasant guards. It is the red-coats, not the rebels, who duck and quail as the dragon's shadow sweeps over them.

The dragon hisses deep in his throat. COWARDS! TRAITORS! THEY'RE SWORN TO FIGHT TO THE DEATH! HAVE THEY FORGOTTEN? WHERE ARE MY FAITHFUL? WHERE IS MY VICTORY?

As they glide past, only meters above the fighters' heads, Paia tries to direct Fire's furious disbelieving glare. There are men and women, Tinkers and farmers, fighting side by side, some of them wearing little

more than rags. Where is Leif Cauldwell, she wonders. Up at the front lines, or at the rear, directing
the attack? Where is Dolph Hoffman?

Ahead, the tall plate-metal gates to the Inner Court
are closed against a steady onslaught. Fire slows,
spinning tighter circles above the sun-baked plaza
where the remnants of the Honor Guard and a handful of priests and priestesses battle for control of the
entrance to the Temple.

HERE ARE MY HEROES, MY FAITHFUL! HERE
THE INVADER WILL BE TURNED BACK AND
DESTROYED!

Can he really believe that, Paia wonders? She
knows little of war, but she can tell a rout when she
sees one. Siege ladders are being relayed hand over
hand up the Grand Stair. Reinforcements have arrived, probably from the outlying villages that suffered so under the dragon's tyranny. Fat metal tubes
are carried up on men's shoulders, gleaming dully
in the sun. Guns of some sort, Paia is sure of it.
Who could have guessed that the rebels would be so
well armed?

With another thundering roar, Fire sweeps low
over the gates. His rage and his body are a united
force. Paia feels his chest expand with his fury to
exhale a long fiery breath. Flame splashes across the
heads and backs of the attackers. A few trailing
screams as the beast wings by, but most of the fighters duck, then just move onward. They're wearing
some sort of shielding, a wide-brimmed helmet flex-
ing into riveted plates down along their backs, like
a turtle's shell. *Or the scales of a dragon.* Paia reflects
on the difficulty of defending the Citadel from the
very man who held it against all attackers for so long.

Leif Cauldwell has not sent his rebels into battle unprepared.

The ladders swing up against the walls. The defenders scale the inner sides to shove them away, but the weight of the rebels swarming upward holds the ladders firmly in place. Inside the courtyard, three red-robed priestesses scurry out of the Temple, their arms loaded with the gold ware from the altar. Paia assumes they're saving the Temple's treasures from the marauders, but as they race past the fighting into the tunnel to the Citadel, their guilty backward glances tell her otherwise.

No, they're looting. Under the Temple portico, in the shade, she sees two priests arguing. She wonders what political dispute could be more important than fighting for their lives.

The dragon wheels, shrieking, and swoops in for another searing pass. As he reaches the gates, a sharp popping sound rips the air. Several of the defenders pitch forward silently and topple into the mass of rebels climbing the siege ladders. Paia has seen this before, watching the news feed during the endless days of the Final Collapse. Projectile weapons, primitive compared to the little laser pistol the dragon gave her, but effective, nonetheless.

Where is it now, that pistol? She follows the thought in order to distract herself from the continuing murder of the Temple staff. Men and women she has spent most of her life with. It doesn't matter that she never befriended any of them. The God—no, the *dragon*—always discouraged that. It doesn't matter that she considered them fools. Or that the ones she did like turned out to be rebels undercover, like Son Luco, aka Leif Cauldwell, and are probably the ones out there gunning down their former colleagues. Death is awful and final, no matter whose side you're on.

Another rattle of gunfire. This time, it follows the dragon's flight, falling around his body and gilded wings like a scatter of hail.

Falling. Gunfire from *above.*

As Paia comprehends this, so does the dragon. He tilts his fiery glance upward. A line of dark shapes, the heads and shoulders of men, roughens the worn profile of the cliff top. Again, the popping, then the sharp clatter against his scales. The dragon bellows and pumps his wings, soaring upward and away, then wheeling back, aiming himself like a missile at the heights. He skims low above the plateau, laying down a line of flame hot enough to scorch the rocks, but the sharpshooters have taken cover beneath deeply protruding ledges. As Fire passes, Paia hears a shout, a man's voice raised in command. Another rain of metal chases the dragon's tail.

For the first time since they joined the battle, Paia is afraid. Not for herself, but for the man down there, with the voice she recognized. The dragon banks sharply, turning back. One man stands higher than the rest, his blond hair and broad shoulders exposed, silhouetted against the sky. In his raised fist, an ancient weapon. Paia knows it well. The dragon-hilted sword.

Fire knows it, too.

HA! THAT ONE!

She'd cry out to Köthen if she could. *Get down! Get down! Your guns cannot hurt him!* But she has no voice now but the dragon's. Panic swirls around her, floodwaters. She will drown in it. Then she recalls Köthen on the mountaintop, how his steadiness and

calm lent her the strength she needed to deny Fire
the first time. Not a physical strength. A strength of
mind. Too late now to wheedle, seduce, or beg. She
must find that strength again, immediately. She must
bargain with the devil.

Fire pulls up, then settles slowly onto a wind-
carved pinnacle of rock. He stares at Köthen, considering. Köthen gestures to his men to stay under cover
and hold their fire, then lowers his sword to the
ground, point first. He leans easily against the hilt,
and stares back. Paia feels the dragon shudder with
outrage. She bends all her will against the hard wall
of his innermost being.

You will not hurt him, my Fire!

I WILL!

*He cannot hurt you. An unequal fight would be
cowardly.*

WHO CARES? I'M AT WAR! HE'S MY ENEMY!

*If you harm this man, I will know that your siblings
are right. That all you've told me is lies! That you are a
coward and a murderer and you care for nothing but yourself and your own pleasure!*

HE IS YOUR LOVER!

*No, though he might have been. Instead, you won me
back again.*

YOU BETRAYED ME WITH HIM! YOU LOVE
HIM STILL! HE SHALL NOT *LIVE!*

Is it love she feels, gazing at Köthen's sturdy, im-
perturbable stance, or gratitude?

But I chose to follow you instead.

HE DARED TO CHALLENGE ME! HE SHALL
NOT LIVE!

Her own person is her only currency. The threat
of leaving is her only weapon. Such as they are, Paia
knows her Duty is to use them.

If he dies, you will lose me again, and this time, forever! You can only hold me if I come to you willingly!

The dragon screams, his tail carving the air like a giant's scimitar. Flame spews across the seamed and broken granite but dies at Köthen's feet. The hot wind ruffles his hair. The men cry out from their shadowed refuge. Köthen doesn't stir.

Spare him, my Fire, and I will not desert you, ever. If you kill him, you kill me also.

Fire's rage and incredulity burn through her like a fever.

MY FAITHFUL DESERT ME! MY ARMIES SPLIT AND SCATTER! MY FORTRESS IS TAKEN! AND NOW YOU . . . AGAIN? GIVE ME A REASON I SHOULD SPARE HIM!

What good is reason, my Fire, at the end of the world?

NO! TELL ME! WHY THIS ONE?

Let your own standard apply. Spare him because he is worthy. Because he is not weak. Spare him because he is what you would have been, had you been human. Because he taught me that love is possible only between equals, and that to love you, I must cease to fear you.

Paia feels the molten light of the dragon's rage fade just slightly. Köthen waits, puzzled and wary. Why doesn't it attack, this enemy he does not comprehend? But Paia thinks that man and dragon actually understand each other very well. She'd like to be able to explain it to him, how they are alike. How loving the dragon does not mean loving him less. How she is a creature of Destiny, and must follow its call. With no language between them, it would be a daunting task. With a language, it would be heartbreaking. Paia is grateful to be spared the pain. Köthen stands defiant on his rock, a brave man facing down a dragon. The absurdity of it makes her love him all the more. He'll never know she's saved his life. He doesn't know she's there.

In her heart, Paia bids the soldier good-bye, and wishes him well.

Come, my Fire. There's no place for us here.

His swift agreement leaves her feeling dizzy and confused.

YOU'RE RIGHT! THERE ARE OTHER PLACES. BETTER PLACES! WHERE MY SERVANTS ARE STILL LOYAL! WHERE THEY'LL WELCOME AND WORSHIP US! LEADERS OF MEN WHO'VE NOT YET LOST THEIR FAITH IN THEIR GOD!

But that's not what . . .

AND THERE WE'LL RAISE A REAL ARMY AND BRING IT HERE TO CHASE THIS FAINTHEARTED BAND OF MARAUDERS BACK INTO THE HILLS THEY SPRANG FROM!

And keep on fighting and fighting? When will it ever stop?

STOP? Inside his pause, a returning echo of exhaustion. A longing or despair. IN THE END, BELOVED, EVERYTHING WILL STOP. AT LAST. THE CYCLE WILL BE ENDED. UNTIL THEN, WE MUST PERSEVERE. PREPARE YOURSELF, MY PRIESTESS, FOR ANOTHER JOURNEY!

Chapter Thirty-one

S now blows up again, mixed with needles of sleet, and Captain Wender bellows for a horse. One of the chastened boys materializes from behind a stack of firewood. "A horse for milady!"

Erde lays a hand on his muddied sleeve. "No, Captain, we should not wait. I can walk perfectly well. I've walked this far, after all. The dragon will follow as soon as we've made room for him."

"As you wish." The captain peers at her to be sure, but he's anxious enough not to stand on ceremony. "Hot water, then, lad. And clean cloths, if you can find any!" He sends the boy packing with a gesture, and offers her his arm. "If you will allow me. It isn't far."

Erde is relieved that he sets a stiff pace. She'd be dragging him along herself if he felt it necessary to observe a more ladylike stride. "Are you fighting in the king's name now, Captain?"

Wender grips her elbow to guide her past a crowd milling around the chirugeon's tent. The moans from behind the stained canvas make Erde shudder and quicken her step. The dragon could do much good here, though it would exhaust him desperately. And where would food be found to fuel the recovery of his strength?

"I serve the Knight now, as my father did before me," Wender replies solemnly.

She glances up at his stern, ruddy face. A weathered face, weary but without complaint, though frost rimes his mustache and his eyes are slitted against the biting snow. "I didn't know."

Wender nods. "I was apprenticed at the armory at Weisstrasse when my young lord of Köthen came to squire in the Knight's household. Being just a few years older, I was assigned to look after the boy, keep his horse, spar with him in the training yard, back him up in fights. The usual sort of thing." Conversation with a lady is clearly not the captain's favorite exercise. He seems glad for a subject he can pursue without discomfort. "But we were . . . a good match, you might say. And his lordship was still young when he was called home to assume his title. The Knight judged he could use some backup while the power issues were being sorted out. So I came to Castle Köthen. And I stayed."

"An excellent match, indeed," says Erde politely, while her mind's eye fills with the dark dream-vision she'd had, little more than a month ago, of Baron Köthen, Wender, and the bloodied body of the murdered prince. A month for her, perhaps, but not for Wender.

The captain paces in silence for a moment, then asks humbly, "Can you offer any news of his lordship, milady?"

"Oh, forgive me! Of course you will be wondering! The Baron is well, Captain." She will not mention how changed Köthen is, or how he'd refused her plea to return with her to Deep Moor, alas too late. "He's fighting the dragons' battles now."

One small portion of Wender's anxiety seems relieved by this knowledge. "The Knight will be glad to hear it. And so . . . we are nearly there."

Ahead, smoke rises damply from a large cook fire, canopied against the snow. Men huddle close around it, while their horses stamp in the cold. Several canvas-draped wagons stand like a barricade between the fire and a faded red pavilion set a bit apart. The pavilion is larger than the tents clustered on the other side of the cook fire, but shows no other sign of luxury.

Erde expects to find men hurrying about, servants or healers caring for the wounded knight. But the door flap hangs flat and still, and silence lies like a pall around the pavilion. Perhaps the knight's retainers are respecting his slumber, but Erde senses something chillier than that. As they pass the cook fire, Wender calls to some of the gathered men. They mutter, and answer him as sullenly as the boys, but a few leave their place at the fire to do his bidding. Erde shivers, watching them approach. Their hands and faces are chapped raw, their postures lank and suspicious. Brusquely, the captain orders them to clear the area in front of the red pavilion.

"It's fear keeps them away, milady," he tells her, correctly reading her questioning glance.

"Of sickness?"

"Of him, milady. When the battle turns, they blame him now. He's . . ."

"He's what?" Disfigured? Delirious? Can it be the captain was not exaggerating? Is the dear old knight really dying?

"Well, you will see for yourself." He strides to the flap, then hesitates. "Your pardon, milady. Let me go in first and prepare him."

"Captain, let us not delay! I'd rather . . ."

"A moment only, milady." Wender ducks through the loose canvas as if intent on concealing the pavilion's interior from all eyes. Shivering now from cold as well as dismay, Erde gathers her woolen layers about her against the snow and icy wind, and reports all she's seen and learned to the dragon, waiting far out in the drifted meadow.

Wender soon reappears as promised, but remains at the door, blocking the way. "Milady, you will find him . . . most changed."

"Of course, Captain. He is weak from the wound, I suppose. Is there fever?" This, of course, would be the worst: the wound inflamed.

"Fever, yes, and more." Still, he hesitates. "Even before the wound."

"Surely I'll not be in any danger?" she demands in a shocked whisper.

Wender's gruff face twists, with doubt or caution. Or it could simply be grief, Erde decides. Without further comment, he steps aside, gathering the limp canvas in one hand for her to pass.

After the bleak gray of the snowy afternoon, Erde expects a greater darkness inside. Instead, her gloom-adjusted eyes are stunned by the glare of a score of lanterns, oil lamps, and candles, arrayed about the interior of the pavilion as if for some saint's day celebration. Their many points of light are misted by smoke from the braziers set at the corners. Squinting into the brightness, Erde doesn't see the knight at first. She see books, piles of books, as well as loose sheaths of parchment and the rolled scrolls of vellum maps, piled on rickety camp tables, spilling out of trunks, scattered across the muddied rugs that only partially cover the frozen meadow grasses matting the ground.

"Has he brought his entire library?" she exclaims.

"Most of it." Wender has come in behind her and closed the flap, pulling it tight against invading wind and snow, and prying glances.

"My lord? Sir Hal?" Erde looks for a sickbed and finds it—rumpled, mud-stained, bloodstained, and . . . empty, but for a litter of books and occultish charts. "Are you here?"

"He's here."

She thinks Wender's tone is very dire. She steps farther in, her eyes adjusting to the flickering, smoky light. She sees motion among the candle flames, and then, a stooped old man, thin past all reason, his gray hair unkempt, his chin ragged with bristles, totters toward her with an armload of leather-bound tomes.

"Is that you, girl?"

She knows the voice only because she expects to hear it. But it was never so cracked and wheezy. *He* was never . . .

"Yes, it's me." She is numbed to a whisper.

"Good! Kurt told me you'd come back."

She clears her throat and tries again. "Yes. I'm back."

"Well, I've got one of you at least! And not a moment too soon!" He dumps the books onto an unoccupied corner of the nearest table and stands breathing hard. When he seems more confident of his balance, he snatches the top book off the stack and shakes it at her like a fist. "Come! You must help me call the others! There's not a moment to lose!"

Wender murmurs, "He won't sit still even long enough to let me shave him."

Surely this is some imposter! Where is her tall, stern, red-leathered knight? Erde cannot comprehend how a man so strong and vital could have aged so greatly in so short a time. Could the injury alone be responsible? Didn't the captain say he was wounded but a day ago? She notes the flush of fever on his cheek and in his eyes. His skin is stretched taut, as if from a wasting sickness, or from the denial of constant and agonizing pain. Beneath the masking scents of burning tallow and charcoal, Erde detects the sour-sweet odor of decay. She turns wide, horrified eyes back to Wender.

"Oh, Captain, go bid your men to hurry, I beg you! I'll be all right here with him."

Wender nods briskly, and ducks out.

Erde turns back to the knight with the most encouraging smile she can muster. He has thrown the book down where a small cleared space is ringed with the golden cylinders of altar candles. He props himself against the table and leans in to study the pages. His arms quiver with the effort, and he bends so low that she fears his scrawl of untrimmed hair will catch in the circle of leaping flames. He appears to have forgotten her entirely.

"Sir Hal?"

Without looking up, he beckons her over impatiently, as if she's been away but a minute, not the several months that she calculates have actually passed. Winter should have been gone long ago, but she knows from Raven that it went on and on. How long actually? She must remember to ask the captain. Weather so freakish cannot provide a reliable calendar.

"Come, child! Look!"

As Erde approaches, the musty stench grows sharper. He is wearing a rumpled but clean tunic—the captain has managed that much, at least—but the right side, across his shoulder blade and down along his ribs, is damply stained: rouge, yellow, russet. Erde struggles for composure, and a steady stomach.

"Look here!" Hal insists. His finger trembles on a brightly illuminated page. "See here where it says . . . well, the translation is clumsy, but this passage . . ." He shoves several smaller books aside, reaching for an older, tattered volume stuffed with torn strips of parchment. He fumbles with the markers. "Where is it? Where?"

"My lord, you needn't tell me now. . . ."

"No, we must . . . Here! Here it is! The same, you see? The very same passage reoccurs, encapsulated within this earlier text!" He holds the ragged little book out for her perusal. Every inch of margin is crammed with his carefully inked annotations.

Erde nods weakly. His bright mad grin has brought her to the verge of tears. "What does it say, good knight?"

"Listen!" He brings the page up close to his eyes, then peers aside at her apologetically. "My own translation, you understand. An improvement, but . . . well." He turns back, clearing his throat and squinting to read his notes. " 'In the beginning, four mighty dragons' . . . four, my girl! You hear that? It speaks of them. It must be them! It goes on, ' . . . raised of elemental energies, were put to work . . .' " He stops to cough and ends up gasping for breath.

"No more, dear knight, I beg you! You will kill yourself with this!"

"But the text breaks off there! It's a fragment

only!" He turns to her with crazed intensity. "A damned illusive fragment! But then, I found . . ." He fumbles again among the many books, but his fingers seem to have lost the will to grasp. He gives up and leans against the tabletop, shuddering and heaving.

"Dearest Sir Hal, you are not well!" Now Erde cannot keep the horror from her voice. "Has the chirurgeon seen to your wound?"

He waves his hand, a jerky half-controlled motion. "Yes, yes. A fool. I called for Linden, but . . ." He frowns, having lost his train of thought. "A fool! He'd have me drugged on my couch if I let him!"

"With good reason! You're sorely hurt and should be resting!"

"No time for that, girl! No time!" He reaches for another book. "It's here somewhere, and I shall find it.

"What is?"

"Did they tell you? The hell-priest is in the Grove. Cursed be the day I took that devil into my household!" He drops the book convulsively and grips his head with both hands. "Aiii, I am to blame! I am to blame! The priest is in the Grove and we cannot pry him out!"

"You are not to blame," she protests, but uselessly, for he isn't listening.

His hands fall back to rustle among the books and papers. "It's his damned black magic, of course. Like he's done with the weather. Somehow the Grove's own magic has been subdued. I've been searching for a proper conjure to lend it strength, but you will help me find it. Now that you and Lord Earth are here, we shall . . ." He looks up, and then wildly around the tent, his whole body sagging in a seizure of doubt. "He is here, isn't he?"

Erde nearly rushes to catch his fall. "He is, dear knight! He surely is, and the first task he must undertake is to make you well again! Then we shall worry about the hell-priest." She moves closer, to take his arm and lead him from the distraction of his books. He tries to wave her away, but there is no strength in him. His wrist is as frail as a willow twig beneath his fevered skin. He shudders as if her touch is agony.

"No time, no time! The answer is here! I had it, almost, and then . . . !" He coughs, a dire rattle clogging his throat.

Erde panics. "Captain Wender!" Hal's face is rigid with suppressed pain. "Captain! Will you come, please?" She sees that the knight's every breath is an effort, a battle won. She cannot imagine what's keeping him upright. She will not ask what answer he seeks so desperately, for he will try to tell her and only wreck himself further. "Please, dear Hal, time for answers when you are well! The dragon will be here soon. Let him see to you, or there'll be no time for you at all!"

"Milady?" Wender appears at the tent flap, then hurries in to help her support the old man's lanky, sagging frame. He grabs up a soft and thickly woven blanket and drapes it over Hal's stooped shoulders like a cloak.

Hal struggles within the enveloping folds. "No! Leave me! My work is not done! I'm so close, Kurt! Let me go!"

"Good, my lord," Wender murmurs. "Behave yourself now."

"Will you not come out and greet the dragon?" Erde asks brightly.

The fever-glaze in Hal's eyes clears long enough to

let a ray of his old joy and awe shine through. "The dragon! Yes! He will know! Wender! My sword!"

"No need for that, my lord."

"My sword, I say! I must make my obeisance!"

Wender sighs. Balancing the knight on one arm, he reaches behind him for the sword hung by sheath and belt on a tent pole. Erde catches just a glimpse of the familiar dragon-shaped hilt before Wender presses it to Hal's chest, then wraps sword, sheath, and knight up soundly in the woolen blanket. "We've cleared as large a space as we're likely to get, milady. I'm hoping it will do."

"It will have to, Captain. Let us hurry! I'll go outside and call the dragon now." She stays a moment to stroke Hal's bruised hand. "Soon, dear knight. Soon all will be well."

"Soon all will be over," Hal mutters.

"Not at all! You mustn't say so. It's only the fever bringing you to such madness and despair!"

"And a good thing, too," he continues. "It's the only way. The texts are very clear in that regard." He begins to cough again, so racked by it this time that his mouth is stained with blood.

Wender gently wipes it away with a corner of the blanket, while Erde turns her glance away. "You go ahead, milady. Go call in your magic beast."

Outside, Erde steals a moment to compose herself, to brush away the tears she's allowed herself only once she's turned her back, to breathe in air—no matter how icy cold—that's free of smoke and the rank stink of infection. The wind has died, and the snow falls more gently, like a caress rather than a punishment.

Oh, dragon! Just when I think I've known every sadness possible!

DO NOT DESPAIR.

Never! Not while you are here. They've made room for you. Will you join us? You are sorely needed!

She gazes across the rutted stretch of field in front of the tent. Wender has ordered the supply wagons drawn aside, and several of the smaller tents and lean-tos moved farther down the line. Word of a happening has obviously been passed through the camp. A sullen throng of infantrymen and squires has gathered around the perimeter to speculate and stare. Erde does not feel particularly welcomed. She has never called the dragon into a crowd of strangers before, except at Erfurt, to snatch Margit from the stake. The men have brought their pikes and crossbows, she notes, but these are soldiers, after all, and they are at war. It is their duty to be armed. Swallowing her dread, Erde images the trampled field, the tents and all the onlookers, clearly and in precise detail.

Are you ready, dragon?

I AM . . . HERE.

And he is. Crouching neatly in the center of the space, with little room to spare. The ranks of the curious gasp and draw back. Prayers and blessings are mumbled. Weapons rattle as their owners' fists tighten on them in terror. Horses neigh and the dogs bark or quickly slink away. The dragon looms over the camp, a bronzy mountain. The squared plates of his hide shine as the gloomy daylight picks out its concentric ridges, like the coffering in a cathedral ceiling. Erde's heart warms to see him, so vast and magnificent, but her joy is not shared by those around her. She hears the words "witch" and "antichrist" muttered around the field. She'd like to scold them all for their foolishness and superstition, but men do not like to be told they're wrong about something, especially by a girl.

The dragon, too, is nervous. He's never liked crowds. Nonetheless, he is soothing the panicked animals, smothering the fright signals they've picked up from the humans with calming messages of his own. Soon, the dogs and horses are quiet, but the men have grown restless, ashamed of their fear and resentful of the dragon that caused it. Emboldened by his placidity, several of them step forward, halberds gleaming wickedly. Erde sees crossbows armed and cocked, and guesses herself to be the most likely target, though enough arrows shot at close range could do serious harm to the dragon as well, perhaps before he could stop them or remove himself from danger. His legend has followed him, she surmises. They've all heard he doesn't fly or breathe fire.

Can't they see we're trying to help them?

THEY COULD . . . IF THEY LOOKED FAR ENOUGH.

Erde decides she might actually be in danger. She glances back at the silent pavilion. She tries to sound casual. "Captain Wender?"

The men with the halberds advance more boldly. One of them mimics her call to the captain in falsetto.

"That's it!" calls another. "Bring the damned turncoat out here!"

Behind them, the crowd murmurs encouragement. Erde understands that her arrival has fanned the flames of an already existing animosity toward Wender and the man he now serves. What has become of the king's once noble army? She'd like to give them a piece of her mind about the nature of duty and loyalty, but recent months have taught her the value of discretion. Instead, she strides to the tent flap and draws it aside. "Captain?"

Wender stoops out from under the gathered canvas with the limp and shrouded knight cradled in his arms like a child. He looks anguished, and Erde sees no sign of life on Hal's slack face.

"Oh! Is he . . . he isn't . . . ?"

"Collapsed. But there's still a breath. It's very close, milady."

The emboldened soldiers are moving in to cut the pavilion off from the center of the field and the dragon.

Wender scowls at them. "What's going on here? Out of my way! We have vital business to attend to!"

"The devil's business!" snarls one, stepping forward and leveling the point of his halberd like a spear. "There's no denying your witchcraft now!"

The crowd calls out its agreement with raucous threats and cheers.

"This man is dying!" says Wender angrily.

"Let him, then!"

"Then maybe our luck will change!"

Wender growls, "If you fought with more heart, you'd change your own luck! Out of my way, I say!"

Small wonder these men resent him, Erde muses. He's brought with him some of his old master's arrogance. She hears shouts in the distance, and the pounding of hooves. She prays it's not more bad news. The crowd's grumble rises like a nest of hornets. A string thunks and an arrow slams into the mud at Wender's feet.

"I am unarmed!" Wender fumes, his arms sagging with the knight's dead weight.

"So much the better," calls the man with the halberd, advancing another step. The shouts and hoofbeats are nearing.

Dragon! We need your help!

He could transport the three of them to safety, but she needs to be touching him. And where would they go? Four more foot soldiers have moved to stand beside the man with the halberd, blocking the way.

I WILL COME FOR YOU.

Earth slews his giant horned head toward the pavilion and lumbers to his feet. Simultaneously, the approaching shouts resolve themselves into audible words. "Make way for the king! Stand aside for His Majesty!"

The king! The crowd parts hastily as two mounted knights trot into the open. Behind them, Erde sees another pair of knights, a flurry of banners and color, and a flash of gold warming the dull air. Then the entire throng is kneeling, herself included. Even Wender manages to sink to one knee while holding his unconscious burden well above the snow and icy mud. Erde is more than grateful for the interruption, which has probably saved their lives, but Sir Hal's failing health is of equal concern. His Majesty has heard about the dragon, no doubt, and has come to see it for himself. She is glad that the ailing old monarch is well enough to travel on horseback, but she prays that he will not require too lengthy a show of ceremony. If Hal is to live, the dragon must get on with his healing.

Her head bowed with the proper respect, she hears horses approaching, murmured commands, then a single horse coming nearer. It halts and two pairs of muddy boots race up to catch its bridle. She hears the soft clink of mail and the creaking of harness. The rider dismounts, more easily than she'd expect from a sick old man.

"Well, little sister. We meet again at last."

She forgets all the protocols drilled into her as a baron's child. She looks up, gaping at the man standing in front of her, helmetless, a thin, bright band of gold embracing his brow. He looks older, less by the march of years than with the maturity gained from the weight of his royal responsibilities. He is still tall and thin, but his boyish beauty has sobered into something more august, as befits a king.

Dragon! It's Rainer! Alive!

"You . . . Your Majesty?" she splutters.

Rainer grins down at her, enjoying her astonishment, then spreads his hands apologetically. "You see? I have regained my heritage. Are you surprised?"

"Yes . . . no . . . I . . ." *I'm just so glad to see you well!* A thousand memories come flooding back, not all of them comfortable. "So you are . . . ?"

"I am. The lost prince." His shoulders twitch in the faintest of shrugs. He lowers his voice. "Or so they believe. In that case, what does it really matter?"

She stares at him. Why does he greet her with such ambiguity? Does he fear she'll challenge his legitimacy? "It matters not at all . . . my liege."

Rainer smiles, satisfied. "You're looking well, little sister."

Erde recalls her reasons for urgency. She must put her discomfiture and wonderment aside for later. She gazes up at the new king imploringly, gesturing behind to Wender and the man in his arms. "Please . . . it's Hal . . . he . . ."

Rainer frowns. "Yes, I was in to see him yesterday

when they brought him from the field. Is he worse?"
He offers her his hand, not so that she might kiss
the royal ring, but outstretched to help her up. "Is it
true your dragon is a healer? Hal has told me some
amazing tales. Can you help him?"

"Lord Earth will do what . . ." she begins weakly.

But Rainer has moved past her to Wender, waving
him also to his feet. "How is he, Kurt?"

"It's very bad, Sire."

"We must hurry, then!" Erde blurts. "Oh, forgive
my rudeness . . . Sire."

"No, we must. You're right." For a moment, the
king looks very young again, and at a loss. "What
do we do?"

"Bring him here. Oh, Captain, hurry!" The way to
the dragon is clear. Erde shows Wender where to
place his burden, between Earth's massive forelegs.
Rainer paces along beside them, silencing the mutters
of the crowd with a few well-placed scowls. But between the scowls are precautionary gestures to his
men. A dozen or so of the king's knights take up
stations around the perimeter.

Dark times indeed, Erde mourns, when the people
will not bow to the word of a strong, young king.
And Rainer will be a strong king, and a good one.
She is sure of it. No matter if he's Otto's true son
or not. Even further in his favor is that he knows
how to greet a dragon. He halts where he can comfortably look up at the huge jaw and golden eyes.
He bows slightly, not a subservience but a paying
of respects.

"Lord Earth," he declares, in a voice he intends to
carry into the surrounding throng of doubters and
dragon haters. "I never thanked you properly for
saving my life back there in Erfurt. But for you,

there'd be a priest on the throne today! Our gratitude is boundless!"

To further his point, he rests his hand easily on the curve of the dragon's foreclaw. Wender watches apprehensively, still cradling the dying knight. He's never stood this close to the dragon before. His jaw works as he masters his fear.

"You may set him down and step back, if you wish, Captain," Erde tells him. "Lord Earth will keep him warm."

"I'll stay." Wender kneels, eyeing the stout pickets of ivory enclosing him on either side, taller than his head. "He's grown some, all right, milady."

Erde allows herself the ghost of a smile. Perhaps even in the midst of horror and crisis, a touch of wonder will lighten the heart of this stalwart and deserving soldier. She kneels beside him to murmur, "You must expose the wound, Captain."

Wender stretches Hal out on the frozen mud, with the blanket under him and the dragon-hilted sword clasped long-ways on his chest. Erde shudders because he so resembles the funerary statues of her ancestors in the crypt of Tor Alte. The dragon lowers his head.

Dragon, is it bad?

VERY BAD INDEED.

Oh, but not . . . you can help him, can't you?

I CAN HEAL THE WOUND AND QUIET THE FEVER, BUT HE HAS DONE MUCH INNER DAMAGE WITH HIS GUILT AND WORRYING.

But he will live . . . ?

HE WILL, I THINK. BUT HE MUST REST, AND TAKE BETTER CARE OF HIMSELF. HE IS NO LONGER YOUNG.

Just like you to be worrying about the long term, when all I can think of is, will he live now?

HE WILL.

Erde's eyes squeeze shut against a threatened flood of grateful tears. If only this was to be the end of it, and the revived Sir Hal could ride off home to Deep Moor to rest and recover in the care of his loving lady Rose. Happily ever after in Deep Moor. A vision rises of Erde's vanished paradise, so sweet that it pierces her heart like love, and the hot tears prick her eyes again.

Not to be, not to be. Not ever. Deep Moor is in ashes, and Fra Guill is cutting down the Grove!

And then she is dragged from her mournful reverie by Wender's glad cry. "He wakes!"

The exclamation is repeated among the watching soldiers, passed around the circle like a prayer and a prophecy. Hal's chest heaves as if drawing his first true breath in days. He coughs but the sound is functional rather than strangulated. He opens his eyes. He's staring straight up into the dragon's golden gaze. "My lord Earth! You've returned at last! Thank good Providence for that! There's not a moment to be spared!"

He struggles to sit up, brushing the sword aside in his haste and confusion. Wender supports the elder knight with one arm, and snatches the sword up from the mud with the other. He cannot repress a quick accusing glance at Erde. "Is it the fever still?"

Erde rests her palm on Hal's brow. "I feel no fever now."

"Fever? What fever?" Hal's eyes narrow in suspicion, then clear, and he gently lifts her hand away. "I recall. I took a blade." He looks to Wender.

"Indeed you did, milord."

"And it went bad."

"Aye, milord. And before that . . ." Wender reconsiders and falls silent.

"Before that, what?"

"You've . . . been unwell, milord. For a while."

Hal rakes a thin hand through his hair, his habitual gesture of bewonderment. "Well, I'm fit as a fiddle now, and a good thing, too. We have much to discuss! I beg you, Kurt, help me to rise."

"You mustn't . . . !" Erde and the king speak simultaneously.

"But I must," replies Hal. On his feet but tottering, he grabs the dragon's claw for balance. He squares his starved shoulders, lifts his stubbled chin. "Lord Earth! At last I can repay you for the many favors you've done me and my king! I believe I have uncovered the final purpose of your Quest!"

Chapter Thirty-two

The Librarian is grateful to Water for retaining her human shape while in the garden at the Ur-Deep Moor. It reflects an empathetic understanding of human sensibilities that his own dragon appears incapable of. And it gives him something to do while the two dragons greet and debrief, strolling up and down the lawn: the tall black man and the stubby bearish one, walking side by side among clusters of sober observers without speaking. N'Doch and the two Tinkers can easily imagine the silent conversation going on at light speed, but it must look peculiar to the Deep Moor ladies, who aren't so used to dragon oddities. The Librarian listened in on the dialogue eagerly enough at first, and then with waning concentration as he realized that, despite Water's obvious advantages, the process of communicating with Air is not a whole lot easier for her than it has been for himself. If all these avid watchers have expectations of immediate answers, they will be disappointed.

So the Librarian listens with a part of his brain,

and concentrates on his balance and footing with the rest. He constantly has to counteract Air's tendency to let her intensity spill over into his physical being. Twice he has nearly slammed his elbow into Sedou's ribs. Without warning, any one of his limbs might be flung suddenly outward, or his head made to nod violently, as the dragon struggles to convey to her sister a certain crucial point. In sympathy, Sedou/Water now grips his arm, for support as well as gentle restraint.

So the Librarian is not the first to see it happen, though he is the most likely to comprehend what it means. It's the murmur that snags his attention, beginning as an ominous undercurrent to the hushed fits and starts of conversation across the lawn. Soon enough, however, it rises to a descant of wonder and dismay that can no longer be ignored by man or dragon.

Beside him, Sedou lets out an involuntary grunt of surprise.

The Librarian glances up from his stumbling toes. The women are staring and pointing. Above the sloping roof of the Deep Moor farmhouse, the background profile of barns and trees is mutating, sector by sector. Leaf, branch, and human architecture are being replaced, three dimensions by two, organic by inorganic, natural randomness by abstract symmetry. The new is no less beautiful than the old, the Librarian observes impartially. But it's not human.

"Ask her," he suggests to Sedou. "Would she keep the nanos in line a while longer?"

Sedou frowns, but does not say, "Why don't you ask her?" He's silent for a space, then his mouth draws tight in concern. "She feels it is not important."

"But the women are frightened. They have no understanding of this."

"I've little more myself. But I mentioned the ladies. And actually, my sister didn't say it was unimportant. I said that. She just refuses to focus on anything peripheral to her central priority: gathering the eight. The only words involved in this transaction were . . ."

"I know. *Hurry, hurry.*"

Sedou nods. "Perhaps this is her way of forcing us into action. She's going to let the city fall apart around us, and we'll have no choice but to go where she wishes."

The Librarian is not surprised. He's concluded already that the dragon inside him is heartless. As in, lacking any sort of human pity. Or if she has any heart at all, it's his. Not the physiological organ so much as the awareness of a connection to others, to life-forms that it might be one's duty to protect. If she were human, she would be called driven, obsessive, perhaps even autistic. But Air is hardly even a dragon, in the organic sense. She is an impulse, an eternal intention housed in pure intellect. A force not entirely immovable but requiring his constant surveillance and direction. Otherwise, she would mow down everyone and everything in her path.

The Librarian accepts this because he must, but he finds it perplexing in the extreme. He has supposed that the dragons' great Purpose of saving the Earth inevitably involves the rescue of humanity. Yet because she has no further use for it, Air is letting the White City disassemble itself. She has withdrawn from its systems, now that she has his own organic circuitry to inhabit. Her energies no longer direct the nanos' programming, so the nanos are taking the city back. They're reassembling it according to nanomech standards, which will soon render it inhospitable to human survival. What need, after all, have the nanomechs for the sort of life-support systems that once served the City's human population? Nanomechs can function quite successfully in lethal doses of ultraviolet, or in the thin and poisonous vapor which, in this far future, is all that remains of Earth's atmosphere.

It's a delicate line he has to walk, the Librarian reflects. He can't allow Air to ride roughshod, but neither can he point her too boldly away from the line of her Purpose. It will seem to her like resistance or rebellion, and she has no time for that. She'll simply hijack his body again, and get him and everyone else killed in the process.

What is it, then, that she's so hell-bent on saving? Is her concern only for the Earth itself and its ecosystems? If so, it seems to the Librarian that the chance for that rescue has already long gone by.

And what is he to tell the others, who are turning to him now with frightened, questioning eyes? Where will he find the words? He looks to Sedou, and breathes a sigh of relief. The engaging black man whose shape Water has borrowed is already busy soothing and explaining, revealing little that might distress, without ever seeming to conceal, all this far more articulately than the Librarian could ever manage. At last, a dragon that can speak for itself.

Meanwhile, if Air will not see to the welfare of the humans she has dragged to this fatal place, he must do it himself. According to Luther, the Grove is currently a perilous location in its own right. But if Air insists on going there, the Librarian will not be able to stop her. Still, a little resistance is in order. He must put the dragon off long enough to prepare everyone for the journey. Then he must make sure that the portal stays open long enough for all to pass through it safely.

Most important, he must let them know that they'll have to be ready to fight the minute they get there.

Chapter Thirty-three

The sultry heat is familiar, way more humid than the Citadel. The ruddy skies are what reminded Paia of home the first time she came here, but it's the tired, dusty palm trees that tell her for sure she's back in Africa. The smell of dead fish and carrion is strong even this high. As the dragon soars along the curving borderline of bleached sand and ocean, Paia is assailed by the memory of N'Doch closing his dead mother's eyes. She'd weep for them if she could, tears of rage and guilt. But a dragon has no tears. Especially this dragon.

Fire materializes in man-form in a deserted hall-way of a vast marble palace, in full dress uniform, his most stunning confection of red and gold. Paia finds herself beside him, corporeal, separate, as if her moment of despising him so totally has flung them apart. She lays her fingers to her cheeks in wonder. Her own skin, her own being. A sigh of relief escapes her so audibly that Fire stares down at her and scowls.

"You're to be gorgeous, quiet, and submissive.

This will indicate my high honor and status, as well as assuring your safety. Can you manage that?"

Paia nods, distracted by the joy of being herself again.

"All right, then. Two steps behind me always. So they'll see you as a virtuous woman, not for sale, and belonging to me. Understand?"

She makes a face, gazing up at him impudently, and curtsies. "Yes, my Fire."

"You used to call me 'my lord.' "

"Yes, well . . ."

He turns on his booted heel and strides off down the hall. Paia hurries after him, but her surroundings are a distraction. Double ranks of polished marble columns support heavy gilt cornices and a long coffered vault stretching toward a distant pair of gilded doors. The marble is heavily veined in rich reds and blues, so gaudy that Paia wanders closer to see if it's painted. This is architecture on a grandiose scale, built with one intention in mind: to impress. Paia has only seen its like in picture histories of ancient empires. Between the columns, arched panels of beveled mirror reflect the glimmer of crystal chandeliers. She's reminded of old videos of Versailles, in her day half-submerged by the rising water. This is how it must have felt to walk its glittering corridors during the reign of the Sun King. But there's also a lot that Louis would not have recognized. Surveillance cameras swivel to keep the intruders in sight as they pass. Hidden speakers fill the long arching hall with sound and music. Huge video screens are set into the mirrored panels between every other column, a different image playing on every screen. Paia lags behind. She hasn't seen advertising since the earliest days of her youth, and the only actual programming she's known is what's archived in the House Computer's library. Very little of it looks like this. She slows in front of a graphic battlefield scene. A cacophony of screams and explosions leaps at her in stereo from behind the columns.

"So real . . ." Paia stares, fascinated. Perhaps it's actually a news report?

Down the hallway, Fire glances back, then stops, his tall silhouette perfectly reflected in the shine of the marble floor. He hisses at her to hurry. Paia trots dutifully after him. Along the way, she glimpses nude bodies intertwined on one screen, and some indescribable carnage involving small animals on another.

"Where are we?" she demands, catching up. Her whisper dances like soft light across the gilded coffering to join the bellows and moans of the mingled sound tracks.

Fire waves her back. "Two steps behind, remember! If anyone sees, I'll lose face immediately!"

Paia complies, trying not to sulk. "What *is* this place?"

"You like it?"

"Not really. I think it's creepy."

"Get used to it. We'll be staying a while."

"But what is it? Did you see what's on those screens?"

"What do you expect? We're in the headquarters of the Media King." Fire gestures grandly around. "A gallery of his current work, I assume. A new addition. And the decor is much improved since I was here last. My minion has obviously come up in the world. You see? There are still places where my favors can make a leader out of an ordinary man."

He pauses, irritably adjusting the high tight collar of his tunic. "It's hot here."

Paia stares at him. Is that sweat beading on his red-gold forehead? "What did you say?"

He looks amazed and vulnerable for about a nanosecond, then snaps, "I know, I know. Permit me the discovery of climatic discomfort, now that I'm actually embodied."

She can't keep the wonder from her face, and the hope from her eyes. "You actually feel the heat?"

"What's so wonderful about that?"

"Well, it's so . . . so human."

"Damned inconvenient."

Paia shakes her head, and then, very deliberately, she goes to him, slides her arm up around his neck and draws his head down to hers to kiss him deeply and lovingly. She feels his astonishment, his delight, the rising of his desire, and then his fury and resistance. He breaks the hold of her arm and pushes her roughly away. "Not here! You'll ruin my image!"

Smiling to herself, Paia keeps pace with him as he turns away, following respectfully in his wake. She's made her point, and she doesn't want to be left behind in this salesman's palace. Despite its luxury and scale and the omnipresent security cameras, it doesn't feel safe.

Just short of the gilded doors at the end of the corridor, a wide crossing hall intersects. Fire wheels right, his sharp heels resounding with military precision. Paia represses a grin. How the dragon must be enjoying this new ability of his man-form to make sound in the material world! Another tool of intimidation added to his arsenal, to compensate for his sudden vulnerability to the heat. She follows him cheerfully around the corner.

A broad staircase rises ahead of them, its elaborately carved newels sporting twin logos in polished brass. The bottom step is flanked by two beefy guards, smartly dressed, despite the humidity, in close fitting black and gray. Their collective gaze is fixed on one of the nearby wall screens. Their jaws are slack with fascination. Paia cannot see the screen from her sidelong angle, but she hears cries and weeping, and a woman's desperate begging. The sentries snap to quick attention as Fire cruises to a halt in front of them.

"General! Sir!" exclaims one, saluting so abruptly that Paia is surprised he hasn't broken his wrist. "You are welcome! Sir!"

"I should hope so." Fire breezes past to mount the stairs two at a time. Only at the top does he wait for Paia to trudge up after him, by which time the sentries have returned their attention to the screen. At the top of the stairs, more guards and more wall screens, this time offering a selection of programming: the battle scene again, and a young girl being beaten, then an elaborate costume drama where only the women go without clothing. Paia glances at the final screen and away again, shocked. Surely this is far too intimate to be viewed among strangers! Worst of all are the actress' screams of pain. So convincing. The soldiers watch in avid silence, their eyes constantly flicking from one screen to the other. Behind them, several doorways lead into other huge rooms and brightly lighted hallways, with other open doors beyond that.

Again, the uniformed sentries snap to with brisk salutes. They are boys, really. Sweating beneath their chic uniforms. While the rest stare openly at Paia and make whispered suggestions among themselves, the oldest steps forward.

"Welcome, General. Are you expected?"

"Expected?" Fire offers a lofty but complicit grin. "Mr. Baraga would soon grow bored, Lieutenant, if I showed up only when expected."

The young man nods politely, but Paia can see he's repressing a frown. He can't bring himself to meet the man/dragon's glance directly, so he stares intently at the middle button on Fire's red tunic, taking another step forward to lean in and murmur, "Begging your pardon, General, but it's His Excellency, the President, now."

"Really? I'll be sure to remember." Fire turns to Paia with a sly wink. "Didn't I tell you he's come up in the world?" To the lieutenant, he says, "Yes, it's been a while. Sorry I missed the coup, but I gather it all went as planned. Is *His Excellency* about?"

The frown mutates into a tight and awkward smile. "His Excellency is shooting live at the moment, sir." The lieutenant waves vaguely at the screens, then slides his gaze past Fire's chest to where Paia has stopped the prescribed two steps behind. "Perhaps you would care to join him."

"Perhaps I will."

The other guards have turned away from this mundane conversation, and the passing diversion of a merely live woman. And though the lieutenant steadfastly faces front, his concentration is faltering, drawn away by the bright, beckoning screens and the promise of drama. "Shall I accompany you to the studio, sir?" he asks unhappily.

"No need." Fire moves past him, beckoning Paia to follow. "I know the way."

A succession of gilt-ceilinged salons leads to a parquet-floored ballroom and rows of gold chairs with plush maroon velvet upholstery. A larger chair resembling a throne rests on a dais at the far end. The ubiquitous wall screens are even larger here, with each sound track trying to overwhelm its neighbors with excesses of volume and pitch.

Passing out of the ballroom into another corridor lined with doors, Fire gestures into the wedding cake of cornices and chandeliers. "There's an entire wing down that way I'm sure he'll be happy to give us."

Paia smiles up at him. He's looking damp and a bit disheveled. She'd like to wipe his forehead, and maybe nibble a little on his perfect, chiseled mouth. "Perhaps you can negotiate for air-conditioning."

"Stop looking at me like that!"

"But why, my Fire?"

He looks away. "It clouds my thinking."

Paia laughs delightedly.

Fire scowls, looming over her. "You don't realize how limited our options are, do you?"

"Perhaps I don't."

"Then let me do what I must to find a place for us! There's time for pleasure later."

Paia damps her seductive grin. "Forgive me, my Fire. I will."

More corridors and rooms, then, and finally, a large door, distinctive by being steel-plated and closed, and by the group of men who stand around outside it, drinking and smoking. A few of them watch the bank of screens that lights up the entire adjacent wall, but most of them are chatting, or playing cards or e-games. Above the door, a lighted panel reads: ON AIR.

The men glance up at the click of Fire's boots

across the polished marble. These are not spiffy, boyish soldiers. They are older, and casually dressed.
Their pragmatic, world-weary expressions remind
Paia of the Tinkers she has met. They observe Fire's
approach with mild disinterest, and yet ease imper-
ceptibly aside so that a passage is cleared to the door
without anyone actually greeting him or even ac-
knowledging his presence.

"You see how they know me," Fire murmurs, and
though Paia is steps behind, she hears him as if his
lips were at her ear. "Perhaps I should have made
my kingdom here."

He processes grandly through the crowd of men
and stops at the metal door. By habit, Paia steps up
to open it for him, as she has ever done when the
God wished to pass through a closed door without
the awkwardness of vanishing on one side and reappearing on the other. Then she hesitates. Perhaps
he'd like the novelty of opening it for himself, now
that he's material enough? But he nods, as if granting
her permission.

"Let it be as usual," he says quietly. "That way, I
can surprise him."

The space inside is cavernous and cool and dark,
filled with the bustle of men and machinery focused
like bees around a central, brightly-lit hive. Paia actually shivers in the draft from the huge vents pumping
in cold air. A mist of condensation rimes the
trusswork below the ceiling.

Again, space clears magically as Fire moves among
the rolling scaffolds and lighting instruments and the
thick bundles of cable snaking across the smooth
gray floor. But soft catcalls and laughter follow in
their wake, dark male laughter that Paia does not
like the sound of. Hands reach for her uninvited. Not

like the soft touch of the Faithful of the Temple. These hands are rougher, grasping, and presumptuous. Paia closes the gap between herself and the man/dragon until she's nearly treading on his heels.

"Don't be concerned," says his voice in her ear. "They will not harm what belongs to me."

Paia twists away and into him with a cry of pain as a stray palm cups her breast and squeezes hard. Fire turns. It's not hard to pick out the perpetrator. He's guffawing and moving in for more. Fire glares at him, and instantly, the man yowls and doubles over to cradle his arm in pain and terror. The grabbing, rubbing hands withdraw.

I AM STILL YOUR PROTECTOR, AM I NOT, BELOVED?

Paia nods, knowing it would be unproductive to point out to him his penchant for putting her into situations where she will *require* a protector. "I don't like it here," she mutters instead. "But it is cooler."

"Like I said: get used to it." He continues onward, toward the center brightness.

Peering past him, Paia sees a short but powerfully built man in a crisp white shirt, the sleeves rolled up to his elbows. He's talking to a man with a clipboard, describing something with impatient, expressive hands. The bright lights fall on him as if besotted by his hair, which is pure black and glossy and straighter than any Paia has ever seen. She knows instantly that this is Kenzo Baraga, once a big-time media baron, now (apparently) president of his country. And more significantly, once N'Doch's hero and role model, now the scourge of his entire family. She studies him carefully as they approach. The man doesn't look like a murderer of helpless old women, even though she knows he is. He's neat and clean, and looks to be stylish within the standards of his era. Nor does he look insane, as is said of Fire's other known henchman, the "hell-priest" of Erde's time. Baraga looks like . . . a businessman. Paia's father used to entertain such men—powerful and rich—at the Citadel in the days before the Final Collapse. But they were never his particular friends.

If Baraga senses the dampening of the bustle that Fire's sudden punishing of the grabber has caused, he gives no sign. He continues his emphatic explanation to the man with the clipboard, who notes Fire's advance with slightly widened eyes but keeps nodding at his boss as if nothing else was on his mind. Only when Fire has come to an august and expectant halt several paces away, does the Media King glance up.

"Well, look who's here!" He offers a faint but genial bow. "El Fiero. It's been a long time."

Paia searches for fear in him, and finds not a hint.

"Kenzo." Fire nods in greeting. "Congratulations on your recent . . . elevation. I hear you're running the place now."

Baraga laughs. "Somebody's got to maintain order around here. Got so I couldn't get any work done. And so, you see? Here I am, back in the traces." He spreads his arms to embrace men, equipment, and studio, then brings his palms together to rub them jovially, looking Paia up and down. "What have you brought me?"

"Ah, my old friend, this one is not for you. Personal property, I'm afraid."

Baraga eyes him as if suspecting a joke. He laughs, but sees no answering gleam in Fire's golden eyes. "But, your pardon, old boy . . . what will *you* do with her? A waste of a gorgeous woman, if she cannot feel your touch and thrust, eh?" He nudges the man with the clipboard, who's frozen to the spot by the man/dragon's proximity.

Paia's distaste deepens. *At least the rest of these creeps have the sense to be afraid of him!*

"Kenzo," says Fire. "You presume too much."

Baraga laughs. "I do, I do! It's your own fault, Fiero! What man could resist such beauty?" He elbows the clipboard man aside and steps past Fire to walk around Paia as if contemplating her purchase. Unlike his underlings, he keeps his hands to himself, though he does lift her chin with his thumb to appraise her face. He seems intrigued by the cool dislike in her gaze. "Hmmm. A live one! Surely you don't really mean to keep all this to yourself!"

Fire says, "Kenzo, we need to talk."

"Such perfect skin! Café au lait! My favorite! Looks marvelous on camera, you know."

Appalling that a mere thumb can feel so possessive! Paia looks away, distracted by the sounds coming from behind Baraga, in the circle of bright light. Somewhere over there, a woman is sobbing.

"Kenzo, a word in private, if you please."

"Let me guess: you've come to claim your piece of the action."

"In a manner of speaking."

"No problem." Baraga shoves gently against Paia's chin, simultaneously a gesture of challenge and dismissal. "But let's talk over dinner, when I can concentrate. Okay by you, Fiero, old boy?" He gestures toward the light and the sobbing, screened from Paia's glance by a barricade of men and equipment. "I'm right in the middle of the final sequence, the devil to get right, you know, under the circumstances. Stick around and watch, then we'll talk.

You'll enjoy it. I've revived an old industry tradition to stir up those jaded pricks out there. It's right down your alley. I'd have a chair brought for you, but . . ."

"Kenzo, I need your full attention right now."

Paia is amazed by how reasonable the man/ dragon is being. A flash of hot temper is more his style, rather than this calm insistence.

But either Baraga does not hear the menace building in Fire's tone, or he chooses to ignore it. "Five minutes. No more than ten. Soon as I get this shot. Time is money, y'know, and we're in a real time crunch here. I can't afford to have our star, ah . . . leave us . . . before we're finished." He walks away, waving various subordinates into line, and the crowd flows after him, opening a view into the center of the studio. What Paia sees there makes her start violently and bury her face in Fire's side.

A young woman, no, a girl, just a girl, lies naked on a blood-soaked mattress. The mattress is raised off the floor on a sturdy wooden platform so that the cameras can cozy in for close-ups. The platform also carries the metal rings to which the girl's manacles are fastened, hands and feet. A big man stands beside the bed with a knife in his hand. Both hand and knife are as blood-drenched as the bedding, but the man isn't looking at her, though she's sobbing and moaning, and has been sliced in several awful and private places. He's turned away to a mirror, gazing at himself intently while a makeup man blots and powders his face, and touches up his hair.

Paia takes refuge in the assurance that it's all make-believe, truly inspired special effects. But the cameras are currently at rest, and the girl on the bed still wears the terror-stricken glaze of a trapped animal. What did they used to call it? Method acting?

And now Paia notices the two men crouching on either side of the bed, whom the first shock of revulsion had hidden from her. They're wearing white lab coats. One applies a pressure bandage to the deepest wounds, while the other monitors the girl's pulse and other vital signs. Well, the girl must be all right if the medics aren't rushing her off to the nearest hospital. But the sticky-sweet smell of carnage under the hot studio lights is nauseatingly real. In her stomach-turning daze of horror, Paia can only wonder how they've kept their white coats so clean.

Baraga strides over to stare down at the girl. "How much longer do we have?"

One of the technicians shrugs. "If you hurry, you'll get the shot."

"Good. Stay in tight until I tell you to clear." He turns to the clipboard man, who is dogging his heels. "Time?"

The man checks a stopwatch. "Commercial break ends in three minutes."

Baraga nods and turns to the big camera, which has been rolled up beside him. He adjusts it slightly, presses a few buttons. "Take the master from here," he says to the operator. He crosses to the second camera, positioned for a close-up of the girl's face. When he's arranged it to his satisfaction, he touches the nearest white-coated medic on the shoulder. "Don't let her die on me too soon. Let her go as slow as you can. We need the footage."

"Yessir, Mr. Baraga."

Die? Don't let her die too soon? Paia's elaborate rationale crumbles. Dizzy and terrified, she snatches at Fire for support, but he's not there. He's moving toward the circle of light, and Paia supposes with a sinking heart that he's zeroing in to enjoy a closer look. But his back is more than usually erect, and he glides rather than walks, a reversion to less human phases of his man-form. He stops just inside the bright circle, taller than any man in the room. The light falls on him as it had on Baraga earlier, setting his red tunic and red-gold hair aglow, glinting off his golden nails and on the faint gilded profile of the scales that have risen up like hackles on his cheeks and neck.

"Kenzo. What is this?"

"What's what?" Baraga barely glances away from the third camera's view screen as he lines up the shot.

"What are you doing here?"

Baraga chuckles into the little screen. "I knew you'd approve. It's kind of an underground thing from the early days of video. Used to call it a snuff flick. I figure people out there are tired of holos and sims. If this doesn't boost the ratings, nothing will."

"You will stop this now."

"Don't make a scene, now. You'll throw off my actors. Don't worry, I'll give you all the time you want when I'm done."

Baraga eases the camera this way, then that, oblivious to what everyone else in the big dark room sees and is backing away from: Fire's ominous glow, his increasingly towering height, the angry hiss of his serpentine curls. The bloody knife clatters to the floor as the big actor shoves past the makeup man and flees into the shadowed perimeter of the room.

"Listen to me, Kenzo Baraga. You will stop this abomination now!"

"What? What?" Baraga lifts his head from the screen at last. He sees he's suddenly alone with a bunch of equipment in a big open space. His only companions are the bleeding girl and the medic whose hands are staunching the flow. Apparently that one fears Baraga's wrath more than the dragon's. Baraga seems unruffled, except for his irritation at the delay. Paia thinks he is either very dense or very confident. He plants his hands on his hips, gazing point-blank into Fire's chill fury, and sighs. "What *is* the problem?"

"Bind her wounds. Let her go."

"What? No way. I have a ton of money invested in this."

"Do it!"

"Wait a minute!" Baraga looks incredulous. "I'm hearing this from you? My evil angel is getting squeamish? The flaming demon of my dreams is suddenly bothered by a little reality video? I can't believe it!"

Paia is not sure she can believe it either. Astonishment shoves horror into the background temporarily. What's come over Fire? Is this another of his poses, or a genuine change of heart?

"Don't argue about it," growls Fire. "Just stop it. Now."

"No." Having moved past his surprise, Baraga is getting angry. "Absolutely not. I've done nothing illegal here. The girl is bought and paid for. Now her father will be able to feed the rest of his family for the next six months, maybe even a year if he isn't reckless. She has three younger brothers who might now make it to adulthood. She's fortunate she can offer them such a gift! Besides, who are you to object?"

Paia hears strong echoes of the God's rationalizing rhetoric in Baraga's justification. She wonders if Fire hears them, too.

"This is not a necessary death, Kenzo. She is no threat to you."

"She'd have died on the streets anyway before she was twenty."

"This is torture, for the pleasure of it."

"Hey, she's not in pain. Scared, maybe, but we've got her on an anesthetic. What do you think I am?"

"A monster."

Baraga laughs. "Oh, that's rich. I'm the monster now. You're going soft, I swear. Look at you all puffed up and furious. What's going on? I've never known you to mind a little mayhem."

"I mind when you misuse the power I gave you."

"You didn't call it misuse when I took care of those little odds and ends you wanted dealt with."

"Those deaths served a larger purpose. A kill should always be *necessary*. And it should be done quickly and cleanly."

"Oh, it's predator's ethics we're talking about here? How old-fashioned. Well, this isn't about ethics, it's about money. My money." Baraga goes into motion now, pacing about, shaking an angry finger at the scaled giant towering over him. "What do you know about what's necessary? What do you know about what sells? What do you know about human tastes?"

"More than I ever cared to."

"Ah, now we're into aesthetics. Look, I'm the sales expert here, and I'll tell you what: people don't *want* a clean kill. Or a justified one. They want it the way they see it in the world: random, messy, and violent. They don't want it noble, and they don't want it metaphorical. They want it real and dirty. They want to see every drop of blood. They want to hear every last gasp." Still pacing, Baraga shrugs elaborately.

"Who am I to question? I just give them what they want."

On the shadow's edge, Paia shudders in empathy. Fire cannot fail to hear the echoes now. These are his own words flung back at him.

"And I've given you what you want. So bind her wounds or end it quickly. Otherwise, I'll withdraw my patronage."

The Media King's head snaps up, and his full mouth tightens. "Yeah? Terrific. You go ahead. I can manage without you just fine."

"Kenzo, I'm warning you. No patronage means no protection. Do not take my mercy for granted."

"Threats, Fiero?" Baraga folds his arms and leans against the boxy camera in a show of swagger. "I've got the greatest security organization around."

"Indeed? And where are they now?"

Baraga waves a negligent hand. "I've only to raise the alarm."

Fire shakes his head solemnly. His bleak and implacable gaze makes the circuit of the empty room, boring into the tiered ranks of faces at the control room window, into the crowd at the half open door. "They're watching, oh, so eagerly, but they're not helping, are they? You're just another thrilling episode of reality video as far as they're concerned. The truth is, Kenzo, you've been deserted, as I was, in your last hour."

"What last hour? What are you talking about?"

"If I'm finally going to destroy the monster that is humanity, I might as well start with those of my own creation."

"Threats again? Remember, I know what you are! You can't pick up a glass or open your own door! What're you gonna do to me? You're a vision, a non-thing. Your psychic laser only hurts if the victim believes it will. You may have the rest of them pissing in their pants, but me? I know better." He steps away from the camera and stoops for the knife dropped by the frightened actor. It leaves a puddle of blood behind as he snatches it up. "You can't even stop me if . . ." Faster than Paia has time to comprehend and react, Baraga is beside her, has grabbed her and put the knife to her throat. "If I decide to use this pretty lady as a substitute when the first one's gone wasted?"

The knife is no mere prop. It's actually done the cutting so horribly evident on the dying girl's body. Paia feels its edge as a thin, cold line against her skin. She knows better than to struggle. She'd be terrified, but she knows something else that Kenzo Baraga does not.

An interesting thing happens during the suspended moment while Baraga grips her tight against him, breathing hard from defiance and adrenaline, while the knife blade warms from her own nervous heat, while Fire watches and watches, each second stretching into an eternity. As he watches, the visible signs of his fury diminish. His snarl fades, and with it, his gilded glow and his scales. The wildfires of outrage die in his eyes, leaving them empty and remote, no longer golden but as black as the eternal void. It's a look of failure, of profound defeat.

When at last he moves, it's like Time restarting. Only a pace or two between them, but this also seems to take forever until, with the speed of a snake strike, Fire grabs Baraga's arm, jerks the knife clear and crushes the Media King's wrist to pulp in his gilt-clawed fist.

Baraga cries out in pain and shock and disbelief.

The knife spins through the air, away into darkness, clattering wetly against nameless machinery. Paia is flung out of Baraga's grasp, stumbling against the camera. Fire has him by the throat and he's writhing, gasping for help. But those watching from the shadows are not soldiers. Their only loyalty is to their paychecks. And if a few of them are concerned enough to alert the sentries in the outer halls, it's too late by the time those boys in uniform storm the door of the studio, automatic weapons raised before them like talismans of their faith.

By then, Fire has already taken Baraga's head between both hands, as if the stunned and struggling man was straw or feathers, and twisted once. The crunch is like sticks breaking. Fire holds the limp weight aloft for a moment, shakes it gently, then lets it drop. He steps over the corpse, man-sized again but no less intimidating. He stops beside the bleeding girl and pins the terrified medic with a surprisingly gentle regard. "Can you save her?"

The man swallows. "I'll sure try."

"See that you do."

With a deft and iron twisting of his fingers, Fire snaps the girl's manacles, then turns away toward Paia.

"Come, beloved," he says with a tired sigh. "We have an appointment to keep."

Chapter Thirty-four

"**W**hat is it, dear knight?" Erde cannot imagine how the old man could have succeeded where the dragons so far have failed. But she's just seen Captain Wender turn away with a grim look, and she refuses to join these men in their gloom and despair. Hal's scholarly side has proved useful before. "What is their Purpose?"

The wind has come up again, flinging snow into Hal's haggard face as he stares up at the dragon and struggles to speak.

"Milady," Wender pleads. "Let me bring him inside, out of this damnable weather, before you get him started again with theories and explanations!"

"Of course, Captain! Though he would be warm enough, tucked next to the dragon."

"And what about the rest of us?" complains Rainer, dryly amused.

"Oh! I . . . forgive me! I . . . !" Again, Erde is too flustered to continue. It seems she will never get a full sentence out in the young king's presence.

"Come, Kurt," he says briskly. "Shelter for all."

He orders the braziers stoked, food and wine brought, then gestures his knights into position around the pavilion. Graciously, he offers his own arm to support the protesting but still tottering Hal through the thickening snow into the comparative warmth of the tent. Inside, Wender hangs Hal's sword back on its hook, and draws up a circle of fur-draped camp chairs. Hal stalls at the doorway, staring in dismay at the chaos of books and papers and lanterns and jumbled furniture. Erde sees him calculating the depth of his plunge into fevered unreason. He lets Rainer lower him into the nearest chair.

"How long, Kurt?" he asks quietly.

"Milord?"

"How long was I . . . unwell?"

Wender decides to play it lightly. "Depends, milord."

"On what?"

"On where you think the borderline might be." Wender gestures toward the higher, messier stacks of books. "It all sounds crazy to me, so who am I to judge?"

"You're a patient man, Kurt." Hal's shoulders relax, and he smiles, rubbing his chin. "I sure need a trim."

"Indeed, milord."

The smile and the calmer manner bring back the elder knight of Erde's fond memory. She settles into the chair next to him once the king has indicated that he prefers to remain standing for a while. "I'm so relieved."

"No more than I." He glances at his hands, sees that they're smeared with mud and dried blood. "Kurt, some hot water, when you have the chance." Wender has it ready, and a clean cloth, and is just clearing space on one of the tables when a boy appears with food and warmed wine. Hal washes intently, as if a proper scrubbing might scour away the shame of his madness. With dripping hands, he slicks back his unkempt hair, then turns stiffly in his chair to eye his king, who leans against a tent pole, watching.

"You're very quiet, my liege."

"I'm savoring the relief of having you back again."

"You're very kind to say so. And I, of course, have no idea of how to apologize."

"No apologies needed."

"If not for the dragon . . ."

"If not for the dragon, you'd be dead of a sword thrust, in my service. And I would have lost my good right hand."

"Well . . ." Hal looks down again to study his palms, clean this time, at least visibly. "It's not all madness, you know. And I really do believe I've found some answers."

"No one doubts you, dear knight!" Erde leans toward him, her hand on his arm. "Tell us! That is, if you're feeling well enough."

Her eager concern and the warm cup of wine that Wender thrusts into his fist are all the encouragement the old soldier requires. He takes a long swig, then sets the cup aside. "You recall, my girl, way back when we pondered the meaning of the answers that odd fellow Gerrasch gave us?"

Erde nods. "You'd think him all the odder if you could see him now."

Hal looks stunned. "You've *seen* him? I thought he'd died, or gone away. Where did you see him?"

"When is actually the question, my knight. Very far in the future, where he has become . . . almost a man, but still very much Gerrasch. You'd recognize him. He is Air's dragon guide."

"Ahhhhhhh. No wonder! A sort of . . . immortal, is he?"

"A hafling creature. Part man, part dragon-stuff."

Hal's stare goes inward for a moment, contemplating this new miracle. "But, remember, when we asked what the Purpose was, he said, 'to fix what's broken'?"

"Of course."

"Well, I know now what's broken."

Erde is too concerned for his delicate health to simply declare this mystery already solved, that it's the Earth itself that's broken, and the question is how to fix it. Nor is this the time to describe to him just how broken. Can these men, for whom disaster means a really bad winter, ever comprehend the devastation that Rose intuited, outside the White City? Instead, she refills his wine cup and hands it to him, putting on her listening expression, while inside she battles with the dragon's impatience as well as her own. Now that Hal is healed to the best of his abilities, Earth wants to get back to the Grove, and it's hard for her to disagree with him. "Tell me your theory, good knight."

"It's all in the book, if only I'd read more carefully, though the understanding is a bit buried by metaphor, perhaps so that it would not fall into the wrong hands. For it is, you see, rather heretical."

"My whole life is heretical, Sir Hal. After all, I consort with dragons."

"Indeed you do." He smiles. "Lucky girl. Anyhow, according to my study, the world was not created by God directly, as it says in the Bible, but by elemental dragons. Four dragons: Earth, Water, Fire, and Air.

Whether they be His creatures or not is, I believe, an article of faith."

"Yes, of course." Erde accepts the wine cup that Wender has poured for her. Perhaps sipping it will help her to greater calm.

"When these four created the world, the tale goes, it was in perfect balance. All the elements of Nature in harmony, like musical notes. Then the dragons' work was finished, and they retired to the various depths of the world to sleep. This much was easy to put together, once I accepted its heretical message." He glances at the cup in his hand as if surprised to find it there, and takes a sip. "Then I came to the question of why the dragons waked at all. It seemed obvious that something must have gone wrong."

"Yes. Something has 'broken.' "

"Well, what do you get when you 'break' a perfect balance?" Hal regards her owlishly over the rim of his wine cup.

Erde frowns gently. "I don't know. A mess? Like broken eggs?"

"Anarchy," chimes in Wender, with a sweeping gesture around the tent.

"Imbalance," says the king, with certitude.

"Right as rain, my liege!" Hal exclaims. "Acute as always. You have Nature out of balance. Freakish storms, flood, and drought, the seasons off their cycle. So the dragons' obvious Purpose is to restore that balance."

This is still old news to Erde, though she sees it a bit differently when expressed in Hal's language. "But how, dear sir, how? Isn't that really the question?"

"Of course, importunate child! I'm just getting to that!"

Erde subsides with her wine cup warming her lips. Outside, the wind shakes the heavy canvas of the pavilion so that the tent poles sway. Rainer drops into the chair on Hal's other side, listening expectantly.

"In order to know the cure, as the healers say, one must know the cause. What is the *cause* of this imbalance?" Hal gazes around the small circle of faces as though he was a tutor testing their aptitude. "What presence in the world most often works against the laws of Nature?"

"Evil," Erde declares.

"True, true. But evil in what form? Be careful, now. The evil that's done may not always be present in the *intent*." He eyes them again. "Come, come! You've all of you suffered at its hand!"

"War?" suggest Wender.

"The Church," Erde murmurs.

The young king shifts in his chair, recrossing his long legs. "It's men you speak of, isn't it?"

"Surely, it is!" the old knight crows. "Allow me to kneel to you yet again, Sire, and offer my sword in your service!"

Rainer flushes, not angry but visibly annoyed. "There are faster ways than guessing games to get at the heart of a matter, my knight."

Hal nods, unrepentant. "Indeed there are, but indulge an old retainer a moment longer. If, as you so astutely surmise, it is men who create the imbalance, it is men who must be corrected." Now when he looks around, he's greeted with glum silence. "Ah. I see you perceive the dilemma."

"People have been trying to do that since the year One."

"And before!" exclaims Hal, as if the notion offers him great satisfaction.

"But surely men are part of Nature," Kurt Wender protests.

Hal shakes his shaggy head. "Set above the rest of Creation, according to the Book. The natural world is intended for his use and sustenance. But in return, man is pledged to act as steward of these resources, to protect Nature, and sustain her. Somewhere along the line, the bargain was forgotten."

He sits back to take another long pull at his wine cup, then collects a hunk of cheese from the platter beside his knee. "Now, here's where I begin to fly off into the ethereal heights of wild speculation. Think of it from the point of view of bridge building or barn raising. Any balanced structure will have some natural flex to keep it from snapping in the gales, or in ice heaves in the winter. So at first, the depredations of man come and go without dire effect. Contemplating this one day, it occurred to me that if I were the master builder of the 'bridge' of Nature, I'd try to build in some sort of signal that would raise the alarm if the bridge was about to fail. Let's say such a signal exists, and it woke the dragons . . ." He leans forward, his eyes alight. ". . . at the point when the balance tipped too far for the natural flex to be able to restore it."

Erde feels a small implosion of insight inside her head. She's unsure if it's hers, or the dragon's, or both. "But that would be now . . . or, just a while ago, when . . ."

"Yes. When you found Lord Earth, and not long after, I found you."

"It's *now*," Erde repeats, aware that her attack of

insight is still in process. "Oh!" She grabs her head
as if her growing comprehension might split it apart.
"That's why Air called us back to the Grove! That's
where the balance tipped, and it's going on right
now! It's Brother Guillemo cutting down the trees!"

"Among other things." Hal nods, gone suddenly
solemn. "Guillemo isn't the cause himself, so much
as its final incarnation."

"Guillemo!" Erde stares at him, wide-eyed. "The
dragons are coming, Air and Water and their guides.
Earth and I will go, too. To the Grove. What will we
do there?"

"Teach the race of men to honor their bargain, or
destroy them. Those seem to be the only possible
options."

Captain Wender shakes his head at such grandiose
imaginings. Erde can see him wondering if the old
knight's mind is once again wandering. "We can't
do away with the one man, never mind the whole
race of 'em!"

She sees it come over them, all three of them, as
visible as the shadow of a cloud over sunlight. Their
shoulders slump as if choreographed together. Their
mouths and brows turn gently down.

Hal says, "True enough. The hell-priest's magic
has protected him damnably well." He squints at his
book-laden camp desk and a hint of his former confusion returns to his eyes. "I was looking for some
sort of countermeasure. It's as if he reached out and
corrupted my search."

"Can't kill the bastard," Wender mutters. "Begging
your pardon, milady."

"But how can it be," Erde asks, "that you have
him surrounded and still cannot finish him?"

"Our forces are demoralized," Rainer admits,

"both men and knights, by weather and hunger and disease. We've had victories everywhere else, but this siege has proved, well, intractable."

Hal adds glumly, "And as long as Guillemo lives, many will believe in him."

"The men are afraid for their souls," offers Wender.

"In a way," continues Rainer, the rationalist, "Guillemo's turned the trees against us. We have the advantage of numbers, but you can't send an army in there. There's no room to fight. The men get picked off from above before they're a horse's length into the trees."

"But we have to stop him! He's destroying the Grove!"

Hal glances up suddenly, remembering. "Did you say Air called you to the Grove? Have you found all four dragons, then? There are four, as I said?"

"Yes, dear knight. Though we have yet to win Fire to our cause. Yet we are summoned, all of us, so sometime soon—Lord Earth and I are unsure of the timing—Brother Guillemo will have surprise visitors."

The men exchange glances.

"An unusual opportunity," notes Rainer.

"The perfect time for a fresh offensive," Wender agrees.

"But perhaps the dragons will not need our help," Hal observes.

"Do not say so!" Erde exclaims. "All help is welcome and necessary!"

Wender drops his chin into his palms and rests his elbows on his knees. "It'll take some time to get the men ready . . ."

Rainer rises from his chair and wanders away,

stretching his long back. "The barons always resist fighting in this weather."

"Again?" Erde is unable to restrain herself further. She leaps up from her chair. "Listen to you all! For shame! Will you give up so easily?" The men blink at her and glance away, and she knows they're ashamed for her breach of ettiquette. It's not her place, as a young girl, to be scolding her elders, or advising seasoned fighting men, or for that matter, berating her king. But she sees no one else around willing to do it, and something must be done to stir them out of their gloom!

She tries to moderate her voice, and keep her whirling arms under more ladylike control. "I'd think Fra Guill has put a spell on you, but I don't believe in such spells, not anymore! Cease your search for magic, good knight. There is no magic but dragon magic, the magic of the elements that made the world. If you seek to understand the success of the hell-priest, look no further. It's right here, in this camp, in this tent, in your own hearts! Your true enemy is despair! Your men won't fight because they have no faith that they can win. They and you—now, don't deny it! I can see it in your eyes—believe that evil is the stronger force, and therefore the hell-priest triumphs!"

"Little sister, little sister," Rainer chides. "You are as always passionate in your ideals. But real life is not so simple."

"No, listen!" Is it treason, she wonders briefly, to argue with your king? "Sometimes we must *make* it simple! Sometimes we must speak in absolutes! Rainer . . . your pardon, I mean, Sire . . . you think me naïve, and perhaps I am, though not nearly so as I was when you saw me last. I have seen how 'real life' wears down the great Ideals: with this excuse, that pragmatic consideration, the several 'necessary' concessions. Soon, the clean and noble marble edifice is worn and weary, crumbling at the edges so that all manner of petty evils and cynicisms enter unheeded through the cracks!"

She pauses, breathless, and the discomfort on their faces nearly stalls her momentum. She's embarrassing herself in front of them, her mentor and the young man she once thought she loved. No matter! She must finish what she's begun. "Well, all that may be 'real' and day-to-day, and we must live with it. And perhaps the smaller evils will most often triumph. But this is not day-to-day, and the greater evil cannot be allowed to triumph! Good must win, or the world will not survive!"

She faces the young king, who regards her stony-faced. "My liege! Go to your barons and your captains! Inspire them with your faith and vigor! If we believe, they'll believe!

"And you, dear Sir Hal, whose tireless conviction in the rightness of dragons saved our Quest from early disaster . . . I know the winter has been desperate and long, and the battle endless, but surely you'll not give up when that end is now in sight?"

Then, all of a sudden, she's out of words. The last drop has poured out of the wine jug. She feels as if she's run a long foot race, and has no idea if she's lost or won. She sits down again, and lapsing into silence, she wraps her arms around herself and gently rocks. The men are silent, too, and for a while they all sit listening to the wind howl and the snow rattle against the canvas. Captain Wender sips his wine. Hal stares morosely into his upturned palms as if hoping to read his fortune. Rainer stares off into the shadow at the corners of the tent, probably wrestling with the weight of his new responsibilities.

Finally, he stirs. "Can you say with any accuracy when the other dragons will arrive?"

Erde can see the brilliance of her smile reflected in the men's eyes. "Not when it will happen, Sire, but surely we will know the exact moment when it *is* happening. If we are ready. . . ."

"Then we'll be ready." The king rises, and Wender with him, drawn upward by respect and the strength of the younger man's returned resolve. "Wender, alert the captains, rouse the men and the knights. Drag the barons from their beds if need be."

"Aye, my liege!" Wender wraps his heavy cloak about him and ducks out of the tent.

Rainer lifts the canvas door flap. "It's near night already."

Hal consults the water clock on his camp desk. "No, Sire. It's just past noon. It's an unnatural night."

"The moment will be soon, then," Erde murmurs, feeling the stirrings of a terror she cannot even name.

"So be it," Rainer replies with conviction, and follows Wender through the doorway into snow and darkness.

Chapter Thirty-five

N'Doch stares through the iron grille set in the stone gateway. Only this frail barrier and Gerrasch's chunky body stand between him and what used to be a dank castle courtyard. Now it looks like the insides of a computer. The nanos have been hard at work out there.

He tugs nervously at his heavy vest and leggings. The Deep Moor ladies have once again managed to outfit him against the cold, this time by giving up various layers of their own, since the fake Deep Moor neglected to include the storage closets. So, he's sweating in wool and sheepskin, but shivering in his heart. Least, that's how it feels to him. The word "endgame" keeps cycling through his brain like some kind of fiendish audio loop.

This time, he tells himself, *the shit really is gonna hit the fan.*

The truth is, he doesn't know what to expect. If this was a vid, there'd be smart nukes and laser weapons and robotic armored vehicles. But this little assault force, except for himself, is all women and old men. Well, old-ish. He knows Stoksie and Luther wouldn't appreciate the designation. As for Gerrasch, who knows what he is.

Women, old men . . . and two dragons.

He's spent the last few hours helping with the flurry of preparation, getting everyone briefed, provisioned, and armed with whatever was available, which wasn't much. Having had their way with the outer courtyard, the nanos are taking down the farmstead at an ever-increasing rate. The house is gone, but for remnants of the rose arbor. The central tree is a last holdout, as if the nanos have preserved its sinuous branches and green tapestry of leaves as some kind of museum exhibit of the extinct characteristics of organic life-forms.

N'Doch shivers again, then gathers himself sternly, leaning on the shaft of the pike he's been assigned, and grins down at his grandfather, who stands as calm and composed as ever.

"Well, it was sure great being back at the Rive 'n all, but I won't mind seeing the last of this burg."

Djawara crinkles his eyes, as if a full-tilt smile might show disrespect for this serious occasion. "All my life, I never traveled abroad, just from the bush to the city, the city to the bush. Now, in my old age, fifteen centuries in what's seemed like an afternoon."

"We ain't there yet, Papa." But he knows getting there is not the problem. It's what happens after. Behind them, the women are falling into formation. A ragtag army, but N'Doch can't help feeling proud of these women. A few of them look scared—after all, they're headed right back to the place they ran from in terror not too long ago—but no one's complaining. They're used to having to defend themselves, and they have faith in the dragons. Probably more than he does.

A big hand lands on his shoulder. "Ready to sing, bro?"

"Damn, I thought you were gonna send me in there on my lonesome." Despite his doubts, N'Doch feels a lot better with the dragon beside him. "Gettin' near time?"

Sedou nods. "G won't be able to hold her back much longer."

"What's gonna go down? You got something spectacular planned? I keep pushing to hear some strategy." He jerks his thumb toward the silent Librarian, who stares intently through the gate like he was entirely alone in the world. "But G tells me that sort of thinking's too structured for Air."

"My plan is, we'll rout the bastard." Sedou grins wickedly.

"Yeah, yeah." He tries to conjure up his old pawn-of-destiny resentment. Do him good to toss out a few antidragon slogans right now, just to keep up appearances. But, truth is, he's about used all that up. Given that he's pretty sure he'll never see home again, given all this "mutual annihilation" business, still he'd have to say that what he's feeling is a kind of gratitude. If he was told he could go home tomorrow, he'd probably tell 'em he wasn't interested. How could he say otherwise? Thanks to these dragons, he's had the adventure of his life.

He scratches his jaw uneasily, leveling an accusing stare at the back of Gerrasch's hairy head. Something's happening to him, no question about it. Ever since Air came on-line with the dragon internet, he's felt different. He'd mention it to Erde or Paia, if they were around, see what they say. Like, maybe they're feeling it, too. Sounds too stupid to come out and say it to anyone who isn't a dragon guide, not the way he really feels it. Which is, like he's got more . . . air . . . in him now. Like, when he looks at these gutsy women, instead of thinking how uncool they are, he feels vast and generous inside, and like he can see to infinity. The real way to describe it is, he feels more like a dragon now. But he knows if he told that to Sedou, he'd get laughed out of town.

So instead, he tucks the pike shaft against his chest and drapes his free arm around his grandfather's slim shoulders. The dragon-as-Sedou stands behind them both. Like a family portrait, N'Doch muses. One that never got taken while Sedou was actually alive.

In front of him, Gerrasch stirs, and the hand on his own shoulder tightens. "Here we go."

And through the stone gateway, the view is no longer nanomech abstract art, but the drifts and snow-laden branches of the Grove.

Erde yawns, despite her nerves being stretched taut with waiting. She'd caught a few hours' sleep in Hal's tent while the armies prepared, and was woken later in the afternoon by the dragon's rumblings. Now, at the king's insistence, she sits wrapped in a royal cloak and astride a royal horse, even though she'd have preferred to walk out to the field alongside the dragon, and even though the poor horse will be suddenly riderless when the others arrive, and she

and the dragon go to join them in the Grove. Earth
expects that Air will reopen the portal at the far end
of the meadow. What will happen after that is anybody's guess, but Earth made sure to build up his
strength by easing the death of two badly wounded
horses and a starving dog, having first asked their
permission to consume them afterward.

For now, the king has arrayed his men in a wide
circle around the Grove, just outside the range of the
archers who've been lurking among the first rank of
trees. The strategy is simple: to rush in when the
dragon signals that the portal is opening. He says he
hears nothing specific, but senses his sibling's preparations as a very faint echo rolling down the years
from the far future. When the portal opens, it will
be as if the echo has become a shout from across
the valley.

Earth crouches to Erde's right, huge and dark
against the white snow, a wall of shadow in the afternoon gloom. Both the barons and their knights resisted the notion of fighting at night, no matter that
success would rely on coinciding the assault with the
arrival of the other dragons. Their young king finally
won them over with a stirring paean to the value of
surprise. Now each foot soldier carries both his
weapon and a torch. Erde hopes the ancient trees of
the Grove will forgive her for allowing this ancient
enemy into their sacred precincts, but they've with-
stood fire before. The saws and axes of Brother Guillemo present a much more present danger.

Hal lopes down along the line and noses his horse
in beside her. "Any word?" He regards the dragon
eagerly, almost lovingly, for a sign. His horse dances,
restless for action.

Erde shakes her head. She rejoices to see the knight

hale again, washed and barbered and clad in his worn red leathers from the old king's service, looking like the warrior who taught her the skills that kept her alive once she'd fled her father's castle. He's looking especially inspired at the moment because she'd finally found the time to let him know that Rose and the other women were not killed or taken prisoner during the burning of Deep Moor—as he had assumed, swearing that this was what had driven him over the edge. Erde could privately have added a number of reasons for the knight's sanity to be vulnerable. The news in Hal's life, despite his great virtue and cleverness, has most often been bad, especially lately. Though, perhaps Hal himself would not say so. After all, one of his most cherished ambitions has been fulfilled: he's consorted with dragons. Right now he's even smiling, in his stern sort of way, as if recalling the good news she has given him, and savoring it all over again.

How wonderful to love, Erde muses, and love in return. Perhaps Rose and Hal are each other's consolation prize for not having dragons of their own. And, as visions of love always conjure Adophus of Köthen, there he is, like a mirage before her eyes. But instead of banishing his handsome visage, as she has learned to do the moment a thought of him arrives, Erde lets her memories of him fill her senses, just for now, a sort of farewell. A true love must be all-consuming, and perhaps she would not have had proper room in her heart for both a dragon and a man.

Still, she wishes he was here, less for her sake than for Hal's, to have one more agile sword fighting by their side. But he has chosen other battles, as is his right. Erde wishes him well, and godspeed.

The Librarian's arm answers the dragon's signal. Before he has time to think about it, he's gripped the iron grille and swung it wide. He's lost all sense of independent existence, of owning his own life. He is Air's conveyance, yes, but not just some mindless mechanism. That would be easier to bear. No, he's her smart-car, programmed with all the rules of the road, and the assignment of keeping his reckless driver from veering off the highway.

As the portal opens, long stored memories awaken. The bite of the cold, the dry scent of the winter trees. The Librarian sees/hears/feels the forest as the dragon senses it, as a tapestry of sensual data. He adds to that his emotional connection with this old place of safety and retreat, his first Refuge.

And then, peering into the dim late light, he sees what has been done to it. Raw stumps, hewn logs lying scattered about like giant matchsticks, piles of broken branches, the trampled ground gouged from the dragging. The wide wounds of a road, bleeding mud, leading from the base of the meadow to the spread of tents and campfires at the farther end.

He opens his mouth, gasping like a fish on land. He'll spew up his cry of rage and grief like vomit. And then, between one despairing breath and the next, he's alone in his head again.

The Librarian nearly collapses. Behind him, Luther sees him flag and shoulders past N'Doch to grab him under the arms and drag him through the gate so that the others will not crush him, rushing through.

"Yu all ri', G?"

The Librarian hasn't a clue. Has the portal malfunctioned? No, here he is, knee-deep in snow. And there's N'Doch with one arm around his grandfather, and Sedou/Water, even now morphing into numberless and nameless tiny motes. After them, the two trackers, and Stoksie and Rose and the other ladies of Deep Moor. He has to keep count, make sure they all get through before the portal closes. But where is the dragon? Where is Air? Who will revenge this awful desecration? A newborn child is no more innocent or worthy than an ancient tree!

"She's left me," he mutters, hearing himself rave like some old drunk who's lost his woman.

"Who has?"

"She . . ." No, there she is. He feels her now. Touching, filling, merging with the trees, with the leafless branches and the sodden earth of the meadow and the snow and the muddied rim of the pond, entering the very substance of the Grove as she had entered him, molecule by molecule.

As she flows into and through, the snowdrifts swirl up and coalesce into the shapes of woodland animals. Pale and huge, they stalk across the meadow. The barren trees writhe like a nest of vipers. The smoke rising from the campfires twists into the form of winged raptors, and the water of the pond leaps up as fish, their gaping mouths lined with teeth.

The sentries bellow their alarm. The quiet camp explodes into action, as the bedded-down troops glance up from their dice games and weapons repair. Voices cry out for light, though it is not yet night. The fires flare high as wood is thrown on in armloads. A hundred torches burst to life. The dark profiles of running men and rearing horses crisscross the brightening glare.

The Librarian hauls himself out of his tumble into grief and outrage. Knowing no other direction but forward, he raises his arm and gestures his little battalion on across the meadow, while around them the trees sway and the whirlwind snow shapes of stag and bear ride guard.

"More light!" the voices cry, now less distant and more frightened. Other commands ring out, but panic deafens the soldiers. They stumble over each other, reaching for their boots, their weapons, their helmets, striking out against shadows and blindly maiming their friends. The campfires swell into bonfires, shooting flame and spark into the thick dark air above the meadow. A man on a tall white horse circles the central fiery tower, yelling threats and encouragement. His white robe takes on the ruddy colors of the fire, and his raised sword throws shards of light far enough to flash in the Librarian's eyes.

The shadows recede before the fire's onslaught. The snow beasts seem less substantial, even flimsy in the glare. Taking heart at the banishing of darkness, the soldiers come to their senses and once again hear the hoarse shouts of their officers, and especially the mounted white-robe, who rides among them like a dog among sheep, herding them into order.

"Illusions only! Pay them no heed! Magic has no force among the righteous!" the white-robe rails, and even through the veil of centuries, the Librarian recognizes the voice of Brother Guillemo.

He glances behind him, with fleeting thoughts of retreat. He is halfway between camp and portal. The last of the women, Margit's twins, each assisting one of the older refugees, hurry through the stone arch hovering insubstantially among the trees. The Librarian grimaces at the finality of it, then releases his stranglehold on a tiny shred of Air's consciousness, which is all that's kept the portal open after his own passage through it. The gateway, its stone pillars and iron grille and its slice of view into the sun and green of Deep Moor, vanishes into snow and air and darkness.

And then, Earth arrives. Water completes her transmutation. Her numberless crystalline motes swirl up into the whirlwinds to be carried over the camp as a glittering cloud with uncanny intent. Raindrops hiss in the bonfires, the early warning of the downpour that follows, quenching the flames with a great whoosh and a belching of black smoke. New cries of dismay rise from the soldiers, blinded again by smoke and oncoming night, and another wave of terror as the ground shudders and sways, jerking them off their feet. Still the white-robed rider, Brother Guillemo, whips his frothing mount through the panic and pandemonium, one moment exhorting his troops to bravery, in the next, promising courts-martial and executions if they do not stand and fight. Many are frightened back to their posts. Even more choose to take their chances with the shadows and the spectral beasts. They flounder off into the drifts between the trees, where their retreat is cut off by a new flare of light. The armies of the king have entered the Grove unchallenged for the first time since the siege began. Surrounding the camp, the foot soldiers light their torches. Fra Guill's army is circled by a ring of bright and steady fire.

Taking advantage of Air's ubiquitous eye, the Librarian observes how, for many of those seeking to flee, the appearance of the enemy seemingly out of nowhere and at night completes the destruction of their fighting spirit. They throw down their weapons, and then themselves, begging rescue from the fury of unnatural forces, and from their mad leader as well. Fear lends others strength enough to hack a way through the enemy line. Mounted squads are immediately sent off in pursuit. But the Librarian knows this is not the real battle. He hopes that the fighting will be over soon, now that it has accomplished its purpose, which was to clear the Grove of this pesky human intrusion so that the important work can begin.

But there is one intrusion more to be reckoned with. Never having dealt with him, and despite the Librarian's warnings, Air has overlooked Brother Guillemo. Until he's done for, this king will not leave the Grove. And the priest sees this is likely his final stand, which makes him a desperate and unpredictable obstacle. Already he has succeeded in reforming a substantial phalanx of his personal guard, his white-robed priest-knights. On their huge and spirited horses, they fill the central clearing, stirring up the pond and spilling out into the snow-swept meadow. But he does not order them to attack. He's stalling for time, the Librarian guesses. Several of the knights have dismounted to build up the largest bonfire, still smoldering damply at its heart. The flames rise high as the dragons pull back, allowing the king's armies to march away their prisoners, clear the wounded, and tighten their ring around the remaining enemy. A respectful space is left for Earth, the only visible dragon, to take his place among them. The men tip their pikes to Erde, who rides proudly on Earth's shoulder. Water glitters among the tree branches like a galaxy of stars. Air waits. She thinks the humans will be gone soon. Again, The Librarian cannot convince her that she's wrong.

The Deep Moor refugees have been spotted, and Hal is racing around the outer ring to greet Rose and draw her up onto his saddle. But he soon sets her down again, signaling Wender over to shepherd them to the safety of the camp outside the Grove. As if in evidence to the Librarian's point, Rose and Raven insist they will stay. Linden joins them, murmuring that a healer might be needed. Stoksie and Luther vow to protect them, while Margit and Lily insist that they will join the fight. Wisely, Hal doesn't argue. He shrugs, kisses Rose soundly, and rides back into the line.

Inside the ring, Brother Guillemo rides around the central bonfire as if celebrating a victory. His white-robes have drawn their mounts up around him in a second ring. Guillemo has thrown back his hood so that his pale face shines in the firelight, cut across sharply by black brows and a black beard that shelters a surprisingly full, red mouth. *A sensual face*, muses the Librarian, whose earlier collisions with the hell-priest left him little time for leisurely observation. The priest's deep voice carries without straining, as an actor's must, lending it a disturbing quality of intimacy, despite its volume and grandiose rhetoric.

"Illusions!" he is bellowing. "If you do not heed them, they can do no harm!"

"But the dragons . . . !" shouts one of the white-robes, as if speaking an assigned role.

"Dragons! A mere creature of Nature! God decrees that man's proper destiny is to rule over Nature! Nature is chaos! Chaos is the enemy! Man brings order and piety and civilization!"

The Librarian's old habits of protest stir in his gut like a nest of hornets. *If cutting down a grove of sacred trees is your idea of piety and civilization,* he wants to shout, *language has lost all its meaning. This is filth, what you've done! You are filth!* But because the dragons still wait, he keeps his silence.

"Man must bend all Nature into harness!" the priest continues, as if he stood in the pulpit of a church and not on the field about to fight his last battle. "Water, wind, the products of the earth! All are created to fuel humankind's drive toward our manifest destiny! I know this to be true and good and righteous! If you believe in me, if you believe in that destiny, they cannot stand against us!" He whirls his horse at the circle of his own men. A way parts for him, as if rehearsed, and he rides boldly into the no-man's-land between the opposing forces. Now his exhortations are aimed at the front ranks of the king's infantry, who stare back at him stonily with pikes at the ready.

"You there!" He singles out one soldier in particular, a boy with sullen eyes. "Most likely you will die tonight! You think you have the advantage of numbers, but hear me! Few can stand against my knights! What will become of your immortal soul if you die fighting for a dragon's cause?"

The Librarian notes several nods among the boy's neighbors. Heads bend together, muttering.

"You there!" The priest spurs down the line, flirting with the archers in the rear by dancing his horse in and out of their range. He pulls up across from an older infantryman. "Is it right that your stripling king forces you into battle in support of *witches,* who should be properly burned in God's name?"

More nods and mutters, even some audible grumbling. The Librarian grinds his teeth. He's just realized what the dragons are waiting for. They're still expecting the fourth of them to arrive.

Erde shivers as Fra Guill evokes the horrors of the stake. She's slipped down from Earth's shoulder to his forearm, avoiding the hell-priest's line of sight, and hopes that the women standing in the warmth of the dragon's shadow will do likewise. Is he looking for her even now? For Rose, or Raven? As he wheels his horse in her direction, Erde shrinks against the dragon's chest, then gasps as a hand grips her ankle.

"Hey, can I come up?" N'Doch grins up at her, his teeth very white against his face and his face very dark against the snow. He vaults up beside her and ruffles her hair, which is his idea of an appropriate greeting. "So far, so good. Was that you brought in the army?"

"Sort of. I mean, they were already out there, waiting."

"Good move. Speaking of waiting, what's going on? Water's too discorporate to make any sense."

"That's what they're doing. Waiting."

"What for? Why don't they just finish the bastard?"

Erde stares at him.

"You're giving me that old surely-you-know-by-now look."

She replies as if reciting a lesson. "A dragon cannot end a life without asking that life's permission."

"I mean the soldiers, not the dragons. How can they stand to sit still for that crap?"

"Oh." Erde frowns gently. She'd stopped listening to the hell-priest long ago. "I think they're waiting for the dragons to do it."

"Well, someone better let them know they could be in for a long wait. Surely Hal knows better."

"Sir Hal answers to his king."

N'Doch rolls his eyes. "The old king thing."

"Don't be disrespectful."

He makes another sour face, tapping the ridges on Earth's chest plate. Erde sees he's anxious, a bit jumpy. "What about the Fire dude?" he asks finally. "You think he'll show?"

"I don't know." She realizes she's disappointed, and yes, nervous, too. Earth had nearly convinced her that Fire would be unable to resist Air's final summons. But if he doesn't come, what next?

"Okay, here we go. Somebody's making a move. It's Hal. What's he up to?"

N'Doch points along the rank of soldiers, and Erde pulls up out of her defensive slouch to look. Hal has urged his horse forward from beside the king, and is riding with slow deliberation around the ring on a path that will bring him face-to-face with Brother Guillemo. His back is erect. His chin is high. The dragon-hilted sword lies unsheathed across his red-leathered thighs. Erde thinks he looks the very picture of a King's Knight.

N'Doch whistles softly. "No chance of one man taking this creep down. What's Hal gonna do, challenge him? I wouldn't trust that dude to fight fair!"

"But no one has more reason to challenge him."
Erde chews her lip, worried. "And he feels this is all
his fault for not seeing what Fra Guill was from the
beginning, and for not putting a stop to him then."

"Hey, hindsight is twenty-twenty."

"Is what?"

"Never mind."

After a moment, Erde says, "Still, I wish he would
let a younger man fight. If only . . ."

She hesitates so long that N'Doch fills in the rest.
"If only Dolph was here?"

"Yes."

"Hey, I'd like that, too." He pats her shoulder.
"Don't worry. If it goes bad, the dragons'll step in
somehow."

There's another pause, so that the sound of Fra
Guill haranguing the troops intrudes like a physical
presence between them. Finally, Erde says, "We put
so much faith in them."

"You're the one who taught me to."

"But what if three is not enough? What if Lord
Fire doesn't come? What if our dragons can't do what
needs to be done?"

"Then the world goes down the tubes, I guess.
Least, that seems to be what they're suggesting."

Miserable, anxious, impatient, but grateful for his
company, she leans into his side, and together they
watch Hal ride to within a dragon's length of the
hell-priest and stop. Guillemo ignores him, or seems
to. But he abandons forward motion in favor of pacing his horse back and forth within a contained area,
as if he's detected a particular source of potential
converts within the enemy's ranks. He's reached the
point in his sermonizing where the "witch-girl"
comes up for specific mention. After a few para-

graphs of choice invective, he turns his horse at the end of a pace and pretends to discover the red-clad knight who sits calmly leaning on the bridge of his saddle, not ten yards away.

"Angels of grace!" the priest exclaims. "It's the dragon lord himself! Are you resurrected, by some black magic? They said you'd fallen on the field not three days ago!"

"It's true I took a blade," replies Hal amiably.

"Then, what devil's bargain keeps you in this world?"

"None but the desire to see you dead and buried, Guillemo."

The priest looks shocked, and shoots a complicit glance at the murmuring soldiers. Erde suspects Fra Guill's spies have told him of the superstitious fears that Hal's eccentricities have inspired in some of the men under his command. "Sir, I am a man of the cloth. You will address me as 'father,' my son."

"Not a chance."

"Though you are lost to Hell for your unrepentant delving into the blackest of magic, yet I will pray for your soul."

Hal smiles blandly. "And that's the surest road to Hell I can think of."

The mutters from the infantry are clearly audible by now.

N'Doch clicks his tongue. "Ease up, Hal. It's not playing too well to the troops."

Hal lifts his sword casually from his lap, letting it hang alongside his horse's flank. "So, what will it be, Guillemo? In the King's name, I can offer you surrender, to save the lives of your men, or certain defeat and no prisoners."

But Brother Guillemo has turned away, listening,

as if to heavenly choirs. Erde nudges N'Doch as the dragon stirs beneath them. "Do you feel it? Something's . . . happening. Someone's . . . it's . . ."

N'Doch hears Water's subvocal warning just as the dark sky above the clearing is split by the flash of gilded wings. He's not sure if Fire's coming is good or bad, but he's relieved to have the waiting over with. Fire circles once, screaming like a jet on a runway approach. The soldiers break ranks and run for cover. Half of Guillemo's knights take advantage of the chaos to kick their horses into a gallop and leap to freedom over the heads of the fleeing men. The rest draw up tight around him, while the king's captains struggle to regain control of their army. With a great splaying of talons tipped in shining gold, Fire hovers above the central bonfire as if born out of its flames. Then he settles on top of it, scattering burned logs and embers among the loyal cluster of white-robes. Only one manages to retain his control of his mount, and his position by Guillemo's side. Two are unhorsed, but steady on their feet. The rest follow their fellows off into darkness.

"Damn!" N'Doch whispers fervently. "Another great entrance! The dude's timing is impeccable!" But Erde is staring at him with her usual mix of horror and condemnation. "I know, I know," he says. "If he's here to save Guillemo's butt, this could be very bad."

Fire hunkers down in the embers for long enough to chill every heart in the Grove with his golden glower and the curl of acrid smoke escaping through the corners of his snarl. N'Doch thinks he couldn't have scripted it better himself. After all, cliches work because they're primal.

To his credit, Brother Guillemo recovers first, his voice steady atop his skittering horse. "You see! He conjures yet another fiend from the fires of Hell!"

Hal replies dryly, "No, Guillemo. I believe this one is yours."

Now what, wonders N'Doch. He spots Water's sparkle migrating toward a gathering point. Gerrasch stands in the open several paces away, still as a statue, a Tinker hovering protectively to either side of him. The king's army is settling into some measure of order, but its ranks have been thinned by desertions, squads sent off in pursuit, and others detailed to escort prisoners back to the main camp. Guillemo's in a tough spot, and N'Doch figures it's about time for him to try sleazing his way to a surrender. He has three men left of his own, and precious few of the king's to preach to. He's likely gained a dragon on his side, but he can't welcome Fire's support without blowing his whole cover. Brandishing his sword hilt as a cross, the priest faces the dragon crouching in the fire with as much ambiguity as he can muster. "Speak, O Fiend! What is your errand?"

As if in answer, flames shoot up to obscure the dragon within a curtain of blinding light that burns so fiercely that the horses squeal in terror and those around it retreat from its sudden heat. Then, just as suddenly, it dies away into smoke and a shower of sparks. A man and a woman stand among the ashes. Or rather, N'Doch observes, a spectacular woman and a great, golden giant.

"Quite the couple," he murmurs, hoping to cheer

Erde with a scandalous remark. Yet, as he watches Fire offer his hand to help Paia through the smoldering remains of the bonfire, N'doch realizes he's not far off the mark. He knows how lovers move together.

The other dragons are still waiting.

The Librarian notes how solicitous Fire is with Paia, but otherwise, the giant's expression is grim and furious as he glares around the clearing, taking stock of who's there and how the confrontation has so far played out. He stalks toward the priest, keeping Paia close behind him. As they leave the circle of embers, the flames spring up again to light their way.

Brother Guillemo's bold facade has been visibly frayed by Fire's transformation, and the Librarian suspects he knows why: it's one thing to rant over a snarling, voiceless reptile, but another thing altogether to handle a walking, talking man. Still, with his trio of knights clustered behind him, Guillemo sits firmly erect on his horse. Only his eyes show the true depths of his terror. Good, good, the Librarian approves. At last we've found something the hell-priest is afraid of.

Fire stops at the point where a perfect triangle could be drawn between himself, the hell-priest and Hal. His towering, muscular body is wrapped in a long robe of cloth-of-gold that reflects the firelight and hisses faintly as he moves, then continues to shimmer and dance long after he's eased to a halt. His glimmering hair is braided and bound at the back of his neck, but it, too, seems to have a life of its own. Despite himself, the Librarian has to admit that if he believed in a god, he'd wish it to look this magnificent. That he has a beautiful and apparently adoring woman draped on his elbow does nothing to disturb the Librarian's notions of deity.

When the giant speaks, his voice is a modulated tenor, a cultivated voice, and in its cool formality, the Librarian hears the echoes of ritual.

"I come to claim the kingdom you promised me," Fire says to the priest.

Guillemo lifts his sword hilt higher, as if its cruciform shape might actually protect him. "Away! I know you not! Why do you speak to me?" He gestures hugely in Hal's direction. "Look there to find your master!"

"I have no master, and seek none. I come for repayment of the favors I've granted, as we agreed."

"I know you not, I say!" Guillemo lowers the sword slightly. "Unless you are one of God's angels sent in disguise to deliver the just from the enemies of righteousness?"

"Will you deny me to my face, ungrateful priest?" Fire throws his massive shoulders back. He seems to be enjoying himself, in a dark sort of way. "Again, I ask: have you prepared my palaces and lands? Is my Temple ready to be consecrated?"

"Begone, vile imagining! Or if you be a true angel, claim your heavenly form and aid me now! Do you not see? I am beset by devils!"

Fire's rigid stance unbends. He motions Paia to remain in the warmth from the bonfire, and moves in on the priest. Guillemo's horse lays his ears back and shudders, but stands admirably still as the giant looms over them. "That's the required three chances,

Guillemo. Do you need a fourth? It looks like you've failed to prepare the Faithful for the arrival of their god, but if you can offer me a comfortable castle toward the south, I'll call it even."

Guillemo turns his horse, circling his three stony-faced knights. "Fear not, men of good faith! A test is sent us from above, but we shall show ourselves equal to it!" Now that he has put the knights between him and the dragon, he faces Fire again. "You! Angel! Prove the truth of your divine origins! Defeat our enemies! Destroy the witch-girl and her warlock mentor! Depose the false king! Then all just believers will bow to you as God's representative on earth!"

Fire says, "The witch-girl. Ah. There's an idea." He turns away, and for the first time, looks around at the scattered ring of watchers. The Librarian knows this is only for show. Fire knows exactly where Erde is, where each dragon and dragon guide stand, awaiting a sign of his true intentions.

Despite the bonfire, Paia is stunned by the cold and the dank sucking mud, and the cinders still half alight beneath her sandaled feet. As usual, the dragon has neglected to clothe her adequately. But this new place he's brought her to seems half familiar, even shrouded in fire-lit darkness, as if remembered from dreams. Or from borrowed memories. Memories from the Meld. For the darkness isn't empty. The others are here. The girl Erde, and N'Doch, and Gerrasch, oddly abstracted. Paia greets them, glad for the company, but only Erde replies.

Why has he come? For our side or theirs?

I don't know!

And then Fire issues his summons.

His voice rises again in its formal pitch. "I call Erde von Alte to speak for the Eight!"

Dragon! What must I do?

YOU MUST ANSWER HIM.

But why?

BECAUSE HONOR REQUIRES IT.

It helps that she feels her own reluctance echoed in his tone. She gathers herself to climb down from the safety of his forearm.

N'Doch grabs her. "You're not going out there!"

"I must."

"Then I'm going, too. We should face him together."

They slip through the whispering crowd of Deep Moor refugees. Rose embraces Erde silently. Raven says, "You'll know what to tell him!" Erde moves into the open, N'Doch a half step behind. On the far side of the smoldering fire, Hal sees them coming.

"No!" He spurs his horse into the path between them and the waiting giant, then dismounts, sheathing his sword. "Lord Fire! If you require a life, I offer you mine!"

Erde breaks into a run. "No, you shall not!" She knows Fire will not be satisfied with just any life, but probably wouldn't mind doing away with one persistent opponent in order to get at the other he intends. She reaches Hal and brushes past him, shaking off his arm when he tries to hold her back. "Earth will protect me," she murmurs. To N'Doch, she says, "Stay with him."

But Hal has made his formal offer, and understands it has been refused. Out of the dark behind him, Gerrasch appears, and Paia moves over to join them, shuddering with cold. N'Doch hauls off his top layer and wraps it around her. What fit him as a vest shelters her as a cloak.

Erde approaches alone. Fire glares down at her from his smoke-wreathed heights. Scales glint on his cheeks. She sees his whispering robe is made of chained links of gold. She's relieved to find him decently clothed for a change. She prepares to meet him glower for glower. Yet it seems that the flames leaping in his golden eyes are fed by exasperation rather than rage.

"Do you come ready to lecture me about my sacred Duty, witch-child?"

Overhearing, Brother Guillemo cries, "His duty is to punish you! And he will, by all that's holy!"

Erde folds her arms across her chest. "You know your Duty better than I, Lord Fire."

Fire sighs. "You virtuous ones. Such a bore, really, but so much more reliable."

Erde frowns. "For what have you Summoned me? Time is passing, and the Purpose requires our attention!"

Much to her discomfiture, Fire drops gracefully into a crouch before her, so that their gazes are level. His is hot and cynical, reflecting the fire behind her. She wishes she could look away. He smiles, as if to a much younger child. "So eager for it to be accomplished, are you? You're not even sure what it is."

"I know it is right." Erde's voice catches slightly, despite her efforts to hold it steady. "Whatever else it is, I'll bear up with."

Fire's eyes lid shut briefly. "Ah. Heroics. Again."

"You shall not stir me to rage with your mockery, Lord Fire."

"Really? Then that fierce little scowl and those

shoulders up to your earlobes have nothing to do with anger?"

Erde smoothes her face, and lifts her chin out of her neck.

"No, keep your anger, witchling! Nurture it. It's a proper righteous anger, after all. You'll need it for the task at hand."

"The Purpose should be accomplished with a calm and glad heart, Lord Fire. I know little, but I know that much."

"Ah, but I mean the task I have for you . . . which must be finished before the other can even be attempted."

The frown returns. She cannot banish it. "What task is that?"

"Ask my brother Earth. He will tell you."

"I'd rather you did."

"So be it, then." He straightens, shifting his glare from Erde back to Hal. "Now, sir knight. Front and center."

Hal glares back, uncomprehending. N'Doch moves to grab hold of him, but Erde shake her head gently, and Gerrasch says, "Yes." N'Doch shrugs and urges the knight forward. "Might as well see what he wants."

Shrugging his tunic and mail into order, Hal hurries to Erde's side. "Lord Fire," he acknowledges crisply.

"I have need of your sword."

Hal's jaw tightens. "My sword is sworn to my king, and to the Great Purpose. I cannot . . ."

"Oh, please! No more lofty rhetoric. I wish only the weapon itself, not your undying loyalty."

Confounded, Hal lays his hand on the sword's gilded hilt.

"Yes, yes, that's the one. Draw it and give it to the girl."

As Hal hesitates, Brother Guillemo crows to his men, "Now you'll see how he'll punish the witch!"

"Do it, dear knight," Erde urges. But when she holds the dragon-hilted blade, so heavy that she must use both hands to keep its tip from being fouled in the mud, she says to Fire, "I will not swear to you either."

"Of course you won't. I'm not that delusional. But hear this: will you accept the gift I offer, in recompense for all you've suffered? In doing so, you will also open the way for the accomplishment of the Purpose which has been the cause of that suffering."

His silky tone alerts her. "I think I must know the gift first, my lord, to see if I am worthy of it."

"Oh, take my word for it, you are."

"Nevertheless . . ."

"By all that's eternal!" Fire snarls, while Brother Guillemo dances his horse into a gloat behind him. "No wonder you people never get anything done!" He turns, picks the stunned priest out of his saddle by the hood of his cloak, and flings him at Erde's feet. His terrified horse careens off into the trio of his knights who have pointedly not ridden to his aid. Resilient as always, Guillemo scrambles up, groping for his own weapon. But he has lost it in the transfer. Erde braces herself and lifts the point of Hal's blade. She faces the priest with the same horrified fascination that he's always aroused in her. His black eyes bore into her. His pouty red lips repel her. He is the thing that, in all of life, she comprehends least: the personification of badness. How can a being so wrong support enough life to draw breath?

"Again I am tested," croaks Guillemo, brushing snow and mud from his cassock.

"This looks like a fair fight," observes Fire to Hal, as if soliciting his approval. "He is the stronger, but she has the weapon."

"But . . ." protests Hal. "You can't . . . this is monstrous!"

Fire only laughs, though his laughter dies when Paia steps back into the glow of the firelight. "This is petty vengeance, my Fire. Do you call this a clean kill?"

The smoldering giant shrugs. "Depends on how good she is." Hal begins another protest, but Fire waves him to silence. "Of course, I could show the further depths of my generosity, I suppose . . ." Abruptly, he shoves Guillemo from behind so that the priest stumbles and falls flat. Before he can rise, Fire places one clawed foot in the middle of his back. ". . . by holding him down for her."

Erde stares at the fallen man. A sudden bloodlust grips her heart, as tightly as she grips the sword. Here, under her blade, is the evil who corrupted her father, murdered her dear nurse, set the barons against their king, destroyed the country and the people with war and famine and superstition. It's an opportunity she should welcome. It would be treason not to. And it would be easy. She has only to lift the blade, the great dragon-hilted sword, and the perfection of its edge plus the weight of it falling would sever the priest's neck with little effort on her part. The sword will do the killing, not her.

Dragon?

She hears only disapproving silence in reply. She glances back at Hal, and his eyes are also saying no.

She turns away angrily. Stupid dragon! Selfish man! He only wishes to do the deed himself! She strains to lift the blade level with her shoulders. She approaches the struggling priest.

BEFORE YOU STRIKE, ASK: IS THIS RIGHT?

Memories of her first encounter with Guillemo rush back. How he ogled her and confused her and made her feel dirty and stupid. She was too innocent then to recognize that his interest in her was sexual. He was a priest, after all. A man of God.

IS IT RIGHT?

Dragon, you were not there!

IT IS DESERVED, BUT IS IT RIGHT? LISTEN TO YOUR HEART.

Dragon, you are my heart! Tell me what to do!

I CANNOT.

But why?

IT IS AGAINST THE RULES.

The rules! How can you talk of rules? This is a mortal decision!

THE DECISION MUST BE YOURS, NOT MINE.

Erde knows that if she was going to do this thing, she would have done it already. As quickly as it came on her, the bloodlust departs, leaving her nauseous and trembling. She lowers the sword, letting the tip sink into the mud and ash and melting snow.

Fire clicks his tongue once, irritably. "I thought you of all of them might have it in you."

Erde looks up at him, spent and lost. "If a dragon cannot kill, then neither shall I."

Brother Guillemo laughs under Fire's claw. The dragon steps back, releasing him. "I give up. I've lost again."

"And righteousness has won!" Guillemo shouts, leaping for Erde and the sword. Fire is there before him, snatching the sword from her shaking hands and leveling it with a smooth backhanded stroke that catches the priest full in the throat and passes through without a sound.

"*This* dragon can kill," Fire mutters, as Guillemo topples to the ground. Paia regards her dragon with somber eyes as he casually thrusts the sword back at Erde, hilt-first. Its blade is almost clean. Cries of triumph and release erupt from the soldiers remaining in the Grove. Fire says, "Well, at least someone thought it was the right thing to do."

Hal steps in and gently takes the sword away. The king rides up to join them as they stare down at the new freshet of red flowing between the footprints pressed into the mud and snow. Then Hal calls over two pikemen to cover the corpse and haul it away. "And treat it with due respect," he growls, just as one of them is about to grasp Guillemo's head by the ear and exhibit it on its own in gory triumph.

Fire braces his fists against his back as if in pain, and starts to pace.

The king watches him, a hint of awe and distaste hiding behind his glad air of relief. He turns back to Hal. "Is our business here complete?"

Hal nods. "The business of the kingdom, yes. You may declare the victory, Sire."

"You deserve that honor, my knight."

"No, better you." Hal glances quickly at Erde. Then, having answered his lord too abruptly, he looks up into the young king's eyes, begging patience. "Your pardon, my liege. There are, ah . . . yet a few details to be settled here. If you'll permit me . . ."

Rainer frowns, thinks better of it, and gathers up his reins. "Of course. Report to me when you're finished." As he turns to go, Hal signals Wender to follow. Erde watches them canter off along the dark road through the trees, the other knights and infantry cheering as they pass, then falling gladly in behind.

Oh, yes, she tells herself again. He'll make them a good king.

Meanwhile, Fire continues to pace.

Chapter Thirty-six

The Grove is liberated! The Librarian can hear the trees sighing in relief. Or perhaps it's his dragon, breathing into their bare, battered limbs and brittle twigs, whispering through the roughness of their bark.

HURRY, HURRY!

Ah, yes, it's Air. The trees are in no hurry. When everything Changes, the sacred, eternal Grove will remain. But it's no rest for the weary. The Eight are assembled. The Work must begin. It will start with the trees. The trees are Air's work, and Earth's. The breath of life, the healing force. The Grove will be restored.

Water has chosen to return to man-form for the debate they all know is coming. While her brother pouts and paces, Water-as-Sedou moves among the stay-behinds, those who sensed that the battle was not yet over and still wish to lend their support: the women of Deep Moor, Djawara, Stoksie and Luther, Hal. She will gather them, help them find a comfortable place around the fire. Already, she's sent Margit and Lily off to raid the enemy tents for food, wine, extra clothing or blankets, stools or kegs to rest on.

Rose sets her women to making a meal. Erde searches out deadfall to bring to the fire, refusing to burn the fresh hewn wood while Earth moves slowly among the great trees, mending broken limbs, cracked trunks, the raw scars of cutting and dragging. Paia sits quietly, letting N'Doch and the Tinkers fuss over her. But she's watching Fire pace.

Finally the purposeful busyness settles into quiet, and Sedou says, "If you wish to open the discussion, brother . . . we haven't much time."

Fire turns. "It's too late. She's already on about her usual business. She's as bad as the humans. She won't listen. It doesn't matter what any of us says." He starts to pace again, then stops in front of Erde. The Librarian sees he's not much taller now than N'Doch, as if his pacing has worn out the rage that earlier swelled his stature. But the fire lord's gaze, as he fixes it on the weary girl, is as scornful as ever. "How do you ever expect to fix things if you can't even take the basic steps?"

"Wha . . . what?"

"Ridding the gene pool of the bad ones." When she stares at him openmouthed, he bends over her, articulating each syllable as if she had trouble hearing. "Kill-ing them off."

"Which is what you'd like to do with all of us."

"Yes. The species is hopelessly flawed."

"You made Guillemo what he was!" N'Doch leaps to Erde's defense, shaking his finger in Fire's face. "You can't blame us! You made Baraga, too!"

"And unmade him as well, which is more than you can claim. But, allow me an addendum: I made them *worse* than they already were, merely by the power of suggestion . . . to prove a point."

"What point?" Erde asks.

"That the defective material was already there. And that humanity is incapable of policing its own ranks. It's futile to run these cycles over and over again. We ought to either quit it completely or start over from scratch. New genes, new species."

The Librarian feels another memory stirring. He's been remembering things, but this is a very long and complicated one. The other dragon guides stare at Fire for a moment, then as a trio, turn questioning eyes to him. "Not yet." He waves away their gaze. "Soon."

Water-as-Sedou calls from beside Rose's soup pot, "He means he hasn't remembered enough yet. But he will. You all will, soon enough."

"Cycles?" Paia asks.

Fire throws up his hands, exasperation on a theatrical scale. "Endless! Pointless! I keep trying to make them see it! We should just play this one out and let that be the end of it. No more cycles!" To Paia, he says more gently, "Your father used to breed dogs, do you remember?"

"Of course."

The Librarian can see she's surprised Fire even knows what a dog is.

"If he bred a dog as mean as Guillemo, what would he do?"

Paia's brow creases prettily. "He'd . . . put it down."

"Exactly! If that whole line turned up mean, what would he do?"

Now she looks away, uneasy. "He'd discontinue that breeding program."

"And if the entire species of dogs turned up mean, what then?"

Sedou brings a tray of steaming soup bowls. "But it's not the entire species. Look at these good people! That's the whole point."

"That's *your* whole point." Fire peers into Paia's bowl, clearly wondering if his newly material manform might be capable of eating. "If we can't get them even as far as the printing press each time without tripping the alarm, I'd say the experiment is a failure, and I'm tired of it. I say no more restarts, no more futures. Let's all go find a comfy den somewhere and enjoy ourselves while the damn planet self-destructs. Let's stop these endless, useless efforts to help mankind get it right, because *they never will*!"

"I don't much like the sound of this," N'Doch admits.

"The Intemperate One." Sedou jerks his head in Fire's direction. "Actually, we get a little further along each time."

Fire dips a gilded nail into Paia's soup. "Not every time. It's two steps forward, three steps backward, if you ask me. Which nobody does."

IT'S NOT OUR PLACE TO MAKE THIS JUDGMENT. OUR DUTY IS LAID OUT FOR US AND WE MUST FOLLOW IT.

"Another county heard from," Fire growls.

"He's hard at work making things better," Erde returns hotly. "All you know how to do is destroy!"

"Burn, consume, *renew*, little girl. It's mankind who does the destroying."

"Wait, wait," begs N'Doch. "Lemme get this straight. This has all happened before?"

"A billion times!" declares Fire. "Humanity fucks

up, we pull the plug and restart the cycle before they can destroy the planet completely."

A BILLION IS UNTRUE. THE ACTUAL COUNT IS . . .

"What does it matter? It's still a waste of our time!"

N'Doch lets out a breath. "Whew. Where do you restart it?"

"That depends." Sedou's voice is steady and quiet. "It's often a matter of debate, but usually, some-where around the end of the last great ice age."

"Too late," says Fire. "They're already men by then."

"As I said . . . a matter of debate."

Along with his returning memories, the Librarian reclaims an idea. Did I mention this after the last cycle, he wonders? Perhaps he didn't have the details quite worked out. If he cannot express it articulately enough, will they listen? "An idea . . . er . . . a proposal."

They all turn to him. He worries that Earth and Air are nearly done among the wounded trees, and it will be time to move on to the next phase of the Work. He worries that the words will not come, or won't come in time. But miraculously, it's all there in his mind, recalled in full, as if he's been handed a prepared speech, or a recording to just flip on and run. "I have an idea," he begins. "What about a compromise?"

"You were our compromise," says Fire. "Don't you remember?"

"Let him speak," Sedou insists.

"How was I?" The Librarian is disturbed beyond measure by Fire's implication that he's failed at a task he's not even been aware of.

YOU ARE CRUEL, BROTHER.

"I am . . . truthful. Uncompromising."

"Mean," Erde mumbles.

"Tell me," the Librarian begs, though he thinks he recalls it now, all of it.

Sedou regards him kindly. "You were to keep the knowledge alive, from generation to generation, evolving with the world. The knowledge of what the planet needs to stay healthy, to survive. Our living library."

A DUTY WHICH YOU PERFORMED ADMIRABLY.

"But it didn't do any good," Fire points out. "Nobody listened."

"Some did," murmurs the Librarian. He'd always found allies in the ecological movement. "But not enough."

N'Doch nods. "No way. Not near enough. I'd still be one of those nonlisteners if I hadn't met the dragons."

"But that's my idea. More people. Our ideas should evolve, too. Don't restart so far back. There's too much room for error if, each time, men must reinvent the wheel."

"Literally," N'Doch puts in.

"It was thought," says Sedou reasonably, "that memories of the former, wrong ways would hamper the evolution of the right ways."

"But why not let memory work to advantage? Let's restart where some already carry the necessary knowledge and understanding. Let the knowledge persist through the Change. Make *sure* that men remember. See what they can become if there are some of us around to explain, to remind, to tell the truth, to spread the warnings."

Fire laughs nastily. "Ha. Prophets. You know what happens to them."

"But the memory of the Change will persist for a while, perhaps long enough. Even as it fades into legend, then myth, it will have its effect on men's behavior, and progress will be made."

Sedou rubs his jaw. "A good idea. But there's a catch. We won't be around."

The Librarian has remembered that, too. "No matter. Some will be." He nods toward the fire, at Hal and Rose and Djawara, listening soberly. At the Tinkers, cleaning up from the meal. At the other women, spreading canvas and blankets to curl into close to the embers. "More than just me."

Rose clears her throat. "Won't be around?"

"Sleeping," Sedou offers gently, "until the next crisis."

"Of course. But the . . . your guides?"

Sedou looks at Fire, and then away. "Why does this always fall to me?"

"Because you do it so well, sister."

Erde lays a hand on Sedou's arm. "I recall it now. I will tell them."

"Heroics," Fire mutters, walking off to the edge of the darkness.

"The guides are . . ." Erde begins. *"We* are . . . extensions of our dragons, born into human form. There are always four such in the world, though they live unaware of it until the Summons comes. To gather the energies necessary to create the Change, the dragons require all their energies. The guides must be . . . reabsorbed."

She sees the shock and protest paling their faces. "No! Don't be sad for us! It's a wonderful . . . a joyous reunion! We will be . . . *be* our dragons again! And we'll rest until it's time to go to work again. So, it is you who have the harder task. You must carry the knowledge into the world. You must struggle to remake the habits of mankind. That is . . ." She looks to Sedou. "If it is agreed to try Gerrasch's idea this time. And I do think it's a very good idea."

"It's a terrible idea," calls Fire from the shadows. "A poor excuse for one more pointless cycle."

"Doan know if yu doan try." Stoksie comes to stand beside Hal and Rose. "Shur gonna be sum surprize out deah, when da wurld getz all green agin . . ." He snaps his fingers. "Jess li' dat. Dat's what'll happin, ri'?"

Sedou nods, a smile softening his solemn gaze. "I guess it will. We've never done it that way before."

"What a lovely vision," murmurs Rose.

"That's why it's a good idea," Erde urges. "People will see a great miracle happen, and they'll be thankful and remember. And with the likes of Rose and Hal around to explain the why and how, surely no one will ever let it happen again!"

Fire's laugh is dry and weary. "There's a sucker born every minute."

Erde scowls at him. "I think I'm a lot happier with hope than you are without any."

"But why sacrifice your lives? You're all young and healthy. Do it my way, and you get to live your lives to the full, and in the end, know that you'll never have to repeat this pointless exercise!"

"You wanted us to take steps," N'Doch reminds him. "So, we're taking one."

Fire shakes his head. "I just wanted it to end."

Earth lumbers out of the darkness and hunkers down beside the fire. A dozen or so stray warhorses wander up behind him, their tack askew.

THE GROVE IS HEALED. I HAVE BROUGHT SOME FRIENDS.

"Time," intones the Librarian. Already, he feels the pull, the dragon's substance calling back its own.

"Already?" breathes Hal.

"Oh, dear," Rose echoes him. "Not so soon!"

Sedou says, "The urgency is at the far end, uptime. There, the world is . . ."

"I saw it," Rose agrees. "Dry, barren, already lifeless. Do what you must. I understand."

HURRY! HURRY!

"Details. Still." The Librarian's internal recording has run out, leaving him terse again. He looks to Sedou to speak for him.

"Yes." Sedou beckons to Stoksie and Luther. "Guess you fellas need a ride home."

Stoksie chuckles, relieved. "Me 'n' Luta wuz shur we'd be lookin' fer digs aroun' heah."

"No way. We need you uptime, to spread the word."

"Yu gottit."

"Now?" The Librarian prepares himself for the effort of slowing Air's momentum long enough to get a portal open. "When?"

"Will you go to the Citadel?" Paia asks. "Will you tell Leif all that's happened? He'll make an excellent messenger of the word."

"Sounds like some crackpot religion," says Fire sourly.

"You oughta know," says N'Doch.

"Shur, gal, we'll go deah. Leif's gonna be wunderin' anyhow."

When the portal opens, it's a discontinuous rectangle of otherness, suspended in thin air, an opening without borders. The Librarian understands that the more formal structure of previous portals—a picture frame, a computer screen, a wooden doorway, a stone gate—has been a concession to human concepts of time and space. But Air has no patience left for the niceties. The view through the opening brings Hal and Erde simultaneously to their feet. They're looking into a richly paneled room, a high dark room lit by a single glowing lamp hanging above a long, polished wooden table. Leif Caldwell sits surrounded by papers and maps. Constanze leans over his shoulder, pointing out something on the paper currently held in his hand. A few of the Blind Rachel Crew are with them, hard at work passing papers back and forth, discussing various issues among themselves. At Cauldwell's right is Adolphus of Köthen, his head cocked with interest as he listens to what Constanze is saying.

"Now," directs the Librarian.

The occupants of the dark room glance up in astonishment as the Tinkers step through the opening. Within half a breath, the portal has closed behind them.

"Oh!" Erde's cry is a single birdlike call of heartbreak. It brings tears to the Librarian's eyes.

Hal frowns, pensive but faintly amused. "He looks more at home there than he ever did here."

Paia takes Erde's hand, squeezes it briefly. "He'll do well. He'll be happy, I think, at last."

HURRY! HURRY!

"Master Djawara!" Sedou calls, then says more fondly, "Grandfather. For I feel that you are, have been. Will you go home to the bush, Papa?"

"Nothing there to go home to," the old man says. "The Change will be welcome, but it will not restore my family." He looks at Rose from under penitent brows. "I thought I might beg shelter of the ladies, to help rebuild Deep Moor. Out of gratitude, you understand, for their hospitality to my grandson. And to live out my life in peace and quiet among people who believe in dragons."

Rose laughs, brushing aside her tears. "You are welcome, good mage!"

HURRY! HURRY!

"Good-byes, then." The human niceties are deserting the Librarian as well now.

The stray horses are commandeered, good-byes said with silent, fervent hugs and the pressing of wet cheeks. The women mount up. Passing on her way to her horse, Rose stops before Fire.

"Perhaps this time, Lord Fire, we will be better able to live up to your high expectations of us."

He inclines his golden head. "Good lady, I wish you all the success in the world."

"Satirical," she scolds him gently. "You lack faith."

"You're right. I do."

HURRY! HURRY!

Djawara declines a mount, swearing he has never yet ridden a horse and is too old to start now. He embraces Erde, then his grandson, then turns away quickly to walk toward the road.

"You be good, Papa," N'Doch calls after him softly.

Hal sees the women onto their horses, then grips Erde's shoulders with both hands. "I swear you're a foot taller than when we first met."

"That was barely a season ago, dear knight."

He smiles, then sobers. "There is no other way?"

"You of all know the answer. It is what we are."

He nods, looking quite at a loss. He brushes a ragged fringe of curl back from her brow. "If I understand this right, you're saving all our lives with this new . . . arrangement. Lives that, like a million others, would otherwise cease to exist at the moment of the Change."

Erde's sad face clears in a wide, joyous grin, as bright as summer sunrise. "Yes! I hadn't thought of that! I guess we are! All the more reason!"

Hal presses his lips to her forehead. "Our thanks to you, lady of the dragons."

Then he flings himself on his horse and leads his little band down the dark road back to Deep Moor.

The Eight are alone. Paia sighs. The wind whispers in the branches. Sedou calls down a brief shower to douse the campfires.

"Don't want the place catching *fire*, after all," N'Doch quips.

They have no further need of light. They are as aware of each other as if they stood in an open field at noon. They feel eternity coming upon them, as the inevitability that haunted Erde from the beginning, as the annihilation that N'Doch dreaded, as the Librarian's perennial sense of drifting unmoored in time and space. But fear, dread, confusion . . . all that dissipates before the anticipated coming together. Union. Reunion. The joy of oneness.

Paia slides her arms around Fire's waist and lays her head on his chest. She thinks he might push her away, not yet released of his rage and frustration. Instead, he draws her tightly against him, his breath hot on her neck.

"Alas, my Fire," she whispers, for his ears only. "I fear you would rather be human."

HURRY! HURRY!

Earth, Water, Air and . . .

Fire?

I am here.

It will be easy, Erde tells them fleetingly. *It will be just like the Meld, except that it will. . . .*

Epilogue

He knows they've succeeded when the pair of Tinkers comes bursting out of thin air, breathless, grinning like fools. They've barely greeted anyone before they're dragging him and Cauldwell out of the room and down the corridor to the Great Hall with its wide windows overlooking the valley.

For a while they all stare through the dusty glass, and nothing happens. Leif starts muttering about getting back to work. Stokes dances up and down on his crooked hip, insisting, "Yu'll see! Yu'll see!"

At the first hint of change, Köthen understands she isn't coming back, or she'd have come with Stokes and Luther. She'd have wanted to see this for herself, if there was any way she could have. He'll ask Stokes later what's happened to her. He'd had visions of a life, children. He doesn't want to think about it now. Right now, the only thought he's got room for is wonder.

They throw open the windows and hang out in the hot, dry gusts, gawking, pointing. The hint becomes a fuzz of amber softening the hills, which cools into pale yellow, then an undeniable haze of green. Green! As he watches the hard red rock smooth over with a patina of new life—lichens, grass, wildflowers, leaves—in his mind he's seeing the snow melting on the battlefields, along the rutted roads, on the ramparts of Castle Köthen. He hopes Heinrich is alive to see it. And the brat. The two of them. What a pair.

Though it pains him to admit it, he's grateful to the brat for yanking him out of what Constanze Cauldwell calls his "narcissistic descent into suicidal despair." He shakes his head. He likes talking with Constanze. It's like talking to another man, but . . . not quite. And these people have phrases and elaborate explanations for notions he's never even thought of.

The valley below has become a vast windswept meadow. The sky is losing its ruddy glare. Beyond the crenellation of mountains, he sees the rounder profile of approaching clouds. Perhaps it will even rain. Rain! That thought makes him smile, and once he's started, he can't hold it back. His jaw just keeps spreading, his eyes crinkling, his mouth curling up, of their own accord. He knows what it is. It's joy.

Adolphus Michael von Hoffman, Baron of Köthen, has long been a stranger to joy. But Dolph Hoffman thinks he's willing to let it into his vocabulary.

He sees what's happening, but he'll never comprehend it. He'll accept the reality of it, but never be able to quite encompass the *possibility*. Why bust his head about it? Instead, he mutters something soft and obscene. It snags Stokes' attention, and they share a winner's grin.

"Das sumpin, yah, Dolf?"

"Yah. Das sumpin."

MERCEDES LACKEY

The Novels of Valdemar

To Order Call: 1-800-788-6262

Tanya Huff

The Finest in Fantasy

DAW 21

Curt Benjamin

Seven Brothers

"Rousing fantasy adventure."
—*Publishers Weekly*

Llesho, the youngest prince of Thebin, was only seven
when the Harn invaded, deposing and murdering his
family and selling the boy into slavery. On Pearl Island,
he was trained as a diver—until a vision changed his life
completely. The spirit of his long-dead teacher revealed
the truth about Llesho's family—his brothers were alive,
but enslaved, living in distant lands. Now, to free his
brothers, and himself, Llesho must become a gladiator.
And he must go face to face with sorcerers...and gods.

Book One:
THE PRINCE OF SHADOWS   0-7564-0054-6
Book Two:
THE PRINCE OF DREAMS   0-7564-0114-3
Book Three:
THE GATES OF HEAVEN   0-7564-0156-9
(hardcover)

To Order Call: 1-800-788-6262

Irene Radford

"A mesmerizing storyteller." —*Romantic Times*

THE DRAGON NIMBUS

THE GLASS DRAGON
0-88677-634-1

THE PERFECT PRINCESS
0-88677-678-3

THE LONELIEST MAGICIAN
0-88677-709-7

THE WIZARD'S TREASURE
0-88677-913-8

THE DRAGON NIMBUS HISTORY

THE DRAGON'S TOUCHSTONE
0-88677-744-5

THE LAST BATTLEMAGE
0-88677-774-7

THE RENEGADE DRAGON
0-88677-855-7

THE STAR GODS

THE HIDDEN DRAGON
0-7564-0051-1

To Order Call: 1-800-788-6262

Kristen Britain

GREEN RIDER

As Karigan G'ladheon, on the run from school, makes her way through the deep forest, a galloping horse plunges out of the brush, its rider impaled by two black arrows. With his dying breath, he tells her he is a Green Rider, one of the king's special messengers. Giving her his green coat with its symbolic brooch of office, he makes Karigan swear to deliver the message he was carrying. Pursued by unknown assassins, following a path only the horse seems to know, Karigan finds herself thrust into in a world of danger and complex magic....   0-88677-858-1

FIRST RIDER'S CALL

With evil forces once again at large in the kingdom and with the messenger service depleted and weakened, can Karigan reach through the walls of time to get help from the First Rider, a woman dead for a millennium?   0-7564-0209-3

To Order Call: 1-800-788-6262

DAW 7